Pete Sheterline (signature)

A Liking for Chocolate

Peter Sheterline

To Emmy, Alex, Harry and Ella-Mae

Acknowledgements

Many people have unwittingly and quite randomly contributed characteristics and foibles that motivate the characters in this story. The characters play out the plot in and around Swansea and Gower, the latter a place of endless beauty. The locations are quite real, but rather less dangerous than this story might indicate.

I thank the Gower Starsky, who I am certain also rolled over car bonnets in his prime, for useful information regarding the local police service. Where procedural or other police issues are inaccurate, I have simply substituted plausibility for fact and take full responsibility.

The image panned across stuccoed buildings. It closed in on a woman, leaning against the ornate ironwork of a balcony, smoking languidly, bathed in pink evening sunshine. Her head slowly filled the frame. As she turned to look at him, a puzzled expression appeared on her face, quickly followed by shock, as she slipped downwards out of view.

He pressed the pause button on his computer and sat back smiling.

Monday

Huw worked the wet salty sand towards his lips with his tongue until he could spit most of it out. He raised himself carefully to his knees and wiped his lips on his sleeve. He could still feel the sand against his teeth. Had he fainted? The thump of helicopter blades and vicious spray of sand became the diminuendo whine of the turbine running down. He could feel piss cooling inside his wetsuit. The surf thudded and hissed onto the beach close by.

The paramedics in their green overalls jumped down from the air ambulance and ran towards him. The man shouted over his shoulder to his colleague.

'Take this one Tracy, I'll check the other one'.
She knelt down beside him.

'You're OK now love, can you hear me? Just sit still. Where's the blood coming from, where does it hurt?' His response, that it wasn't his blood at all and that he was fine, was drowned out by her colleague, who was leaning over the prone body.

'Christ almighty Tracy, this one's had it.' She immediately stiffened up. 'Are you OK with him?' He jerked his thumb to indicate Huw, 'I need to call this in'. He ran across to the helicopter and started an urgent conversation on the radio. As he talked he looked steadily across at Huw, nodding into the microphone.

The red air ambulance stood some 30 metres away and Huw could hear the chatter from the radio as Tracy helped him to stand.

'Take your time love.'

He stood gingerly, his heart rate settling back towards normal as he recalled the events of the last; what, ten minutes? Half an hour? He really wasn't sure.

'Look, the police will be here soon love and they will want to have a talk with you, we'll wait quietly for them b'there shall we?' she said leading him towards the air ambulance. 'I've got a flask of coffee'.

He started shivering as soon as he had climbed inside and started to relax; shock. The sweet coffee helped. He wanted to sleep. He remembered sitting in the dunes looking out over the beach at Llangennith; the swell curling cleanly onto the sand, deciding where to take the break with his surf board. Early morning mist lay over the grey water, all but obscuring The Worm. A light north-easterly blew and a big swell was coming in almost lazily off the Atlantic, to hump and fold onto the beach in perfect arcs. It was the first obstacle they had met on their journey from Newfoundland. Perfect conditions and yet he was the only other person on the beach; brilliant. The other; a man by his gait, was some way off, walking north on the tide line from the stream towards Burry Holm. He was skipping in and away from the curls of spent waves as they moved up the beach and then slid back to be reclaimed by the sea. The other person seemed to throw his arms upwards for joy. Huw had responded with a smile. But the figure followed through the movement backwards until he lay still in the surf. Huw jumped up and shielded his eyes with his hand as if it would somehow aid his vision. He willed him to get up, but the surf, oblivious to the drama, lapped against and over the body. Huw shoved his mobile into the pocket of his hoodie, skidded down the front of the dune and ran across the beach towards the prone figure. As he got closer, he could see that a faint smudge of pink coloured the foam swirling around his head. His heart raced from the exercise and from a rising panic. He reached the figure and waded around him to find a purchase to pull him from the surf. The face was leaking blood into the water and onto Huw as he struggled to pull the limp body from the sea. He knew that the tide was still on the flood and dragged the stranger beyond the line of wrack left by last night's tide. He would probably be safe from the waves. Only then did he force himself to look into the man's face to see a small round hole, still leaking blood in the centre of his forehead. Fucking hell, he thought, Llangennith beach. The man was young, just a bit older than himself.

He felt for a pulse, but he was too panicked to be certain one way or the other. He looked intently for any sign of movement and saw none. He started running back the way he had come, trying to make some sense of what to do. Get the mobile out stupid, call for an ambulance; and the police. His mind became clearer as he forced himself to order the events into a narrative for the dispatcher. Stay calm he said to himself, stay calm the dispatcher had said.

If the man had been shot, he must have been shot by somebody. He turned and stared back at the dunes a long way behind, from where he knew immediately the shot must have come. He suddenly knew that there was also the very real possibility that he might also be a target and there he was standing in the middle of a few square miles of open sand. He was ridiculously vulnerable and felt a wave of physical panic sweep through his body as he tried to curl up and sink down into the very sand. He imagined the feel of a bullet ripping into him at any second.

The police helicopter arrived some minutes later, blue and yellow. Two coloured toys on the beach with a body and the waves.

Three police officers walked across to the air ambulance and had a word with the second medic, a conversation which involved much nodding and shaking of heads. The one in the suit identified himself as DI Kevin Bryn and sat with one of the constables, Constable Williams, inside the ambulance opposite Huw. The third policeman, not in uniform, another Williams, donned a white sterile over-suit and gloves and rummaged in his briefcase.

'So, what's your name son? What are you doing here?' a bit brusque thought Huw, who at that moment thought he deserved and had expected sympathy.

'Huw Thomas, I came here to surf.'

'And your friend?' said Bryn angling his head towards the body.

'He's not a friend. I don't know him Inspector.' His voice quavered, 'he was just walking on the beach and I saw him get shot. I thought he was just messing about.' DI Bryn rubbed his hand over his face and his eyeballs went skywards as if he'd heard this very line many times before. He looked exaggeratedly around him indicating that apart from Huw, there weren't many suspects.

'So, did you see anyone else on the beach? There's nobody else now.'

'No, he was the only person I saw, he was walking along the shore.'

'The blood on your wetsuit, how did that get there?'

Huw described how the victim had bled over him as he dragged him up the beach above the high tide line.

'So where did you throw the gun?' The corners of Bryn's mouth twitched into a smile as if suggesting to Huw that to divulge just this one simple fact, would clear the whole thing up and Huw could go home and forget about it.

It was only then that Huw really saw himself as the suspect, of course he was a suspect, *the* suspect, who else could it have been? The realisation seeped like a chill through his body.

'I didn't have a gun,' His voice was faint now; shock. 'Don't have a gun'.

'We'll see about that' said Bryn, 'swab his hands Dai. The DC was affectionately known as Dai Swab, which also conveniently solved the Williams dilemma. 'Throw it in the sea did you? Been trespassing on your patch had he? Playing around with your girlfriend?' Huw put out his hands, but his shoulders slumped and his head drooped. Bryn looked at the wetsuit; he never could see the pleasure in them.

'Do you have any other clothes? How did you get here?'

'I've got my clothes in the van,' Huw pointed over towards the car park. 'I drove from Swansea'

'OK Dai, take the lad over to his van, bag his wetsuit, take the keys'

'How'm I going to get home?'

'Oh you won't be home for a while son. Run along now, back here in five,' the detective said merrily.

Huw and Dai Swab jogged up the beach, picked up Huw's board and his bag from the dunes and went back to the van. The car park was empty. It vaguely occurred to Huw that the van which had been there when he arrived and that he had subconsciously assumed belonged to the shot man, could not have done. It also occurred to him, as he fought off his wetsuit and donned his jeans, that he had not seen anyone except the victim since he had arrived and that it was at least a couple of hundred metres from the dunes to the tide line. The word sniper fizzled around uneasily at the edge of his consciousness. The van must have belonged to the killer.

Dai nudged him along back to the beach. 'Into the blue one *bwt*, you'll be coming with us'

'Do you have a computer?' Bryn, leaned towards him and watched his response.

'A laptop at home; can I call home?' said Huw, pulling out his mobile again.

'I don't see why not, and you can give me that phone when you've finished, if that's OK with you son?' Huw was about to argue, then nodded listlessly.

'Where are we going?'

'Swansea Central, OK?' Huw called his dad outlining in hurried phrases what had happened and where he was going and why.

'Ask your dad to bring in the computer; our techies will want to look at it.' It too wasn't really a question.

Dai Swab took his phone and bagged it. Bryn was on his radio checking on the arrival of the SOCOs from Swansea.

'Dai, you've got the gear on, tape what you can and stay here 'till the SOCOs arrive.' Bryn knew that the tide would cover the murder site for a couple of hours or more so there was not much he could do there. 'Wait 'til the hairy man arrives and then drive Mr Thomas's van back to the compound in Cockett. Meet me at Central.' Dai pulled some tape and a few stakes from the helicopter and retrieved his flask of tea. 'Constable Williams,' Bryn nodded across to him, 'you come with me and Mr Thomas.'

It was Huw's first time in a helicopter. Not quite the adventure he had imagined, but enough to enjoy the helicopter looping over the Burry inlet and back into Swansea Airport. Three minutes by helicopter 20 minutes by car on a good day. A squad car, Volvo, quick by the look of it, appeared by the door as soon as the helicopter landed. He was led across the tarmac to the car and his head was pushed down to clear the door lintel and into the back between DI Bryn and Constable Williams for the

11

ten minute ride into town. His father arrived at Central Police Station about 15 minutes after him and was told to wait in the foyer. The sergeant told him Huw was being held for questioning in an interview room, was fine, had not been charged with anything and was helping them with their enquiries. Newsreaders and policemen, lawyers and nurses, all seemed to pick up by osmosis the patois peculiar to their professions and the sergeant was a master of his. He was also a decent man and so Huw's father was offered tea, as was Huw in the interview room. Bryn and Dai Swab sat and stood respectively opposite him.

'Interview commencing 11.02 am, Monday 13th May, 2013.' Got to be; Huw thought with a wry smile. Not much else was funny.

'Present; Huw Thomas, DI Kevin Bryn and DC David Williams; please confirm your name and address for the tape.'

'Huw Thomas, I live with my parents at 45, Knoll Avenue in the Uplands'

The interview established other family and personal information, age, brief history, work; that sort of thing.

'You arrived at the beach at what time?' Bryn rattled his fingers on the table and watched Huw Thomas intently.

'About nine I think, I left Uplands about eight thirty'

'Was anyone with you? Did anyone see you arrive? Can anyone vouch for these times?'

Huw looked upwards, inwardly playing back his recollection of the journey and of his arrival at the car park in the Hillend campsite in Llangennith. 'My dad knew when I left; I shouted out. I came on my own. Hillend was pretty quiet, a couple of tents in the field with their cars and a white van in the car park. I didn't talk to anybody; I don't suppose anybody noticed me.' The recollection of the morning immediately triggered a rapid rise in his heartbeat and the other sensible physiological things animals do when they experience fear.

'The van wasn't b'there sir when we collected his clothes.' Dai Swab was no fool.

'You've said that you didn't know the victim, did you recognise the face? Surfing pal or acquaintance perhaps?' The repeat of this question raised a faint sense of disquiet in Huw, he didn't think he knew him.

'I had a pretty good look at him. I didn't recognise him at all'.

Again Huw looked up at the ceiling and into his inner video; 'not at all,' Huw finally concluded and experienced a slight relaxing of tension.

Bryn stood up. 'Constable Williams, get a statement down and signed by Mr Thomas would you? Get him to sign a consent form for us to look at his computer and mobile phone. Thank you for your assistance, but don't go out of town for the next few days, we will want to talk to you again. We will let you have your phone and computer back as soon as the techies have had a look. The SOCOs will want a look at your van. We thank you for your cooperation; we should have the swab results in a couple of days. Stop by at the desk, the sergeant will take you for fingerprinting and DNA. Routine stuff sir, it will be deleted if you are not charged. Dai,' he looked across, 'swab time again.'

At home, after a silent drive, Huw told the story again, shaky now that the tension had been released. About the drive out, the wonderful waves and then the shooting of the victim, the two helicopters, the holding of his van. The first swab must have been for gunshot residue; he had read enough to realise this, and he knew that they wouldn't find anything, would they?

'The detective said I mustn't leave town for a few days. I don't have my phone or my computer, or my van, so I don't have much choice really.' The concept of ordering his life in the absence of the internet had long been extinguished.

'There is one thing that's bothering me dad; I was sat on the dunes, you know, near the path from the car park looking over the beach. You can see the whole beach from there and there was only one person on it, the bloke who got shot. How did he get shot? It must be a couple of hundred yards to the sea where he was walking, so whoever shot him must have been in the dunes, right? I mean, that's a pretty serious shot, two hundred or more yards, smack in the middle of the forehead, I didn't hear the shot. Has to be a trained sniper, army or something, right? I was terrified when I'd realised that he could shoot me too, so I just kind of broke down and curled up on the sand. And then the helicopter came...' His dad held his shoulders and he shivered away some more of his shock.

'A hot bath with a stiff drink for you son; medicinal whisky only, Penderyn special. Have a soak, get yourself down in front of the fire and I'll phone for some food. Sound alright to you? We'll sort this out.' His father looked at him intently. 'We will, so go take this up' he said, as he handed over a generous two fingers of his favourite whisky in his best cut glass tumbler. A coming of age.

Kevin Bryn called the team into the ops room. The uniforms had put up some basic information on the two display boards standing at one end of the room, beside a white board, in case somebody had an inspiration. 'Right ladies and gentlemen, what do we have? A witness who is still a suspect, calls in at? Dai?'

'Seventeen minutes past nine sir, according to the dispatcher. Said he sounded terrified and that he had seen someone shot and had pulled him up the beach, out of the sea sir'

'We were there at what, Dai?' DI Bryn and Dai had their little party piece where Bryn would cock his head towards Dai and raise his left eyebrow in a theatrical manner. Others in the room weren't quite sure if this was merely irritating or comfortably familiar. Dai had been one of the DI's chosen ones, a local lad with an avuncular manner who could talk with anyone and elicit information others could not. He also acted as a convenient mirror for the profound thoughts of his master and it was not unknown for him to exploit this for his own advantage.

'Twenty minutes to sir, about five minutes after the air ambulance.' It was Dai Swab's turn to raise an eyebrow. It was a point of some friction that the ambulance which had to fly from Swansea airport, the same base as the police helicopter, would often get to a scene of mutual interest a couple of minutes before it. In fact, the desk sergeant ran a book on such discrepancies and stood to make some beer money for the evening. It was Constable Williams' turn.

'The victim is, sir, according to the wallet he had in his inside pocket, Michael Green.'

'Do we have an address Constable Williams?'

'We do sir, and more; both the credit card with Visa and a library card from the University confirm the name, and both the bank and the University confirm his address in the marina; flat on the front, very nice sir. Thirty two years old. The victim that is sir'

'Well done Williams.' Bryn did a small, but definite mock bow towards the constable. Was he being ironic, or worse, was he a thespian?

'There's more sir.' Williams chirped. Bryn sat down with his hand on his head looking amazed, 'Go on.'

'Michael Green worked in the University; Engineering Department, it's meant to be very good sir'.

'You are able to discriminate one University Department of Engineering from another are you constable. What is their particular speciality? Quantum bedsprings, atomic bridges, cordless curlers? Enlighten us.' A faint snicker or two emerged anonymously from the gathering.

'Actually sir, there are cordless curlers, my wife has some,' said Williams, looking around for approval. Even Bryn grinned.

'He is in the robotics group sir, computer control systems for robots,' Williams read from his notes. 'A bit of a star sir, brought in 'specially from the big city.'

A faint whistle emerged between Bryn's thin lips; 'London eh?'

'No sir, Cardiff.'

'Well done again Williams, you may sleep soundly in your bed tonight. Go now, get me next of kin, on my desk as soon as. I'll need the names of collaborators and colleagues in the University; find out who his drinking

16

pals are. Take Ferrari with you and talk to them. Who does he confide in, who does he tweet, text or facecloth or whatever?' He said, waving Williams away. Looks of faint surprise at this previously unexpected, but clearly imperfect familiarity with the cyber world, appeared on the faces of his colleagues.

DS Lucy Evans was the team techie. She was probably the only one in the room who was familiar with the inside of a computer, the strings of code which told them what to do and the reclusive kinds of people who shared her interests and skills. She also had a wide network of acquaintances scattered over the globe, with whom she communicated, and with whom she often undertook clandestine discussions and projects to find out this or that, or to crack this or that problem. In her view, you had to be one to know one, to talk with one and be trusted by one. She was very careful not to interfere with things which were not her business in this twilight world. It was not something she discussed with her DI. She had been one of the bright young things recruited into the South Wales Police force on the rapid advancement scheme for bright graduates. She had a first in physics from Bristol University and was energetically lobbied by both the University, who expected her to continue her studies with a PhD, and the financial institutions who vacuumed up some of the best talent in the UK; merely it seemed, to make more money for those who already had too much. Neither of those life paths appealed to a strongly independent thinker with a social conscience. To the disappointment of both parents and her commercial suitors, she joined the force. Tough it was, but boring and unchallenging it was not. She had become a mostly self-taught specialist in latent data on computer equipment and on security and access to sensitive data storage systems. She admired the quick decisive manner of her superior and enjoyed his quirky humour. Because DI Bryn gave her a lot of independence and backed her up when she needed it, she was happy in the team.

The remaining member of the murder team was sitting in the corner looking both bored and distracted. The appearance was deceptive, but it was hard to be fully convinced of that. DS Graham Crossman leaned forwards and looked across at Bryn and swung his eyes past Lucy. 'Assassination. Pros. Not your usual grudge, passion or drugs killing. Not surfer,' he pronounced. He seemed to have absorbed over the years the persona suggested by his surname. He sat back and resumed his former expression. Gray Crossman was wise in the way of a detective who has seen everything a small city could throw up in twenty five years. He was also never going to be DI; not because of his value as a detective, but because he pretty much followed his own hunches regardless of instruction from his superiors and did not take rank into account when arguing against weak hypotheses. Something his seniors found particularly irksome. He valued experience and contacts over intellect and computers. He didn't value the brass at all. Sometimes he was right; mostly he was right. Crossman was old enough to have missed the university boats that floated off from council estates after the second war. He had taken the longer and grittier route into The Force. The police service was certainly that, but he didn't regret the decision for a moment and had plenty of opportunities to exercise the creative bits of his brain. He came from Port Tennant, an old industrial corner of Swansea in which grit was both a given and a necessity.

Bryn stood and did an expansive spreading of his hands to applaud the gnomic words of his junior in rank, but significantly senior in age, colleague. 'You took away my very words Detective Sergeant Crossman and added your very own flowery nuances to the language, reminding me of our only true son Dylan. It's very likely not our Huw Thomas, I agree, but let's see what's on his phone and computer. Lucy, see me at the end about that. As to the possibility of a professional hit, well, university boffin, hole in the head, it feels right. There aren't many in this neck of the woods though.' He walked over to the white board and wrote 'Suspects' and underlined it. Below, he wrote 'Huw Thomas?' and below that, 'Sniper?' and 'Colleague?'

'Michael Green, walking along the beach, nobody else in sight according to our friend and a head shot from at least the distance of the dunes. Is it an ex-army sniper? There must be plenty of those running around these days, caught between wars. Dai, contact local army regiments, they should have records of snipers both discharged, on leave and active. Make a list; names, addresses, contacts, we need to talk to them now, where were they Monday between 6am and 10am? Who can back them up?' Bryn paced, as he talked, as he thought, playing out on the floor the complicated directions and bifurcations his thoughts were taking in his head. 'Gray, get uniforms round to his flat to seal it now, get the SOCOs in, take computers, phones, anything else you find. I'll join you when I've talked to his mother, father or girlfriend whatever.' He waved his hand around in the air. 'We need to think about 'the why' and 'the who'. Is it connected with his work? He pointed at 'Colleague?' It seems a likely start given that not many young men get shot on beaches by marksmen. Not a squabble over Scrabble or skunk; that would be handguns. Dai, young Huw's phone, computer and van, what's happening?'

'We have his computer and phone by'ere sir, SOCOs are looking at the van, it's in the compound; haven't found anything unusual except a tin of sex wax.' Dai looked around puzzled, looking for enlightenment. He was definitely interested. The group techie, Lucy Evans popped up her hand.

'I use that stuff sir.' There was the sound of suppressed giggles; 'it stops you sliding around on your surfboard sir, lots of people use it. But it tends to give you a rash from the friction, it's not well named.' Real giggles, Bryn broke through them.

'Thanks Lucy, for that insight.' He paused; 'OK, take a quick look at Thomas's phone and computer. What can we get quickly that will help? I don't want to waste valuable resources on him for long, I still don't have him down for the shooter.'

'I'll look at the easy stuff; email, phone contacts and texts, voice mails and make a list, I'll look out for unusual files or software, encrypted stuff and the like, see if anything stands out..'

'Good, no more than an hour or two. Gray will give you heads up on any computer at Michael Green's flat, do the same with that when we get it, but dig a bit deeper and work with Williams and Ferrari to make up a network of his contacts and how he ticks. You know the sort of thing.

Liaise with the University to get access to his work computer. Take it away if you can, I'll sort the paperwork.' Bryn hooked the index finger of his right hand over his chin. 'We also need to know how he got to Llangennith; there was only the white van and Thomas' VW in the car park. Did he get the bus and walk? What car does he drive? Does everyone know what they're doing?' he said swinging round to look at each member of his team in turn. 'Good, off you go.'

The body of Michael Green had been taken to the pathology labs at Singleton hospital and a part of a 0.22 calibre bullet was at this moment falling from a pair of tweezers into a stainless dish to make a sharp ding.

'I haven't seen one of these since Belfast. A 0.22 calibre by the looks of it, copper jacketed, lead-filled; not standard issue though' he said, turning it round in the tweezers. 'This one has been cut at the front, do you see?' he said wafting it in front of Bryn. 'It broke into fragments as it passed through the skull, the bits rattled around inside his head. I'll probably find three other pieces; ballistics will enjoy this one.' The pathologist turned his eyes on Bryn to gauge the effect.

Bryn had not had much luck on the case up until then, 'So this isn't widely available then?' he asked the large, bearded pathologist optimistically.

'It is my boy; standard 0.22 calibre ammunition is freely available in the States. My guess is that someone has bought it and modified it themselves. If it hits you in the head, it's an almost guaranteed kill.'

'The sort of thing a sniper might use then Geoffrey?' he offered even more optimistically.

'No dear boy,' he slowly shook his head. 'So you didn't do the ballistics course then? A sniper likes to use high velocity ammunition which doesn't get blown around by the wind and the like and still has enough go to make a hole in the target at the other end. This is effectively the opposite' said Geoffrey Jones, swivelling his eyes, partly hidden by a voluminous beard, towards Bryn for full effect. Attached below the eyes was an idiotic smile. 'I'm not a ballistics expert,' he mused, 'but a few years in Belfast gives one an eclectic lesson in gunshot wounds.' Geoffrey, who had grown up in Monmouth, had an accent halfway between those of the previous generation of the royal family and Richard Burton. He was a large man with some presence who probably scared the daylights out of his students when he was a pathology professor in Cardiff. He was one of the best students Guy's had produced. His charm was laced with a bit of Beelzebub. The large, and now greying beard, camouflaged the twinkly eyes, in a way that his green scrubs did not hide the results of the many dinners and much wine he had consumed over his long career. Bryn was one of the few detectives that he had any time for and they had worked together many times over the ten years from when Bryn was a DC with so very much to learn. Geoffrey shifted his attention back to the task at hand.

'Well' said Bryn, fiddling with his chin and looking skywards and contemplating the consequences of challenging Geoffrey's assertion. 'That's very interesting; but from what we know, which isn't much, the weapon was fired from at least 200 metres away,' he looked carefully at Geoffrey to judge the effect. '220 yards to you non-metric dinosaurs,' he risked.

'218 yards actually; umm, quite. So it's a bit of a conundrum eh? Didn't you say there was a witness on the beach? Maybe he's not just a witness then?' Suggested Geoffrey, swivelling back and raising his eyebrow; this could have been where Bryn had picked up his various facial tics.

Bryn gave a little shiver, 'I didn't have him down as anything other than witness. Better have another think on that one.'

Geoffrey was now re-engaged with the skull and didn't look up. 'Well good luck with that. Nothing other than the gunshot wound to report as yet. It was that which killed him, stirred his brain into porridge. Like shaking ball-bearings inside a paint can. Otherwise, a healthy man in his thirties I would guess;' He swivelled his eyes to Bryn, 'wouldn't have felt a thing if that makes it any easier.'

'It might for someone,' said Bryn, who paused and looked up, 'especially his parents.' He knew from Williams that they had retired to Spain and had asked the local Spanish police to break the news. They weren't happy, nobody liked that job. The parents should be over tomorrow to identify the body. Bryn started walking away, 'if it is Michael Green then well done; he's 32 years old'

Geoffrey went back to the opened skull and his tweezers. 'I'll see you cock, need to find the other pieces; full report on your desk soonest.'

Bryn nodded his thanks, shook his head and raised his eyes and went quickly out of the morgue, the paint can image refusing to die.

Bryn had met Gray at Michael Green's flat; a two bedroom flat on the first floor facing out over the Bristol

Channel. To the left, the green and red navigation lights twinkled under the grey sky. Green starboard, port wine red; they guided vessels into the mouth of the River Tawe. For the bigger ships, they provided access to the King's Dock and the mooring for the Cork Ferry, for the yachts and fishing boats, access to the Tawe basin marina. The Cork Ferry had been a regular daily service to Ireland. It was ten hours of often bucking sea, which took cars and passengers to the wild delights of South West Cork. To Kinsale, twinned with Mumbles just along the bay from Swansea and to Skibbereen and out to Cape Clear. This would have been the first sight of land for passengers on an eastbound transatlantic voyage. Just off Cape Clear was the Fastnet lighthouse perched alone on a nub of rock lashed by the Atlantic rollers. The ferry service had been on and off in recent years and Bryn still missed the sight of the Innisfallen, sliding in at dusk along the south coast of Gower, fairy lights in the fading light. The marina though, and the cafes and restaurants that had sprung up around it and the Kings Dock in the new developments of SA1, seemed to be flourishing. Student gold.

'Where's his computer Gray? He's a computer specialist, works on computers at the University, but no bloody computers. My ten year old nephew has a laptop, even if he only uses it to stand on to reach the biscuits'. Bryn and Crossman had gone carefully through the flat. There were lots of books on computing, lots of technical magazines, files of technical notes, at present undecipherable to the detectives; all neatly arranged on shelves. It was a serious working office, but no computer.

There was even a wireless printer on the desk. He must have one.

'Office, University?' asked Gray. Gray was no more fluent outside of the station.

'Would you?' Bryn said, looking at Gray. 'He'll have a university machine, a terminal connected to the University system.' Bryn was on soft ground here, 'he must have one he takes home, to conferences and the like.'

The SOCOs had nearly finished dusting for prints, looking for any signs which might help, collecting trace evidence. They had found some scratches around the front door lock and similar ones on a desk drawer but not much else, except from some fine brown fibres around the desk. Probably they were just the kind of key scratches that we all make as we stumble in the door after a night out. The photographer was snapping pictures of everywhere and everything. Nobody was raising high fives.

'We'll check out the prints,' Bill looked at Bryn, 'there aren't that many actually, it wasn't a flat visited by many people. There was plenty of dust on surfaces, so it doesn't seem to have been purposely cleaned down. Fibres, scratches; we'll have a closer look.' Bill Wood sighed; Bill was head SOCO. 'But that's about it for now. No other signs of break-in or disturbance, but that's not very unusual if a thief was careful.' He held Bryn's gaze, 'if there was a thief that is.'.

'Thanks Bill. So, exactly the sort of flat a single university lecturer might live in, but no signs of a girlfriend, no contraceptives, not even any make-up or extra toothbrushes; everything where it should be. BUT NO BLOODY COMPUTER,' he shouted. 'Let's check with neighbours and anyone who overlooks the entrance to see if anyone saw or heard anything.' He scanned the bleak communal car park, 'I'm not optimistic.'

Just then Gray's mobile rang; he talked for a few minutes then jotted something down on his pad, leaning against the door post. 'Good timing' said Gray, 'Volvo S60, silver metallic.' He showed Bryn the number he had written down.

'Might as well start here then' said Bryn walking towards the cars remaining now that most people had gone off to work.' They spent ten minutes walking around the car park with their numbered slots; the one corresponding to Michaels Green's flat was empty, but they continued around the whole space and into adjacent parking areas. Nothing. They then knocked on doors of all the adjacent flats and those from where the entrance to Green's block of six flats could be seen. Only five people were in and nobody had seen anything. Most of those up and about early and who may therefore have seen something were now at work, so someone needed to go around again in the evening.

He had hired the van in Birmingham; the hire office suitably busy so that they would be unlikely to remember him. They gave only a cursory glance at the forged licence and credit card, both apparently belonging to a man living in Wolverhampton, who would later receive both a visit from the police and a nasty shock to his bank balance. This didn't worry the driver unduly, in fact, not at all. He drove a few miles and parked the van on a busy street in Edgbaston. He locked the van and squeezed a single key with a blob of blu-tack behind the handle which opened the rear door, as if checking that it was locked. He then walked a mile or so away into a public car park, dropping the hire company fob into a drain grating on the way and drove off in his SUV.

An hour or two later, another man arrived at the van, felt for the key and removed it. He carried his small overnight bag a few yards along the street and checked in to a scruffy commercial B&B. A rep, he said. He was friendly, but not interested in small talk. This was his job and he was good at it. He told Mrs. Wallace that he would have to be off early in the morning and that he had to get to Carlisle. There would be no time for breakfast, but would she be kind enough to fill his flask with coffee, milk and sugar, and leave it outside his room. He could pay now and he would leave the keys in his door when he left. Monday tomorrow, off to work early thought Mrs. Wallace, who pocketed the cash in her housecoat jacket and showed him his dowdy room, which smelt just the bearable side of a rugby changing room. He thanked her, shoved his small bag onto the bed and went out almost immediately for some food. Fish and chips would do for tonight, with a pot of tea. He received and sent a text while he was eating. He was back in his bed by eight, and finished with the last pages of a novel by nine. He slept almost immediately.

In the morning, he crept out and was driving south along the M5 by 4.30am towards the junction with the M50 and thence through Ross-on-Wye towards the looming mountains of Wales. He didn't like to rush, a property he shared with the bottom-of-the-range 2 year old Ford van in regulation white. The van laboured on the Heads of the Valleys road which switch-backed across the tops of each of the major South Wales mining valleys. To the north, the open moorland of the Brecon Beacons National Park, to the south, the valleys, once carved by glaciers, but now laced with rows of terraced houses clinging to the contours and disappearing into the mist below, towards Cardiff and the sea. The Valleys once proud, which churned with life and industry, rugby and boxing, music and dancing, early death, were now learning slowly to sing the quieter song of life after coal. Some became suburbs to Cardiff and Swansea less than an hour away; others, like Merthyr swallowed the bitter pill of unemployment and disillusionment. They were skilled men with nothing for their skills and many still carried the scars of mining to keep them awake into the night. The rush hour, if that is what you could call it, had just started and was feeding traffic down into Neath, Port Talbot and Swansea. He dropped steadily now through the drama of the Vale of Neath which opened up in front of him, scooped out by the same ice sheet. He drove unknowing past the hidden waterfalls on the rivers draining south from the Brecon Beacons as they carved through the carboniferous limestone, meeting layers of harder rock on their journey. He met the M4 close to where the Neath and Tennant canals ran side-by-side, once carrying coal and copper, to and from the city, past Gray's ancestral home. It was then only ten minutes into the centre of Swansea where he parked close to the marina. He opened the back of his van and carefully checked the contents. He then texted a long message on his second mobile and waited for a reply, which came some 10 minutes later. I probably woke him up, he thought. He looked at it, grunted and nodded, then looked at his watch. The arrangement was to meet was in just over an hour at Llangennith at the very North West corner of the Gower peninsular, some half hour's drive away. He had done his homework and had a fair idea of the detailed layout of the area, the car park at Hillend and the path through to the beach. Google Earth was a pretty useful tool. He even had photographs which surfers and walkers had taken. He unscrewed the lid of his flask and poured himself a coffee. He leaned back in his seat and ate with obvious relish the chocolate bar he had taken from his pocket.

A little later he checked and reset the sat nav on his iPhone and set off for Llangennith. He entered Hillend, which he knew was a caravan park and campsite, but also had a car park by the beach regularly used by surfers. He pulled into the car park, empty at this time. He checked his watch, 15 minutes to go yet. The instructions in the text he had sent, the content of which he had only received by secure email himself the previous evening, made quite clear that the timing was to be observed absolutely. The victim was to travel alone and make his way to Llangennith beach and walk from the stream crossing the beach close to Hillend towards Burry Holm. He would be expecting to be joined at some point along the route to receive some information. He would know that the meeting was clandestine, that is how he had been groomed. He looked around, checked the wing mirrors, then got out from the van, opened the rear doors and took a rucksack from the back. He walked towards and then onto the dunes to the north of the beach footpath. He found a comfortable nook in the dunes out of site from the path and car park but with an unrestricted view of the beach. Not many people walked this way. He set out his gear and and waited and watched. He saw him walking out by the stream and starting along the tide line towards Burry Holm, as instructed. He was a couple of hundred yards away, it was time to act.

Some minutes later, he gathered his gear together again and was about to return to the van when he saw another figure in a wetsuit running across the beach towards the body. Damn, damn, damn, he thought. He watched as the figure dragged the body; he alone knew for certain it was a body, up the beach. He had to hurry now, when he had expected to take his time, think ahead and act carefully as he usually did. The wetsuit must have been camping or in one of the caravans or had arrived just after he had. Wetsuit would contact the police, soon, he was sure of that. He gathered his rucksack and

29

walked purposefully across the dunes, just another walker coming back from the coast path. He saw the VW; bloody hippies. So wetsuit had arrived just after him and would have seen his van. He was reasonably sure, but not enough to risk his life on it, that the wetsuit hadn't seen him in the dunes, although he did look up to exactly where he had sat after he had dragged the body up the beach. He might have taken the van number; not likely, but possible. He memorised the number of the VW van then drove off the campsite and, using the north Gower road, took the route off Gower to Swansea by a back route via Cockett. It was a risk, but he was pretty sure that by the time the police arrived and had realised that the white van in the car park may have been significant, he would be a long way away. He also thought that if they did twig quickly, which he considered unlikely, that they would expect him to get to the M4 by the quickest route and look for him along there. He parked the van back in the marina and called his contact, 'job done,' he said.

'You have the recording?' He confirmed that he did. 'OK, send it the normal way.' The phone disconnected. The recording was the proof. He took out the SIM card and burned it with his lighter, got out of the van and took his rucksack out from the back. He locked the van then dropped both the mobile and the van key into the marina as he walked across towards the railway station. He bought a return ticket to London with cash. He got off the train at Cardiff, bought another ticket and then got onto another train to Portsmouth Harbour. He checked into one of the anonymous hotels on Gunwharf Quays. Here, he unpacked his bag and connected his phone to his tablet to download the video. He recorded the file onto a microSD card and slid it into an envelope wrapped in hotel notepaper. He then sent a message using an encrypted email server to Colossus with the registration number of the VW van telling him that the owner had witnessed the killing and suggested what he *thought was necessary. He then deleted everything on his tablet except for the operating system which he would restore later at his leisure. Fool proof certainly, police proof probably; but not a big problem for one of his hacker friends to find evidence of his recent activities on his tablet.*

He was hungry now and wandered out of the hotel to explore the emerging nightlife of this sailors' city. Food and companionship in that order he thought as he dropped the envelope into a post box. He would savour the discomfort about to descend on wetsuit over a fine dinner. He shouldn't have been in the wrong place at the wrong time. The interventions he had requested Colossus to make would certainly muddy the picture for the police; in the unlikely event that they had found anything that might incriminate him. Tomorrow he would catch the ferry.

Michael dragged himself from an unsatisfactory sleep to pick up his mobile which was playing the drone and beeps from O Superman, announcing a text message. Not a good way to wake when you were jumpy anyway, but maybe it was his contact in the organisation. He had been told to expect a message to arrange a meeting at short notice. It was a misty dawn, but the smooth surface of the sea, rippled only by the remains of an Atlantic swell, lay magnificent before him through his picture window as he sat up to grope for the phone. He had bought the flat three years ago, after he had accepted the University post, when he found how many were for sale and at what decent prices. The result of the recession caused by the great bank deception whereby they lent too much money with too little collateral to too many people buying too many flats like his in the hope that prices would rise forever. The economists, professors, pundits, treasury mandarins, ministers and the FSA boffins who had applauded the economic miracle, now, and only now, had raised their voices in alarm and surprise at what was its inevitable outcome. The bankers quietly rubbed their hands and winked. It was a good result for Michael though. He read the message, a long one, with a mixture of fear and excitement, memorising the complex message and realising that he had to move now. He had spent many months cultivating contacts within the various hacking communities and was to meet one of the movers and shakers. These people rarely appeared as themselves out in the real world. He did not know and never expected to know, who the people he communicated with as alias names on forums, really were. This was, for a university specialist in this area, a bit of a coup. He hoped to use any information he gleaned to improve security against some of the technically advanced crime syndicates who used in part, the very hackers he communicated with. Penetration testers they were called in the trade; who sat on the fine line dividing the legal from the illegal. The escalating security war between legitimate banking and commercial users and the criminal gangs, rages on out of sight in servers around the world. They both have access to exactly the same technology. It is a battle fought not with guns and padlocks, but with programming code. Programs that had evolved like life and where only the fossils of previous code could be discerned in the multiple layers laid subsequently one on top of the other. Michael was well aware of the overlap between the individuals who were both on the side of the goodies and of the baddies. He was excited as he got dressed quickly into casual walking gear and set off in his Volvo, a combination of solidity and menace that he and clearly the police too, quite liked. He was parked by half past and on the footpath a couple of minutes later, soon he was walking along the beach. Soon after, he was dead.

Bryn compiled a statement for the press and had the sergeant communicate it to the press officer. The statement declared that a murder had been committed on Llangennith beach between eight thirty and ten in the morning and asked that any potential witnesses who were around the car park at Hillend during these times to get in contact with the police. It would just make the deadline for tomorrow's Post and might get an airing on the regional TV news and radio this evening. Bryn and his crew gathered late in the afternoon in the ops room to swap notes. Everyone was tired and it was clear from the atmosphere that no one had any revelations or had found anything that might point a clear way forward.

'Constable Ferrari, I trust you had a rewarding day with Constable Williams and have tales of derring-do to offer?'

'Fine sir, we are making our way through his colleagues at the university and email and phone contacts. Nothing stands out sir, colleagues all say bright as hell, conscientious, good teacher. No known bad habits. Only has the odd lunch with colleagues, he's not a drinker. He's described as friendly, but not one of the gang. Nobody knows of any girlfriends or partners. He got the job here three years ago, was the best candidate by far, everyone was pleased to have him in the Department. He has brought in lots of new grant money; this is the thing that matters apparently, and some lucrative hook-ups with

British Aerospace, the defence and communications company. He has lots of links with government, GCHQ and the like. He does seem to have a side-line in hacking techniques,' the audience stiffened with interest now, 'on the good guys' side. His PhD student Jennifer Flowers says he needs to keep contact with some of the online groups. She says that they are mostly nerds proving that they can crack the system; but of course some of them are actively illegal. That's about it. We will look at anything related to these contacts with Lucy when she has had more time on the lab computer.'

Bryn clapped, 'splendid oration, concise, eloquent and free from chaff. Old Gray better watch out or we'll have to give his bardic scroll to you. Have you anything to add Constable Williams; some nugget of evidence perhaps?'

'Nothing sir, sorry sir, Ceri got it all in. We have lots of people to talk to tomorrow, maybe something will turn up.'

Bryn wrung his hands 'We need to talk to the caravan people and campers tonight to see if anybody has seen anything. Sorry you two; do it before it gets dark then finish off tomorrow. We would particularly like to know anything about the white van and its driver. It may be nothing, but it may have carried the killer. Get contact details of any campers who left last night. Work your way from closest to further caravans. It's the only lead we have at present. Word would have got around the site about the killing by now, there will have been a lot of gossip. Avoid the tittle-tattle. You'd better get off now.' Bryn turned to his left, 'Lucy, since you were mentioned in despatches. What have you got?'

'I looked mostly at Huw Thomas' phone and laptop. I've compiled a list of phone and email contacts which I will run past him tomorrow, nothing shouting at me from the computer. I've had a quick look at his web history, which is anything from surf sites and weather to technology stuff, mainly computers, though; he seems to be a buff. I'll know more when I've looked a bit deeper. That's it I'm afraid, sir, until I look a bit harder.'

'Glad you can do this stuff Lucy, all a bit hocus pocus to me love. Hold back on Mr Thomas for the moment; crack on with the lab computer. You're doing fine. Now, Gray, help Lucy with a bit more digging into his phone and email contacts. Oh, we need a warrant to look at his financial stuff, bank accounts, building society accounts; same with Michael Green.' The almost complete dependence on web phones by all but the disenfranchised, the very old and the genuinely disinterested; a category in which Bryn included himself, was a bit of a godsend to the foot-weary detective. Most people kept almost their entire social network and history plotted in their address books and web search records, Facebook pages and Twitter accounts mobiles. It was long way from the chance discovery of an address book or diary or the often inaccurate knowledge about friend, relative, parent or child expressed by one about the other, which was the only way possible before that. Perhaps their actual social lives were there too he mused, recalling the many occasions he had sat in a bar or pub surrounded by young people tapping away on their phones like techno Trappists; not talking at all, or hardly at all, to each other.

'Now, to what is probably the only new information. Our jovial friend Geoffrey, of the spattered green scrubs and St Nicholas beard, has confirmed that Michael Green was killed by a single gunshot wound to the middle of his forehead; pretty much dead centre,' he said, to faint clapping and groans, nodding to acknowledge the applause. 'There is a little more. The bullet is small calibre, our hirsute friend thinks that although it looks like standard ammo and makes holes like standard ammo it has been modified, probably by cutting slots in the nose so that it broke up on impact and just ricocheted around the inside of his skull. Shaken and stirred then.' More groans. 'We should hear tomorrow from ballistics.'

'White van; only link with killer?' Gray as usual got there with very little fuss.

'Just so, Gray. Lucy, ask Mr Thomas if he can tell us anything more about the van. Was the van involved at all? It was apparently there when Mr Thomas arrived and was not when he came back to collect his stuff with Dai Swab. Since Mr Thomas saw nobody else on the beach, then it may have been used by the killer. If it was involved, he would have driven off sharpish when he saw Mr Thomas. Which way would you go Dai? Not many roads off Gower.' Dai looked to his inner map.

'I'd take the North Gower Road out to the M4 then away; twenty five minutes maybe? He could be almost anywhere by now. There aren't any cameras on Gower, so unless he went to town, no records. Not much chance of anyone noticing a white van. If he's a pro, then he might see the risk that somebody at Hillend takes the number and we use the cameras on the motorways clock him.' Dai shrugged and said 'so maybe he hired it locally, maybe he dumped the van. My money would be on stealing or hiring a van and coming in for the hit and out as soon as.

I'd leave the van somewhere not very far away and catch a bus or train or swap cars or get picked up somewhere, which probably means Swansea or Llanelli.' There were sage nods from the audience who were pleased that their thinking had already been done for them.

'Thank you Dai. Gray, since you effectively volunteered yourself, talk to Traffic, alert them to look out for a white van abandoned in Swansea or Llanelli. If we get a description of the driver from the caravan folk, talk to Constables Williams and Ferrari, they can ask around at the railway and bus stations. If we were good when we were young then we might even have a registration number.' He looked around at the motley crew, 'but probably not.'

'He might be a she sir.'

'Quite so Lucy, we would regret a road not taken. Last thing,' he paused, 'we don't yet know how Michael Green got to Llangennith. He has a Volvo S60, silver metallic, Gray has the number. Traffic are looking, keep an eye out. There is a bus leaves Swansea seven forty, arrives Llangennith just before nine; tight, but possible. Dai, get a picture of Michael Green from DVLC and show it to the driver of the early bus, there aren't many people going out to Gower on the early one. Anything else anyone wants to say?' Silence, he looked around quickly. 'OK, finish what you started today, get some sleep, be up and at it tomorrow. Here at eight please. Go!' Bryn rubbed his eyes and sat down for a few minutes. There was nothing more he could do tonight; he hoped that there would be new information tomorrow. He would let the small amount they did have roll around his head overnight. Something useful usually emerged. He got up, collected his bag and coat in the office and nodding at the sergeant on his way out, walked across to his car.

The light blue Bentley sat between the Mondeos and Skodas looking like a beneficent uncle, as well it might because it was roughly the same age as one, thirty four next birthday. The kind of car that might make somebody stop at a used car display. Apart from Lucy's green mini Cooper, the car park was almost a uniform sea of silver. Next year it would be white. The car was an indulgence; not excessively in cost. To buy five years ago it was roughly the price of a Ford Fiesta. Maintenance was the real problem and parts were expensive and not always easy to get hold of. When Paul at the garage in Cilibion handed in his spanner, he might just have to let it go. Until then he would enjoy the smell of leather and machinery which greeted him every time he opened the door and that particular kind of clunk that only heavy and well-made doors could make when they were closed. He jumped with annoyance when passengers casually shoved the door back hard. Steady now, he wanted to say, treat the old boy with respect, it's not a bloody Vauxhall. Fuel was an issue; the six litre V8 had lots of things going for it, but economy was not one of them. He used it only in the summer, the rest of the time it stood in his well-appointed garage, whilst its substitute, a truly dilapidated Corsa battled out the winters.

He made his way out of town towards Gower on the main road out through Uplands, then on through to the outskirts of town at Upper Killay. Here the road effectively forked to either the north Gower road to

Llangennith or the south Gower road to Port Einon, past the magnificent sand and limestone cliff beaches that made Gower the first area in the UK to achieve the status of Area of Outstanding Natural Beauty. The south Gower villages were prettier and the beaches more dramatic, but that very lure had destroyed the community heart of the southern villages. The shocking discrepancy between wages in rural areas and big cities, particularly the voracious maw of London, meant that many people had, inadvertently, destroyed piece-by-piece the fabric of local communities by buying second homes. These irregular visitors not only deprived the villages of another live-in family with children growing up, using the local schools, buying at the local store and creating a whole and changing community, but did not significantly contribute to the local economy, often bringing food in the boot of their car from city supermarkets. In contrast, the north Gower villages away from the pretty beaches were now the cultural hub of Gower with strong local communities which flourished in the winter as well as summer. Even so, the comparatively high prices of houses on Gower were mostly out of reach of the sons and daughters of local farmers whose incomes have not changed much for years and who must either find other things to do with the land or move away.

Kevin Bryn lived in Landimore, only a few miles from the very murder he was investigating. He had lived there since he split up with his first and only wife in the early years of the Millennium. It was the usual story of the job eventually squeezing out the other parts of his life. The mental freedom to do his job without hindrance was definitely better than having to continually explain that he would be late back and the quarrels that ensued. But he dearly missed his ex wife and was pleased that they had become reliable friends after the bitter months had run their course. Landimore had no pub and no church but sat on the edge of a salt marsh, grazed by herds of wild Welsh cobs and sheep whose flesh was sold by a local farm and enjoyed in local restaurants. Before the salt marsh had taken over the estuary, probably over the last couple of hundred years, the village had been a fishing and minor industrial port shipping mostly lime to Carmarthenshire in return for coal. There were two local pubs within five minutes' drive; one to the east and one to the west, both selling very decent beer. The one to the east had even started making their own. The access to walking was the thing that sold the house to Bryn. He could walk from the front door in several different directions. The coast of Gower was part of the Wales coast path which embraced the whole coastline uninterrupted from Chepstow to Chester. He had walked large stretches of it and contemplated the day when he could walk the whole distance in one sitting. Inland, the paths took him to the Burry valley and out towards Fairy Hill and the south coast or in the other direction upland walks across the tops of Llanmadoc Hill and Rhosilli Down to the west coast. The house was a typical stone-built workers' cottage which was barely two up and two down and was probably built in the eighteenth or early nineteenth century. His cottage had an extension to the rear for a kitchen, which was its only real concession to the twentieth and twenty first centuries.

Bryn set a match to the kindling and paper in the small woodstove which stood at one side of the space which was both kitchen and living area. In May it was still cool at night and anyway, a lit woodstove cheered the spirit on any night of the year. He was fond of cooking and did so whenever the opportunity was presented at a reasonable hour by his work. It was nearly nine o'clock now, so he simply put some pasta on the stove which he would consume with pesto and a liberal grating of his chunk of Parmigiano cheese. He would make a tomato salad sliced with some olive oil. He poured himself a glass of merlot and checked the news on his tablet. He would watch the nine o'clock news occasionally, but preferred to read and do, rather than watch and listen. He ate his supper then cleared up. Always leave things as you found them his mother would say. He plodded up the stairs to continue with his novel, a crime fiction set in Australia; brutal, funny. It made him laugh out loud. Within the hour he was asleep, after the inevitable hazy questions about who and why, that were drifting around at the edge of his subconscious, had subsided.

Tuesday

He arose early, ordered coffee and croissants on room service then made his way to the ferry terminal by taxi. He checked in as a foot passenger for the 9.00am sailing on the fast ferry to Cherbourg.

Bryn was back at his office in Swansea by seven thirty the next morning, missing most of the modest commuter traffic between Gower and the centre of town. On his desk was the ballistics report which, almost to the letter, matched the thoughts of Geoffrey Jones. The extra information was that the tampering Geoffrey had suspected seemed to be confirmed by fine scratches on the copper jacket where a cross had been sawn part way into the nose of the bullet. The modifications with the saw would have resulted in the bullet fragmenting on impact. Bloody Santa Claus was spot on. His smirk when he told him might well be unbearable, so perhaps Bryn would wait for him to ask. Ballistics also noted that this type of bullet could not be fired from a high velocity rifle, it would fragment in the barrel and so was strictly a hand gun, close range modification, which they speculated would ensure a fatal wound if it entered the skull, as it had in this case. Geoffrey would be pretty pleased with this report. The paint can image returned to haunt him. There was another anomaly. According to ballistics, there were no clear marks on the outside of the fragments that would normally have been made by the spiral rifling inside the barrel of the gun. They were puzzled by this; they would come back to him after doing some trawling, see if they couldn't find some precedents. This confirmation of the short range nature of the bullet, made what they knew about the case so far, almost impossible to put together, unless the Uplands lad had fired the shot from a hand gun. He made a note to ask ballistics more about the type of weapon which could have fired the fatal shot. Hell and damnation, he should have mapped footprints to and from the body on the beach, should have put our Mr Thomas to the torch in the first interview. Everything he had done now seemed absurdly gentle, even negligent, with the only witness now a likely suspect and all evidence washed away by the tide. He had been led astray by the natural and straightforward responses by Thomas, as he now thought of him and the fact that he had been the one to call the emergency services and to remain by the body. A very cool performance, if Thomas was their man, although he still baulked at the idea of him as a contract killer. He would wait to see what else emerged when the team arrived in the next few minutes. Evidence was king; but every fibre of his intuitive self, that subconscious machine that collates nuances and details had Thomas down as only a witness. However, Occam had been here before, so he sat with some coffee and ate the Danish, which he had bought at the metro store, his jaw stopping momentarily, as each thought passed across the narrative in his mind's eye and was evaluated.

Bryn clapped his hands to slow and eventually stop the chatter of new thoughts which had been generated miraculously in the night and which were now swapping between brains using mere pressure waves of air.

'Our first development I think, ladies and gentlemen. Ballistics have confirmed in almost every detail the speculations of our hirsute Mr Jones. The bullet has been tampered with by cutting grooves in the nose and in the opinion of our technical betters; these bullets could not have been fired from a high velocity rifle, only from a pistol. It means that it is not possible for the shot to have been fired from the dunes, *ergo*, it must have been from close range and the only person there, as far as we know, was Mr Thomas. Why the bullet was cut we don't know yet; ballistics think maybe to reduce range and possible collateral damage; maybe to ensure all head shots are fatal. So Dai, no need at present to bother our khaki friends, who would have probably ignored our enquiries anyway. I conclude, tentatively, that Mr Thomas therefore is either the killer or was working with the killer. I was of the strong opinion that he was simply a witness, but it seems I am wrong. I would very much like some corroborating evidence, but we will go to arrest him this morning with or without.' There was a hum of conversation, trying on the new information for size.

'Sir, I have something which seems much more interesting now, than it seemed to me last night.'

'Lucy, bringer of solace, spit it out.' Bryn's heart rate went up a notch; Lucy didn't deal in trivia.

'I checked Mr Thomas's bank details last night before I left. A sum of ten thousand pounds appeared as credit in his account an hour or two before I made the search. Directly below, two sums of five thousand pounds were debited to different unidentified accounts; could be offshore accounts, could be somewhere else. Anyway, not the sort of stuff you find in the average bank account.' There was complete silence and just as Bryn was about to issue a further eulogy, Lucy spoke again.

'It looks to me like a payoff for the killing.'

'This knocks some of the guesswork out Lucy, *iawn*, bloody *dda iawn*' flapped Bryn as he did his Celtic knot thinking dance around and amongst his colleagues. 'We left a contract killer loose in the law abiding western suburbs of Swansea. Mothers and Osprey's's supporters would have shaken in their beds with good reason. Right, unless anyone has something of equal significance and urgency to impart, I suggest that you, constables Williams and Ferrari, get down and commandeer a nice four seater car for us to bring the slippery Mr Thomas back here for a chat. The rest of you will need to change priorities somewhat. Put all your efforts on Mr Thomas for the next couple of hours. Gray; he must have thrown the gun and the empty cartridge case into the sea. We need to find it as a priority.' He looked at his watch, 'unfortunately, the tide should still be on the flood, judging by yesterday; bloody nuisance. Ask the SOCOs what to do. There must be some metal detector gadget they or we can use when the tide ebbs. We want SOCO data from the gunshot swab, the VW and the bagged clothes, as soon as. Lucy, carry on digging at his contacts. Anything you can find which will sharpen the interview appreciated. We have twenty four hours to either charge or release him. Go!' With that, he stormed out of the room on his way to Uplands. Gray shook his head slowly, all this rushing about was not his way of doing things, more brain, less boots. He was surprised at what had emerged but suspicious too. He got on the phone to the SOCOs

The police car arrived ostentatiously, as they do, outside number 45 Knoll Avenue. Curtains would be twitching, parents, with their children on the swings and slides would be stopping to look across from Brynmill Park. Williams knocked firmly on the front door and watched as a figure opened the inner door and then seeing the posse at the front door, opened it quickly.

'Detective Inspector Kevin Bryn again,' said Mr Thomas senior rather uncertainly, 'you'd better come in.' They all squeezed through, first the front door and then the inner door into a hallway to the back of the house. The stairs went up to the first floor to the right. Here they found themselves in the same position as demonstrators kettled by the Metropolitan police. Mrs Thomas came out into the hall from the kitchen looking anxiously between her husband and the group of police.

'It's your son Huw we would like to talk to Mr Thomas, is he here?'

Mr Thomas senior nodded, 'he's upstairs; HUW! He shouted. Huw appeared at the top of the stairs and seeing the posse looked a little taken aback. He walked down the stairs towards DI Bryn whose eyes followed him all the way.

'Some new information has come to light Huw, I am arresting you for the suspected murder of Michael Green, yesterday, the 13th of May at Llangennith. You have the right to remain silent but anything you say may be used in evidence against you and your silence may count against you.' Huw's mouth opened in disbelief as did his father's. His mother put her hands to her face, only the wide open eyes visible above.

'Inspector, surely you must be making some mistake, Huw a killer?' Was the best that he could manage.

46

'Huw is coming with us now, Mr Thomas, we will be going to Central, you may of course come along, but he is under arrest. You will not be able to talk to him or see him until we have finished our questioning. We have twenty four hours and can request another twenty four hours if necessary. He won't be coming home tonight. If you have a family solicitor you might want him to be present, if so, send him there now, otherwise we'll provide somebody from the pool.' Huw nodded resignedly to his father.

'We do, I'll contact him now.' With that, Bryn guided Huw's shoulder towards the front door and out into the street. He was helped gently, but firmly into the back seat between the two constables. Mr Thomas senior and his wife were left looking shocked at the front door.

Huw was wise enough not to make small talk in the back and he uttered no words until they got into the station and he gave his details to the custody sergeant who wrote them in his book. He also listed the contents of Huw's pockets and asked Huw to sign for them. 'Escort Mr Thomas to cell four constable' and he walked, arm held by Williams along the corridor and out of sight.

'OK team, well done, let's get back to the ops room and see if we have any more information. Dai and I will do the interview, say half an hour, room 2; Ferrari, you can sit in.' They walked off. Word went round that Thomas was now in custody and the team filed into the ops room in dribs and drabs, depending on what they were doing. The display boards had undergone something of a transformation now that there was a focus for the enquiry. A photograph of Huw Thomas was pinned at the top, personal details, a picture of his van and the inside, contact names, numbers and email addresses from his mobile. On the other side, pictures of the victim, Michael Green, at the beach, his personal details, information about his work at the university, his contacts and a photograph of the pieces of bullet in a dish, a couple of comments from ballistics.

Bryn, Gray and Dai Swab sat around a table and went through an interview scenario until they were happy with the structure. Bryn to lead, Dai to back up and Gray in the observation room ready to send down notes if anything profound occurred to him. Lucy was there too to help with any technical stuff if it arose; but otherwise to just observe. They were ready.

Huw was sitting in a metal-framed chair at one end of the table with constable Ferrari standing by the door. Bryn and Dai Swab let themselves in. Bryn sat opposite Huw and Dai stood up against the wall. Mr Parker, the solicitor who had done their first family conveyance, but had never yet had to act for them in any criminal capacity, had been apprised of the situation and was sitting next to Huw with his notepad on the desk. Bryn introduced the assembled company to the tape as before. It was almost exactly twenty four hours ago that Huw had been sat in that very seat. He felt decidedly less sure of himself this time, but strangely resigned. He knew he couldn't stop what was happening and knew that he had done nothing. He knew equally well that innocent people were convicted. Bryn nodded to the solicitor.

'Huw, you know why you are here, would you like to tell us about it.' Huw looked at his solicitor and said 'I told you everything I know yesterday, I saw someone being shot, I ran to help and I let you look at my mobile and computer. I have nothing to hide.'

'How do you make a living Mr Thomas?' Huw looked to his right again, Mr Parker nodded.

'I don't make much of one actually. I work lunchtimes and some evenings at the Tav, sorry, the Uplands Tavern three days a week. I get some labouring work with a couple of the local builders when they are busy. I'm still looking for the right thing, haven't found it yet; it was silly to leave university.'

'How much do you make a year?' Huw hesitated. 'I'm not the tax man Mr Thomas. Let me guess, minimum wage at the pub, cash in hand for the labouring. What; five thousand pounds, six thousand a year?' Huw hung his head a little, 'something like that, maybe a bit more'

'Give your dad rent?' tilting his head to one side, 'food, heating, that kind of thing?' Huw looked miserable now as he reflected on the worthlessness of his contributions.

'Not a lot, no. I give my dad some rent,' he blushed, 'a token rent. I'm looking for a job, have been for a year, there's not much out there.'

'Inspector, is this economic discussion leading anywhere?'

'It is Mr Parker.' Bryn adjusted his position on the seat as he leaned forward to look at Huw. 'Do you have any savings Huw?' He gave a hollow laugh.

'I've got some premium bonds, fifty pounds, never won a penny.'

'Bank account, building society accounts, shares, rich aunties?' Bryn continued to lean forward looking at Huw

'Offshore investment accounts?' Chipped in Dai, 'Brokers, financial advisors?' Huw shook his head slowly looking at the table.

'For the tape Huw please,' said Bryn.

'No, a bank account and a few hundred pounds in a building society account. I try to put some by.' Huw turned to his solicitor with a questioning look.

'Bank account in credit is it Huw?'

'Mostly it is,' said Huw.

'How much? One hundred, five hundred, what's in there now do you think?'

'Haven't looked this week, but maybe two hundred pounds,' Huw didn't look very interested.

'Oh I think you did look this week Huw' Bryn looked down at his notes. 'It says here that ten thousand pounds was deposited into your account electronically just after 5pm yesterday evening and that shortly afterwards, two lots of five thousand pounds were parcelled out to two different accounts, probably offshore accounts. We don't know where yet Huw, but we will.'

Both Huw and the solicitor looked up and then at each other, with the same expressions of astonishment on their faces, but for two completely different reasons.

'Now perhaps you would you like to tell us what is going on? Why did you kill him? Who hired you?' Huw shook his head and looked helplessly at his solicitor.

'Inspector, I think you can see that Mr Thomas knows nothing of this and frankly, knowing the family, I find it very hard to believe. There must be a mistake somewhere, a big mistake. I need a discussion with my client before we proceed, otherwise I will instruct him to say nothing more.'

Bryn sighed. 'As you will Mr Parker; you have thirty minutes. Interview terminated at eleven twenty hours. Constable Ferrari, would you please escort Mr Parker and Mr Thomas back to cell four?'

Gray and Lucy made their way down to the interview room after watching. 'What did you make of that Gray, Lucy?' Bryn asked.

'Lawrence bloody Olivier or telling truth.' Another bloody soliloquy, thought Bryn.

'Lucy?' Bryn arched his eyebrow again.

'Same sir, I'm afraid; if he is the killer he's pretty cool. Professional killers are usually self-controlled and controlling psychopaths. Sometimes even their friends or family don't see anything wrong. They are clever, can live comparatively normal lives, but do tend to the autistic and obsessive side of human behaviour. Does this seem to be the behaviour pattern of Mr Thomas?' She said, indicating that she certainly did not think so. Why these words were spilling out from her mouth she had no idea. If anything he seemed vulnerable not controlling. She was flustered, but could not articulate why. She tried to imagine how he might have felt. What did you say when you were accused and knew you'd done nothing. But at the same moment she also imagined talking to him in a bar, at the beach. It was this that had made her flustered and she hoped that she wasn't blushing. Lucy had often thought about the injustice of the parole system where prisoners could not be granted parole unless they showed true remorse for the crime they had been accused and convicted of. What about those who could not show remorse because they had been wrongly convicted They had to suffer the

51

double burden of having to serve the full sentence as an innocent person. How did those people survive? It was a hard and unforgiving system and it also got it wrong far too many times. She'd been in court on enough occasions to know this. Even Bryn had been taken aback by Lucy's passionate outburst; it was physics she did, not bloody psychology.

'Thank you Lucy. No we don't know enough.' Bryn got up to pace again, but turned to look at her with a puzzled expression before he moved on. 'We have direct evidence in the form of a payment of ten thousand pounds to his account on the afternoon of the killing. We have to think of that as payment for the killing, his denial is would be what we might expect if he thought he was beyond suspicion.' He raised his eyes in her direction again, 'we need to know more about the payment details Lucy. We know the bullet that killed Michael Green could not have been fired from as far as the dunes, so apparently there couldn't have been a sniper and Thomas himself has signed a statement saying that nobody else was on the beach. Again, he would say that if he thought that we would have to assume a sniper based on his 'nobody else there' claim. He may not have thought that we have the ballistics evidence.'

'The van in the car park b'there is also rather convenient sir, and it's only his word that it exists at all let alone that it disappeared. He could have set us up very nicely sir.' Dai sat back and looked at each of his colleagues to check that his icing had sat happily on their respective cakes.

The four of them were silent for a few minutes weighing up what they knew and playing with the options.

But they all knew that it was not quite enough to be certain of anything, not enough for a conviction.

'OK, we need the gunshot residue results and we need the SOCOs to find the gun. The tide should be low enough early this afternoon. If we get that, we get our killer. Gray, offer money, beer or even free tickets to the ball to your pals to make sure we get this stuff today latest. Remind them that we have only,' Bryn looked at his watch, 'about twenty two hours before we may need to release him and I definitely do not want to do that. OK Gray and Lucy, SOCOs and payment details, off you go, chop chop.'

Ferrari escorted Mr Parker and Huw Thomas back into the interview room, both looking a little pale and subdued. Bryn would dearly have liked to know what the conversation had been like. Was Parker trying to weigh up his client's guilt? Did they talk about mitigation of sentence? Did Huw Thomas tell his solicitor that it was up to the police to provide evidence, not for him to deny it, and for his solicitor to back him whatever the weather? Bryn reintroduced the players to the tape machine.

'Chief Inspector, we have heard what you and your colleague had to say. My client denies any knowledge of the payments into his account and stands by the signed statement he made at his first interview yesterday. You know that you don't have enough to charge him and you know that he will need to be released tomorrow morning if you don't. The ball is firmly in your court Chief Inspector.'

Bryn grimaced. 'OK, Detective Williams, ask Constable Ferrari to return Mr Thomas to his cell. We will talk again Mr Parker.' He terminated the interview.

They stood up and Ferrari led Thomas and Parker out of the room. Bryn sat down again. The waiting was always the hardest part of this game, the only relief was to get on and do something. That relief appeared in the form of Constable Williams.

'Mr and Mrs Green sir, Michael Green's father and mother; they've just come in from Bristol airport on the train, they're sitting with the sergeant.' He pointed back out of the room.

'Thank you constable; Dai, help Lucy or Gray, whoever wants some extra hands. Be back here in about half an hour. You can come with me out to Llangennith to see how the SOCOs are getting on. Tell Williams to bring a cuppa and some biscuits along here for Mr and Mrs Green and to be ready to go with Ferrari to take them to the mortuary, we need a formal identification.' Bryn went along to bring the Greens back to the interview room, where he sat them down and offered his sincere condolences, not worth much he knew if you had been told only yesterday that your son had been murdered. He told them only that somebody was helping out with their enquiries and that the motive was completely unknown at present. He asked them if they were aware of any problems Michael had or anything at all that might help them to understand the murder. He asked them if they knew a Huw Thomas, to which they looked at each other and both shook their heads. They said that they saw their son only once or twice a year and that they were simply baffled as to possible motive. Bryn thanked them and asked Williams and Ferrari to take them to the mortuary and then for them to go on out to Hillend to question potential witnesses in nearby caravans.

'Are you staying locally?' he asked as they were leaving. They had booked three days in the Marriott Hotel. He would contact them there if he needed to ask more questions or if he had any news.

Bryn and Dai Swab made their way in the pool Mondeo out to Llangennith. Neither said much. They stopped at the café on the Hillend site for take-away coffees and bacon baps and carried on down to the beach car park. The SOCOs van was there along with several other cars, mostly belonging to walkers Bryn supposed. The surf wouldn't be much good at this state of the tide. He walked, still chewing his sandwich along the sandy path out to the windy beach. The sound of the surf nearly drowned out the chirruping of larks singing their territory above the low-lying meadows behind the dunes. The breeze drifted the shadows of white cumulus smoothly across the beach, and then reluctantly it seemed, as if tired by all that blowing, up and over the dunes behind. The SOCOs could be seen, three of them with metal detectors quartering the large patch of sand. It was marked off by tape and string lines, to ensure that they didn't miss a single square foot of sand, because sod's law would ensure that it was that very square foot of sand under which lay the gun. The sea beat the sand twenty yards away now and was receding. Bryn and Dai walked steadily towards them and when close up shouted and waved to Bill Wood, the head of the team. Just one word from the SOCOs and they had their man. He half expected that the shear electricity crackling round his brain would set off the metal detectors.

'How's it going Bill? This has got to be better than scraping around in plastic bin bags in Blaen y Maes?'

'Bryn, it's good to see you,' and in anticipation of his question, 'nothing yet, but we haven't finished the first sweep. The tide is on the ebb for about another three hours, so we will keep sweeping this area for a couple of hours, then add fifty yards or so west when the tide turns, in case it has been dragged towards Burry Holm. The tidal sweep tends to be northwards because of the Worm.'

'How deep do you think it might be?'

'Well, it's suffered two tides since it was thrown into the sea, so it could be as much as two feet down. The detectors are pretty sensitive, they should be able to pick up the gun down to maybe three feet, but might not pick up a cartridge case if it was ejected.' The Worm is a tidal island in the form of a hump-backed rock ridge which is easy to imagine as some giant dragon or creature basking in the sea. This rock wall marks the southern end of Rhosilli beach and is home to nesting guillemots and shearwaters and to thrift and dune flowers on the sea-sprayed turf. It is a wild place in a storm, but a heavenly picnic spot in summer.

Bryn's mobile rang. It was the simulation of the ringing telephone bell of the 1960s, a sound he curiously found familiar even though he had not even been born then.

'Bryn,' he said, looking up 'right, go on, yes, yes, only one witness to that? OK. Good work Williams. Get as much of a description as you can, probably only a walker.'

56

He pressed the red button and looked at the phone as if it might give him some further information; lead him on the true path. He put it in his pocket. 'Right Dai,' he said rubbing his hands together in anticipation, 'the white van does exist and it was seen by a caravanner with his dog at the right time, in the right place. Unfortunately, the dog walker went off south towards the Worm, so he didn't see anything else. He didn't recall seeing the VW, so either he just doesn't remember or the white van was there first, just as Thomas said. But, he also said that he saw a man, medium build, outdoor gear on take a rucksack out from the rear of the van and walk off towards the beach; that's it.' Bryn licked his finger and held it up to determine the wind direction. It was simply a displacement activity to hide his need to be doing something. 'Williams is getting a formal statement. Williams and Ferrari still have other people to talk to on the site, so there may be more.' He glanced around him at the ripples and pools on the beach and noticed his wet shoes with a grimace. 'We don't yet know even if Thomas had an accomplice; it would be good to get a sighting of anyone leaving the VW.' Bryn looked up the beach towards where the caravans are and where Williams and Ferrari would be walking amongst them. 'We'll leave them all to it, nothing much more we can do here, just sit on our hands.' Bryn had needed to come to the beach to relieve the tension, he now needed to leave.

They arrived back in Central after lunch. The identification of Michael Green by his parents was positive. It was never much in doubt, but it was another uncertainty ticked off. Lucy was on the telephone with

Thomas's computer on the desk in front of her and Gray was moping behind his desk tapping his pencil.

'Is there anything on the gunshot swab Gray?' Gray shook his head. 'We have a positive sighting of the van by one of the caravanners; it appears that it may have been there before Thomas said he arrived in the VW, but not by very much. He also saw a man get out of the van and take a rucksack from the boot. Could be important, could just be a walker off on a hike.'

'Not walker,' said Gray categorically. Bryn twitched round to face him, a hand cupped behind one ear.

'Go on Gray, my antennae are quivering, hit me.'

'Walker wouldn't take rucksack on short walk.'

'That's it Gray; thought provoking.' Lucy had put down her telephone and was following the stilted conversation.

'He's right sir, if the white van got there just before Thomas, ten minutes, twenty minutes, doesn't really matter, we know it was gone by what, twenty past nine? You don't need a rucksack for that kind of walk.' Bryn was now meandering around the space.

'So; if he wasn't a walker then what? Lucy?'

'He is a candidate for the sniper sir.'

'Not sniper; Bullet not right,' mumbled Gray looking aside.

'Here we have the central conundrum, the exquisite twist that makes our jobs so engaging on the one hand and so bloody frustrating on the other. We have no other suspect but Thomas and we have the unaccounted for payment of money. He says another white van was there, we now know that this is true. We also know that a man with a rucksack left the van just before Thomas arrived

58

and left before Thomas and Dai here collected his clothes from the VW. Is the rucksack man our killer or is he just a walker, to keep us awake at night?' Bryn spread his hands in supplication to his colleagues.

Gray answered; 'Money went into account and straight out, somebody setting him up?'

Kevin Bryn shut his eyes and looked upwards stroking his chin. 'Gray, I'm glad you're on our side; useful thought. You should have considered a career in science, making sense of the apparently senseless, never being seduced by the obvious.' He paused, 'So, not only setting Mr Thomas up Gray, but us too,' Bryn got up to do his thinking dance. 'We don't know enough yet though, do we?' said Bryn, still pacing.

'We will when we get the gunshot residue results sir,' said Lucy. Bryn nodded.

'We will Lucy, we will;' he left the room chewing his lip.

Bryn knocked on the door to his Super's office. She was just back from a management course at training headquarters in Bridgend 'Enter.' Bryn walked towards Superintendent Maureen Fellows who was sitting at her desk. 'Thanks for calling Inspector,' she said, still unpacking her briefcase onto the desk. 'A shootin' on Llangennith beach Kevin. Whatever next eh?'

Bryn went through the events of the last day and a half, what little, but significant evidence they had, the puzzles which were not yet resolved and the arrest of Huw Thomas.

'Mm, you don't sound as jubilant as you might be about Mr Thomas.'

'I'm not, Ma'am, I'm not at all sure, despite what the evidence says so far. He is either extremely good at acting innocent or he actually is. The gunshot residue analysis is due in any time and that should tell us for sure if he fired the shot.' Bryn described the ballistics data and the bank payment. 'We have no witnesses yet to his arrival at the scene. We don't even know if he was alone, as he says he was.'

Bryn went over the white van and rucksack man ideas and the lack of any corroborating evidence either way.

'I have asked the sergeant to run a news conference at six tonight, here. It would be good to have you there Ma'am.' The Superintendent nodded her assent. 'Nae bother Kevin. Drop off a summary of what you have on my desk and what you want me focus on at the meeting. You'll be there I trust Kevin?' It was Bryn's turn to nod. Maureen Fellows had been recruited from Glasgow, outside the force, to try to sweep away the remnants of the old copper's rugby club network which had pretty much run the show up until recently and which had become complacent and resistant to change. The idea was to bring in both a female and new ideas at the same time in a *donner und blitzen* tactic. It had seemed to work; some of the disaffected had left early or on the sick. Against all the tenets of station folklore, Bryn was developing a great respect for his Super.

Lucy had worked last night to get the bank information and encrypted message data and had been working for most of the afternoon looking at the way the bank transaction had been executed and trying to identify the overseas accounts into which the money had been transferred via Thomas's bank account. She had talked to the technical people in the bank and they confirmed that the payment was listed as a CHAPS payment; the rapid cash transfer system that many customers can now use, at a price, to transfer their own money around. Who, she wanted to know had sent it. On the account, the payment had been listed as 'automatic credit', the same as payments into her own account from her police salary, except with the identifier tag WHO. Was this a joke? The technical person at the bank promised to investigate further; they would also look at the two payments out. She floated the credit and debit payment details that she had to some of her trusted contacts out there in her unofficial hacking world to see if any of them had come across similar payment codes or could help identify them. She had watched his behaviour minutely in the interviews and like most of the rest of team, all her experience of interviews and criminals had said that he was genuinely shocked and telling the truth. Gray was right, the money was no longer in his account, it went in and it went out. Lucy realised that someone with the knowledge to get behind the encrypted money transfer system or the ability to make non-existent transactions appear in the records could just make it look as if he had been paid. If that was true, what else was there to incriminate Huw Thomas? There was nothing; certainly not enough evidence to charge or convict him.

Bryn appeared over her right shoulder; 'No gunshot residue on either Huw Thomas's hands or clothing, the lab just called.' He sat on the corner of her desk; 'we can't hold Thomas, we certainly won't get an extension unless we have much more. How's the computer search going?'

'Nothing new sir, his bank can identify neither the sender of cash nor the two recipient accounts. This really could be a diversion couldn't it?' Bryn nodded reluctantly, feeling like the Duke of York, neither up nor down.

'We decided that he must be lying, but there are too many ifs for my liking and my gut still tells me he is an unlikely killer. Would there have been an accomplice who fired the gun? Why drag Michael Green up the beach? Where did the accomplice disappear to? I'll check with the Super, but I'll recommend releasing him on police bail; bloody press conference at six. Shit!'

Lucy left the room with a little skip feeling slightly confused as she had after her outburst. He wasn't one hundred percent in the clear, but she was very pleased that this particular suspect was demoted again to witness.

The rest of the bad news emerged whilst Bryn was explaining the new situation to Fellows. The press conference would be postponed and a statement issued asking for witnesses of firstly a white van or the VW van in Hillend or driving across Gower yesterday morning and secondly, to look out for Michael Green's Volvo which was still missing. The public were invited to phone in. Fellows agreed that they had no further grounds to hold Huw Thomas and police bail would allow them to keep tags on where he was and to call him back in if any new evidence emerged. They would hold on to the phone and computer, but he could have his van back. Bill had called Gray to say that the trawl with the metal detectors had found nothing so far except a few fishing weights, which as he pointed out, confirmed that the detectors were working properly. They had extended the area of search and would continue until darkness fell in an hour or so, but he thought it unlikely that a gun had been thrown there. Bryn asked the sergeant to show him into Mr Thomas's cell and to prepare to release him on bail. He had him telephone both his father and his solicitor with the news that Huw was being released on bail now and that they might like to come to collect him to avoid another police car in the street. He walked into the cell and explained to a deeply relieved young man that he was being released now and the terms of his bail. The sergeant would return his belongings and he was free to go home.

An unusually quiet Kevin Bryn gathered his team for the last meeting of day two. His subdued mood was infectious.

'Two bits of news, one confirmed, one to be confirmed. No gunshot residue on Mr Thomas or on his clothing. He couldn't have fired the gun. There is also no sign of the gun on the beach. The SOCOs are still searching, but Bill is not optimistic and Bill is rarely wrong. Remember that this was only a supposition to square a circle. If he had fired the shot, but there was no gun found at the scene, he must therefore have tossed it into the sea. So the new evidence seems to rule that supposition out. We have only the apparent deposit of money into his account, but Lucy is even getting cold feet about that, leaning towards him and us, being set up.' He looked across at Lucy who nodded. 'We will want to know the why of that.' Bryn got up and walked to a space and turned back on the team. 'So we are left with the mystery white van, a man with a rucksack, Thomas's laptop and Michael Green's university PC. We don't know how Michael Green got to Llangennith, in fact we don't know very much. Bryn looked up as Ferrari and Williams came in to the back of the room.

'Welcome weary wanderers, what titbits do you have for me from the western front?' His banter was a little less enthusiastic than usual.

'Sir, we talked to everybody in the occupied vans close to the car park, apart from two or three whose vans looked in use, but we couldn't contact. Apart from the dog walker, we have two other witnesses, one saw the white van arrive to park on its own at, he estimates some time before, but close to nine; he just happened to glance out of his window and connected the time to the radio programme he was listening to, thought nothing suspicious about it. The second witness saw the VW van arrive and somebody, presumably Mr Thomas, getting out. I asked him whether he saw any other person get out or any other vehicles in the car park at the same time. He was certain that only one person got out, with a shoulder bag and surfboard, he didn't remember seeing anything else parked. None of the campers were awake apparently. Nobody saw anyone else or any other vehicles around the car park at that time.' Bryn bowed towards Ferrari and Williams in turn.

'Useful work you two. This confirms then, that the white van arrived before the VW and as we know, left before Thomas and Dai Swab got back to the car park. It confirms what Mr Thomas has told us in his statement that he was alone in the VW, there was no accomplice.

This pretty much rules out him out as anything but a witness.' Bryn outlined the negative results on the gunshot residue and the absence of a gun on the beach.

'We concentrate on the white van and the rucksack man. A press statement has gone out requesting sightings of the van, the VW and Michael's car. Traffic are out there keeping their eyes open. Lucy will continue to work with the computers and phones. That's it, until eight again tomorrow, bright eyed and bushytailed.' He turned and walked out of the room.

They had hit an impasse when all seemed to be rolling along nicely. He knew as soon as he looked at what had happened through the clarifying lens of hindsight, that they had been building paper castles. They had done the right things, interpreted the evidence fairly, but had built paper castles. Bryn needed to refresh his mind; it had been beating against the same evidence for too long now. He hated these doldrums which occurred in almost every case and left him wired and frustrated until something broke. He decided to call in for a pint on the way home, to think about something completely different, to talk to a few of his pals and neighbours. The Dog he decided, only a mile or two from his house. It was, in the back bar at least, very much a local's pub, did decent food and had a tradition for conversation in the round. Pretty much everybody talked to everybody else at some stage of the proceedings and apart from a few stools and the tables at the sides, it was a standing bar. The friendly fug and hum of conversation slapped him warmly on the cheek as he entered. Not so many pubs like this these days. It was also the place where rugby would be watched by those who could squeeze into the bar or had had the foresight to book a space in one of the eating rooms. A big passion here and for Bryn; there had been quite a lot to cheer about in 2013, and when he could make it to watch, cheer he did. The grand slam and a good chunk of the Lions win; but on gloomier years just groans. A few of the current and ex Wales internationals lived nearby and were quietly appreciated, their privacy scrupulously upheld by the locals. The landlord had started brewing his own beer recently and he ordered a pint of the weaker one, conscious that someone might be counting how much the policeman drank; and he dearly wanted to drink two. He leaned back against the familiar bar and chatted to the farmers, the milkmen, the barristers, the hustlers, the business people, the professors, the bar staff and the builders. It was conversation which could be considered to be either of trivial importance or conversation which was the very essence of community life. Past him were carried plates of food; the smell of which persuaded him that he didn't feel in the mood to cook at home tonight. He ordered fish and chips and moved onto one of the tables at the back with his second pint when the plate arrived, nodding then to new arrivals as they came in. He relaxed completely and didn't think about the murder until he was at home scanning the web news on his tablet and noticed the brief mention in the Wales section; 'Police release suspect in Llangennith shooting'. He took his book to bed with him hoping that crime fiction might displace his worries about crime reality.

Huw had gone back home in the family car, relieved and still shaking from his second encounter with the police. His mum squeezed his shoulder from the back of the car. Huw's dad looked at her in the mirror and held her eyes. Huw stared straight ahead.

'I can't really think straight; one part of me was terrified, the other deathly calm and saying that nothing could possible happen because I've haven't done anything wrong.'

'Did they tell you what made them arrest you, it must have been something they found?' Huw's dad was looking intently at him, 'You haven't done anything Huw?'

'Nothing like that dad, they found some money transfers on my bank account, lots of money. I don't know anything about it.' He paused for a few seconds. 'I must have been hacked. They thought that I'd been paid for a contract killing.' Huw burst out with a peal of nervous laughter. 'They didn't find anything on my hands for the gunshot residue test so they had to let me go. They thought that I'd shot him and thrown the gun into the sea. I have no idea why they're not considering a sniper. It had to be.' He looked at his parents in turn to check that they had understood. 'The sergeant said I'd get my van back tomorrow and my phone and computer. That's something at least.'

'Can't we do anything? Can they just come along and arrest you and tell you nothing, and then release you, just like that?' Mrs Thomas asked incredulously.

'We'll talk to Mr Parker' said her husband. They said nothing more until they returned home a few minutes later. Mr Thomas had talked earlier in the day to Huw's builder mate Gareth, who had simply called to see if Huw wanted work next week. Mr Thomas had then told him briefly about Huw having witnessed a murder, the one that he had probably read about that morning in the paper or heard on radio. So after that, word had got around and Huw's friends and surfing pals had been ringing the house all day. A city of a quarter of a million people it might be on paper, but a collection of villages with a strong sense of shared community it was on the ground. Huw's name, 'you know the one, computer whizz, surfer, wavy hair; his dad used to teach chemistry in Olchfa School, lives in Uplands, went out with Karen….' passed in more or less the same form through many lips into many a receptive ear. The wave of knowledge moved out from the centre and had probably reached the outer limits of the city by the end of the day. Later, Mr Thomas had called Gareth again, to say that Huw had been arrested for the murder. This second wave of knowledge carried a much more impressive item and probably overtook the first wave. 'Accused of murder on Llangennith Beach' was now being added to the list of identifying features causing many exhalations and low whistles, 'you mean Huw Thomas? Wow!' It would change many aspects of his life in the coming months.

Wednesday

The somewhat quieter murder team made their way with muted whispers and shrugging into the ops room. The atmosphere had definitely lost some of the anticipatory buzz of the previous morning. Williams and Ferrari were not present; they were manning the telephone lines set up to respond to calls from the public relating to the white van and Michael Green's Volvo. Bryn had called in to see them before the meeting and only a few calls had come in so far.

Bryn started the briefing in a subdued tone of voice.

'We were moving along what we thought was a line of evidence and it has gone sour. Mr Thomas is, in my opinion, no longer a suspect, but there remain some unexplained issues which are almost certainly linked to the murder and which have involved him. Primarily, we need to know about the funds which appeared and disappeared in his bank account. It was these that led us to suppose that he had been paid for a contract killing; that and the absence of any other plausible suspects.' Bryn looked across at Lucy Evans 'Lucy will be working on this today, so no distractions for her please. Ferrari and Williams are on the telephones as we speak taking calls from the public. We hope for information about the sighting of the van and the Volvo…' A mobile rang from the depths of Bryn's silk and linen jacket; he showed exaggerated signs of annoyance as he first tried to dig it out from his pocket and then put the phone to his ear, his eyes raised; 'yes Bill, ahh! Well; that explains that then.' He meandered around the floor. 'OK, thanks Bill' and he slipped the phone back into his pocket. 'Michael Green's computer Gray, it wasn't there because it had been stolen. The lab has been looking at the blow ups of the scratches on his front door lock and on the lock of one of the drawers on his desk found by the SOCOs. The lab boys are pretty sure that they were made very recently by somebody using a pick. So, more free tickets to the ball. Who the hell was our burglar then?'

'After Green left for beach, before uniforms sealed off flat' Gray offered, peering around the room for dissenters.

'When would that be then Gray, exactly?' Bryn asked, arms folded, eyebrow raised.

'Murder after nine, forty minute drive, between eight thirty and midday.' Bryn nodded.

'Could be the killer then, went back after the beach; knew Green wouldn't be there.' a smile flickered across Bryn's face when he realised that he had inadvertently mimicked the sparse locution of DS Crossman.

'Plausible sir' said Dai, 'there might be information he wants on the computer.'

'Thanks Dai, yes possible, it could even be the motive for the killing; something which Green knew and that was important to or might incriminate the killer, or whoever hired him. A professional hit job, kill the guy, steal his computer to tidy up the loose ends. They must be pretty pissed off.' He sidestepped then turned round. 'We didn't get much from his neighbours first time round, probably because most of them were at work. I'll get Williams and Ferrari to knock doors again after six this evening; we have a better idea of a time window now. When did Michael Green leave his flat? Did he drive away to the beach? Did anyone see the possible intruder arrive or leave?' Bryn tapped his teeth with the biro he had been gesticulating with.

'This shifts the centre of gravity towards what Green knows or does, or who he associates with. Let's call it a contract killing shall we? We were distracted by Mr Thomas. So again Lucy, much falls on you. We also need to re-evaluate information from Mr Green's mobile on his contacts and we need to talk in more detail to his colleagues in the university, dig into his history. Gray and Dai please. Go off to Singleton after the meeting; talk to his Professor, fellow lecturers, Jennifer whatever, his PhD student, who does he talk to online and on his phone? Lucy will feed you information as she gets leads. I'll help out as things emerge. OK team, off you go'

Bryn spent an hour or so with Lucy to map out a strategy; first get numbers and contacts updated on Green's phone and his laboratory PC then check out his browser search history, erased files. She would look for anything unusual; it was a priority now to find out who this man was and who he mixed with. Bryn planned to talk to his parents, to find out more about him. These things hadn't seemed so important when they thought they had a killer in their cells, who would eventually lead them to the motive. He called reception in the Marriott, who confirmed that the Greens had not yet left. He left a message to tell them that DI Bryn was on his way.

They talked in the Green's room on the third floor overlooking Swansea Bay. The old fishing village of Mumbles was to the right with its tidal islands barely clinging to the headland with their rocky fingertips. A lighthouse was perched on the outermost hump which warned incoming sailing ships of the dangers of this string of islands and shallows on this lee shore. The land curved around from the headland towards the city to form Swansea Bay, hiding the houses and villas tucked into the wooded hillside, giving them splendid views across the sea to the east. On a clear night, the views from anywhere along here were spectacular, with the necklace of lights on the Mumbles Road reflected off the sea and mingling with the lights of the city. The dark mass of Town Hill hulked to the north as a backdrop. When the blast furnaces were emptying at the steelworks in Port Talbot beyond the eastern side of the bay, fiery red flames and sparks could be seen jumping into the sky on the horizon. Now, the view east was dominated by the new Tower. It housed expensive flats with a restaurant and bar at the top which looked over and lorded the rows of terraces below. Groups of friends would be sipping coffees, gossiping, but all distracted by the vista, just as Bryn and Mr and Mrs Green were now in their room overlooking the sea. The Greens had moved to Spain when Mr Green had retired as a financial advisor in Cardiff. They had been there for a few years and loved it. Two kinds of people seem to emigrate; those who enthusiastically seek a new life in a new culture, learn the language, make new local friends and have an adventure. The others drag their cultural baggage with them and bemoan the lack of things they left behind. The Greens were of the former persuasion and whilst they missed having friends and family close by, saw them often enough in their new home. They said that Michael had been over two or three times since they had moved and had himself moved from Cardiff to Swansea.

His parents knew relatively little about his daily life since they had left; the academic and technical world he lived in was not familiar to them. He was single, had had relationships but was effectively wedded to his ideas, focussed on his career. He'd been top of his class at Barry Boys in every year, strolled into the Computer Science Department at Imperial College with 4 A's and took the inevitable first class degree. He was made an offer by Cardiff University that he couldn't refuse, to go there for his PhD which examined algorithms for interactive computer control of machines. He was one of the youngest lecturers appointed there after he had finished his thesis. He was pleased to be back near to home. *Hiraeth*, a love of home, is strong in Welsh culture. As a child, he had always been completely entranced by computers and gadgets and had designed and made electronic circuits, his own computer and written program code. He joined computer clubs, chat forums and online discussions from an early age to talk to like-minded people all over the world. The Internet was as much home to him as the things he saw, smelt and touched in the real world around him. His parents had always been a bit wary of his online activities, partly because it isolated him from many of his peers, but also because they had a natural suspicion of things they barely understood. They were well aware of the potential for fraud and deception and of the infiltration by criminal gangs into the fabric of the internet. As to his contacts and colleagues, there were a few friends, mostly those from his time at school and Cardiff University whom his parents knew. They were mostly other computer-crazy friends. There was another from school who they thought had moved to France, but they hadn't seen or heard from him since school and they'd not seen much of him then. His parents gave Bryn a list of those they could remember, just three, who they thought still lived around Cardiff. He had a sister; but since she was a few years younger, they didn't think she would have anything much to add to their list of friends. Bryn thanked them for their time and for the coffee. As he got up to leave, he apologised, as he always had to do, to friends and relatives of victims, for the seeming lack of progress. He knew that whatever he did, it wouldn't be enough. The prickles of guilt and remorse had and probably never would, go away. The Greens told him that they would go back to Spain after the funeral the following week when the body had been released from the post mortem. The service and wake were to be held in Barry.

He had been following all the media output so far on the case with interest, it wasn't often he watched the news or listened to local radio online, he even read some of the local rag. He congratulated himself on the arrest of Huw Thomas, the little decoys he had left on his computer had done better than he could ever have imagined. The police would first be congratulating themselves, then would be running round in circles for days chasing their own tails. He smiled at his audacity. The other police forces hadn't made any progress on his other exploits and they'd been fumbling around for a few years now. It felt sometimes as if he were choreographing his own comic opera; a little bit of tragedy, a lot of humour. He didn't expect anything different from the Swansea police. He dearly wanted somebody he could talk to about his perfect crimes, to explain how he did it, to tell them what fun it was; but you couldn't always have everything you *wanted could you? Thomas's picture had been on the front page; he didn't think he'd be looking as chirpy now as he did in his photograph after a night in the cells. Not a bad looking boy; he would be released eventually, but you never could be sure with the British justice system. Everybody got a bit overexcited after a murder and that's when you made mistakes.*

Bryn went back to talk to Ferrari and Williams, manning the telephones at Central, to see what had come in. Bingo; Michael Green's Volvo had been found in a car park in Broughton, the next bay around the headland from Llangennith. The caravan site owner adjacent had noticed it there for two nights and was going to call it in when he had heard the request for information on the radio the previous evening.

'Good work; anything else?' said Bryn looking at the notes. There had been two calls reporting the possible sighting of the Volvo, one at Caswell and one at Llanrhidian, where it was seen at the garage. Both sightings were at the right time of around half past eight. The latter was on the direct route from Swansea to Llangennith. Caswell, a bay on the south coast, was not on that route. Had he been there for some reason on the way or was it just a sighting of another Volvo? The Caswell sighting had two people in the car, at Llanrhidian garage, it was only a sighting of the empty car. Bryn was aware that this might be important. Most garages had CCTV these days didn't they?

'Give the garage a ring Ceri and ask if they have footage of visitors to the garage on their CCTV system and whether they still have the tape or disc or whatever for Monday morning. Go there anyway to see if the staff remember anything more about the car or who was driving it, bring back the tape. You can cope on your own Williams?' Constable Williams nodded disconsolately as he listened to another call. Bryn rubbed his hands together, they had some momentum again. It felt good. So Bryn wandered a complex route determined by his thought patterns back to the ops room, during which journey he stopped and realised suddenly with a jump of adrenalin, that Michael Green had been asked specifically to park at Broughton, the only other parking access to Llangennith beach, so that he wouldn't meet his attacker parked in the white van at Hillend. Of course! He blocked the corridor for the couple of minutes it took him to realise the implications. Had Michael been lured to a meeting of some kind which went wrong, or had the killer told him where to be at a particular time so that he could murder him, making sure that Michael Green would not see him or his van beforehand? In Bryn's mind, the circumstances of the murder had solidified from supposition into fact. Bryn could visualise Michael's arrival and subsequent walk to the beach from Broughton along the smooth turf footpath across the sandy meadows behind the dunes. They would be starting now to erupt with wild sweet pea and ragged robin and later with purple loosestrife. Michael would have walked the ten or fifteen minutes across the meadow to where the stream cut through the dunes onto the beach and fanned out to meet and join with the sea, to sustain its own rebirth. Maybe he noticed the flowers, maybe he heard the skylarks trilling above. Bryn hoped so. He very probably didn't hear the gunshot above the sound of the surf in the milliseconds before it wiped out all thought. But where did the bullet come from? Either both

76

ballistics and Geoffrey Jones were wrong somehow or? Or what? Bryn put it aside; he had suffered enough discontinuities during cases. Niggles that left the same hovering anxiety at the back of his mind as those he suffered when he lost his wallet or car keys. Niggles that wouldn't go away until they were found.

He went to the canteen where his left brain told him to eat a salad and his right something filling and greasy. He had a ham salad sandwich, which he considered to be a rational victory, or at least a compromise. The coffee was not as good as that in the Marriott. It shouldn't be difficult he thought for the hundredth time to have good coffee, but the habitual expression on the face of the canteen manageress, had dissuaded him from ever voicing this opinion, or of even bringing in his own flask, which she would certainly interpret as rebellion. He went back to see how Lucy and her colleagues were getting on. Gray and Dai were at the university talking to colleagues, they probably wouldn't be back until late afternoon, in time for the six o'clock team meeting. He would go through the names Michael Green's parents had given him, leaving the sister for the time being. He searched names and addresses and, as Mrs Green had said, all were living in and around Cardiff except one, who he was pleased to see was in Swansea. He started to call them on the numbers he had been given to arrange a meeting. He would drive into Cardiff this afternoon. He would leave interviewing the one who had moved to Swansea until the end.

Michael's three friends and computer buddies in Cardiff were all doing alright for themselves. It is the era of the nerd, thought Bryn, they should be. The first was working in the University Computer Services Department which provided the bread and butter service that staff and students in the university used day in and day out. A twenty four hour service seven days a week which needed continual management, bug fixing and upgrading. The system that Colin Watkins ran was the high speed system. Supercomputers, they would have been called at one time, which ran the complex modelling and simulations required by science departments. Bryn found Watkins an affable nerd; he remembered Michael well and had been shocked by news of his death, passed on by his colleagues at Swansea University. Michael was extremely talented, he said, was considered to be the brightest in their group with that rarer of talents, a deep and creative knowledge of programming and of complex electromechanical equipment, but with a sufficiently broad overview to join the two together into useable systems. Bryn pressed Colin on their connections to forums and online groups. Colin was rather less forthcoming, but acknowledged that some of the cutting edge work was being done by people who trod along that fine line between the dark and light side of the internet. If you wanted to stay up there yourself, you needed to share to some extent with these people. After some pressure from Bryn, Colin promised to compile a short list of sites and activities with the strict understanding that his name was never, never to be connected with them. Bryn hoped that his promise could be kept. Colin said that to run a complex computer network, required evasive action on occasion against hacking attempts of one kind or another, perhaps by the very people that Colin and his peers talked to about avoiding them. It was tricky. They both used the same toolkit for attack and defence. Bryn asked about other computing contacts in Michael's group and he gave him the same list of names as Michael's mother had. He knew where only one of his Cardiff friends lived and knew that Bob Hughes had upped and left for Swansea, but had no idea where to or why. Their social contact was virtual, via blogs and technical forums where they were known only by their online aliases. They were savvy enough not to use social media. They preferred to operate outside the mainstream social network. They didn't even drink together except on rare occasions. We were a tight group he said, but not in a pub crowd way. He didn't have any idea of who might have wanted to kill Michael or for what reason. He concurred provisionally with the DI, that this was a legal world infiltrated by an illegal world, with potential gains for criminal gangs which exceeded even those made more traditionally by drugs or people smuggling. So, the stakes were high and double-dealing, betrayal and exploitation were all there. Maybe murder was an inevitable consequence. Bryn shivered a little, it looked as though this case was going to brush up against all of that. Bryn looked at his notes again.

'Michael Green's parents mentioned a school friend who moved to France.' Colin showed faint signs of distaste.

'That was probably Cut Price. Michael talked about this nasty little bugger he was at school with. He just came up in a conversation. I've never met him, he ran away Michael said.'

'Cut? Is that his real name?' Colin made a thin whistling noise which could have been a laugh.

'It was the name Michael called him; apparently, as a kid, he liked to dissect animals if he found them by the road or in the woods. It must have stuck, he never mentioned any other name for him.'

The other colleagues of Michael on the list did not significantly add to the results of the discussion with Colin, again, they gave the same set of names. A very tight group thought Bryn with a similar slant to the same questions. They had apparently all used the same online contacts in the twilight world of computer programming and hacking, insofar as Bryn was able to follow the conversation. One of them, Tom Carver, ran a small business as a consultant for debugging and problem solving for technical users. The other, Majit Kahn, ran a research group in the Meteorology Department. They all knew the other one, Bob Hughes and that he had moved to Swansea, but were unable to say what for and were surprisingly incurious to find out. They all thought Michael Green a straightforward character, incapable of getting involved with any illegal online activities. Who really knows what their friends think, Bryn pondered? He asked about Price and neither of them recalled his name. He was still left with an unsatisfactory aftertaste from these meetings. It wasn't as if he felt that they had colluded to agree a story exactly, but the neat image of a group of clever friends, who thought together, but rarely drank together or had much idea of the details of each other's private lives, grated. Welcome to nerdland he thought.

The whereabouts of a white van, the van which may have been used at Llangennith, became known during the afternoon. A van similar to that described by Huw Thomas had been found parked near to the Lipstick, the local moniker for the tallest building in Swansea, in a public car parking space in the Marina. It had been there for a while, the witness who called in had said. She lived in one of the new terraced houses opposite; but for how long it had been there exactly, she couldn't say. Ferrari had run the number through DVLA and it belonged to a small car hire business in Birmingham and had been hired out on the Sunday, the day before the murder. The hirer had said it would be returned on the Tuesday, so it was overdue, but that was not uncommon, the manager said; they hadn't been concerned. Ferrari took driving licence number and credit card details of the hirer, a man from Wolverhampton. They all tallied. She called the contact number. No answer. A tricky one; this was in Birmingham's territory and the man might simply be working here in Swansea. This was just a white van, they certainly didn't know whether it was the van seen in Llangennith. She decided to go the official route and talked to a sergeant in the Midlands force, who passed her on to a DI. She told him that the name had cropped up during an ongoing murder enquiry, as a hirer of a van which may have been used in the murder. She asked him if they could send an officer round to check out the address of the hirer and talk to anybody there, to see if the van driver was working in Swansea. The DI recognised the address, was helpful and said that he would call her back as soon as the nearest mobile unit had called by. They could always go up there, if the visit turned up anything interesting, Ceri thought. She went to talk to Gray, who perked up at the information.

'Mightn't be right van; not much to go on. Bill from SOCOs should have a look; need a uniform to protect it,' said Gray, dispensing advice freely. Ferrari said that she would get a car out there and alert the SOCOs. She'd then take Williams and go to talk to the witness who had reported the van. She would ask her and any neighbours who also overlooked the parking area, if they had seen anybody leaving the van. She would alert the camera surveillance team to see if any cameras overlooked the site. Ferrari was an asset. She and Williams were due to knock on doors around Michaels Green's flat around six when more people had returned home from work, so they would grab their tea at the café in the Marina too. Williams was not at all unhappy about a trip out. Four hours on the telephones had lost its glamour. His face muscles hurt, from maintaining the smile he felt he needed, to make him sound interested when completely irrelevant, longwinded information was offered him by seemingly demented members of the public. He had seriously considered the possibility at one stage, that there were people, or perhaps even only one person with many voices, out there amusing themselves on a grey morning, at his expense.

Gray phoned Bill Wood; head SOCO, to tell him that a white van had been reported as apparently abandoned in the Marina. Not of great interest in itself, but that Ferrari had traced the van to a Birmingham hire company and that her enquiries with the Midlands Force had provided some very useful information. Apparently, the supposed hirer of the van himself answered the door to his house in Wolverhampton and knew nothing at all about hiring a van and had never been to Swansea. His wife looked similarly confused. He showed the officers his driving licence and his credit card which matched the information given to them by Ferrari and obtained from the hire company. He had been at work all that week he said, again backed up by his wife and then by his boss, who the officers had talked to by telephone there and then. They were all equally puzzled, but the officers judged that taking a statement would be sufficient for now and said that they might well be back. They left the couple looking out of their living room window at them as they left.

Bill Wood went out to the van himself, with his briefcase full of tricks, for a preliminary look. He was aware that the only thing that linked this van to the murder was the colour and that it had been there for a couple or more days. He nodded to the two officers sitting in their car keeping watch and walked around the van, looking carefully at everything, at the interior which he could see and most particularly, the tyres. The sand and soil from every location has its own chemistry and character and he was looking for residues trapped in the tread. There was usually something left even if the vehicle had been driven some way over roads. He scraped several bits of dirt and sand from the treads and from the sidewall where he could see mud stains as if the van had been through a muddy puddle. These he put into sealable plastic bags which he labelled with a felt tip pen. The van was locked, but that didn't inhibit Bill unduly. He ran through his selection of Ford keys and within ten minutes had operated the central locking with a clunk. He poked his head inside and smelt an unpleasant acrid stench, not strong but obvious. It could be an old van driven hard, burnt oil maybe, electrical fault maybe. He knelt on the ground and with gloved hands examined meticulously first each seat in turn and then the floor. Both seats yielded some textile fluff caught in the join between seat and back. He bagged some of that and he also bagged from the floor on the passenger side a wrapper, a foil and paper from a Kit Kat chocolate bar. There was also a small piece of burnt material which was just a twist of carbon, but with some flecks of metallic material in its folds. This he bagged carefully with tweezers. He would take this away for the lab boys to look at and if the soil samples confirmed the van as having been in Llangennith, they would take the whole thing back to the depot in Cockett on a loader. He shut and locked the doors and had a few words with the traffic officers in their squad car. He was back in the labs within fifteen minutes. Bill got on the telephone and arranged for a flatbed to pick up the van and bring it in and alerted the dispatcher that they would be collecting it and that the lads guarding the car would be able to leave soon. Bill thought that they had probably found the car which was there on Monday morning at Llangennith. The earth and sand would confirm it or rule it out. He had a feeling, and it seldom let him down. He did a little skip as he left the lab.

Bryn returned from Cardiff just in time for the six o'clock meeting. The team were assembled and there was a distinct buzz in the air, far removed from the relative gloom of the morning. Gray came up to him and motioned him aside by the door. He told him about the witness who had telephoned in about a van left at the Marina. Bryn perked up noticeably.

'So we're moving again' he said, sliding his hands up and down against each other. He almost couldn't contain his movements, jerking, as Gray told him about the false name of the hirer in Birmingham and that Bill was collecting the van for deep SOCO treatment.

'Brothers and sisters, providence in the form of a member of the public and the first rate research by Constable Ferrari has, as you probably know by now, been kind to us. The person who actually hired the van is very likely to be the killer, but he is not the man named on the driving licence and credit card. When was that Gray? Let those words roll over your tongue one more time, this is something you will be able to tell your grandchildren.' The floor is yours he gestured.

With a rare smile on his face, Gray said 'registration number had van belonging to hire company central Birmingham. Van hired three thirty Sunday, small business, specialises in cheap and cheerful. Sunday, busy with people wanting to get off early on Monday mornings. Owner doesn't remember much about hirer. Bloke, mid-thirties, not Midlands accent, showed licence, paid credit card, above average height, medium build, darkish features and hair, not foreign. Wearing driving gloves' he said looking up at Bryn to see if he had caught the significance and could keep up with the pace. 'Licence and credit card, belong to same person, lives in Wolverhampton. Midland Force called round, name on card answered the door, didn't know about hiring van, had his licence and credit card, showed them; at work all week. They believed him;

good alibis from his boss, telephoned cold there and then and from his wife; will follow up with a visit to his work, but sure that someone impersonated him. Hire company have form he signed.'

'So' Bryn said doing a visual touché to Gray, 'the gloves mean that we are unlikely to have either prints or DNA on the form, which is a pity and suggests again that we are dealing with pros. But, who knows? There may be just a flake or two of skin from his hand or a whisp of dandruff. Can you ask Midlands to bag and send the form and we'd like to know the results of their visit to his work; we need to know for certain that he has been set up.' He stopped and looked at his team one by one, 'Somebody has been seriously taking the Michael' Bryn said smiling until he realised the inappropriate choice of expression and had the grace to apologise, to a low background tittering. 'Is it too much to hope that the hire company has CCTV in the shop?' Bryn looked expectantly at Gray.

'Too much,' Gray mumbled, the soliloquy had obviously tired him out, or perhaps he was contemplating the huge pile of unused pronouns, articles and conjunctions lurking somewhere in the universe, which belonged to him, but which he had never had the inclination to use.

'Have we got Michael Green's car back at the compound yet?'

'We have' said Gray, 'Keys fit, found victim's pocket, no computer, old car park tickets'

'Well we didn't have any reason to think there would be much for us in the car, I hadn't thought of the computer though, I was swayed by the break-in to his flat.' He paused to think, 'nothing that helps us then. I suppose we can release the car back to his parent's custody, can you sort that Gray. I don't think we have any more use for it. Check with Bill Wood to see if he has any more he needs to do, then arrange to hand the car over to his parents. They will be at the Marriott until after the funeral. I've no idea what they will do with it, part of the estate I suppose.' He glanced for long enough to see the barest of nods, the nod of somebody who has done quite enough for the day.

'So Bill Wood has taken samples from the van tyres to see if he can find bits of Llangennith on them,' he turned slowly on the spot, 'he said there was little else in the van to offer us hope. But, even the scruffy hire companies usually clean out the inside before a re-hire, so what he found probably belonged to our man; or' he said looking over at Lucy, 'woman'. He continued to turn; 'he will do prints, but I think we know enough now to expect that our killer is not that daft. But, everybody makes a blunder. So Williams and Ferrari back on the telephone lines just for tomorrow morning. Dai, check the town cameras to see if any cover the car park where the white van was parked, I don't think they will, but you know what to look for if they do. Let us hope that tomorrow brings fresh revelations.' He said rubbing his hands in anticipation, 'meeting, ten tomorrow, here.'

Bryn had a word with Lucy when the others had filed out. 'Anything to report Lucy, you were not your usual bouncy self I thought.'

'Well I have had a response from the bank. Neither the paying in data on Mr Thomas's account nor the accounts into which it was transferred seem to exist in reality. The records simply disappear when they try to follow the transactions beyond their own server. It makes them pretty nervous as you can imagine; that they can be hacked in this way. I expect a lot of people will not get much sleep tonight, but it rules Thomas out of the picture.'

Bryn with pursed lips, 'makes me nervous too Lucy, I bank with them' he said. He didn't sleep so well anyway.

'Thomas *is* a computer buff; his search records and contacts are full of geeky websites and chat rooms, actually some the same as those Michaels Green used, but I don't really think this is relevant to this case, just the usual boy..' 'Or girl' Bryn interjected with his customary raised brow. '..nerdiness.' Lucy laughed at herself and with Bryn.

'OK, are you happy to return the computer and phone? I don't have any reason to keep them now' said Bryn, turning towards the door.

'No, fine' said Lucy 'I'll drop them off tomorrow.'

'I talked to some of Michael's computer buddies in Cardiff this afternoon, funny bunch, nothing to make me suspicious, just a feeling that they are being thrifty with the truth. They all know each other online but don't do much real socialising. We'll talk more on this tomorrow Lucy, can you go through these names,' he handed her his list of names of the Cardiff group, 'see what you can find out.'

Bryn walked out.

Lucy had been working on Huw's laptop when she'd had time and was looking forward to doing a couple more hours this evening after the others had left, since she was handing it back tomorrow. She found it almost impossible to do her best work with others around her even if she wasn't disturbed. She needed silence and an uncluttered space and was suspicious of people who said they could do complex analytical tasks with the radio on or music playing. This requirement did not endear her to her flat mates at University. But when the degree grades appeared on the noticeboard of her department in Bristol, the validity of her assertions seemed to have been vindicated; which further annoyed her flat mates. Lucy was as much an enthusiast of life as she was of her science. Whilst she could and did party with the best of them, she drew a line; mostly, at getting drunk enough to spoil the next day. She also avoided the various drugs which did the rounds during her time there. She had tried them a few times, but disliked the sensation of not being in control. She also knew enough fellow students who used drugs regularly and reckoned that she could identify most of them by their behavioural tics. Lucy was deemed a desirable person by her peers and she had not lacked for attention. She'd had a couple of enjoyable relationships as a student. There were some very attractive boys there. How often do you get to spend three years with a bunch of bright and bouncy people your own age away from your parents? The relationships eventually fizzled away so that the inevitable parting had been less of a trauma and more of an expectation. One of the boys had simply assumed that they were an item and would continue to be after university. The other couldn't quite separate his work from his fun, a particular hazard if you mixed with maths and physics students. She had wanted neither the obligation of the first nor the irritation of the second.

She booted up the PC and continued with the searches for concealed data and contact information, her face lit by the unearthly glow of the backlit screen, her eyes probing across the lines of script and code. She would not get to bed until nearly one o'clock.

Bryn left Central in the secure and fragrant womb which was his Bentley. He had diverted back through Crofty on his way back from Cardiff and had two pots of laverbread and two bags of fresh cockles in his boot. He would make one of his favourite dishes for supper and open a bottle of wine. He had been on the brink many times of asking Lucy if she would like to join him one evening. He admired her as a colleague and was attracted to her as a woman. She had the dark, high cheek boned features which were common in Wales, with lustrous dark hair and a curvaceous body shape. Both of which; given that he had imagination and that he was male, he could sometimes quite literally feel. The DI part of him though, realised that such a relationship could and almost certainly would, be a disaster within the group and for the independence of both their careers. It would end in tears. He'd watched it happen to others. Despite this, his mind; that part of his mind at least, was not so easily dissuaded and he continued to dream. He pulled his car in beside the cottage and looked sideways at the tide flooding across the salt marsh. Nearly nine metre tides here on the springs, thirteen in Swansea. Big like all tides in the Bristol Channel.

He threw his briefcase onto the sofa and lit the woodstove. He made his way into the kitchen area pulling out a bottle of Viognier from the fridge and a pack of bacon. He took out the cork and poured himself a glass. Since holidaying in France, he had taken to using the small fluted tumblers which you got in most of the Tabacs or cafés if you ordered wine. The glass not only pleased him with its chunky feel, but he drank less without even noticing it. He took a rasher of bacon and cut it into narrow slices and then into small chunks. He put these in the frying pan with a splash of olive oil and fried them until they were just browning; the room filling with the aroma of bacon. He tossed in one of the bags of cockles and moved them around until he heard the first few start popping. He shifted the pan over and replaced it over the heat with a small saucepan in which he melted some butter and stirred in a spoon or so of cornflour to make a paste. He turned the heat down and moved this around with a wooden spatula until it had bubbled for a few minutes and then took it off the heat. He grated some cheese. Just what he had in the fridge; a bit of old cheddar and some Perl Las well past its best and put it in the pan with about a half pint of milk and a few turns of the pepper mill. He stirred the pan carefully back on the heat until the cheese sauce thickened. He threw in the cooked bacon and cockles and a whole pot of laverbread and stirred it all in. He leaned against the counter and sipped his wine while it heated through then cut four slices of stale baguette he had left over from the weekend and put them into the toaster. He put a napkin and cutlery on the table near the woodstove, moved over the bottle and his glass of wine and after laying out the toast on a plate, poured and spooned over the gratin. He ate the food and drank about half the bottle of wine with great pleasure, watching dusk creep over the draining marsh.

Thursday

Lucy was up early, a little bounce in her step which she didn't want to think too hard about, but which left a whisper of a smile on her face which wouldn't go away. She had stayed up late to finish her analysis of Huw's computer. She felt like a bit of a voyeur now that she was sure he was innocent, having looked at his private world. Two things had emerged; he was very keen and probably pretty competent with his computer skills. He spent a lot of time swapping knowledge with the online community. There were a few encrypted files and he used one of the encrypted email systems, but as she had said to Bryn, they were commonly used by lots of computer buffs who simply thought that their private communications should remain private. Lucy used them, lots of people used them. She would talk to him about that though. Secondly, he loved to surf, judging by the photographs that she had no professional reason to look at, but could not prevent herself from doing. He had done the European surf tour when he was a student, to almost exactly the same beaches as had Lucy at the same time; Biarritz, Nazare. Atlantic waves bigger than anything she'd seen at home. She remembered the shear excitement when she first saw the enormous waves in Portugal. They were way out of her league except on calmer days. She remembered the vinho verde which she and the other surfers drank sitting at beachside cafés with plates of grilled sardines and potatoes watching the evening sun sink into the waves. Even now she could feel the salt drying on her skin.

Lucy grabbed Huw's phone and computer and left her flat in Caswell to drive to Uplands. She had called to say she that she would arrive sometime after eight and got there about twenty past. She knocked on the door and Mrs Thomas answered.

'Come in love, Huw's in the kitchen.' She walked to the back of the house with Lucy in tow. Huw was sat at the table, wavy hair flopping over his ears and one side of his face. He looked much like his father, who also had a smiley face, but Huw's features were more defined, his nose more Roman. 'Coffee, tea?' asked his mother.

'Tea would be lovely, thank you Mrs Thomas. I need to have a talk with Huw , can we use the front room?' Mrs Thomas was good at picking up hints.

'No I'll make the tea then you two stay here, I've got things to do upstairs. Mr Thomas walked to Uplands for the paper, so you won't be disturbed for a while.'

Mrs Thomas busied herself with the tea while Lucy pulled out the laptop and phone from her bag, a little flustered.

'So sorry about keeping your computer and phone Mr Thomas, I'm sure it's been a nuisance, but in the circumstances we had to look. We also appreciate you letting us have them voluntarily.' She wasn't sure how to begin apologising for the arrest, but Mrs Thomas broke the silence by proffering tea and biscuits.

'I'll be off then' she said and went out of the room shutting the door.

'The arrest must have been very hard for you and your family, we didn't have any choice at the time with the payment information from your bank account, but I can assure you now that you are no longer regarded as a suspect in any way.' Huw was looking at her, head tilted slightly to one side. 'Detective Inspector Bryn will be writing to you personally to explain the circumstances,' Lucy had definitely reddened a little, 'as much as he is able to at the moment with an ongoing enquiry.' She blurted.

'My mother was very upset at the time, she has talked to our solicitor about doing something about it,' he said continuing to examine her, making her squirm a little.

'Mr Parker, yes; well we acted as we had to Mr Thomas, I don't think there is any likelihood of an unfair arrest case, but that is your decision.'

'That's what I told mum' he said regarding her with interest. 'It was pretty scary, but I knew I hadn't done anything wrong and that it would be sorted out eventually. I have nothing to hide.' We all do, thought Lucy. Nobody can really withstand a detailed analysis of their lives without something emerging. Even if it was a just an undeclared cash payment or the proverbial biro borrowed from work.

'That's good Mr Thomas.'

'No, call me Huw.' He smiled and held her gaze.

'That's good Huw' she said smiling in return. She slid the computer and phone across the table 'I had a good look at your computer Huw.' She blushed again thinking of the photos of him on the beach that she had looked at. 'I can see that you are interested in computer technology, is that something you did at university?' She looked up at him.

Huw brushed the hair away from his face, 'It's part of any course now, but I did the first year in Chemistry, which is pretty computer intensive and I did a module on programming too. I've had an itch to programme since I was allowed to use dad's computer. I used to write programs to look at chemical reactions, you know, rates and concentrations and things, simple stuff really.' Lucy was happy with code, but not with molecules.

'Actually, I couldn't persuade myself to buckle down and study for exams. It was easy to be distracted by the surf crowd who just did their day jobs and partied and surfed in the gaps. They didn't need to spend evenings studying and finishing coursework.' Lucy knew all about that, but she had been able to put her social life to one side. 'I realise now that I should have chosen a university away from home, but just couldn't drag myself away from this.' He swung his arm round in an arc to indicate the beaches that spread from Swansea city centre itself out west to Gower. It was part of the reason why Swansea and Gower were known as the graveyard of ambition by smitten youth. 'So, I didn't go back for the second year.'

'I can really understand that Huw,' she said looking at him, 'I went to Bristol, for physics actually, lots of maths and computing in that. I missed all this too and I couldn't settle properly being away from the sea. The difference with you was that I was able to shut out the siren calls until I'd finished.' Lucy was leaning forward a little too eagerly she realised and settled back and dragged her style back into police officer mode.

'I did find a lot of stuff on your computer relating to tech forums, hacker groups and some encrypted email software. At the time you were a suspect, these made us very interested, it gave you a gateway to knowing Michael Green. That's how we thought about it. If you knew Michael Green, then you could have had some kind of conflict or grudge with him.' Lucy watched him closely.

'Yeah, I dip in there sometimes. There are some clever people out there and, I know, probably some bad guys too,' 'and gals' Lucy couldn't resist interjecting, because she was one.

'Ha, ha, yes of course, just an expression' said Huw laughing with his head thrown back. His expression became serious.

'Look Lucy, I saw it happen, I want to know who did it. That guy nearly got me put away, he hacked my computer. I want to nail him.' Huw said that with genuine anger and looked like he meant it. 'I have run through the same thoughts every night, I was going to have a root around out there in the chatrooms and forums as soon as I got my computer back, I wasn't going to do it on dad's.' He shifted position on his chair, held the edge of the table.

'I go there too; I have to really for my work, but it is definitely not official and frankly, the DI prefers it that way. I don't care how you do it, but get the result is his view.' Lucy looked serious now, 'Look Huw, this is me talking, not Swansea police, maybe we can swap information, strictly on an informal basis. You get any whispers through your contacts about Michael Green, you let me know. I will let you know as much as I can about the case as we go along. You deserve that much I think, you watched him being killed.' Huw flinched recalling the scene again. He looked back at Lucy.

'Deal' he said, putting out his hand. Lucy hesitated then put hers out.

'Deal' said Lucy, grinning. 'You surf, I surf,' they snickered easily at the ambiguity like naughty school kids. 'Why don't we meet up on Sunday; at Caswell if the waves are any good? We can get coffee and a burger afterward. It will be my treat as a peace offering from the police.' Huw grinned, nodded and only then let go of her hand and broke eye contact. Lucy got up and walked out looking over her shoulder. Yes, she thought, we might make some progress on the case. But that wasn't what was making her smile. She arrived at the ten o'clock meeting just on time, still smiling.

Bryn came into the ops room early, just after Mike Williams and Ceri Ferrari, who definitely had the demeanour of people with something to say.

'OK Williams, you look like a feline with dairy product, what have you got?' enquired Bryn; Williams looked somewhat puzzled, as well he might, his first language was Welsh and he looked quizzically at Ferrari as if to indicate that the DI had finally flipped, as he knew he must.

'Oh, sir, yes, we talked to most of the neighbours close to the parking area where we found the van at the Marina, two people saw a man leave the van somewhere between about 10am and 10.30am on the Monday, both said different times, but close enough. They both noticed the man because he carried away a rucksack from the back of the van.' Gray and Dai came in to see Bryn standing by Ferrari and Williams looking upwards with an almost seraphic expression on his face. 'OK, Gray and Dai, our trusty colleagues have excelled with their legwork again. You'll appreciate this Gray, no computers, no profilers, just a good pair of legs, two pairs; well one actually' he said sailing very close to the wind by modern standards, 'and cool heads' he said recovering a little. 'Our two friends have witnesses who saw a man leave the van at the right time with a large rucksack. Ring a bell, Gray, Dai?'

'Same rucksack man at Llangennith' said Gray, leaving his pile of unused articles untouched.

'You had a theory Dai if I recall?' Bryn looked across at one of his protégés.

'Yes sir, I would leg it to the railway station or bus station sir.'

'Good, we're getting somewhere here. Dai, get onto CCTV surveillance office and look at all the footage between say 9.30 and 11am. Was there any information on which way he walked Williams?'

Williams looked at his notes to make sure.

'One of the witnesses saw him walk out to the Oystermouth Road.' Bryn turned back to Dai.

'So could be either rail or bus then; you know which cameras to look at first. I want to know as soon as you see anything; go with Gray, four eyes are better than two.' Ferrari was waving her hand at Bryn. 'Yes Ceri?'

'We also talked to neighbours of Michael Green's flat, the ones which overlook the entrance, after six in the evening as you asked us, to catch neighbours who would have been at work when you and DI Crossman went there. Several neighbours noticed people walking out of the entrance between about 8am and 11am, a couple thought they saw people walking in too. Nobody had any specific recollections; it is the time when people leave their flats to go to work or later on to go shopping. We pressed them to remember details, but nothing really. Maybe if or when we get a description from CCTV we can ask around again?' Bryn started to meander, both inside and out.

'Rucksack man wouldn't cross Oystermouth Road to flat' said Gray. Bryn's meanders turned into oxbow lakes.

'Quite so Gray, but that leaves us with the unpleasant conclusion that the killer was rucksack man and the burglar, if there was one, is somebody else. Bloody messy,' said Bryn and looked up as if he had made a great breakthrough in the understanding of human behaviour. 'So Dai and Gray, get off to surveillance and come back to me soon as.' They started to leave, but Ceri raised her hand again.

'One more thing sir, you asked me to ask around at the garage in Llanrhidian, to get the CCTV tape? Nobody in the shop remembers who came in with a silver Volvo, a busy time for them, but the tape shows a man getting out of the car at eight forty two and back in again two minutes later. I'd say it was Michael Green sir, judging by the photos we have of him' she said sitting down.

'Right, so we can be pretty sure now that the killer arrived in the white van and that Michael Green made his own way, alone, to the rendezvous and to his death in his own Volvo. It tidies up a loose end Ceri, good.' Bryn was rubbing his chin as Lucy arrived, a little breathless.

'Welcome Lucy, we have witnesses who saw a man, who is probably the same man with the rucksack at Llangennith, leave the white van at the Marina. Dai and Gray are going to look at the camera tapes, see if they can follow him through town. I think you should come with me to the University to talk to colleagues, see if we can dig anything else out. Williams and Ferrari, good work; look up these names on the records, see if anything jumps out at you, computer pals of Michael Green. I've talked to some of them in Cardiff. There's actually one moved here to Swansea,' Bryn looked at his notes

'Bob Hughes. Get whatever you can on all of them.' He passed over a sheet of A4 paper covered in notes.

Bryn and Lucy walked along the promenade to the University of Swansea, on a lovely May morning with the sea glittering to their left and walkers, joggers and dogs gambolling around on the sand; happy to be bathed in warm sunshine after an unseasonably cold spring. Bryn was enjoying the proximity of Lucy, but Lucy was feeling, for the first time, guilt at the arrangements she had made with Huw Thomas; the collusion, the inference that she would share information on the case with him. She must be mad. Bryn, if he ever got to find out, would be furious, he could suspend her. She might have felt less guilty, had she known that Bryn was simultaneously playing with the idea of himself enjoying a walk with Lucy on a spring weekend, holding her hand. She had no idea that Bryn had ever thought of her as anything other than a colleague. Whilst he was far from unattractive to her, she'd somehow never thought of him as anything other than the boss. It was now Bryn's turn to feel a pang of guilt as he jogged back into DI mode.

'I wanted you along Lucy, to field any technical issues with the computing. If you want to butt in and ask something technical, just give me a nod. This case must have something to do with this bunch of computer geeks and their interests; I feel it in my waters.'

'I saw Mr Thomas this morning sir, to give him back his computer and telephone. He said that his mother had talked to their solicitor about whether the arrest was kosher. He himself didn't think it unfair, accepted that we were doing our job.'

'Don't get many like that Lucy.'

'No, we don't. I said that it was their decision of course, but that I thought that we had acted reasonably and that that is how the Super would view it. I don't think there will be any comeback.'

'Good Lucy, well done. They wouldn't have a case, but it could have been a lot of messing about with bits of paper; anything else?' Lucy coloured, but Bryn was enjoying the spring air and his fantasy and didn't notice.

'Huw is very angry at the killer implicating him in the murder and at least as much at having been the victim of a hacking, which is what it was. He feels like a dupe for not being able to protect himself from whoever hacked in. My view is that behind this, is a much bigger criminal operation, where hacking is normal and murder not ruled out, I suspect he feels the same.' In fact I know he feels the same she thought.

'We have a killing with all the hallmarks of a professional hit even if we have no idea how it was actually done; anything on that sir?' Bryn shook his head slowly.

'No, no idea yet;' he put up a finger, 'we have an assassination on the beach which we can't understand.' He put up a second finger. 'We have a killer with a rucksack, we have a burglar at Michael Green's flat where we assume that a computer was stolen and who knows what else.' He put a third finger up, one finger too few, 'and we have a group of people who were definitely close with each other and Green, dabbled in computer occult and who aren't telling us everything.' He put his hand down and shook his head slowly. 'And that's about it.' He sighed and shrugged his shoulders, 'Let's see what his colleagues have to say.'

They walked up the entrance road into the University, past the security barriers, showing their badges at the porters' lodge. They then walked on towards the students' union and to the right into the taller of the two slightly faded sixties buildings which comprised the Engineering and Computing Departments. Even as they walked, excavators were digging the foundations and starting to put up the steelwork, for the entirely new second university campus in SA1; the logo for the old dock area of Swansea, which stretched east from the river Tawe past the docks and into the flat dune area at the eastern end of the city. This new development would centre on the new Engineering Departments and would comprise a complete campus area with residences, shops and academic facilities. The residents of Port Tennant would see the first new building in that area since the completion of the Amazon warehouse a few years ago. House prices would go up as landlords competed for the pleasure of taking students' money. The price of pasties in Port Tennant might even go up too. He recalled that Gray had been brought up there close at the foot of Kilvey Hill in a fiercely working class community. He would talk about it in his more mellow moments. His grandfather kept pigs on the hill during the war, a practice tolerated by local police knowing how hard it was bring up a family of six on rations. He said that they would have pork in the autumn, then bacon and black pudding through the winter. He had said he remembered the squeals of the pig, as its throat was cut and the bright red blood gushed and spattered into a bowl of oatmeal for black pudding. He had swum in the Tennant Canal which connected Swansea to the Neath valley as a child; receiving a clip around the ear from his mother if she smelt canal water on him. He said that it didn't stop him. He had played in and around the industrial railways and coal and gravel yards which occupied the area which was now destined for the new university campus. How would this new university site have seemed to him and his family then? Bryn could see that he had retained his spiritual connection to that society, that community, even when he had moved west when he had married, to the greener lands of Derwen Fawr, the lands of the big oak. He had been nostalgic about his roots but Bryn didn't think it had blinded him to the improvements in the quality of life he had now. He didn't think he would want to go back, except to that sense of freedom that we probably all feel sometimes, like a pressure in the chest, of just being young again. It took a few seconds for Bryn to retreat from his reverie.

They took the lift up to the fifth floor where Michael Green had his laboratory and office. They went first to see Jennifer Flowers, his now mentor-less Ph.D student. She indicated stools against the bench supporting a row of computer terminals for them to sit on, Bryn moved very carefully to avoid touching any keys or buttons. He was slightly allergic to these sleeping beasts with flashing lights.

'Thank you for seeing us Ms Flower. We are sorry to disturb you, but we need to try to find out if anything about Michael's work was involved in his death. At present we have very little to suggest motive, although I can tell you that we have made some progress on the murder.' Bryn looked around at the laboratory humming with computing power and thought how quickly one can become a dinosaur. It didn't need a volcanic eruption or an asteroid collision. A rapid decrease in the price and a rapid increase in the speed of computer chips was all that was required.

'Who did Michael spend most of his time with at work, who was his closest confidante?' Jennifer, who had been looking at him expectantly with clear bright eyes, dropped them to look at the hands in her lap. Bloody hell, big fat policemen's boots treading all over some lovely young woman's soul, Bryn thought too late. Lucy looked across at him, compressed her lips. He had no reason to know or suspect anything before, but he did now. Lucy stepped in.

'Look Jennifer, your private life is your own, we have no interest in it except that it might help us to understand the motive and to find the killer.' Lucy had spoken in a quiet voice, was looking at her. Jennifer looked up at Lucy and Bryn, tears in her eyes.

'He was a lovely man, bright, funny, and not so much older than me. We got close through the work of course and then we'd meet for a drink after some special day when a problem was cracked, just to celebrate. Then we started going out socially. We've been close for a few months now.' Jennifer sniffed back the tears and wiped her eyes.

'I know you've been hurt terribly by this and will need a good while to sort things out, but we need to get as

105

much information as we can now to find his killer. You do want that?' Lucy asked gently. Jennifer nodded.

'Did he talk about anyone in a way that made you think he was scared or angry with them?' Bryn was now in the lead again. 'I know academics are pretty competitive. You don't want somebody else to get your prize or your publication' Bryn encouraged.

'Oh yes, well we always talked about work we wanted to publish, who else might be doing the same thing, whether they were ahead of us or not, that sort of thing; normal lab banter. The publications are like,' she looked up at Bryn, 'like your success at solving crimes. It's what gets you promoted, gets us research income.' Bryn twitched and then nodded.

'Anyone particular he talked about?'

'He was in a group of mates from around his student days, they thought they were pretty sharp, could do anything, crack anything, all now working with computers in one way or another, used to be pretty well known on the chat room circuit according to Michael.' Bryn took his notebook from his pocket and read out the names he had been given by Michael's mother and that Colin Watkins had given him in Cardiff.

'Yes, those are some of the names; he didn't talk about them much, as if they were no longer very important to him.'

'Did you meet any of them?' Bryn asked.

'Yes actually, all of them. We went to Cardiff, to the University for a lecture about strategies to counter hacking attempts, it was Colin Watkins talking. He's good.' She looked up, 'but I did sense something more than the usual competitiveness between them, you know rutting stags kind of thing; something which made them uneasy in each other's company. It was just a feeling, probably nothing.'

'Any other names you'd like to add to the list, what about?' Bryn looked at his notes, 'Bob Hughes, was he there?'

'He was, but I didn't talk to him much, he didn't talk to Michael much either.'

'Did you know he had moved to Swansea? Does Michael keep in touch here?'

'No, I didn't know that, Michael never mentioned his name in a local context nor ever said he was meeting with him; perhaps he doesn't know. No, I can't think of any other names. He collaborated with various people around the university, work stuff only as far as I know.'

'What about forums, internet contacts, that sort of thing?' asked Lucy.

'He didn't spend time online when I was around, here or in my flat. Lucy hesitated, 'maybe in his?' Bryn picked it up.

'But I got the impression that he had contacts out there in geek world, he definitely would have. Nobody in particular though. I can't help you there.'

'Did you stay at his flat in the Marina?' Jennifer looked briefly up at Bryn and Lucy.

'No actually, he said it was his hermit's cave where he could escape the university and social life, a place he could think. He wasn't a socialite, only with me I think. We always met at my flat in Brynmill. He was, you know, a bit nerdy, needed things to be just so, tidy; liked his routines.'

'You weren't suspicious that he was married or had another girlfriend he didn't want you to meet?' Jennifer didn't seem put out by this. She was bright; of course she had thought it. 'No, I had absolutely no reason to think that, I just accepted his reasons. Knowing him, it didn't seem odd. In fact I would have been surprised if he'd had another girlfriend. A wife?' She pursed her lips and shook her head slowly.

'No way.' Bryn cast a rapid glance at Lucy; they both believed her. Bryn and Lucy got up from the stools and thanked Jennifer for her help.

'What happens now you have lost your supervisor?'

'The grant is still there for another two years; I can probably choose one of the other lecturers in the department. There are a lot of people here who could give me guidance and they'll all muck in I think; and I'm pretty independent. But it won't be easy for a bit.'

'Oh, one last thing' said Bryn turning back, 'did Michael have a computer?'

'Oh yes, he wouldn't want to be far from one for very long. He had some slick laptop and I think a tablet of some kind. I saw them sometimes, but he mostly used the lab terminals and his lab PC here. He must have kept them in his flat.' They both nodded thanks and left the room. Bryn and Lucy walked along the corridor towards the office of Michael's Head of Department.

'Well that explains the complete absence of makeup, toothbrushes or even hints of any visitors. I wondered at the time if the intruder had done a good cleanup job to remove stuff; probably not then. So it looks as though the break-in was for the computers. OK, let's see what his boss has to say.' After a rather unproductive half an hour where it became obvious that whilst he hardly knew Green, the HoD endeavoured to gain as much credit as he could from his association with his successful colleague. Bryn and Lucy left.

'There's something going on with that gang, but I'm damned if I can put my finger on it.' Bryn scratched his chin. Lucy nodded,

'I feel the same about their online cruising, there's something we're not being told; not lies, but just kept on the edge of the truth.' They were both silent for the next few minutes as they digested their intuitions, tried to make something tangible from them. Bryn's body twitching a bit this way and then a bit that as if his physical body was forced to follow his thoughts and only a strong will prevented it from getting away entirely.

'Let's get something to eat at that new café on the front, have you been there?' Lucy shook her head and then nodded to say, yes, why not. Just as they had found a table amongst the walkers, joggers and ramblers they had seen on the beach on the way out to the university, Bryn's mobile rang. He mouthed burger and chips and coffee to Lucy as he went outside. Lucy shrugged and joined the queue to order the same for both of them. Bryn came back looking more pleased, less pensive and sat down at the table. Lucy joined him after a few minutes from the queue.

'We've got a fix on rucksack man, on Princess Way and then at Swansea station. He caught the 10.58 to Paddington, bought his ticket before he left. Dai and Gray must be cross-eyed by now looking at all that video.' The waiter brought their lunch and placed it on the table. 'Arrived at 14.04; they're getting the transport police there to look at cameras on the platform and in the concourse at Paddington. The rucksack is big. We'll see it.' Bryn rubbed his hands together examining the food in detail as if to precisely identify the morsel he most fancied, and picking up his knife and fork, he speared it; a chip. They ate in silence and with enjoyment. The sun was still shining and they had a handle on the killer. When Bryn had finished his plate, he wiped his hands carefully with his handkerchief and sipped his coffee. 'With a bit of a fair wind, we'll be able to follow him in London onto the tube or out to a taxi or even onto the streets. If he lives there, then we're in with a chance. He's been pretty good at keeping out of our way so far. Maybe he just got complacent, but I somehow doubt it.' He pushed his plate away, 'so we know for sure now that he didn't burgle Michael's flat, didn't have time.' Lucy nodded again, still eating 'Who was that then I wonder?' Bryn asked.

'Do you know?' she said, putting her knife and fork down, 'we have been getting little bits of evidence here and little bits there since we started the case. The optimist in me says we are closing in bit by bit. The pessimist says we are still just skating round the edges. We may have a lead on the killer but we don't know how he was killed yet, we have no idea about motive. Who broke into his flat? I think it does have something to do with the group, but it also feels like it has the hand of organised crime waving in the background.' Lucy just stopped, shaking her head slowly.

'Just how I feel' said Bryn; surreptitiously swallowing a piece of tendon he had worked from between his teeth with his tongue.

Dai and Gray were back in the ops room when Bryn and Lucy got back, both on the telephone and talking, both nodded as they went past.

'Nothing from Paddington yet sir' said Dai. Gray merely cast his eyeballs upwards; 'not looking good; they've had the best part of an hour and they know which platform to look on. Those midday trains aren't that busy.' Dai held the handset as if it might point to where he was.

'Got off somewhere else, dumped rucksack?' If Gray didn't like pissing on other people's parades he was always extremely unfortunate.

'Much as it spoils our fun, it is a distinct possibility Gray. He could simply have left the bag on the train, chucked it out of the window or got off somewhere else, plenty of choice. He's having a little titter at our expense no doubt. OK Dai, you know what to do, let the Transport bods decide how to spend their time.' He sat and looked at the large array of images and dry board markings with times and places and lots of question marks at the end of the room.

'No news from our SOCO friend I suppose?' It was Bryn's last attempt at positive thinking for the moment. Dai shook his head, Gray didn't bother to move. Bryn had that post lunch, low activity feeling that early afternoon often brought these days. But knew he had to get more information on Bob Hughes, the only member of the geek club to move to Swansea and the only one he had yet to talk to.

He had arrived home on Sunday evening and guided his SUV into the garage. He shut the garage door with his remote and let himself into the house. He tried to settle, but was unable to relax after the drive from Birmingham in heavy traffic. He checked his mobile for messages and then sent a single text, receiving a reply a little later which seemed to satisfy him. He opened a tin of Scotch broth and heated it on the stove. He ate it from the pan with a slice of bread from a packet. Comfort food, the warm soup in his stomach, it always worked. He went through the plans in his head, step by step, assessing risk at each stage, setting the timings in his head for tomorrow. He would need to be ready to go early; so far so good then. He slept soundly and awoke early; breakfast, toast from the same loaf and coffee. The meeting was arranged for 9am so he could be sure that nobody would be there from about 8.30 onwards. He checked his collection of picks and the address, checked his watch again and headed out to the flat.

Lucy had been trying to collect information on Bob Hughes, a common name in this area. She had started with DVLA for all people with those names living in the SA postcode, which actually extends out into Carmarthenshire and Pembrokeshire, even if the population was clustered around Swansea, Llanelli and Carmarthen. She checked police records and council tax information for the local authority areas around Swansea. She had a list of about twenty names, which were fewer than she had feared and she could cut down these down to nine by ignoring males under twenty five and over forty. None of them had police records; all but one owned a car. She collected the addresses and telephone numbers and began to call them. She would ask them if the name Michael Green meant anything to them. After an hour of calls, she had got no further forwards, nobody she had talked to claimed to know Michael Green; two of the Bobs were not available by telephone. OK Lucy she said to herself, would the right Bob admit to knowing Michael Green if he had something to do with the murder? If one of the Bobs did know Michael Green would it mean anything? She was tired and couldn't answer this question in a satisfactory way; but she knew she had to tie this one down. So while she was typing the Bob information into her laptop she continued to call the two numbers which hadn't answered; half an hour later one of them did answer. He did know Michael Green and asked what it was about. He was surprised and sounded shocked when Lucy told him he had been killed, it had been on the news she'd said. He didn't read the local newspapers much or listen to local news and hadn't heard. He knew Michael Green from his school days, they both were into computers and yes, he knew some of the other names in the Cardiff group that she had asked him about, but didn't see them much. They had communicated by blog and mail, nerdy stuff he said, hadn't seen them since a lecture in Cardiff last year. Could Lucy and Bryn come to talk to him? Of course they could, they knew his address didn't they? Of course they did, courtesy of DVLC. Tomorrow then.

Bill Wood called Bryn mid-afternoon, about the white van; his voice had that little lift in it that Bryn had learned to interpret as progress.

'Good news and bad news Bryn, as ever. We found no useful fingerprints on the contract the hire company in Birmingham sent down, just a few smudges. There were none at all in the van or on the sweet wrapper we found inside the van.' Bryn stood tense looking ahead, he sensed more, the good news. 'We have though recovered two

113

useable DNA samples, the first from the contract, if you remember, signed by the hirer.' Bryn had remembered on prompting, but had thought getting evidence from the contract as likely as having tea on Pluto and had put it to the back of his mind. He was rubbing his hand against his side now in anticipation as Bill continued.

'Well, he had gloves on as you know, but there were two eyelashes, complete with follicles just stuck to the paper.' Bryn continued to rub his hand expectantly.

'My theory is that somebody may have rubbed their eyes while they were leaning over it and they probably stuck as the contract was folded and filed. Sorry, Bryn, but we don't really know whether it was from the hirer, the hire company boss or anyone else who had handled the forms.' Bill's last comment had taken a little of the shine off Bryn's apple and he stopped rubbing his hand.

'We also have DNA from the sweet wrapper found in the van; it was a Kit Kat wrapper; paper sleeve and foil inner. Now our hit man has been a pro throughout, given us very little to go on, but he fouled up on this one. He obviously held the sweet wrapper with gloves on, but he couldn't resist licking the last smear of chocolate off the foil, he left some epithelial cells from his tongue. He must have done it automatically, just liked chocolate.' Bryn's heart beat went up to a rate which might be common in part-time athletes, but was distinctly dangerous in DIs. He even had an urge to run.

'Unfortunately, the two samples do not match each other and neither are they in the database. My guess is that the contract DNA is from the hire company boss, or from a secretary or whoever.' Bryn heart rate slowly went down to his habitual 70 beats a second and he didn't want to run any more. He walked with the phone around the room in figures of eight, his thoughts churning the same thoughts in a complex loop to match his footsteps.

'So, we have the DNA of the killer on the wrapper, is that right Bill?'

'Most likely. For what it's worth, the hire boss confirmed that they clean out rubbish from the previous hirer, so the wrapper should be from whoever drove to Llangennith and killed Michael Green. No record on the database though, so we are not much further forward in actually finding him. But if we find him, we've got him. Sorry Bryn' Bryn continued his meandering.

'So, one step onwards. Can you ask Midlands CID to get a cheek swab from the hire company staff to compare with the contract sample? Tell them 24h courier, no expense spared. Is it worth sending the data to check Europol records?'

'It's easy to do Bryn, I'll see to it, but a long shot I'd say.' Bryn should have been excited, they actually had a physical bit of the killer in their labs and it had told its tale. It wouldn't help to find him, but would be crucial if it came to trial. They also seemed to have a sample from an employee at the hire company.

'Oh, another interesting find; when I opened the door of the van, there was a faint smell like burning electrical circuit, I put it down to old van, knackered electrics, but I found a small piece of carbon on the floor as if something had been burned. Turns out to be a SIM card, burned, but with flecks of the gold contacts which connected it to the phone mixed in. So our man was doing everything right, but he liked chocolate too much. He probably chucked the phone in the dock.'

The team gathered for their nightly lessons at about half past six and Bryn gave a rather brief summary of the interview with Jennifer Flowers and the trace evidence from the van. There was a hum of interest as he relayed the finds, but it quietened down when he gave the results. 'A tease' was how Bryn put it in conclusion.

'We know how both the killer and victim got to the scene of the murder, we have seen him on video, we have his DNA, but we're still not clear on how he killed him or where or who he is. We also have DNA from the hire contract; probably some staff member there. We have a group of slightly dodgy university friends, no real reason for suspicion, but I feel it nonetheless. Have we got any more on the sightings Dai?' Dai sat forward with a definite smile on his face.

'London found nothing at Paddington sir, so I started at Neath, the first stop of the train after Swansea and asked the transport people to look at the video at the time the London train would have arrived, nothing b'there. Went on to Port Talbot and Bridgend…'

'Know the route Dai, hungry now' Gray growled. Dai merely paused, looked disdainfully at Gray, then continued.

'The lovely boy, I found him at Cardiff station sir, I haven't seen the video yet, I'll go and collect it tomorrow but it sounds like him from the description.' Bryn danced a little on his tiptoes, nothing like ending the day on a high, perhaps a pirouette would be in order, just the one.

'He got on a train to Portsmouth sir.' Dai sat back in his chair looking pleased with himself.

'You look like a porcine in poo Dai, and so you should.' Bryn made an expansive gesture with his arms.

'In France' said Gray looking at his fingertips.

'Why so Gray, can you see into the future, are you born to strange sight, things invisible to see?'

'Ferries.' Gray continued to evaluate his cuticles. Bryn stroked his chin.

'Cogent argument Gray, beautifully constructed argument and eloquently delivered too. Since you are obviously drawn to the place where too many sailors drink too many beers, why don't you check with the ferry people there to see if they can find our man on their cameras. I'm sure they've got them on all the boats to stop hanky panky in the couchettes.' Bryn looked more serious.

'But if we see him, what can we do? He used a false name and documents to hire the van. Presumably, he will use a false passport on the ferry; he'll disappear from the boat and that will be that. The ferry port of itself will tell us little.' He tapped his teeth with his pen; 'Still, if it does nothing else, it will justify our request for Europol and the French police to check out the DNA data we have, if he's on their books maybe we can revive the trail. Can you see to that Dai, since you sleuthed him to the border.' Bryn waved his arms about, 'anything else anybody?' he looked around; 'no? Off you go then; tomorrow at eight.'

Bryn made his way home at dusk again; he barely looked out across the marsh, frustration with the case lurking just below the surface of his routines. Light the fire, put some potatoes in the microwave to pre-cook, turn the oven on hot then knock up a salad with the bits of lettuce, tomatoes and onion he had in the fridge. Waste

117

not, want not his mother had said. He took some of his irritation out on the dressing, beating the vinegar and mustard ruthlessly into the olive oil. He pulled out the remaining lump of cheddar and the grater. At the ping of the microwave, he put the potatoes into the oven to bake. Only now did he relax his shoulders a little and feel that particular enjoyment of being in control of the little things in life, in his own house, with his own dinner sorting itself out in the oven. It was time for a glass of the Viognier from the fridge. Cooking and looking after myself is one thing, I need to do more than just working and eating he thought. He sat back on the sofa reflecting that he was always saying to himself that he would do more of the things he got satisfaction and fulfilment from when he got home. Cooking was one of these, not only the sense of independence by being responsible for his own food, but the genuine enjoyment and creativity of the preparation. It meant that he ate good fresh food too. He always felt a twinge of guilt in a supermarket. It was money to shareholders when it should be to his local farmers and small shops who struggled against them. He had little enough time to do things carefully in the whirlwind of work. It was either glut or famine, but he could be thoughtful with his cooking. He had considered joining the local choir which he had heard was going well, who put on concerts in the local church at Christmas and in summer. They had even put on an outdoor concert in Weobley castle, the fortified Norman house overlooking the Burry inlet. He liked to make things too; he could put his hand to anything practical but had a yearning for stained glass. He resolved to do something this very weekend. He would check out suppliers and 'how to' books on the weekend and have a word with someone in the choir. The thought calmed him. He was finally roused by the aroma of baking potatoes. He laid the table and served himself supper. He sat for an hour or so on the sofa after eating and clearing up. He sipped his wine and let thoughts pass unhindered across his mind. He suddenly sat up straight with a 'eureka' expression on his face, French, France, Cut Price; surely it's worth a look, surely not just coincidence? They had the DNA of the killer, there was a good chance he had gone to France on the ferry, one of Michael's friends, a not very savoury friend by all accounts, had moved to France. They needed Price's DNA, they needed Price's current alias. They needed Price's parents. His shoulders relaxed as the thought lifted a weighty load from them. He got up, washed his glass and skipped off to bed feeling distinctly chirpy and looking forward to the morning.

Friday

The team were again subdued, expecting the morning meeting to be uneventful. It was too early for any results from across the Channel, they were just checking back over anything that might have been missed in the list of contacts. There was always more work for Lucy on the computers. Williams and Ferrari had been poached by Fellows for a day or two to help CID with a spate of burglaries in town, more legwork for them. Kevin Bryn clapped his hands as was customary and shared his thoughts from the previous evening.

'We may have a candidate for our killer,' it was possible to detect an immediate and distinct upgrading of interest, from reluctant listener, to all ears. 'One of the people alluded to by Michael Green's parents and confirmed by reputation at least by the geek team in Cardiff was a Mr Price, Cut Price to his friends because of certain alleged unsavoury practices in his school days.' Bryn looked around to see what the puerile minds of his team made of this, not a lot it seemed, they were used to hyperbole. 'He apparently disappeared from school in the sixth form. Moved to France they said, but nobody knows anything more than the rumour. He was, Colin Watkins said, in a group with Michael Green and Bob Hughes at school. None of the group knows his real first name. Now, the combination of naughty boy, France and Michael Green associate is enough to twitch my antennae. It's certainly a long shot, but dismissing coincidence, we might speculate that Price could be the one who got onto the ferry to France and, may therefore be the killer.'

Before the rumble of scepticism could grow too loud, Bryn darted, 'I think we can test this, Dai, how?' Bryn rarely caught out his pupil and didn't on this occasion.

'We have the killer's DNA sir, if it is his, from the sweet wrapper. We need to find out who Price is and where he lives or lived. Be difficult to get to him in France, if that's where he is, but if we can find his parents or siblings sir, we can match DNA.' Bryn was extremely impressed; that's my boy he thought but did not articulate it. He reflected again how breakthroughs, if that is what this was, usually occur when a simple, but not obvious, leap over a hurdle knitted disparate pieces of a puzzle into a coherent whole. The infuriating thing was that the leap looked entirely obvious in hindsight.

'Dai, that took me three glasses of wine and a nice supper to sort out and here you are fresh from breakfast and only needing a hint to set you off galloping along the right track.' Bryn was animated now and if not dancing quite like Fred Astaire, he was light and mobile on his feet. 'So to the victor the spoils, Dai, you are doing the Europol thing with the DNA data?' Dai nodded; 'and Gray, you were sorting timetables and routes out of Portsmouth, ferries to France, video information, that sort of thing? Is that right Gray?' A faint grumble could be heard, but it was enough to satisfy Bryn. 'Good' said Bryn rubbing his hands. 'Lucy, can you concentrate now on the records, see if we can't pin down this Mr Price amongst all the other Prices. He should be the lowest Price,' he couldn't avoid blurting out. Lucy rewarded him with an insincere smile.

Lucy knew Michael had been to Barry Boy's school and so telephoned the school secretary and explained who she was and that she was on an enquiry and wanted to trace a Mr Price, who would have been in the sixth form of the school in and around 1999. The secretary said unnecessarily that there would be lots of Prices in the school records and that she needed his first name to shorten the odds. Price is a corruption of the Welsh naming system before it became subject to the English crown; people were named with reference to their father and grandfather or to where they lived, so a person whose given name was Morgan might be Morgan ap Llwyd ap Rhys; Morgan, the son of Lloyd who was the son of Rees in English vernacular. This nomenclature served perfectly well to identify individuals in a small society, maybe better than just first and second name as the secretary had just indicated, but gave no formal identification of family line which has always been of great interest to the state. So ap Rhys became corrupted in English to Price; Probert and Bevan were other corruptions, ap Robert and ap Evan; the 'b' and 'p' being somewhat interchangeable in Welsh. The secretary's tone became more defensive when Lucy said that they didn't have a first name or they would have looked for him themselves in the national records and that she, the secretary, would be receiving a signed warrant from the Chief Superintendent in Swansea. She was finally persuaded to search from 1997 up to 2002 and would email a list as soon as she could. 'This is a serious crime enquiry Mrs. Howell; this morning would be good,' said Lucy 'before 10am,' just to ram the point home. She put the telephone down drumming her fingers on the desk, then grabbed her coat and left.

Bryn and Lucy went out to Penmaen to meet Bob Hughes at his home, a rather fine house overlooking Three Cliffs Bay, a sandy bay named after a striking cluster of blunt rock spires at its eastern end. The bay was featured in many a postcard with its stream curving round the beach and set against the wooded valley. The ruins of Pennard Castle, perched on the eastern ridge of the valley, made sure all was well below and served as a marker for wayward golfers on Pennard golf course. Lucy pressed the doorbell, which resulted in the front door opening shortly afterwards to reveal a well-built, in the rugby prop sense of the expression, man in his early thirties; thirty three as they knew from the records. He wore scruffy expensive clothes and had not shaved. He looked like magazine fashion advertisements did these days, thought Bryn scowling unconsciously.

'Robert Hughes?' Lucy asked.

'Yup, come on in, coffee in the kitchen.' He led them across a living space with an area on one side which was the kitchen. A couple of rugs adorned the wooden floors, the space uncluttered except for a number of simple items of furniture. Some fine paintings by Glenys Cour added colour and verve. He gestured them to the kitchen table.

'Nice,' said Lucy circling her arm around the space and the view, 'been here long?'

'I moved from Cardiff about four years ago, got fed up with the city in the end, did well there, consultancy work, systems stuff for companies; pays well. I mostly work from home here, same sort of stuff. The technical end gets more complex every year so people like me are in demand and probably always will be. Small companies need advice on how to spend their money wisely and need help keeping out the bad boys. That's something I can do.' Hughes settled back into his chair, arm around the back.

'You said that you knew Michael Green, in what way?' it was Bryn this time; holding his cup out.

'Michael and I went to school together, of course, near Cardiff. We were always interested in the same things and both pretty good at it. There were a bunch of us who would write code, try a bit of low level hacking, just to test ourselves really. Build our own computers, faster and cheaper than the ones you could buy. I still do this sometimes, that one over there is one of mine.' He pointed to a black box with winking blue lights which hummed with the sound of its many fans. 'Runs faster than anything you can buy, five hard drives running in parallel, fastest CPUs on the market; if a faster one comes out, I can usually just swap it.' Bryn stifled a yawn, but Lucy looked interested. 'The joke is,' Hughes continued, 'that broadband here is not much faster than the old dial up, so it's definitely quicker to surf on a board here.' He laughed at himself. It reminded Lucy of her quip to Huw Thomas. Were all nerds limited to puns?

'The bunch of you would be who exactly?' Bryn asked looking straight at him.

'Well, Michael as I've said, Colin Watkins who works in Cardiff University for their Computer Services; we were the close ones, then there were Tom Carver and Majit Kahn, both still in Cardiff when I last saw them. That's about it.'

'Which was when?' Bryn angled his head.

'Last year, Colin gave a lecture. I turned up for old time's sake.'

'You don't meet often?'

'Hardly at all, we were computer friends, not really pub and party friends; we met often online, but rarely in the flesh. It wasn't what we did.' Bryn reminded himself to get Lucy to look at the websites and blogs that Colin had given them in Cardiff; rather reluctantly if he recalled correctly.

'Would you care to tell us where you met online?' Lucy asked, since she was the only one who might understand the answer. 'Would you like to show me?' she said nodding her head towards the black box which hummed. There was a brief hesitation.

'Sure, I can show you some sites people like us use, but, as I said the broadband is not very broad so it will take a while.' Lucy went over with Hughes and stood to the side as he booted up the beast.

'Linux' said Lucy, 'what's that?'

'Yeh, use it all the time, less hassle with viruses and spam. It's a freeware operating system which programmers like me can modify or patch into. We don't want to be giving Mr Gates more of our money than we need to and Apple is not much good for programmers. Apple want to keep total control over their operating system and everything else' he added. He clicked rapidly over the keys until the browser started to come up with technical forums where live ongoing conversations scrolled down the screen filled with technical information, mostly gossip about how to patch faults in software, how to get this driver to work with that operating system and sometimes if anyone knows how to unlock commercial

125

software. Stuff which Lucy was familiar with; it was a site she used, the names of the correspondents things like Jakewhizz and Hotmandy. He went to other similar sites, all creaking along with the narrow bandwidth.

'That help?' He said. Lucy nodded, 'yes, thanks, all a bit over my head' she said. She wanted to hide her knowledge from Bob Hughes, to pretend she was just a plod.

'I think we've seen enough Dr Hughes, thank you for your time' Lucy turned towards Bryn and got up to go. Bryn and Hughes also stood and the party made their way towards the door.

'By the way Dr Hughes, some of your pals in Cardiff said you moved here to set up a business; anything interesting?' Bob Hughes hesitated slightly during the step he was in the process of taking towards the door; giving himself time to think.

'The business I described Inspector when you came in, mostly freelance consultancy stuff.' Bryn nodded.

'They also mentioned a Mr Price who left school, left home and apparently went to live in France, did you know him?' Hughes again hesitated for a fraction of a second then turned to look at Bryn.

'I remember Mr Price, Cut Price they called him, I never heard him called anything else. Not a very nice boy if I recall. We only spent time together in the sixth form, he was a year below me, he was just a face in the school before that. He was into computers, not that good. Nobody was sad to see the back of him. The word was that he had left and gone to live in France. Nobody queried it, I didn't and nobody seemed to know anything about it either. I got the impression that even his parents were completely taken aback.' He opened the door and ushered them out. He watched them to their car and only shut the door when they had moved off. He went back inside to the black box and typed out a message which he sent speeding along the inadequate broadband cable.

Bryn and Lucy pulled into the café at Parkmill on their way back to the station. It was part of a general store that used to be run by Don Shepherd's family, the cricketer who played for Glamorgan for over twenty years and was born just down the road at Port Einon. They ordered coffee and two pasties. They were on their own in the café.

'What did you make of that, Lucy?' Bryn took a bite of pasty and chewed.

'He's pretty confident certainly, but I think he's not being entirely open with us; the sites he showed me on the computer were Noddy stuff.'

'I could see that you didn't burden him with your knowledge Lucy, I kind of assumed you wanted him to think you were just a punter.' Bryn chewed some more, Lucy hadn't touched hers. 'He acts just like the Cardiff crowd I talked to, confident, but not entirely open.' They both chewed on that.

'I thought he might let slip something he wouldn't have otherwise. It didn't work the way I'd hoped it would. He just showed me stuff that most school kids probably know, thinking that we'd been privileged to look into his world, which I suppose is good, that he underestimates us, I mean.' Lucy looked at her watch, 'I'm expecting some information from Price's school, name, address, any other information they might have. We can start tracing him properly then and his relatives.' Bryn nodded, yes they could move on then; he was optimistic again. He had forgotten all the other false trails.

She ate her pasty quickly, lifting the stubborn flakes of pastry from her lips after each bite with her finger. They drank their coffee, wiped their hands and mouths on the paper napkins and left. They listened to the news on the way back and to the chatter and callouts on the police frequencies each in their own world.

Lucy went straight to her computer and Bryn walked into the ops room where Gray was sitting at his desk alongside the desk of Dai Swab. He stood up and walked over to Bryn. 'Cherbourg, 9.00am' he said. 'Had bag, Ronald Walker, baby, died 1985, Poole.' Gray looked intently at Bryn for a few seconds to see if his complicated prose had been registered and analysed, shorn as it was of the grease of syntax. Apparently satisfied that it had, he sat down and pressed some keys on the computer, job done. Dai didn't bother to look up having had the pleasure of Gray's eloquence a little earlier, but turned with interest to see what Bryn's response would be. He wasn't disappointed, Bryn started to move, sideways at first, but corrected to straight ahead, moving away from Gray.

'Well done Gray,' Bryn turned his head back towards him, 'let me see if I've got this right; they've seen him on one of the ferries and identified him by the bag. If I'm not mistaken, he caught the one that goes to Cherbourg at 9.00am.' He stopped and turned around to face Gray, then continued with one hand flat on his head. 'He was carrying a false passport made out in the name of Ronald Walker, who was simultaneously and silently feeding the carbon cycle somewhere in a graveyard in Dorset; he used his birth certificate. How am I doing?' Bryn smiled his biggest smile. He was rewarded with one of Gray's less ambiguous grunts. He reciprocated by saying, 'you will be pleased to hear then, that Lucy is probably reading an email as we speak telling us who Mr Walker actually is; what his name was when he was a baby. Is there anything from your end Dai, from the Foreign Legion; those doughty desert defenders, or the bureaucrats from Brussels maybe, M. Maigret on Rue d'Orfevres?' Bryn adopted his characteristic arms out, palms up plea position, knees slightly flexed.

'Not yet sir' said Dai keeping a neutral expression; it didn't do to encourage his Inspector unduly. 'But I have two contacts now and have sent emails b'there with the DNA data; they hope to be back to us tomorrow latest.' Dai carried on typing too. Bryn sat back on the edge of a desk. 'Good, good. I suppose there were no sightings in Cherbourg on camera?' Gray didn't move except for the slightest sideways movement of his head which he repeated only once. 'Didn't think there would be' said Bryn as he waltzed out to Lucy's computer office.

Lucy put down the telephone and turned as he entered, 'Mark Price,' she said, 'born and lived in Barry, went to school in Barry. The school secretary was pretty helpful after I'd emailed the signed request from the Super. He left school in 2000; bright kid from the subject teacher reports, Bs at AS level, maths, computing and physics; expected to get an A or two in the second year exams, but he didn't turn up at all after April so blew that. Lots of behavioural comments suggesting that he had a cruel streak, things left in lockers, unprovoked violence; nothing very serious, but not a nice well balanced kid it seems. One sister, parents still alive and still at the family home; one of our rare bits of luck sir. He, Mark Price on the other hand, doesn't have a registered address in the UK on the standard databases, no car, no bank account, no convictions. His parents haven't heard from him since he left home unannounced in that year, no trace since. They are beginning to think that he is dead. He was a problem child, apparently he had a couple of unofficial brushes with the local police, but I've only just had a few minutes talk with them after the searches, so I'm on my way to Barry now to find out more.' Bryn had that feeling in his chest which meant they were on the move.

'He fits Lucy, the first person that has. I'll come with you if I may. Can you let Dai and Gray know his name and details, Dai can pass it on to his continental colleagues and Gray can dig a bit deeper while we're in Barry; see if missing persons have any more information, that sort of thing.' Bryn went off to get his coat and they went down to collect a metallic, silver Mondeo from the pool. Forty minutes, substantial rain and a few jams later they pulled into Barry.

He walked through the entrance door to the block of six flats and walked casually up to the first floor where he used his picks to open the front door, clumsy with his gloves on. He slipped inside and closed it behind him. He had seen nobody in the car park and nobody on the stairs; his car was parked in one of the public car parks by the Marina. He carried a parcel wrapped in brown paper and labelled with Michael Green and the address of the flat, in case anybody stopped or queried him on the stairs. The parcel contained

130

an overnight bag. He looked around the flat; it was the first time he had been here and it had that unremarkable look of a flat owned by a male who used it as a private bolt hole. By somebody who used IKEA as a style guide. There were no magazines lying around, no squashed cushions on the leather sofas, no flowers, no washing-up on the surfaces. The office room, the second bedroom he guessed, had a large stark desk with a printer on a shelf slung underneath. The drawers were all unlocked except one, which proved a rather easier challenge than the front door lock. It contained, as he had hoped, the computer, two computers in fact; a laptop and a tablet. He un-wrapped the parcel and put the brown paper and computers into the overnight bag along with some memory sticks, CDs, loose notes and a folder he had found in the other drawers. He looked carefully around, mentally looking for places he might have left trace evidence and found none. He left the flat preparing to say that he had stayed with Michael last night indicating his bag if anyone had queried him on the stairs; but they didn't, because the stairwell was empty again. He came out of the entrance door and walked across the car park. He would take his moustache and hat off in the car; simple but effective, the best way.

They parked outside an ugly 1970s corporation house on an estate close to Barry. It looked like similar estates built all over the UK when the enthusiasm for dormer houses with tiled wall facings and timber clad sections was at its height. Possibly the worst architecture ever built. It was a great pity that the style coincided with the fastest building period in recent history. They knocked on the door after deciding that the bell was not working and eventually the door was opened by a woman who looked to be in her sixties, but was probably in her fifties. She nodded at them to indicate that she was expecting them and led them into the front room laid out with old and scruffy sofas and some post war utility furniture. Everything was clean, but life was clearly hard. Mr Price sat on the sofa and barely acknowledged their presence, a younger woman, Mark's sister perhaps was sitting on the other sofa. Lucy sat next to the sister and Bryn on a wooden dining chair. Bryn introduced himself and Lucy.

'We're very sorry for the upset we must have brought Mrs Price, I gather from DS Evans that you had come to believe that Mark was dead, no contact for what, fourteen years?' Bryn adjusted his position on the hard chair, 'We have no firm evidence that he is alive, but his name has come up in an enquiry in Swansea and we would like to confirm his identity. We have a DNA profile for this person who might be your son and we would like to take a DNA sample from both you and your husband. We have come here to ask you for this and to explain what the consequences of this might be; Lucy?' Lucy leaned forward on the sofa towards Mrs Price.

'You have probably heard about DNA profiles,' Mrs Price looked intently at Lucy, 'they are effectively unique to every person, but because a child will have DNA from both his mother and father, some of the same patterns will occur in both parent and child; so we can use your DNA and your husband's DNA to establish whether the DNA sample we have in Swansea is from your son. Does that make sense to you Mrs Price?' Mrs Price sat back in the sofa and looked across at her husband who hadn't shown any sign of recognition or interest in the question.

'You won't be needin' 'is, he's not the father of Mark,' she thumbed at the young woman next to Lucy; 'she's 'is and a fat lot of use she is too.' Bryn and Lucy looked at

132

each other, both working hard to suppress any inappropriate expressions.

'This is a delicate point Mrs Price,' said Lucy looking intently again, 'If the result is positive, that is if the DNA samples match, it will prove that your son is alive and may prove that he is involved in a serious crime which took place in Swansea earlier this week. If they don't match, then you will not know whether your son is alive, but he will not be the suspect we are following.' Mrs Price slumped back again looking shaken. Lucy did not mention France or the possibility that he may have committed crimes elsewhere; they would have to wait for a response from across the Channel.

'I need to know if 'e's alive, even if 'e's done something bad. Not knowing 'as been torture. What do you need to do love?' She stood up. Lucy pulled her briefcase onto her lap; 'I will just wipe a cotton wool swab inside your mouth Mrs Price, no pain, two seconds; is that alright?' Mrs Price nodded and Lucy stood up, pulled on some gloves and removed the sterile swab from its plastic sleeve. When she had taken the swab she returned it to the plastic sleeve; 'all done, thank you Mrs Price; not an easy decision.' Mrs Price sat down again. 'What 'as he done?' Lucy wrung her hands together 'We are investigating a murder Mrs Price and I can't tell you anything else at present. We will give you the results as soon as we know them, it will be a difficult couple of days for you all.' Bryn leaned forward to talk.

'Have you had any contact since Mark left home? Could you describe the circumstances of his disappearance?' Mrs Price stared at her fingernails and looked close to tears.

'He just wasn't home when I got back from work one day. He usually got 'ome from school before me, left 'is bag and coat b'there,' she indicated around with her arm, 'then went off to play computers with his bwt; mad about those. He always came back for dinner at six,' she indicated Mark's stepfather; 'he was working then and wanted 'is dinner when he came in.'

'That would be when Mrs Price?' said Lucy.

'April in 2000, I can't remember when.' Lucy leaned forward again in support.

'Don't worry Mrs Price; we'll deal with that when it comes up.' Bryn stood up and nodded to Lucy.

'One more thing Mrs Price, we would appreciate a photograph of Mark just before he left if you've got one; we will return it.' Mrs Price thought for a few seconds then stood up and went out of the room. Lucy and Bryn stood there looking a little foolish, but both of them thought it too late to initiate a conversation with the silent witnesses. Mrs Price returned holding a large colour photograph.

'This is the only one from then, 'e's with his class at the comp; don't matter does it?' She pointed at a short lad with a slick of dark hair hanging over one side of his forehead. Bryn said it was fine and thanked her for her assistance. Both of them nodded at the father and sister and receiving no sign of response, walked out through the door held open by Mrs Price. They walked across to the car.

'Christ that was depressing; poor woman, grieving for a lost son who might be dead for nearly fifteen years and now she has the choice between a live son who's a murderer or carrying on in no man's land as before.' Bryn was quite shaken; it was a long way in every sense from his cottage and his life. He resolved not to moan as much in future.

'One murderer and two zombies' Said Lucy with feeling, strapping herself in. 'Was I right to say nothing about the case sir?' Bryn turned towards her.

'Oh yes, quite right, we can't say anything about the victim until we know it was him. But, we've got a class picture of 1999; that's a real bonus. Michael Green and Hughes should be there' he said looking at the photograph as Lucy drove off, running his finger along the row of 17 pupils. 17? Those were the days.

They stopped off at the forensics laboratory in Bridgend to drop off the DNA sample and were back in Swansea by midday. Lucy scanned the photograph as soon as she sat down and cropped it so that only Mark Price was visible. She emailed it to her colleagues then went around the office with prints. Dai immediately typed a note and emailed it with a copy of the image attached to his new continental friends. Lucy glimpsed a 'bonjour' on his email and smiled; this could change Dai's life. As far as she knew, he had never been outside the UK, perhaps not even outside of Swansea. Dai looked at Lucy over his shoulder.

'Nothing from France yet, Jules said he hoped to finish the DNA search this afternoon. They have a picture now too.' Lucy laughed.

'Good luck,' She went back to her computer to contact her anthropologist friend in the Museum in Cardiff, who she hoped would age the photograph ten years to give an impression of what he might look like now. Bryn had identified Green and Hughes in the photograph on the way back; bright kid and slick bastard he said. Bryn rarely swore. They hadn't changed that much from when they were eighteen and now one was dead. But, he was sure that they had the killer, and, ironically, he was standing next to his victim in the school photograph. Dai was now attending to the more prosaic task of comparing the image of Price in the photograph with images caught by the CCTV cameras in Swansea and Cardiff. He might need to ask Lucy to do something more sophisticated than just look, he was sure that she had some computer trick that she could use. He saved some stills from the video that showed the best views of his face.

He went along to the main post office which instead of inhabiting the rather fine stone building on the Kingsway which proclaimed to all the quality of the service offered, was now on the first floor of WH Smith in a less salubrious 70s building, part of the scruffy shopping centre, which spoke for itself. He collected just one letter; first class, from his PO box and drove back home. Here, he removed a microSD memory card from a folded piece of notepaper and put it into the drive on the front of his computer. He opened the file and watched the three minutes of video, flinching at the end. It doesn't take long to kill someone he thought, then removed it into a small plastic case which he put inside a standard envelope on which he wrote 'Llangennith May 2013' in felt tip pen. He unlocked a drawer in the desk and placed it alongside the others. He relaxed as he always did when loose ends were tidied up. He arranged his pens on the desk in celebration, then set up a cash transfer from his euro account in Guernsey to one in France. He loaded duckduckgo, a web browser which saved no cookies, saved no history and ignored most restrictions on access. It left no significant trail for somebody to follow. He typed in his username and password and entered his favourite forum, the one in which he was known as Colossus, the one he used to find out what the latest gossip was on the dark web, who was doing what to whom and where. The circle of contacts was extremely useful for solving technical problems, but it also acted as a personal message network and kept him in the loop. He used the encrypted email server Tor, short for The Onion Router, for all his communications online. It was a free access mailer which encrypted messages and then routed them through an ever changing sequence of volunteer servers dotted around the globe, re-encrypting at each server so no server could identify either the ones before. It made identification of the sender and recipient of the email extremely difficult and the content effectively inaccessible; hence the metaphor with the layers of an onion. This was his world, this was his social life.

Gray had been looking after Holmes, the UK crime database, an acronym of Home Office Large Major Enquiry System for the team and spent an hour or two each day feeding in information at the terminals in Cockett; names, locations, forensic data and feeding back suggestions for enquiry avenues back to Bryn from its intelligent reasoning engine which collates a wide range of information and draws conclusions and suggests strategies which can maximise the use of evidence. So far, apart from the obvious comparison with other gunshot cases, it had found no cases with similar characteristics, and none of the key names; Thomas, Price or Green had led anywhere. Dai was also feeding information to Europol headquarters in Lyon and was waiting at Central in the ops room. Bryn, Dai and Lucy had eaten a far from gourmet lunch in the canteen and returned to the ops room, their earlier enthusiasm and appetites having been completely replaced by torpor. Dai sat at his terminal and almost immediately swivelled round to shout that the DNA was a match with a crime in Naples. Dai had only a brief email which said that a matching sample of DNA to the one found on the sweet wrapper in the van had been isolated from skin cells on a seat belt in a hire car; the belt presumably having grazed the killer's face as he left the car. The car itself was found in a back street in Naples and believed to be associated with a shooting nearby from witness statements. The date was March 2010; no further progress had been made on the case since then. He stood up and rushed over to Lucy and Bryn who had stood, eyes wide, waiting. Bryn could hardly control his twitching body and actually laughed. 'Mark Price, school friend of Michael Green, lost in France, may be an international serial killer; an infamous son of Barry; *Duw Duw.*' He sat down, his hands around his face.

'We don't know whether it's Mark Price yet sir' said Dai, bringing the whole hot air balloon back down safely to its tether. Bryn had calmly stood up and walked out of the room to his office to let Maureen Fellows know the possible widening scope of the enquiry. She also cautioned patience, whilst being secretly almost as excited as Bryn. It would be her first murder success and suppress some of the old school mutterings from the rugby brigade.

Lucy had gone into her computer retreat after the excitement had died down. Bryn had wanted to see Mrs Price this afternoon but Lucy and Dai persuaded him to wait until the DNA sample from Mrs Price had been analysed and compared with the sample from the sweet wrapper. It would likely be tomorrow; the technology had moved on in leaps. Mrs Price would not appreciate being told that her son might not only be a murderer in Swansea but also in Italy, but to not get too excited, because the police were not sure yet. Bryn had just got a little overawed by the match; it meant only that the Llangennith killer was a hit man, as they had supposed, but who had also killed in Italy. It said nothing about it being Mark Price. Lucy worked with the stills from the street camera videos and those at Cardiff railway station which Dai had emailed across to her; they were the noisy images that she usually saw, but improved when she used some simple enhancement software to sharpen and add contrast. She then applied OpenCV face recognition software, which was an open source program she used to compare the video faces with the school photograph. The software was not entirely convinced that these were the same person, but rather more so than it would have been comparing random faces. This was a good start Lucy thought; she would repeat the comparison when she received the aged images from her colleague in Cardiff Museum. All this data was being fed to Gray and the team of specialist users there for entry into Holmes. At last they had material to work with. Lucy stayed late tidying the data and writing the material up for the case notes to order the evidence in her mind. She was starting to think about how the evidence would look in a trial now, how a defence barrister would attempt to undermine it. This would be a far more rigorous test than the banter in the ops room in Central.

She would stay later that she had hoped and arrive at her flat completely finished. Lucy liked good food but only if someone else cooked it. She had picked up a chilled meal in the metro store next to Central and heated it up in the microwave when she got home. She ate it whilst she made a last circuit of local and national news on her tablet. She would clear up in the morning. Her last conscious thoughts before sleep were whether she would offer Huw a meal here on Sunday after surfing or whether they should go out somewhere?

Bryn asked Dai if he wanted a quick beer on his way home, something he did not do often, with anyone, but he was itchy with the change in tempo of the chase and wanted to wind down with somebody he could talk to about it. That was another thing he missed about his wife, before the hours made both their lives difficult; she had been a good and sympathetic listener. Dai was both pleased to be asked and reluctant to go. His wife of only just over a year would be looking forward to seeing him and disappointed when he said he would be a little later, which indeed she was when he told her. He resolved that he would say no next time, but might as well enjoy this unexpected treat. Bryn was sensitive enough to see the difficult decision Dai had made and so they had just the one drink in the No Sign bar next to Salubrious Passage, a name at the centre of many quips, which branched off Wind Street. By half past nine, Dai was eating with his wife and Bryn was drinking the last glass of wine remaining in the Viognier bottle after a eating a ham sandwich made with the last of his stale bread. Both of them were still slightly wired from the day's events. Sleep would only come much later to both of them, but in each case, for entirely different reasons.

Saturday

The atmosphere on Saturday morning was upbeat, considering that many of them would, in an average week, be thinking about reading the paper in bed at that time, not gathering around their screens or drinking machine coffee. Most of the team were already in when Bryn arrived. Lucy had received a ten year older reconstruction of Mark Price from her colleague in Cardiff which she was busy comparing with the captured CCTV images using the face recognition software. She was leaning back drinking coffee and waiting for the analysis to finish. Dai had walked in and straight up to his terminal where he logged in to his email inbox. The second mail was a long message with several attachments from Jules Lefebre in Lyon. Dai could scarcely make his fingers work fast enough. The message said that Jules had spent several hours searching the ICPO database using very particular criteria which matched the ones Dai had described to him for the murder in Llangennith to the one where DNA data had been found in Naples in 2010. The features that he had picked out were the fact that in both cases the victim had been killed by a 0.22 calibre bullet modified to fragment, there were many of those over the years he had noted, but the crucial extra criterion was for crimes where there was no reasonable explanation as to how the killer had approached and shot the victim. The latter had left both investigations hanging in mid air at an early stage. This had been Lefebre's stroke of genius. The new search, using those criteria, threw up three more murders, all of high profile people, all of whom were killed in apparently secure environments, ones to which the killer had no reasonable means of access. Although in Michael Green's case, there was plenty of access but nobody there at all to fire the shot. Dai first sent off a rapid *diolch yn fawr* to Jules. He thought that he would very much like to meet this man who could see so clearly through the mist. He said that he would respond more fully as soon as he had time to read everything. The second thing he did was to run into the ops room to announce to all, that Europol, well Jules actually, had come up with something very useful. Gray sensing intuitively an opportunity to dampen any dangerous signs of enthusiasm said 'found more crimes' which left poor Dai floundering in the centre of the room. Bryn brought some order.

'Gray, would you mind asking Lucy in, I think she might like to hear this.' Gray reluctantly stood up and walked out to the computer office. 'Sorry Dai, he's a cantankerous old bastard, it's too late for him to change, but I'm impressed with his foresight though, as I suppose you are. He didn't have to steal your thunder though. Jealousy I expect, he was probably like you once,' he said winking at Dai to lighten the mood. Lucy and Gray walked in, one looking expectant, the other a little sheepish; which was rare.

'Dai has something interesting to say to us; Dai?' Bryn settled back on a wooden chair, balancing it precariously on its back legs.

'Jules Lefebre, our contact at the Europol headquarters in Lyon..' a faint whistle could be heard from the group, 'he had an idea yesterday for searching the ICPO database, The International Criminal Police Organisation, the Europol computer database. He selected the features of these crimes which might make them different from other gun crimes,' he looked up to make sure the others were paying attention, 'of which there are many hundreds on the database. The key features he chose were the calibre and type of bullet, a fragmenting bullet, and the fact that in every case it was not known how the gunman got close enough to kill the victim. The other unusual feature which emerged from the search and which Jules ..' more whistling, '..selected from the results was that all the victims were high profile individuals, some criminals, some business, some political. All had pretty high levels of security, either where they were shot, or in the form of bodyguards protecting the site. None have been solved and the only useful forensic evidence from all four European cases was the DNA sample in Naples which matched the one in the white van. Otherwise, diddly squat' Dai sat down. Bryn stood up and started wandering.

'So, the person who killed Michael Green, who might be Mark Price, might have killed many others, all over Europe. In fact apart from Green, they were only killed in Europe. Things are starting to hang together, even if we can't find the hook' he said rubbing his hands and turning clockwise. 'Dai, can you write us a nice succinct report on those cases and send a copy to all of us. Gray, you could try the same approach in Holmes and when you get your copy from Dai, put that in too.' Gray looked stony faced.

'Did search; nothing' he moaned. Bryn turned more until he was facing Gray.

'You are saying Gray that you had got there too? Well, credit where credit's due, and you couldn't be expected to fly to Lyon to get the names. Let's see what entering the new names from Europe brings out, just in case.' This was as close as he generally got to admonishment, browbeating or excessive discipline Bryn recognised, were not conducive to creative thinking and cooperation. Lucy stood up.

'Sir, I have been comparing the faces Dai picked out from the street cameras with the school photograph and the facial recognition program finds significant similarities, but unfortunately, probably not enough to satisfy a court.' The eyebrows raised in interest returned to their resting positions. 'But I have just received an image from my anthropologist friend in the Museum in Cardiff which uses their software to age the school photograph.' She held the photograph up. 'This has been aged by ten years, to how Mark Price might look now.' She then smiled at Bryn and said, 'the recognition program finds a close match, good enough now I think to use as evidence in court.' Lucy sat down. Bryn tottered to his left.

'This is all looking good, most likely Price is the man, but not quite enough to spoil or brighten Mrs Price's weekend yet I think, but the day is nigh.' He wandered away from the group. 'Bill will call me with the DNA results as soon he has them which will nail it, but we will have to wait until Monday I fear. We still don't have a clue where he is, but we are coming for you Mr Price. Good work all of you, *nessun dorma*.' He turned and walked out. 'See you Monday 8am sharp. Take some rest and relaxation, and Dai; thank your French connection.'

He had been working on the laptop he had stolen for an hour or so now, he tried the easy way in using a memory stick loaded with Linux and a small program to load the foreign operating system.

This ran alongside *Windows* on the laptop becoming the new default operating system and therefore bypassing the entry password system. He could now look at any file he wanted to. It was that easy. He looked first at the browser. There were two, *Chrome* and *Duckduckgo* which he knew and used himself. Green had obviously used *Chrome* for routine stuff, booking train and plane tickets, *BBC* news and financial stuff, his everyday browsing. *Duckduckgo* leaves no history and he knew that there would be little to find even though this was the very place he wanted to look, so he moved on to the email. There were two email systems loaded, the open one *gmail*, which at a glance was used to mail people in the lab and at other universities judging by the many .ac.uk suffixes. He didn't expect any revelations there, although he was interested to note most of the mail was sent to jennifer.flowers391@swansea.ac.uk and a glance at the content told him it wasn't always science being discussed. This part of Green's life he was not interested in, but it did lay waste the image he had of Michael, as a bit of a monk. *Tor* was the system he knew Green would use for his important stuff, the forums and dark web stuff they used to do together and clearly still did; but not together now. He tried using some cracking software downloaded from *xda* developers and *backtrack*, but he knew it was almost impossible to identify recipients without monitoring simultaneously the inputs and output servers used by *Tor*. GCHQ might have the resources and might well use them, but not many other people did. He wanted to find the messages Green had sent to 'Colossus' on the forums and by email. He wanted to make sure that Green had used these computers so that he could destroy any evidence of the communications Green had made while he was grooming him in preparation for his death. You couldn't be too careful. He went back to the public emails, some of which were to Colossus, the emails by which Green had committed suicide. That was the way he liked to think of it, it absolved him from blame completely. He took the

146

laptop apart to remove the memory and mother board chips and these he put into his wood stove along with the screen part of the laptop; he enjoyed the burst of flame and cared not at all for the burst of toxic products released from his chimney; he would bury the metal bits later. He followed it with the tablet. Not much metal in a tablet. There was nobody nearby to complain about the smell or to see him dig his flower bed in the garden later in the afternoon.

Bryn spent the afternoon browsing through the stocks of leaded glass suppliers online and was thrilled at the range of glass on sale; he could enjoy this. He looked then for a couple of books to buy to find out how to make windows and what tools and other materials he might need. He bought three. If working with glass still appealed to him after reading the books, he would order some materials; definitely. He sat back, feeling the minor sense of achievement and catharsis which followed taking action rather than just wishing for something to happen. Life is not a dress rehearsal his mother had said when he had shown signs of procrastination. He might even chat to somebody about the choir the next time he had a pint in the Britannia pub; in fact he might just have a lunchtime pint tomorrow.

Sunday

Kevin Bryn rose late for him and smiled when he saw the sunshine that had been predicted by the weather forecast yesterday, beaming in through his window. He made himself coffee and toast which he ate with some fruit listening to the political discussion on Radio Wales; the only serious non-religious programme at that time of a morning on a Sunday. He would pack sandwiches and a flask and walk up the hill and over the Roman Bridge in the Burry Valley; there would be bluebells in the woods there. The bridge wasn't Roman of course, but medieval, part of a packhorse trail from Landimore to south Gower carrying coal and lime for building and agriculture from the many lime kilns dotted along the north coast, which were in turn fuelled by coal carried across the Burry inlet from Carmarthenshire by boat. He would follow this route past Fairy Hill and then along the ridge to Nicholaston where he would walk down through Crawley Woods to the beach and along the surf line to Oxwich for a coffee or a pint. The afternoon would be spent walking back through Penrice Woods to return to Reynoldston where the twelve or so miles of fine walking would justify the two or three pints of San Miguel at the Merlin Hotel in Reynoldston required to rehydrate him to his satisfaction and to set him up for pie and chips. He never cooked chips at home and so felt it an obligation to consume them whenever he ate in a pub.

Lucy woke up equally excited about the coming day; a feeling that was enhanced, if that were possible when she saw the fine weather and read the excellent surf report on PJ's website. Light winds from the northeast, to hold up the four foot swell. It might not be big, but it might be beautiful she thought. She had arranged with Huw to meet at 10am, when the tide would be coming in, somewhere around the centre of the beach. They'd find each other easily enough. Lucy showered and ate muesli and fruit for breakfast with a cup of Earl Grey tea listening to Radio Three. It would be that or Classic FM. Sometimes one suited, sometimes the other. It was possible to get fed up with the limited play list on Classic FM, but that had to be weighed against the risk of a long and obscure piece on Radio Three. This morning she was receptive to new things. She hummed as she gathered her surf gear together and put it in a shoulder bag. She then brought in her board to wax down. It was a ten minute walk down the hill to the beach and she was there by a quarter to ten.

Huw parked in the small car park at the back of the beach, it was filling fast now on such a fine morning and he was relieved that he didn't have to park up by Newton Church and carry his gear down. He put money in the machine and put the ticket on his dashboard. He too was early and saw Lucy as soon as he had walked past the Café. He walked across the sand towards her with a stupid grin on his face. He had a huge urge to kiss her but held back and shook her hand warmly looking into her face. He was pleased to see that she looked like he felt.

'Wow what a cracker of a day and look at that surf, not big but very beautiful', he beamed at Lucy, who had laughed at the repetition of her own thoughts earlier;

'Let's get at it.' They pulled their summer suits on over their swimming gear and ran down the beach with their boards, whooping as they splashed into the sea, the sun glinting on the waves as if to welcome them. They dived forwards onto the boards and paddled out beyond the break getting the feel of the swell and the looseness in their arms. The breaking surf crashed over the nose of the boards as they paddled through each wave. It felt delicious after a week spent mostly indoors. Lucy was good, flicking the board back to the crest of the wave then pointing downhill again to repeat it. She rarely lost it. Huw considered himself to be not too bad, but in this company, only that. There were many surfers out now, sitting between rides just outside the break bobbing like an unruly row of black corks on the swell. Lucy and Huw rode and bobbed for more than an hour then made a final ride back to the beach, where they went back to their gear, which was now very close to the encroaching waves. They ran the last few yards and throwing their boards further up the beach, grabbed their towels and bags and put them on the boards off the sand. They jogged along the beach for a few minutes to warm up again and to dry off a little. They sat down on their boards.

'Where did you learn to surf?' said Huw with some admiration 'You're good.' Lucy tilted her head and half closed her eyes against the sun, 'A little bit of most places in Europe' she said pleased. She didn't need to ask where Huw had surfed and felt a flush of guilt. 'I don't get so much time with this job, but I'm catching up on the surf here again and loving it. I'd forgotten how different all the beaches are.' She looked steadily at Huw, who didn't turn away. After a small, but significant pause, Huw pulled out

150

a flask of tea, made by his mother. She had noticed a certain air of distraction in her son that morning and to observe it more closely, she had offered to make the tea. He poured one; 'tea?' Lucy held out her hand, 'milk?' He tipped some into her cup then poured one for himself.

'So you're domesticated then' she stated. Huw neglected to put her right about the provenance of the tea and smiled awkwardly. 'What's it like living with your parents again Huw, they seem very nice, but it must be tricky sometimes?' Huw blushed. Christ, what did she mean? She tilted her head again and pointed her twinkly smile at him.

'Not really my choice, been looking for a proper job for over a year now, until that happens I can't afford a flat of my own. I'm not that keen to share with a bunch of mates, it would bring the worst out in us. And anyway, I like doing my own thing. Mum and dad don't really get in the way of much, but my bedroom is the only space that's really mine.' He looked at Lucy to see if she was bored by this domestic stuff; she wasn't. 'They were great after the arrest, all support, but my mum can't stop being my mum and even though I offer, she does the meals and all my washing. I feel slightly institutionalised. It must be what it's like to be in the army.' He smiled at her, they both laughed, it broke the tension. 'What about you,' he said, looking sternly into her face 'I haven't had the chance to grill you in an interview room?' Lucy slapped his arm; an intimate slap; a slap of collusion.

'Not much to tell really. I went away for my degree in London, loved it at first, but got sick of the traffic and the continual pressure to be wearing the newest thing, talking about the latest restaurant and well' she raised her arms 'just London's obsession with itself. Believe it or not, I really missed here. I probably turned down some mega job in a merchant bank to be a police officer; how mad is that?' She looked at Huw.

'Not mad at all from where I sit' he said, resting his chin on his hand.

'What about you Huw, I know you packed in university, you seemed to regret it.' He looked upwards, lips pursed.

'I do, dearly now, but I don't honestly think I could go back to that life, I've grown out of it; the lecture halls, parties, snogging kids. I don't think I could continue with my studies in that way. I want to work in computing, I think I'm pretty competent, I just don't have a bit of paper to say so. I think a lot of people are in my position. How do you get your first job to prove yourself? Catch Twenty Two.' He shrugged, 'anyway, things might be about to change, I've got an interview for a computer technician's job in Swansea Uni tomorrow morning; so fingers crossed.'

Lucy described her year in fast track for the police and her recruitment into the job she had wanted; the one she had now. She said that she was in a good team and her boss was a decent DI. They talked for a long while getting a feel for each other, carefully digging attitudes to life, politics, religion, books, music. Nothing of any consequence seemed to emerge to spoil their increasing attraction to each other.

'Do you fancy a bite and some coffee in Surfside?' Lucy asked as she started to stand up.

Huw laughed; 'sounds good to me.' They took their gear across and leaned their boards against the wall by the café in sight of their table. Huw insisted on buying, he wanted to treat her, but whilst Lucy was quite happy for him to order, she would be paying half. She wanted no obligations this early on. She wouldn't object to him paying for dinner though she thought and giggled to herself.

They discussed over lunch the deal they had outlined in Huw's house; that they might share some information to help assuage Huw's tangible anger at having been set up and arrested. They agreed to go back to Lucy's flat to discuss it. Lucy was well aware that she would be breaking trust at the very least, were she to pass over police information to Huw; a one-time suspect. She had no idea how this might work, but maybe they could combine skills to come up with a strategy where she wouldn't need to compromise her position as a police officer. As Lucy Evans, she was very keen to get to know him some more and maybe to help him work out his frustration in the process, if she could. As a DS, she dreaded to think what Bryn would think of this liaison. Her decision-making had gone haywire.

They drove up to Lucy's flat, the first time in many years that she had been in a surfmobile as she thought of these old vans. She offered Huw the shower first while she tidied around and opened a bottle of wine and put out two glasses onto the table.

'Sorry, red only, help yourself while I shower' she said, as he came back rubbing his hair. This intimacy seemed perfectly normal to Huw, as if they did this every day, but one part of him, the man part, was still amazed and excited. Bloody hell, a very beautiful police sergeant is having a shower just there. He exhaled to ground himself. Lucy came back after a few minutes pink and scrubbed and poured herself a glass.

'So, shall we see what kind of things you think you can do to make some progress, to get some sense of control back,' she was back in police mode and they were both sat at the table. Huw had been thinking hard about this. He was pretty sure that Michael Green, from what he knew, would be known on the geek forums, the places where all computer addicts ended up. He was also pretty sure that Green, and Lucy, come to that, would also dabble in the occult world of the dark web. Logic told him that the authorities would use the same tools as the criminals, unless they had some whole other world of resources he didn't know about.

'I thought that it might be useful to float some information out on the forums to get some kind of response. Lots of people do it and there is usually someone who can give you some kind of answer. You might only know them by their alias, but it's worth a try.' Lucy tilted her head to decant the idea from one side to the other. She liked it.

'Mmm, that's not a bad idea Huw, what did you have in mind?'

'Well, I would start by noting the sad death of Michael Green, implying that I'm one of the team, and ask for tributes. This might let us know either who had dealings with him or who was interested in him or liked him, who thought they were part of the team.' Lucy sat quietly for a few minutes sipping her wine.

'Mmm, yep, I think that's a good start, not provocative and it would seem too naïve to be the work of the police. I don't think it would make some of the less savoury readers suspicious.' Huw was quiet, he hadn't thought of it as naïve, but he supposed on reflection that it was. She continued, 'we are trying to flush out the killer or someone associated with him, so there is some risk that we will alert them to our interest.' She was thoughtful.

'It will just be my alias, but it has to be me doing this. I realise that you can't compromise your position as a police officer, but you might be able to help me to analyse the responses, to see if we can find out who they are, to see if you've come across them somewhere else. I've no idea what resources you guys have and you don't need to tell me, but I will be using an anonymous browser to get to the site if that makes you feel better.' They continued talking over the details and agreed that Huw would put a statement out in the form of a brief obituary inviting further tributes and hinting that there was a killer to be found. Huw would do this when he got home or tomorrow morning on his own computer. Lucy knew that he would use duckduckgo because she had seen his hard drive; the wine made her snort at this unspoken innuendo, which she covered up as a cough. They resolved not to talk any more shop. Lucy put on some Jan Garbarek and both the music and the level of wine in the bottle went down nicely and ensured that when Lucy offered to cook some supper, as she rested against Huw on the sofa, he was completely unable to refuse. They had their first tentative kiss as she leaned over him to stand up and it lasted longer than either of them had anticipated. She decided that she needed to sit down again. Huw left much later, still intoxicated, even after several cups of coffee.

Huw spent half an hour before he went to sleep putting out the agreed message on some of the widely used and less widely used dark forums. The job was done. He was excited, but sleep sucked him into a warm embrace as he reflected happily on the day. There were only the tinges of anxiety leaking into the edges of his consciousness.

Monday

Huw bounded out of bed and made himself some tea. His mother was experienced enough to see that something good had happened and wise enough not to ask what it was. She put some toast in the machine and told him where his clean shirt was, which she had ironed for him yesterday. She then stood back looking at him, her arms folded, waiting for some kind of explanation, if it were to be forthcoming. It wasn't.

'What time is the interview?' She observed her son closely.

'Ten o'clock in the Department. I'll walk through Singleton Park on this lovely morning.' She raised her eyebrows at this uncharacteristic display of early morning enthusiasm.

'Good surf yesterday?' Huw could see his mum's raised eyebrows and knew what they meant. He laughed.

'Yes, a great day, thanks mum,' he smiled at her over his shoulder as he walked out to get smartened up.

Bryn and his team, including a Detective Sergeant with a fixed grin, filed into the ops room. Bryn welcomed them back, hoped that they had a good weekend. He didn't notice Lucy's smile deepen. They had an important day, they all knew this he said, Dai was doing his Europol report, Gray was doing Holmes and Bryn would chase up Bill for the crucial DNA result. Lucy was writing up her report on the photo evidence for Gray.

'Let's meet up as soon as Bill gives us the result, we won't know what to focus on until then; in limbo we are.

Don't leave the building, no telephoning the News of the Screws. Don't panic' he said as he rushed out of the door just resisting the urge to jump.

Bryn made contact with Bill just before 10am, Bryn was hopping by then. He had been going through some of his departmental expenses to stop himself from running around the room keening or even flying out of the window.

'Bill' Bryn said, as if he were just passing the time of day.

'Gotya!' said Bill. Bryn almost dropped the telephone, but clung on by his fingertips.

'Lovely boy Bill, lovely, lovely boy. Certain are you Bill, quite certain?' Bryn was waltzing around the chairs and only slowed down when he realised he had a team to speak to. 'Look forward to the report Bill,' he said then hung up. He hummed some unidentifiable tune as he walked across to the ops room. All heads turned, the humming told them all they needed to know.

'Bill has just told me that the DNA sample taken from Mrs Price confirmed that she is the parent of the owner of the DNA sample found on the sweet wrapper in the van. *Ergo*, Mark Price is our killer.' Bryn rubbed his hands and moved his body from side-to-side.

'So it seems that he is certainly alive and well. How his dear mother will take it I don't know, but we need to go there now, she needs to know and not by telephone. Lucy, you're coming with me. Gray, put this stuff into Holmes if you would be so kind, see if it has anything on him. Talk to Colin Watkins, Bob Hughes and the Cardiff group, press them now that we know it's him for how they knew that he had gone to France in the first place and if he or any of the others ever knew where.' Lucy and Bryn grabbed their jackets and rushed out, Bryn looking back to shout, 'Dai, *dit merci a vos amis* and ask Jules, very nicely, to pull his finger out to look for his name and alias in the ICPO database. Europol will be wanting to look out for him at borders too. Alert Immigration to look out for him here. Lucy has sent you the updated photograph to distribute, so put out a press statement with the photo too.' Dai watched them go, wrestling with the string of commands. He shook his head slowly wondering what Bryn's last slave had died from. Europol now had a real name, a DNA profile and a photograph which captured how he looked now, judging by the recognition software comparison with the videos. It also had one of his presumed multiple aliases in the name of Ronald Walker; what it did not have was the alias Price was using in France on his identity card and his location amongst the sixty or more million people that comprise it. If indeed, that is where he lived.

Bryn had phoned Mrs Price on the way to Barry to warn her of their approach. They didn't specify what the second visit was about, but he supposed that Mrs Price would have her own ideas. She didn't seem a stupid woman. They arrived by eleven and Mrs Price opened the door and let them in to the same living room. It was improved by the absence of her husband and step-daughter. She nodded to the empty spaces and said she'd given them a fiver and told them to go to get some breakfast. They were late risers.

'So, what did it say' Mrs Price said sinking down onto the sofa.

'Your son is alive Mrs Price, his DNA was found in a van in Swansea, a van which was used by the murderer of Michael Green. He went to Swansea railway station after abandoning the van and caught a train to Portsmouth, then the next day, he took a ferry to France; Cherbourg, in Normandy on the north coast.' Bryn chewed his bottom lip.

'I know where bloody Cherbourg is' she said vehemently then dropped her head into her hands and sobbed loudly, her shoulders shaking in spasms. Lucy moved over next to her and put her arm round her shoulders. Eventually, the shudders ceased and she wiped her hands across her cheeks.

'I thought 'e was dead, the little bugger,' she took some deep breath and looked up to Bryn. 'The murder, you're sure?'

'We are sure, the evidence is good, we think a court would convict, except we have no idea where he is. We don't even know if he is in France. Think again Mrs Price, you have not heard from him at all in all the years he's been gone and you have no idea where he is?' Bryn watched her carefully.

'No, no' she said and started sobbing again. Lucy looked across at Bryn, eyebrows raised, Bryn nodded, she turned round to face Mrs Price.

'That is not all Mrs Price, we now know that his DNA was also found at a murder scene in Italy, they didn't catch him, they haven't solved the case. There also several other cases which look like they were committed in the same way. Mark could have been involved in those too. We and Europol will be looking for him, we hope to find him.' Lucy looked distraught herself, 'I'm so sorry to bring you back your son and then take him away again like this.' She put her arm around her again as Mrs Price digested the new information.

'We will send round one of the local community support officers if that would help you,' Bryn was taking out his phone. Mrs Price shook her head firmly.

'*Dim diolch*, no thank you.'

'Do you want us to call one of your relatives, a sister maybe' She shook her head again and sniffed away the last of the tears for the moment.

'She's about as much use as the other two. I'll get by myself as I've always done. My son is alive; whatever else he is, he's still my son.'

'We will need a statement Mrs Price; what you know about the last year or so your son spent in Barry, we'd like to know more about his computer friends, how you found out he had gone. We can do it now if you want or maybe you can write something down today and we'll get one of the local officers to go through it with you tomorrow morning?' Mrs Price looked into the distance as if she was measuring up the future. She nodded.

'Tomorrow, I need to collect my thoughts, bring him back to life again in my own mind, poor dab.' Lucy squeezed her arm and Mrs Price patted her hand, 'thanks love, not nice for you either I suppose.' They left the room nodding goodbye, leaving the mother to contemplate the memories of her son, which she could only now safely revive. Bryn and Lucy were mostly silent on the way back to Central and chewed their garage sandwiches thoughtfully. Bryn was running ideas of how to make progress on the case through his mind. Lucy was still disturbed by the traumas that Mrs Price would face.

Kevin Bryn knocked on the Super's office door and walked in. He told her that the Llangennith killer had now been positively identified as Mark Price, one of Michael Green's computer buddies from his schooldays at Barry Boys along with Bob Hughes. He told her about his unannounced disappearance from home and school before his A levels. That it was thought to be to France, but then hadn't heard any evidence, even from his mother, to back this up. So he wasn't one of the Cardiff group of geeks, of which Michael was a member. Some of them seemed to know of him, but presumably had never met him. Only Michael and Hughes linked the school and university together. Bryn told Maureen Fellows that Europol had come up with at least one other crime in which Price was definitely involved, since they had found his DNA at the scene. This murder was in Italy, but Europol had unearthed several more candidate murders with the same MO. He would report back to her on those later today, Dai was compiling a report. Bryn confirmed that they had a firm trace and DNA evidence trail suitable for the CPS. They just had no idea where he actually was at present or what name he used now. Gray and Dai were giving Immigration and Europol the information they needed to stop him at borders if he attempted to enter the UK again.

'So Barry boy to international criminal' she mused, 'do you have any ideas about motive? Is anybody else involved here in the UK? After all, you have your killer. The whole operation is most likely to have been run from abroad. Mr Green must have seriously pissed off somebody for them to take the risk and cover the expense of launching a hit man.' Fellows sat back in her chair, Bryn massaged his chin.

'You are right ma'am in principle of course. We still have no motive,' he swayed on his feet from side to side; 'but for me the chance that the hit man was launched by some continental gang, some spying or industrial espionage thing; a hit man who turns out to be an old school chum of the victim seems to me unlikely. This has to be a local grudge of some kind. Price and Green were two members of a tight group of three Barry Boys computer nerds. According to Mrs Price they were round each other's houses. We have talked to the third member, Bob Hughes and whilst he said nothing overtly suspicious, he came across as slick and quite capable of lying. DS Evans and I both had the same impression. We have nothing to implicate him in the murder except their shared interest in computers. That goes for the Cardiff group too, they also had things going on with and around Michael Green during the University and post university period, their relationship also centred on computers. I have to say that discussions with them leave the distinct impression of things unsaid.' Bryn leaned on one of the arms of his chair, 'that gives us five suspects, all with a possible reasons to have a grudge against Michael Green.'

'Wouldn't those bright kids be playing with hacking of some kind, if only to prove to themselves that they could do it? Is some criminal link involved? Did they stir up some wasps nest online? Did they piss off some gang?' Fellows was leaning forward, elbows on desk. Bryn took a moment to frame a reply.

'Yes, they've all effectively admitted to dabbling, but if one of them stepped way over that line or in what way the did, we simply don't know. This stuff is DS Evan's bag, but from what she's told me, the use of encrypted software and who knows what else means that digging out useful information is rather like trying to unravel complex financial transactions in a fraud case. Only a few people are capable of digging and they use the same tools as the criminals. It's easy to be outsmarted. I don't trust coincidences ma'am; my money is still on the school connection.'

'So tell me where you want to go.' She said finally, leaning back. Bryn scratched his head.

'I'm going to concentrate on the relationship between the Barry Boys group, this has to be central. We don't have Green's computer, it appears to have been stolen from his flat. That's another loose end, but it wasn't Price. I think that there's a good chance that it was a collaborator here. Lucy has only his university PC to work on and she's already found that it really has only university business on it. I will need a signed authorisation to look at their financial records and we will talk to the Cardiff group again. We'll request school records, DVLC and the like. DS Crossman is communing with Holmes.' Fellows shuffled some papers on her desk to indicate that the meeting was drawing to a close.

'OK Kevin, keep me updated with anything new, come back in ten for the authorisations. What do the press know?'

'Dai is preparing a press statement, but we don't want to name Price yet as a suspect for the murder of Michael Green, I would like to keep that back in case it alerts any accomplices here or abroad. We have a photograph Lucy obtained which ages him to his current appearance. It matches the images from CCTV so we think it's a good likeness. Dai is sending all the information we have to all UK police forces and to Europol.'

'Good work Kevin, you'll get there laddie, I can smell it. Let me know if there's anything I can do to help' Bryn nodded thanks, curtsied and retreated. Did I really just curtsy thought Bryn to himself shaking his head?

Dai presented Bryn with his summary of the Europol data and they went through it together in the ops room. There were at least four murders in addition to that of Michael Green which shared the search characteristics which Lefebre had run through ICPO. The first was the shooting in Naples of the wife of one of the local politicians in his town villa. Not an unusual occurrence in itself by all accounts, but she was found on a balcony with a single bullet wound to her head. The bullet was a fragmentation bullet that had been cut like the one used in Llangennith and had killed her outright and like our one, the police thought only effective at short range. The balcony looked over an enclosed courtyard in the villa. The entrance to the building was guarded by security staff day and night and access to the courtyard was impossible except for family members. The police arrived within minutes and everybody in the building was swabbed, nobody had fired a gun. There was no line of sight to the balcony from anywhere outside the villa.' Bryn paused to flick something off his jacket. It gave him a few seconds to digest the information. 'Price's DNA was found in a van parked two streets away and local witnesses had seen a man leave the van shortly before the killing and walk in the direction of the villa with a bag; he never returned. The local police assumed that he had been the killer, but remain baffled as to how he had done it.' He sat back to catch breath and to see how Bryn was coping with the deluge; he was fine. 'There were three more boss that looked similar, all unsolved. In one an eminent banker was shot whilst sailing a boat on a lake in Berlin in 2011; apparently sailing alone, way out of range of such a bullet and no other boats out according to witnesses. Case not solved. The others also involved the shooting of respectively, a prominent property developer in Geneva and a human rights lawyer in Brussels with a single bullet of a similar type in locations where access for a gunman seemed impossible. Bryn rubbed his head, he wasn't sure at all whether in the absence of Price's DNA, he would have linked the cases, but seeing them all together, it looked like rather more than coincidence. Good old Lefebre.

'We've given Europol all our information Dai?'

'We have sir; I suppose that with the photograph they can interview witnesses again, but the most recent one was four months ago, I wouldn't bet money on their chances and the Naples job was over three year ago.' Dai closed the cover over his folder of notes.

'Has the press statement gone out?' Dai pulled out a sheet and handed to Bryn. 'The Super has OK'd it sir, it's gone out.' Bryn nodded and wandered back to his office.

Lucy had left Central to take a break over at the library in the Civic Centre. The weather was fair; the air warm and she enjoyed her walk down towards the sea. Inside, she had stretched up to slide a book from the top shelf, enjoying the gentle pull at the back of her legs. She smiled to herself and at the same time, feeling herself observed, turned away from the sea towards a man, Huw, who was looking back at her. She held his gaze. She slid the book back into a row of others on the shelf then turned and walked past him smiling and out into the sunshine.

Huw looked across just as she reached on tiptoe for the book, sparkles of sunlight fractured by the waves danced around her. Silhouetted by the sea. He couldn't look away. She sensed at the edge of her vision a movement in the room; his, and turned her head towards him. Huw held her eyes for several long moments. He closed his book carefully and placed it on the table, then followed her out of the room.

She grabbed his hand and they ran along the shore, laughing. 'Well lovely boy, you didn't tell me that you'd be in town today. Did everything work out?' They stopped to face each other.

'Yeh, good,' he laughed incredulously, 'I got it.' He pulled her closer to him. 'I came to bone up on some things in the library, but this is better.' She held his eyes.

'That is wonderful news' she said, kissing him on the cheek, 'really wonderful.' They stood looking at each other. Huw broke the spell.

'Let's celebrate. Have you eaten?'

'No.' She hesitated for just a moment. 'Great idea, yes, we must, let's do it. Something nice I think' she said.

They swung their arms as they walked through town away from the beach. In less than twenty minutes she was sitting with him in the restaurant, her favourite restaurant, drinking a glass of sauvignon blanc and raising her glass for a toast. 'So,' she said, looking into his eyes, 'the job?' she said clinking glasses. Huw beamed.

'Technician grade 3 working with the professor in physics, quantum behaviour in thin films. Ask me next week what it is about, at the moment, I don't have a clue. But you have to admit, the description sounds exciting.' He grinned his boyish grin. 'He didn't choose me for my knowledge of quantum physics, thank God, he just wanted my computing skills so I gave him a demonstration of a few things I can do.' Huw clinked his glass now. 'I thought I'd call into the library to see if there were any idiots' guides to quantum stuff and thin films, I'd like to know the terminology at least, I don't want to make a fool of myself with the other people in the lab. You probably know all about this stuff. But there you were looking lovely in the light. I was so pleased to see you.' It was Lucy's turn to beam.

'You won't make a fool of yourself Huw, you don't come across as pompous or arrogant, those are the people that get shot down, and anyway, you'll have access to the university library pretty soon, which will have shelves of specialist stuff. I've already forgotten anything I might have known. I'm so excited for you; it's a great feeling to be standing on the edge of a new ocean not knowing what's on the other side.'

'Yeh, it really feels like the time I walked into my first university lecture and there was this buzz of talk, everybody thinking that they'd get given the keys to the secrets of the universe. I suppose I threw the keys away for a bit, but I'm not going to again.' They clinked glasses again as a way to defuse the mutual excitement they felt for each other and Huw's obvious delight at getting back in harness.

'When do you start?' Lucy put her napkin over her lap when she saw the waitress approaching.

'Next Monday, I call in to their office sometime this week to sign things and go over the contract, that kind of thing. It's for three years, enough to get me going.' Their food arrived and they started eating with enthusiasm, just looking up every now and then to check that the other was still there. Lucy had obviously been preoccupied as they ate and then finished their meals. She pushed her plate away from her.

'Huw, sorry, but I am working, I just slipped out to get some library books. I don't know when the boss will miss me, but the case is buzzing. The DNA data says that Mark Price was the killer, he was the one in the white van you saw; he was also at school with the victim, so we seem to be closing in. His name is being withheld at present, so I'm giving you information which won't become public yet.' She started to get up from her chair, wiping her face with the napkin and taking some money from her purse. 'Look, I know it's a terrible way to treat a good lunch, but I have to be off, now.' Huw shook his head firmly and took her hand.

'Thanks for acting on impulse Lucy, this has been lovely; to see you again so soon. We'll do it again when you have a whole day.' He held her other hand. 'Let a new member of the salaried classes treat you, really, I insist.' Lucy smiled, pursed her lips and put the money back. She leaned towards him so that she could speak more quietly. 'You might post a further message in the forums asking about Mark Price, asking to make contact, does anybody out there know where he is or how to contact him? It's probably worth a try; it's all we've got to flush somebody out. You should be safe behind your alias.' She blew him a kiss, thinking even that was risky for a DS in the town she worked in. 'I'll call you later, I don't know how much later.' She went out of the door and along Oxford Street back to Central light of step. Huw sat sipping his coffee, he wasn't in a hurry. He mulled over the name Lucy had given him, perhaps she hadn't meant to. He definitely wanted to find the bastard.

He booted up his computer to carry out his routine daily check on his web society over a breakfast of toast and coffee at the desk. He was distracted by a message from Uptownboy noting the sad loss of a friend, Michael Green, from the fraternity of the forum community. Well, well he thought to himself, I've seen you before on the forum 'Uptownboy', I wonder who you are, friend of Michael Green. The message invited tributes or condolences from well-wishers. He spent half an hour looking at other forums in his online territory and found the same message in two other forums. Not very surprising he thought, other enthusiasts used similar networks of chat rooms and forums to keep in touch. He didn't like not knowing what was going on in his domain and Michael Green was definitely in his domain. He loaded some software packages off a memory stick he had collected from the backtrack website which he used regularly to get information which he was not meant to get at all. He had used it before to hack into databases and the package had proved useful for finding out who people were and where they were. He started on the forum he expected to be least well protected. An hour or so later he had the membership list from the forum and the IP address he was looking for. 'Uptownboy' had used a covert browser to get to the site and so he couldn't easily work his way back in through that to his computer, so he compared the IP address with those he had hacked many times from various utility companies and eventually found a name he recognised. He wondered why the IP address had rung some bells when he first saw it and now he knew why.

Lucy returned to the office flustered by Huw and by her unannounced absence. She avoided eye contact with other members of the team as she made her way across the ops room floor. She raised her eyes only when they met a pair of brown brogues standing directly in her way. She knew exactly to whom those belonged and raised her eyes slowly up the legs and body, to look into the face of her Inspector standing three feet away, arms behind his back.

'Ah Sergeant Evans, good of you to join us, we all need a break every now and then, let the nerve cells fire free, get a bit of wind in our hair.' He was looking now at her windswept coiffure. He wasn't a detective for nothing. He continued his examination of her face, using what Lucy thought of as his quizzical expression, for far too long for comfort.

'As I was just going to say to your colleagues' he said sweeping his arm around. Only now did Lucy look up to see the team all sitting looking expectantly at her. 'We have set all the organs of justice off in search of Mr Price with all the tools they need to find him. Let's be realistic here; he was last seen crossing *La Manche* in a southerly direction and we have no reason to suppose that he will make a return trip anytime soon. If he does, then UK Immigration should pick him up from the photograph.' He picked at his fingernails, 'although it seems not to be a happy service at the moment and I've never been told explicitly whether cameras at immigration can do this. So there's a betting chance that he could walk straight through.' He shrugged. 'But, my bet would be on Europol either finding something else out about him or picking him up as he crosses a border on the rare days that anybody bothers to check a passport in the federation of the free. Gray has kindly been looking through Holmes using all the new data and the skills that he has accumulated over the years to see what the old sleuth could provide for us. Can you tell the assembled company and DS Evans,' he glanced across at her with his quizzical expression again, 'what juicy nuggets you have found.' He put out his hands in Gray's direction.

'Nothing,' said Gray.

'There you have it in a nutshell; we have nothing to fear from Mr Price in the mountains and the valleys. A crisp, succinct précis of the many hours DS Gray has spent at the keyboard and the countless lives dedicated to the building and maintaining of this magnificent database. It was just a one off murder in the UK it seems.' Bryn looked around. 'Anybody? So we can assume for the present that the same criminal organisation which resulted in the deaths of the continental victims was used for Michael Green and that Price was the hit man, or at least one of a team.'

'So what about the Cardiff gang?' Bryn looked back over his left shoulder from where he had wandered to, 'any thoughts?' The team were silent, picking their nails or checking their pockets to see whether they'd remembered to bring along a pen. He turned round. 'My money is still on a connection here. There might be a criminal ring, there might not, but somebody other than Price stole Green's computer and the killer was an old school buddy. Let's go talk to Dr Watkins and his friends in Cardiff again and to Hughes, which means you Lucy. Dai, you need to get across to Barry to see Mrs Price, tell her we need to know as much as we can about Price's friends and contacts, even though she hasn't seen him since he left. Get names and whatever else you can. Be gentle Dai, Mrs Price is having a tough time of it. I don't think for a minute that she's involved, but keep your mind open. Oh, and pick up her signed statement if you would from her or from the Cardiff uniforms. Call in at the school and talk to the head, his class and subject teachers in particular, find out as much as you can about who he spent time with.' He turned around towards Gray, 'Gray can you look at every database you can think of and find out all you can about Price; entries may well dry up after 2000, but anything we get could help.' Bryn looked around again, 'OK Lucy, off to the middle-east; our magic carpet awaits.' They wandered out to the silver Mondeo.

He had been mulling over what to do about Uptownboy, Huw Thomas as he now knew him to be. He was the one whose bank account he'd hacked. It had certainly seemed to divert police attention for a while; he laughed at the memory. He was good at that stuff and it gave him a sense of power, even invulnerability to be able to manipulate other people's lives. He could manipulate people through the very machines they thought were their friends, the things they kept in their bedrooms or their pockets, the things they confided their innermost secrets to. He sat back with his hands behind his head; he was a lucky man.

He had left the forum page open on the message screen. As he watched, still warm from his self-congratulatory thoughts, a second message from Uptownboy appeared at the top of the screen.

Bryn and Lucy turned up again at Cardiff University, parking by the National Museum and Gallery where a couple of years ago, Bryn had seen the Graham Sutherland collection which had been left by the artist for the nation. Sutherland had been a war artist and had sketched the devastation of Swansea caused by a series of brutal raids which had reduced a significant area of the small city to rubble in only three nights of intense bombardment in February 1940. Many were killed. Only a few of the finest buildings of old Swansea were left after the raid and remain still, close to the very dock it was the intention of the Luftwaffe to destroy. One is now the Dylan Thomas Centre. Ironically, much of Dylan's old school itself was destroyed in the raid. Sutherland later moved west and had gone on to paint many abstract images of Pembrokeshire, particularly around the Cleddau. These two river valleys of the east and west Cleddau link together to make Milford Haven, a deep water natural harbour, now home to oil terminals and refineries. It was these latter paintings for which Sutherland is best known and it was these that Bryn had seen in the museum.

Lucy had called each member of the Cardiff group to ask them to make themselves available this afternoon. It had been a calculated risk. To not call, risked that nobody would be available, to call ahead, risked collusion. They started as Bryn had before with Colin Watkins. They would take statements this time. He ushered them into his office; Lucy leaned against a desk to the side, Bryn sat in front of him. Bryn introduced DS Evans and asked if Watkins minded the interview being recorded so that they could transcribe it to make a statement that he could sign later. Lucy pulled out her mobile, set it to record and placed it on the desk.

'Sorry to disturb you again Dr Watkins, but we have some new information. Can you tell us more about Mr Price, the one who went to France; we talked briefly about him when I was here last week.' Colin Watkins scratched his head and looked to the sky.

'I pretty much told you all I knew last time. Michael would talk about him occasionally, just enough for me to know that he had been at school with him and that he was a nasty little shit. If I recall, and he really did only figure in a few conversations as a side issue, Michael, Cut Price and Hughes, Bob Hughes were in the sixth form of Barry school?' he queried as he looked at Bryn; Bryn nodded, 'Barry school together and they identified each other as computer nerds and spent time together. I mentioned how Price got his name last time and I don't know anything else; Michael would always flinch slightly when he did come into the conversation. How and when he went to France I don't have a clue; but the way Michael talked, suggested that it was not announced in advance and that even his parents didn't know.' He shifted his feet. 'He didn't think that the Price family had upped and moved to France.'

'When did you actually meet Michael Green for the first time?' Colin Watkins again looked skywards to capture the image he wanted.

'First time, mmm? You know that Michael had a first from Imperial and came here for his PhD.' He looked at Bryn to see if he had known, 'I had done my first degree here and then my PhD, so we met as postgrads in the Department, the Computer Science Department here. The first time we actually talked was I think, at a departmental seminar. We had lectures from outside speakers and from research staff within the Department, every fortnight in term time. We were all expected to go to learn and to meet the great and the good in the field, and I suppose to get experience of what an academic research talk was. They were usually pretty good. The first one was on computer security; encryption, Michael and I found out we had a common interest.'

Bryn nodded and looked at Lucy.

'Dr Watkins, you used to be in a group which included Michael Green. Was it a formal University Society or an informal group?' Lucy asked.

'Oh, completely informal, we just used to hang around the common room or each other's lab spaces and play around. Majit Khan and Tom Carver were also doing a PhD, Majit was a year older; Bob Hughes was brought in as a postdoc researcher, from Birmingham I think. We were, and I'm trying to be as explicit as I can, the usual naughty computer boys. We played a bit on the edge between strictly legal and not legal, but I can say with hand on heart that we, or at least I, did nothing that I'm ashamed of now that I run a serious system which I have to protect against people like I was. The lines between legal and illegal were very blurred. What the internet could do and how to sustain and subvert it were closely related. They still are actually.'

'Was anybody in the group pushing the line a bit further, getting into trouble?'

'Look, really, not that I know of, Tom and Michael were really very straight.' Colin Watkins sat back as if he had finished. Bryn leaned in again.

'Just one more thing, was there any friction, more than usual friction between any of you?'

'Majit was the wild one, he would give us dares, challenge us to get into x or y websites.' Lucy interjected.

'x or y being?'

'Oh,' Colin sighed, 'it could have been Cardiff City Council or some company which had just started using computers and weren't up to speed. Illegal yes, certainly now, but there was no malice or intention to do anything other than be a nuisance or just prove we could do it. At least on my part there wasn't. With the NSA snooping around and GCHQ in hair trigger mode, I would be much more careful now to keep away from most of that stuff; it was just growing pains.'

'Anything else? This is a murder enquiry, we will check; what about Green and Hughes?' Bryn looked sternly at Watkins.

'Hughes was the one who got a kick out of being able to out-think computer systems people. He had similar interests to Michael in that they thought robotics was the future, you know, the intelligent control of machines. They said years ago that machines would replace people on the battlefield before we were thirty. It turns out that they were right. We used to debate the ethics; you know, war is limited to some degree by how much suffering you are prepared to dish out or your soldiers prepared to take to achieve some political or financial goal. If you take away the suffering for your side by using machines from the safety of your bunker, what are the restraints on all-out war? Could it really herald in a period where damage can be inflicted at a distance with no cost to oneself, I mean, think about it, we're about there now? It's a dangerous situation in my view and we've seen already how powerless the so-called democratic controls are against its use. We don't even bloody know most of the time; we certainly aren't asked our opinion.' Colin Watkins slumped back. Bryn wanted to clap.

'Did this thinking influence what they did in the laboratory?' Bryn folded his arms.

'Yes, a bit, Michael and Bob definitely wrote and developed software together, software strategies to control machines. They had gadgets around and would play with them; Michael's thesis veered off in that direction, it was that which Swansea wanted I think.' Bryn made a move to stand up.

'Thank you Dr Watkins, you've been very helpful and very open, I appreciate that. We will send the transcript of this talk for you to sign. I can promise you that we will not follow up your youthful indiscretions, unless they impinge on the case that is.' Bryn turned as he was leaving, Lucy still had her phone switched on but in her hand now, 'One last thing Dr Watkins, what were you doing on last Monday, the 13th, between 7am and midday?' Watkins sat down to think, then picked up his diary and thumbed through it.

'At 7am I was probably shaving or brushing my teeth, then travelling here from Llantwit by train for a nine o'clock lecture to the Chemistry Department staff advising them on how to protect their computers, which means us eventually, from fraud or penetration. I give every department in the university the same lecture spread over the year. After that I don't have anything in the diary, but I think I would have been dealing with the everyday hassles thrown up by a big system. That is basically my job.' Bryn nodded.

'Thank you Dr Watkins, we will be in touch.'

Bryn and Lucy left. They went on to talk to Majit Kahn and Tom Carver, neither of whom had really heard anything about Price and neither of whom was as eloquent and forthcoming as Colin Watkins. Lucy did press Majit Khan about illegal activity on the web. He had the decency to blush, but pretty much echoed the views Colin Watkins had expressed. He had no opinion or view on Michael Green's relationship with the group; just a nice guy he said. Both of them were in work that day, Khan spent most of his time on his research project modelling jet stream data when he wasn't lecturing. He didn't have any lectures that Monday morning. He said he worked in his office alone and so couldn't really suggest anyone who could verify what he said. Carver had a diary full of engagements with clients covering the morning which they could check if they liked. Not rock solid, but they weren't quite in the firing line; yet.

Kevin Bryn and Lucy Evans returned to their car and retrieved their 'Police Business' card which they had left on the dashboard. As they were strapping themselves in Bryn asked Lucy what she had thought of all that. Lucy shrugged a Gallic shrug.

'Colin Watkins came across as straight and open to me, nothing he said twitched any of my bullshit sensors, I did want to cheer after his rather eloquent extemporary analysis of robot warfare.' Bryn nodded and laughed, his head thrown back.

'Same here, I had to restrain myself from clapping. I'm not sure our political seniors would have the same view and if they did, they certainly wouldn't express it.'

'The joys of being an Indian I suppose,' Lucy said.

'The naughty stuff with computers, does it ring true for you?' Lucy felt herself blushing provoking Bryn to laugh again.

'You did that too then' he said. Lucy grinned.

'Of course I did sir, we all did, it was a right of passage; but I'd be grateful if you kept it to yourself.'

'There was one thing that caught my eye' said Bryn; 'Watkins mentioned that Michael Green and Hughes did programming stuff together, I'd quite like to have a look at that; it keeps coming back to the Barry Boys, but we still can't rule any of them out. What did you think of the alibis; it could be any of them who broke into Michael Green's flat.'

'Watkins' lecture seems to rule him out, we can check with the Chemistry Department, but he'd be extremely foolish to offer that in a murder investigation if it were untrue and so easy to check. Carver is running a business, he showed us his diary; it was client meetings about every hour, so I'm inclined to rule him out too. Khan is more interesting, he either was in his office as he said or he has offered us an alibi we can neither prove nor falsify. He was the wild one according to Watkins, but they might all be trying to tilt the evidence away from themselves.' They both mulled over the afternoon's discussions.

'We'll get Ferrari to type this out when we get back if Fellows can spare her, maybe get her to check the alibis for a bit of experience; I'd like to give her more responsibility, she did well sorting out the details of the van hire; dealing with Midlands force, she'll make a DC one day soon if she wants to.'

They drove out onto the M4 past St Fagans and were back in Central by late afternoon in heavy traffic heading west. Lucy put her hand out to the radio and looked across at Bryn, who shrugged and nodded; she put on Radio Wales for traffic news and some light music and banter. They had done enough talking for the afternoon.

Some nagging thoughts abruptly worked their way into his reverie and were suddenly bothering him; it was just too much of a coincidence that Thomas, the only witness to Green's killing had posted an obituary note on the very person who he'd seen killed and then a message asking about Price. How could he possibly know about Price? If the combined police forces of Europe couldn't find Price how did some hippy surfer? Of course it wasn't a coincidence, no sensible person accepted coincidence at face value. Stupid, stupid, he hit his head with his fist, hard, twice for emphasis; but why for Christ's sake? A wave of paranoia swept across him, had he completely misjudged everything? He had hadn't he? He put his head in his hands and grabbed his hair. Who the hell was this Thomas guy, how did he fit in? Was Price working with somebody else, with Thomas? Had he arranged with Thomas to be at the beach so he could help him? Had he completely underestimated Price who he treated like a minion? Had the little bastard been plotting revenge all this time? His brain swirled and switched back and forth as he shook his head. Of course, it was clear as day, Price and Thomas

181

were planning to blackmail him, that's what he'd do in their position, cut him out. He popped a valium out of its foil coffin and swallowed it down with water. The panic slowly subsided as the diazepam leached into his bloodstream. Price was a ruthless bastard, this was right up his street. He liked to see the fear on the faces of his victims, he had seen that on the videos. Thomas, he recalled from his walk around his computer when he hacked it, was no computer novice, he had much of the software he had on his own computer. He threw his head back and laughed. He had thought he was setting Thomas up as a patsy by leaving data on his computer for the police to find, it was bloody Price who asked him to do it. Instead, Price and Thomas were setting him up. He laughed again at the audacity of it, Price trying to get one over him. He clenched his fists in anger, now that he was in Machiavelli mode, rearranging all the pieces to fit what he now knew, he realised that he had an awful lot to lose. His company, his money even his freedom; he wasn't having that, he was the brains not the bloody navvy. He straightened up; 'I am the controller,' he said, 'I will decide.'

Calm, be calm he told himself. He put a Mozart CD in the drive, the repetitive motifs suited his current mind-set, he could work alongside these sounds. He spent some time composing a message, then keyed it to the forum. He felt much better after he had posted it, he would deal with Price when he needed to. One problem at a time, just like when writing software code.

Gray had gone over to Cockett to check with the Holmes team there and to get advice on searching their databases. He had left a message that he would be back in time for the morning meeting at 8am. Dai had not yet returned from Barry and had left no message.

'I'm going out to see Bob Hughes again, let's try to tie up these Price contacts and ask him about the Green connection. I'm going to take my car, it's silly to drive out to Gower then back to town. You might want to take yours Lucy, his house is just around the corner from you isn't it? They drove out to Penmaen in the quieter part of the evening work traffic leaving Swansea and parked outside Hughes's garage. Lights were on; good, they had wanted to arrive unannounced.

Hughes took some time to answer the door and looked surprised to find a large blue Bentley and a Mini parked in front of his house.

'Ah Inspector and Sergeant, come in. Have I missed the veteran car rally again?'

'Only one a veteran Dr Hughes, I think Issigonis might well blanch at the other one.' He said nodding at the mini. Hughes ushered them to chairs in the living area.

'Tea, coffee, something stronger, the sun seems to be over the yardarm.' Hughes stood facing them. They both asked for coffee, small black please. They looked around the room again noting his black box with the blue flashing lights. He returned with coffee.

'So?' He said.

'Dr Hughes, we know a little bit more than we did the last time we saw you, we would like to know more about Mark Price.' He indicated Lucy who had pulled out her phone. 'Do you mind if DS Evans records this, we will type it out as a formal statement for you to sign?' Hughes said it would be fine and sat down on one of the chairs.

'You are one of the few people who we know was close to him. Tell us when you first remember meeting him.' Hughes put his hand to his chin.

'He was in the lower sixth, I was in the upper, but we both joined the computer club which met on Thursdays after school in the physics laboratory. They had soldering irons and stocks of transistors, that kind of stuff. I quite liked making electronic gadgets from components, although nobody does that now. You could get logic gates,' he looked up to get their interest, 'you know, AND and NAND and OR and NOR,' Bryn remained po faced, Lucy reluctantly showed signs of interest. You could make basic computing circuits from scratch. A computer with the power of your mobile phone would probably fill the back of a lorry made from those bits.' He looked genuinely nostalgic.

'Price was into programming and games. I liked the programs, but wasn't at all interested in games. Why would you create a sophisticated machine and write clever software to make a stupid little figure dance around the screen to get clobbered by some alien or bash a ball across a net. I think Price liked the bashing and annihilation. That's about it really.' Bryn nodded.

'So, were there any other people you knew in the computer club?'

'Michael Green of course; he was a gadget man, loved the smell of solder, but a bloody good programmer too; he was also in the year below with Price. There were three or four other lads; I did probably know their names, but I can't recall them now. We were all in the geek set, because that's what we were, didn't rate high on social skills. We used each other for our knowledge and what we could get out of each other. We weren't too interested in each other's souls.' Lucy made a mental note that she should talk to Dai about finding out who was in the computer club from his new school buddies in Barry.

'Did you and Michael do joint projects together?' Bryn looked carefully at Hughes's response as he asked. Hughes held his gaze.

'We did try some programming together. We learned that you can't programme by committee. It's probably why many of the early programs were almost impossible to use. It's the equivalent of driving a car made by a team of people who didn't know what any of the others were doing. Like the useless car, few things we wrote worked properly' He seemed amused by the analogy.

'Did your collaboration with Michael cause friction between you?' Hughes did seem to ponder this a little longer than he had the other questions.

'Yes, a little, we were eighteen, egos were being polished. Competition, even with a smile, was the name of the game between males. We didn't fight physically if that's what you mean.'

'Did your collaborations continue when you met again in Cardiff?' Hughes looked to his left as he thought.

'We definitely swapped ideas back and forth, but we had gone our own ways. I came to the Department as a postdoc, the system separated post docs and postgrads a bit, so like in school, we weren't quite in the same academic or social set.' Lucy tried to break the tone of the questioning.

'Can you think of any reason why Michael Green might have been killed?' Hughes looked a little uncomfortable with this; he wasn't in control of the narrative any more.

'No, it has been a shock, he was a quiet man, it's difficult to think why anyone would want to kill him.' He looked at his fingernails.

'What were you doing on Monday morning, last Monday, the 13th?' Hughes scratched behind his ear and then stood up, seemingly relieved to be moving.

'Let me get my diary, it's in the desk,' he walked over, opened the top drawer and pulled out an A4 diary. 'Yes, I thought so, no client meetings. I went into town to get stationary, in The Uplands, it's where I go regularly. It would have been soon after nine o'clock. I then picked up something for my lunch. I came back here to prepare some notes for a client, had lunch and then went off to see the client in the afternoon.'

'What stationary did you buy in Uplands?' Bryn watched him.

'Let me see... probably A4 notebooks, roller pens, basic stuff. I keep all my records on computer, but I still like to rough things out on paper. Is that enough detail, it's all I can remember?'

Bryn asked and received the names of the shops where he had bought the stationary and his lunch. He and Lucy looked at each other with a faint shake of the head to confirm that neither had any more they wanted to ask, then they stood and walked to the door after thanking him for his time. They would be back if they had any more questions. This time he shut the door after them.

'Slick bugger, but he hasn't given us much. We need to check out the computer club with the school, talk to the others that were there if we can. We should talk to

Michael Green's PhD supervisor and whoever hired Hughes, see what they've got to say.' Lucy said that she had the same thoughts and that Dai will have made some contacts with the school. She would do some rummaging in the Computer Science Department and talk to colleagues. He stopped as he was about to get into his car, 'I'll get Ferrari to follow his alibi up too, to call in the stationary shop and café with a photograph of Hughes, get them to check their sales. If they back it up, he couldn't have been at Green's flat.' He started to get into his car then hesitated.

'We could get something to eat at the Gower Inn if you fancy it, my treat, you've been working hard lately.' Lucy reddened and Bryn saw the reluctance. Bloody fool, how do normal people do this kind of thing? He had to admit to himself that he was not merely asking a colleague to have a bite to eat. 'Only if you've got time of course,' he managed to squeeze out to cover his humiliation.

'Sir, that would have been great, I am absolutely starving, but I'm meeting a friend tonight, we made the arrangement earlier.' Lucy was definitely blushing now.

'Lucy, it's no problem, really, another time. 8am tomorrow?' He tried to bring the copper in him back to the surface to protect himself.

'Thanks sir, tomorrow eight sharp.' She got in to her car and drove off. Bryn waited for her to leave first. Damn. He decided to go into the Gower Inn anyway, where he didn't know anybody and he hoped nobody knew him. He wanted just his own company. He'd have a scotch followed by a pint and eat a sandwich or a pasty. He'd completely lost his appetite for a meal. Then he'd drive home and read, to clear his soul and hope for sleep.

Lucy Evans called Huw on her mobile as soon as she was out of sight of the house, relieved to have extracted herself from the obligation to Bryn. She was not sure whether he'd seen her blush. 'Huw, sorry it's so late, have you eaten yet?' Lucy nodded with the phone clamped illegally to her ear as she negotiated the bends on the hill down into Parkmill. 'OK, I'm on my way back from Gower, why don't you come to Caswell for something to eat?' more nodding. 'Oh, great Huw, would you pick up something on your way over, I'm starving? Yep, I'll do the wine, see you soon.' She mouthed a kiss and smiled. She was back in her flat ten minutes later and opening a bottle of merlot. She poured herself a glass then went into the bathroom to shower and change out of her formal jacket and skirt. She folded them carefully and put them on a hanger for tomorrow. She fussed over what to wear; crikey, I don't normally have to think about this, she chided herself. She even put one frock on and then took it off again; too girly. She ended up in loose cotton trousers and a cashmere cardigan which she thought said casual and relaxed. She hadn't been soppy over a bloke for a long time; it felt good. Huw arrived as she finished her first glass of wine, carrying with him the unmistakeable smell of fish and chips. They kissed until it became obvious to both of them that the supper would have to wait a while. It took only a few seconds to remove the clothes she had so carefully chosen and put on only a few minutes before. She giggled and told Huw the wardrobe story and laughing, he admitted that he'd done exactly the same and opted for 'casual, snogging on a sofa' clothes, but ones that would come off easily. He smiled, looking into her face.

The delayed supper was still edible and they ate it from the paper with their fingers. 'I nearly bought pickled onions, but knew it would counteract the positive effect of my snogging clothes.' He gave her a mischievous look, 'they worked didn't they.' They giggled. They were comfortably *cwtched* in to one another on the sofa, eating warm food. Both were reluctant to change the mood by talking about the investigation but it was Lucy who spoke.

'Any response to your forum messages Huw?' Lucy got up to take the paper and leftovers away into the kitchen. The once appetising smell was now pervasive. She came back with a tea towel to wipe their greasy hands.

'Actually, yes, I'll fire the laptop up and show you.' He went out to his car to pull his laptop out of the bag he'd packed with some overnight things and left there, unsure whether he would be staying the night, but hoping that he would. He again left his bag in the car, unsure about protocol. He returned and plugged the laptop in and waited for it to boot up and find the wireless signal. They snuggled back on the sofa again.

'Here' he said when the forum website loaded. There were five messages in response to the obituary message, all of them saying in a wide range of styles and patois what a fine person Michael Green had been and one even offering condolences to his family; not that they'd get to see it. 'Yo bro, he's the main man,' type of message predominated. There only one response to the request for information on Mark Price and they both stiffened as they read it. It was from Colossus clearly

189

directed to Uptownboy and it made it clear that the sender knew who Uptownboy was and would contact him by email in the next few days to arrange a physical meeting at very short notice and that he should be ready. He would not conduct a discussion online. This was to be his last message as Colossus to the forum. They looked at each other, neither of them had known quite what to expect from the message, maybe just aliases they could try to identify. They hadn't expected a meeting.

'Wow Huw, what do you make of that?' Lucy had gone distinctly pale. Huw was subdued when he responded.

'Yeh, it gave me a bit of a shock too, came in this afternoon. What does it mean do you think?' He looked earnestly at her.

'This puts me in a bit of a spot, I thought it was worth a go to see which aliases knew him, but I must have been a bit fuddled in the restaurant when I said you might try floating Price. I didn't think it through. My Inspector would be furious if he knew I had opened up a line of enquiry on the murderer without clearing it with him first. I daren't think about the Super. Bloody hell.' She bit her lip, Huw touched her arm.

'Look Lucy, it's not you doing this, it's me, I'm a victim in this whole thing and I want to get to the bottom of it. I would have started probing with or without you, but I do realise it would have been harder without your support,' he looked at her and took her hands, 'and a lot less enjoyable. I can't see what you've really done wrong. You only suggested the messages, I could have said no and if these guys are as savvy as we expect, then he,' 'or she' Lucy interrupted; grinning. 'Or she' Huw conceded with a smile, 'could have found out who you are and that would have blown it. They would have thought it was a police trap or something.' Huw sat forward, 'I know he would give you a bollocking if he found out, but it's me he would throw the book at. He looked more pensive, 'he doesn't know we have a relationship either, which might be none of his business, but it would certainly heat the situation up. So I say we follow this along and see where it goes. If anything hits the fan I will make it out to be all my own doing with you warning me off; promise, OK?' He sat back. Lucy moved towards him.

'You need to know,' she said looking him in the eyes and undoing the belt of his trousers, 'that obstructing a police officer in the course of an investigation' she paused for effect, 'is a criminal offence.'

Somewhat later, Huw went out to fetch his bag from the car.

'You must leave early, before six. I've got to get ready for a meeting at 8am and I don't want the neighbours twitching their net curtains in the morning, is that OK?' Huw nodded and they sat down to plan Huw's next move.

'Unless we can find out who Colossus really is I don't see that we can make any useful progress, do you have any tools for that Lucy?' Lucy looked up at him.

'Probably the same ones you know about; backtrack and xda developers, I get my penetration software there,' she snorted out a giggle. 'Unless we pass something on to the spooks, we all pretty much share the same tools.' She snorted again and took a while to get herself under control. Huw slowly shook his head smiling. 'I'll have a go at the forum website, but I don't hold out a lot of hope,' she said.

'That's good, so we can keep in touch about that.' Huw said, 'otherwise we wait to hear from Colossus. This could be pretty important if he does know Price, perhaps he has some score to settle. You said Price was a nasty piece of work. He might also be scared of what he would do if he found out. It must mean Colossus thinks meeting is the safest option and is prepared to come here or suggest some neutral place to meet. I get that he doesn't want to do anything online, but it's risky to meet too.' Huw was staring into space trying to make the pieces fit. 'Maybe he's a part of the organisation which is carrying out these murders. Maybe he worked with Price and is trying to get out of the system. If they can organise murders around Europe without being caught, they could surely find Colossus if he snitched. I don't imagine that they'd be just throwing books at him if they found him.' They both sat back thinking, not wanting to articulate the thoughts that indicated a possible risk to them too.

Lucy suddenly stood up and gave Huw a mischievous grin.

'OK Huw, you can collect your overnight things from the car now.'

'How....?'

Tuesday

The team entered the ops room in dribs and drabs and sat around chatting. Lucy came in looking a little pink and flustered. Bryn arrived a few minutes later and clapped his hands for attention.

'OK team, we have the killer but not the motive, we know there's an organisation behind this but we don't know who or where they are. Michael Green seems to have been on the hit list for this organisation along with the other VIPs that Dai has obtained from Europol.' He looked across to acknowledge Dai. 'There is nothing more on the Holmes database, but our resident poet has been looking further afield; anything to report Gray?' Gray shook his head, 'absolutely nothing?' Gray shook it again. 'So we can conclude that the organisation operates in Europe, which whilst not much, means that we don't have to swap data with our cousins over the water.' Gray showed faint signs of animation.

'Last entry 2000, Education' he said. Bryn wondered if the little fish that Douglas Adams had described which could translate all languages in the universe and which you simply put in your ear, would be able to cope with Gray's terse utterances. He thought probably not, there were simply not enough contextual words to link the ideas together. Bryn acted as the fish.

'I think our friend here has been looking to find entries for Mark Price in government databases and the most recent entry he could find was in the Department of Education database of citizens in full-time education. Tell me I'm right Gray?' Gray offered a nod.

'So, that doesn't get us further forward but seems to rule out interactions between Mr Price and the state after he had left home. He really did disappear and maybe permanently to France. But don't forget that we only know that he went there after the Llangennith murder, we don't have a clue where he lives now. Maybe we'll hear from our continental friends, maybe he's eating croissants as we speak in Montmartre.' Bryn swivelled round to Dai again, realising that he quite subconsciously chose Dai for interviews which required complex explanations and Gray for elucidation of evidence which could be expressed in monosyllables. 'Dai, have you gleaned anything from the green and pleasant lands of the Vale?' Dai stood, which Bryn interpreted as a good sign.

'Sir,' he looked at Bryn and then slowly around. 'I've talked to Mrs Price again about her son's activities in the last year or so before he ran off. Mrs Price was quite chirpy. I think she's finally grasped the fact that her son is still alive. We spent some time going through his friends at that time; Green and Hughes are there, they were his computer mates, the ones he went to computer club with. She didn't know any of the other people that went there, but more of that later sir.' He looked down at his notes, 'He had other friends he did stuff with on weekends. Mrs Price was reluctant to tell me at first, but I said that we would be extremely unlikely to follow up things he had done so long ago, we wouldn't be able to make a case that would stick anyway. I hope that was OK sir?' Bryn nodded at him, 'I didn't like to point out that it couldn't possibly matter anyway, because we had him nicked for murder?' Dai looked up. A gentle titter ran around the company. 'Anyway sir, there were three of them got up to no good on weekends,' he looked down again, 'Darren Bright, a lad from London whose family had been moved from a sink estate in Hackney to Barry. Apparently problem families get swapped around all the time.' Dai looked up and shook his head in dismay, 'and a local lad Rhys Edwards. He seemed to be the really wild one according to Mrs Price, but don't all mothers say it was someone else who corrupted their lovely boy?' He looked around for support, and got it. 'Anyway, this gang went out looking for trouble, sometimes in Barry, but mostly in Cardiff. Mrs Price said it started off as shoplifting, small scale vandalism; she often found things in his pockets, penknives, pens, bits of bling he'd stolen from shops. She got the impression that they'd moved on to more violent stuff, she wasn't sure, but he started going out with a knife in his pocket. She said that she had tried to reason with him, tried to keep him in, but she couldn't really control him. He said he needed the knife for protection. She said he was already bigger than her when he was thirteen. The father was useless she said and then he left anyway. The person you met was his stepfather. He already had a daughter by another woman. She started finding money, sometimes large sums like fifty pounds; a lot for a school lad in those days. He'd come home with blood on his face and cuts on his hands. She was never very sure what they got up to exactly, but the police were involved after a shop robbery where the shopkeeper had been stabbed in the arm. The local police apparently interviewed Mark and several others. Mrs Price thinks that her son and Edwards were involved, but had managed to set up Bright and he was the one arrested and charged. He got six months in a youth offending unit. Her son just got a warning to stay clear of trouble. So he has no formal mention on police records and I doubt we'd find his name anywhere in the station in Cardiff. I will try to find any officers who dealt with him or came across him then, but that might not be easy. It might be useful to know a bit more about Edwards too sir, Mrs Price really did think he was a head case. The juicy bit sir, is that Edwards also disappeared from school around the same time as Price. Mrs Price had no idea where to, the gossip just went around. I've got all this on a statement sir.' Bryn sat back and clapped silently.

'Dai, you have the talent for telling a crisp tale, I was quite engrossed, you did well to see that Mrs Price was ready to talk and better to ease it out of her. This is useful stuff Dai, you might find a Mars bar in your pigeon hole.' Bryn actually did this if one of his team impressed him, they smirked a lot about it, but they were pretty pleased if they got one. 'So in fact we have another possible suspect for the killing. If Edwards was as bad as Mrs Price thinks he was, then he could be pulling the strings? Have Edwards and Price formed a team that murder for money? I'm sure if you have the head for it and the skill, it's a pretty lucrative game and we already know Price can do it. From shoplifter to international hit man wanted by Europol,' Bryn whistled softly. Lucy leaned forwards.

'If Edwards is the driving force behind a professional hit squad, is it just coincidence that one of their school friends was a target? Or is it maybe an old grudge from school days? Michael Green has certainly done well for himself. Was he trying to blackmail them?' Lucy looked around for interest. She continued.

'But Green was their most recent hit, so he can't have been high on their personal revenge list. He doesn't sound like blackmail material to me. It suggests that he was simply another high profile individual whom somebody else wanted out of the way and they were being paid to do it. Just another job, just another punter; the fact he was at school with both of them may even have amused them.' Bryn was up now and moving about, dodging chairs as best he could.

'It may just be a coincidence Lucy that the paid killers know their victim, it remains a possibility. We also have to consider whether the activities of the computer geeks in Cardiff connect up with these two? The only link I can see is that Price did computer club together with Green and Hughes and that both Hughes and Green went on to work in the field and link to the other Cardiff people, but that may be enough. Is there really something to do with computers or hacking or blackmail or whatever which connects three sixth formers at school with a bunch of computer academics in university? Anyone have any views?' Gray shook his head. Bryn leaned his head over in Gray's direction, 'well Gray I agree with you, but we can't ignore it.' Dai had his hand up; 'Dai?'

'Sir, sorry to interrupt, sir, but I did also go along to the school and found the teacher who ran computer club and also some the teachers who taught Price and Edwards. Most of them have retired.'

'Demographic bulge,' said Gray, apropos of nothing. Dai looked uneasily across at Gray; collected himself.

'Mr Bailey was the maths teacher, but he also ran all the computer classes and the computer club. He's a lovely man, enthusiastic and still with twinkly eyes, the kind of teacher I would have liked sir.' He looked up to see if he had gone too far. 'He remembers Price, a difficult lad he said, but his home life wasn't good. He had a waster of a father and a mother who had to take on too much; the house, her son and earn the money too. Price was no computer genius and he had a nasty streak which came out in the odd spat in class or in the playground. Mr Bailey seemed to put this down to home life too and talked fondly enough of him. I mentioned Rhys Edwards. His face dropped noticeably, sir. He said that if Edwards was still alive he'd be in prison, that he was a very nasty boy with violence he just suppressed, but that was visible all the time. I asked him if he knew anything more about him, but he said that he knew he had run away, maybe with Price he had thought at the time, and since nobody had word of them since, that he or they might have been killed in some way. He clearly didn't think it unlikely. Price and Edwards were *Bwttys*, they seemed to get on alright in computer club. I found two others who taught both Price and Edwards; English and *Cymreig* teachers sir. Neither of them had anything nice to say about either of the boys, disruptive in class, rude, often in detention. Price was Jekyll and Hyde, Edwards pure Hyde. The secretary looked up records for me and they were both regular members of the Wednesday and Friday detention classes held by the deputy head. He's retired sir, as has the head.' Dai started to sit down; then remembered something. 'Nobody in the school had any idea that either of them were planning to run off, they went about two days apart sir, Edwards first. Nobody had any idea either as to where they'd gone. Nobody, including Mrs Price knows where the idea of France as a destination came from, but they did all suspect that they had gone off together.'

Bryn almost jumped up as Dai sat down, animated now, executing the steps of a new dance to a new tune playing in his head.

'This opens things up a bit I must say Dai, just at a time when we thought we were closing it down. We have a new player in the drama when we'd have preferred to have some more plot lines.' He tapped his lips with his fingers as he walked. 'OK Dai, follow down Price and Edwards as a team. Find out who else they hung around with, get to see the parents. Go back to the school to get names and addresses of their classmates, see what pops up. I want to know what we can from when they left home and if any of their friends know where they went. Missing persons should have information on Edwards too, dig harder there. Gray, can you follow Edwards down on Holmes and the databases and find out about the shop robbery in Cardiff that the London boy was involved in. Anybody got any comments?' Dai twitched as usual when a question hung in the air for more than a few seconds and failed to stop himself from answering.

'I did get Edward's family details from the school secretary sir; I was going to follow those up today.'

'Of course you were Dai, good lad. Get back to me if anything comes up.' Bryn looked across at Lucy; 'anything to report Lucy?' Lucy felt vulnerable under the gaze.

'Nothing specific sir, I've been looking at the computer forums that Green used again, seeing if I can identify some of the regular contributors.' Lucy felt sweat collect under her arms at this blatant spin on the reality of what she and Huw were doing. Bryn pinched his chin, not appearing to notice her discomfort. They walked off together to Lucy's terminals in her office.

'Don't spend too long on it if nothing comes out Lucy, we may need to switch direction, what do you think about the Edwards boy?' Lucy had trouble assimilating another player in the scenario, they had enough already, all of them potentially involved, all of them with plausible connections to Green. It came back to Price; that she knew. Who he was working with or for? She and Huw might just be able to come up with some answers soon, but there was no way she could tell her DI that.

'Price we have sir, except in body of course. So the story for me goes, who was Price working with or who was he working for? If with, then it could, in principle, be any of the Cardiff mob or even this new boy Edwards. Of the two, maybe I'd put my money on Edwards. He sounds like a criminal in the making and the disappearance of the two of them at the same time makes it likely that they had hatched a joint plot abroad.' She paused and looked at Bryn, 'but that's not such a trivial thing for a couple of eighteen year olds to do who probably hadn't been much further than Cardiff before that. Wouldn't there be records of their leaving the country sir, did they even have passports?' Bryn ducked his head and then shook it slowly.

'Damn fool, I should have looked as soon as France was mentioned, I'll see Gray in a moment; anything else?'

'If, on the other hand, Price and maybe Edwards too, were just freelance assassins, up for hire, then there may be no connection at all with the Cardiff group or anyone else in the UK for that matter. Green was just killed for something he did to seriously threaten or annoy some criminal gang or some villain, who then hired Price and we may never find out what or who. The fact that Price and Green attended the same school may simply be irrelevant.' She paused again to see the effect on Bryn; 'it might be worth getting a DNA sample from Edwards' family and getting it checked here and by Europol though, if he was involved in killings with Price?' Bryn stood thinking for a few moments, unusual for him to be still and think at the same time, then he nodded. He wandered off, a little distracted leaving Lucy stranded at her keyboard looking mildly perplexed. She had seen Bryn go through wringing self-doubt in other cases, not an enjoyable thing to see in any colleague, but he had always come out stronger afterwards. She shrugged, there wasn't much she could do except to keep an eye out and get on with what she had come here for.

Bryn went back to his office in a glum mood; he felt as if he had been trying to fight his way through some viscous liquid for the last few days, like he did every now and then in his dreams, when he could see that his wife desperately needed help just a few yards away from him, but he just couldn't make any progress towards her however hard he worked his arms and legs. He would wake up with an overwhelming feeling of failure and frustration, sweaty and drained and it would take an hour or more to come round. He sat back in his chair with his hands on the table his head hung forward. He was losing confidence in himself. The case was getting on top of him. Every step they took seemed to divide and branch and leave the ideas that sat resolutely in his subconscious just out of reach again and again, just like the dream. The players in the investigation paraded in front of his eyes completely ignoring him, taunting him. How could a mediocre policeman hurt them they seemed to be saying? Perhaps he shouldn't be running murder cases. Perhaps he should do some cold case stuff or go back to good old assault and battery. He should have done the passport checks as soon as he heard the France stories, he should have pushed Michael Green's associates harder; these thoughts reminded him of the conversation he'd had with Lucy walking back from the university; just skating around the periphery she'd said, and she was right. He left a note for Gray to follow up the passport query and for Dai to take DNA samples from Edwards' family if he could find any of them, but both actions seemed somehow pointless in his current frame of mind. He picked up his coat and left the station.

Now, he needed a brisk walk along the beach to clear his head and to persuade himself, if he could, that he was a competent police officer, that he had done most of the right things. They did have the killer didn't they, even if they had no idea how, or why, or who with. He walked quickly down Belle View Place, working his way across town towards the sea, pumping his legs forward and back and swinging his arms, just to feel his body work and succeed at last, heading towards a place where he could breathe.

Lucy spent a couple of hours trying to get inside the various forums for information about contributors. She wanted to find out anything she could about Colossus.

There were a string of messages from him stretching over the last few years in several forums, all of them offering bits of technical advice or requesting software fixes or probing system vulnerabilities. He came across as a controlling kind of person and she had the feeling, which she couldn't justify by logic, that he had some kind of hidden agenda, but much else she couldn't say. Not a very useful few hours. She had tried to call Huw a few times, but his phone responded with a 'not available' message.

Dai had spent much time trawling around telephone directories finding numbers for pupils who were in the class at the same time as Edwards and Price on the list he had been given by the school. He had made many calls to find out what they knew about the two of them. He'd found Bryn's note and would call in at the school again to check on Edwards' family, take samples and drop them off in Bridgend on the way back. He also had an urge to talk to teachers about Green and Hughes who were also in the computer club. He hadn't even mentioned them when he talked to Mr Bailey and he had come to respect Bailey's views on the character of his pupils.

Gray had laboured over his terminal and telephone, communicating with the passport office and when he had the information he'd requested, with Mrs Price, who also confirmed that her son had a passport from a school trip to Paris the year before he disappeared. The trip, Gray noted with a wry grin, overlapped with the Six Nations game between Wales and France. He was prepared to bet that teachers who would normally shun overseas school trips had put their hand up for this one. He'd check with the school to see who supervised the pupils and if Edwards, Green or Hughes had gone. There was no record of Edwards and Price using their passports at the time they disappeared, but Immigration would only have had a record if they had flown to France, not apparently if they had crossed the channel by boat. So, nothing there except that they definitely had the passports they needed to travel south if that is where they went. He went on to ask 'Holmes' about Rhys Edwards and to find the records of the robbery in Cardiff.

Ferrari was back in the ops room checking out alibis of the Cardiff group by telephone and would walk on out to Uplands later to ask about the purchases in there. She had obtained a photograph of Hughes from DVLC to show in the shops.

Bryn was walking, head down along the shoreline towards Mumbles. He didn't notice anything or anyone, but was conscious of the lulling sound of the waves and of the salt and seaweed perfume. He couldn't explain why, but Edwards didn't add anything to the story for him, Price was the killer, he probably worked from abroad and had killed more than once. Whether Edwards was a partner in crime or like Price, another hired killer did not seem important to Bryn. Europol could deal with that, it was off his patch. He was sure that there was somebody here pulling strings. That is what he needed to address. He looked up and around him for the first time since he had started walking, surprised to find himself at Blackpill. He started to feel so much better, having firmly resolved now to push the whole of the Price-Edwards story to one side of his mind as an essentially finished part of the investigation. He could now enjoy the scenery. He turned round and started back towards town. He would clarify and crystallise his views on the return trip. He was drawn, as he had been from the beginning, with the relationship between Green and his colleagues, particularly Watkins, Khan and Hughes; these now successful men with history together. There was something nagging at him from the depths. He realised that it had nagged him for the last few days. It was something he had thought once to remember to check but hadn't. He would get there. He felt sufficiently rejuvenated to stop by at the café and order himself a coffee to drink outside, the same café he had stopped at with Lucy. He smiled a little as he recalled the vanity of his dreaming about Lucy that day, but neither could he convince himself that the dream had entirely gone away. The reminiscence was quickly replaced by a foolish feeling left over from his invitation to her to have supper with him, the invitation she had declined. He was unsure when he challenged himself whether it was truly an invitation to a colleague or an approach to a woman. All approaches to other humans, he thought with the warm sun encouraging philosophical thoughts, particularly to those of the opposite sex, were intrinsically risky and carried, simultaneously within them, both the seeds of humiliation and of promise. All approaches to another human being could be misinterpreted. These everyday risks were the very substance of human interaction. He sat back with the sun on his face thinking of absolutely nothing at all. He sat up suddenly from his reverie. It was that day at the university with Lucy which had triggered the nagging feeling he had been feeling. The sun was reappearing from behind a scudding cloud and as it emerged he said 'Yes!' out loud, causing customers at neighbouring tables to covertly look across at this tall, lanky man with scruffy hair. He finished his coffee, nodded to his neighbours with a wink and left at a brisk pace along the promenade back towards Central. He left behind the satisfactory susurrations of disapproval.

Bryn was intercepted by Gray as he swung his coat off onto the hook.

'Passports 2000, school trip Paris.' Gray looked at Bryn in the slightly challenging way that he had cultivated over the years.

'Right Gray, good, so Price,' he paused and looked at Gray with an eyebrow raised, 'and Edwards?' Gray nodded almost imperceptibly, 'have passports dated 2000 for a school trip to Paris.' Another minute tilt of the head; Bryn looked up to for a moment to recapture something in his memory. 'Well Gray, if they'd gone in March they could have seen the game.' Gray for only a millisecond looked impressed; 'anything else?'

'Two cautions Edwards; extortion, knife.' Bryn nodded.

'Doesn't surprise me Gray, even what we know already says the boy is doomed to prison or worse, doesn't change anything.'

'Paris?' said Gray. Bryn nodded again.

'Yes that occurred to me too, maybe that's where they got the idea to abscond to France. I suppose it's just possible that they made some contacts there.' He looked fondly into his school memories of young French girls, 'I know I tried to when I went to Paris on my school trip.'

He winked at Gray and received a glimmer of a smile for his trouble. 'So thanks Gray, it fills out the story we already know and I don't doubt that eventually we'll hear something from across the water. They are bound to slip up sometime and if not, some alert gendarme will find them by their DNA or their photographs. I am no longer thinking about Price.' Bryn flounced off leaving Gray uncharacteristically flummoxed.

He went straight to his computer terminal, a usually unloved object in his office and fired it up for the first time in several days, glad to be free of Gray and the minutiae of dribs and drabs of evidence about the killers. Motive and opportunity were what mattered to Bryn. Wearing the quietly confident expression of a master sleuth, he typed a name into the search engine on his browser and was genuinely amazed at the huge number of links that appeared almost instantaneously on his screen. There were many pages of them, thousands of them. This would take quite a while; but although he was unused to screening information on lists, he rubbed his hands together and seemed content in his work. He slumped back into a more comfortable, but less ergonomic position and started to work his way down the list, one at a time, leaving out only those that were clearly irrelevant. After a while he realised that there were just too many entries to check so he tried different combinations of names and words together until he found a search that listed only a few hundred links. He was scratching his itch now and he was happy.

Lucy had spent a frustrating few hours trying to get information on Colossus from the forums by fair means and foul and had been entirely unsuccessful. She sat drumming her fingers on the desk. She checked her watch. She would go up to the university to see Jennifer Flowers before the afternoon meeting, she might have come across Colossus if she or Green used the same forum sites. She didn't like being beaten.

Dai had the address of Edwards' mother who lived with a boyfriend on the Ely estate not far from Barry. He was meeting her this afternoon. This was a tough estate and was just a couple of miles from Barry. His mother had moved there after his biological father had left home and after her son had disappeared. Mrs Edwards showed every crease and fold of the wear and tear that she'd experienced in an unhappy life. She said that she had received a postcard from her son about ten years ago from France, saying only that he was fine. She certainly wasn't. She had resigned herself to his absence and didn't really care anymore. She gave Dai a DNA sample with neither enthusiasm nor rancour. They could have it if they wanted. As far as she was concerned, her no good son was either dead or alive somewhere overseas and good riddance. A depressing visit and one Dai was pleased was over as he walked out of the front gate to his car. Mr Bailey would be a tonic in comparison. He sat with Mr Bailey in the common room with a cup of tea. He wanted to know a bit more about Green and Hughes at the computer club. Bailey talked about them as if it were just last week. Price hardly talked to Green at all, he said, treated him as if he wasn't there and Green sneered at

Price. He was more friendly with Hughes. But Hughes and Green probably spent the most time together at the club. They seemed to share the same interests in programming, but, said Bailey, it was a love-hate relationship, very competitive, lots of outbursts.

The afternoon meeting back at Central was a muted affair again with Gray relating the passport information to the group and Dai passing on what were really only snippets of information from Mr Bailey, which joined the large pile of snippets accumulated during the investigation. Bryn had nodded during Dai's delivery as if it was all simply confirming what he already knew. Bryn had listened good-naturedly, nodding and encouraging, but curiously detached. He didn't pace around or make his usual summary of the case at the end. The team weren't quite sure how to take it. Lucy said she had talked to Jennifer Flowers again to find out more about Green's use of forums but it didn't amount to much, but Bryn just nodded, didn't seem to be particularly interested. They broke up and Bryn wandered off back to his office leaving an initially silent gathering of puzzled colleagues behind in the ops room, which slowly erupted into uneasy conversation.

Bryn was on his third cup of coffee and finishing the BLT sandwich he had collected at the metro store nearby, to stretch his legs and get some air. It was nearly eleven o'clock and his initial enthusiasm was waning fast. He came to an item which made him sit up straight. It was an article from a computer magazine describing the setting up of a start-up company specialising in surveying of tall buildings and structures. The company was based less than a mile from Central Police Station, in the Technium Centre in SA1, a centre designed to promote innovation in Wales by supporting technical company start-ups. Incubators they were sometimes called, that provided technical, administrative and some financial support to help companies become independent. He loaded the website. He knew he had found something significant, but he hadn't expected this. He watched the company video on the home page and let out a long whistle. If he didn't know which direction to follow this morning, he certainly did now. Thoughts were tumbling through his head faster than he could process them. It was too late to do anything other than call Maureen Fellow's home number and tell her what he'd found. Fellows said she would prime one of the Magistrates so that they could get a search warrant approved first thing tomorrow. He would have Ferrari and Williams back full-time and they would hit the house and the company offices simultaneously in two teams. Bryn got the desk sergeant to leave messages for the team to come in for six o'clock tomorrow for an early briefing. He sat back down at his desk twitching with energy and forced himself to carefully draft the warrant. Only then did Bryn allow himself a little skipping run down the corridor where, in his mind, he bowled a perfect googly to Viv Richards. He grabbed his coat with a swing of his arm and departed.

Lucy had left Central soon after the meeting, after calling Huw to arrange to meet him at the diner in Uplands. She was hungry and frustrated after what she considered to be a wasted day and could think only of comfort food, greasy food, as some kind of compensation. Huw was there by the time she had found a parking space and walked around the corner to the diner. He was tucked into a corner near the window. He stood up and they self-consciously pecked each other's cheeks and sat down, they weren't used to being together in public places. They both ordered tea with bacon, egg, sausage and chips. Lucy slowly unwound as Huw told her that he had spent most of the morning in the finance office at the university signing bits of contract and then going from office to office arranging for a library card and a pass for the car parks. He collected entry cards for the computer building from his new department and would be starting on the following Monday at 8.30am. He had cycled along the promenade to Mumbles and back then returned home to check his computer for anything from Colossus. There had been nothing so far. Their food arrived and they both concentrated on eating until their initial hunger had been sated and they could leave big enough gaps for talk. Lucy started off.

'I've had a really frustrating day; I spent hours trying to hack into some of the forums to see if I could get a handle on Colossus. I managed to get a list of registered contributors from one of them, just the aliases but there was no other data associated with the names. No other search I made on the name raised anything useful.' Huw put his hand across onto hers and gave it a squeeze.

'I've got nothing either, we don't have much choice but to sit and wait.' They continued eating their meals mulling their own thoughts.

'Have you had any problems with your boss? He still doesn't know about this I take it?' Lucy sat back and grimaced.

'No he doesn't know and I'm finding it pretty uncomfortable not telling him. He was in a strange mood today too; I think sometimes the cases get to him. We haven't made any real progress since last week; it's getting to all of us a bit. Let's see what happens next.' They continued to eat, eyes down on their food until both plates were cleaned.

'Huw, I've loved having you to stay. Last night was pretty good,' she smiled up at him, 'I was humming tunes around the flat this morning after you'd left; how silly is that? But I definitely didn't get enough sleep.' She gave him a knowing look, 'and my housekeeping chores are piling up. What with the lull in the case I just feel I need to pull things together and regroup, does that sound weedy to you?'

'You certainly weren't weedy last night.' Huw laughed and raised his eyes, 'but I forget you work a long hard week and that I can take a break anytime I like; and, as I've told you, my mum insists on doing my chores. Why don't I come and help you sort the flat on the weekend if you are off. Really, I'd love to. You can pay me with supper.' He winked, 'and pudding.' He took her hands again, 'go back and have a quiet evening sorting yourself out. You mustn't ever feel guilty about taking space for yourself Lucy, just tell me.' Huw started taking money from his back pocket.

'Thanks Huw, and the weekend idea sounds great, but I can't be sure yet how the case will go. And you can put that away. It's my turn I think' she said looking at the bill and putting money on the table. They stood and walked out into the dusk. They hugged each other when they were around the corner and kissed properly.

'I'll call you tomorrow and if you fancy it, we can have a simple supper out tomorrow evening, or I'll bring round some of my famous ragu and some pasta. You can do the wine again.' She hugged him closer.

'The ragu sounds good to me,' she kissed him once more, firmly on the lips and disappeared off onto Beechwood Road, turning round to wave. Huw watched her drive off and then followed her along the same road towards home.

He had collected his gear together and checked everything carefully. He knew how it all worked, even if he didn't do it very often. So he spent an hour or so playing with it, making sure he wouldn't cock it up, he only had one chance at this. He had practised until he was sure and then packed it away ready for use and brought it back to his house in the van he had hired. It was dark when he poured himself a brandy and sat down at the keyboard. He wrote a long email, stopping to think as he went and amending it until it was just right. This had to be absolutely right, a bit intimidating, irresistible, no ambiguities. When he was satisfied, he pressed the send button. Let's see what he makes of this he thought, he knew that he would have to be scared to make the meeting. This should scare him.

Huw had gone home and was watching some television with his mother. She had been observing him more closely than usual for the last few days, there was definitely something up and it was definitely in the girlfriend department. She was aware that they had a

213

privileged view of their son's life simply because he lived with them. He might well have been independent by now and be living in a flat with friends or even in with a partner and then they would have seen him only when he decided they could and they would see only what he wanted them to see. She was wary about intruding on his space.

'How did your trip to the university go today, Huw?' Huw sat up to talk to his mother.

'Oh, you know, just admin stuff, but fine. I've got all my cards so I can use the university library, use the car parks and get into the department. They're expecting me Monday morning; so good, yes. You are now speaking to a fully-fledged member of the academic community.' He looked pleased and smiled at his mother.

'You know we're happy for you, you were getting restless doing dribs and drabs. Do you have to give your notice in at the Tavern?' Huw scratched his head.

'Yeh, I'll go and see them tomorrow, tell them it's my last shift, thanks, I'd completely forgotten about that.' Huw's mother looked sideways at him and without changing her tone said 'any come-back from the police?' She watched his face.

'Er, no, not really,' she raised her eyebrows, 'I've had a few chats with DS Evans about the hacking of my computer.' He examined his fingers carefully.

'Is that the tall gangly man?' She said mischievously. Huw laughed.

'Ha, ha, not quite,' he said blushing. She laughed too.

'I thought so' she said and wandered out into the kitchen.

Wednesday

Huw went up to his room and read until late. His computer pinged an incoming email just after midnight; not too late for some of his friends he thought, as he wandered over to open the laptop, slightly annoyed. His heart almost stopped when he read Colossus in the subject line. It took the third reading of the mail for his heart rate to drop back to something sensible and for his brain to start to grasp what it was saying.

Price is a dangerous man. Both you and I need to be wary of him. He would kill me if he knew I was doing this and he would kill you if he knew you were reading it. He is schizophrenic. He kills when he needs to. He will kill you; he always does. Do not work with him. I know where he is, where you can find him and what he's done. I say this as someone who knows, someone who can help you. It is better for you if you do not know who I am. We can meet alone. I can't risk putting information online or talking by phone. You will tell nobody about the meeting before or after. There will not be another meeting if you miss this one or if you do not come alone. Take your car and park it at Cwm Ivy grid reference 439936 at 06.00. You have only a few hours to arrange this. Walk down the track out to the beach and bear right towards the lighthouse. Walk along the beach close to the sea. I will meet you before you get very far along. I will

tell you what I know. You will turn round after we meet and leave by the same route. You must come alone. I will be able to see you all the way.

Huw felt distinctly faint, what on earth had they dug up. He needed to talk to Lucy now. He called her. She took a while answering the telephone and had clearly just been woken up but came round quickly when the adrenaline kicked in as he told her about the email.

'Christ Huw. Can you get here now, we need to act quickly. I'll put some coffee and toast on and we'll decide what to do. See you soon.' She pressed the red button. Crikey he thought, SWAT mode. Huw quickly got together some clothes and his laptop and crept along the landing, past his sleeping parents and down the stairs. He picked up an anorak and his keys from the side table and carefully opened the front door, clicking it shut as quietly as he could behind him. He would call his parents in the morning, when he'd thought of a suitable story. He winced as the starter motor kicked in and the engine started, it sounded like formula one in the quiet street. He drove as quietly as you can drive an ancient VW past the park and out to Caswell, arriving there about ten minutes later. There is not much traffic on a weekday after midnight in Swansea. The flat lights were blazing when he arrived and Lucy was up and dressed and looking distinctly energised.

'This should excite the neighbours then, you'll have vice squad round.' He said as he moved through the front door. Lucy shoved him then grabbed him for a kiss.

'OK show me,' she said as she hustled him into the living room. Huw opened the screen and booted it up.

Lucy sat for while reading it several times through. She was in detective mode. 'It isn't the style of note you or I would write;' she fingered her lips as she spoke. 'Either the author is compromised in some way, maybe language difficulties of some kind or is trying to obscure their natural writing style.' She sat back thinking for a few moments.

'I wonder who he thinks he's communicating with, it looks a bit like he thinks we are in league with Price in some way, which is interesting. He must know that Price is a hired killer or even a serial killer. He might expect that we're involved in some way through some criminal connection. He may be giving us the information that we can use to get rid of Price, maybe that's how he interpreted your posting on the forum. He certainly sounds scared of him and that he'd be happier with Price out of the way. It really is quite a chilling note.' Lucy and Huw sat quietly sipping coffee reflecting on this.

'It suggests that he has also associated with Price, to know so much about him, to be that scared of him. Maybe he's an ex partner in crime who wants rid of him, to get as far away from him as he can?' Huw stopped and peered again at the text looking for meaning. 'The other meaning that comes through to me is that he's just warning us that Price is extremely dangerous and to avoid any dealings with him at all. Maybe he thinks from my request for information that I'm planning to arrange something with Price. He's warning me off. Don't do it he's saying.' That thought hung in the air with the others. 'It can certainly be interpreted in several ways,' Lucy said cradling her coffee, 'but the cryptic style doesn't help.'

'I'm a bit nervous that he...'

'Or she,' Lucy couldn't resist saying with a smile

'..Knew my email address. I only appear on the forum as an alias; what does that mean?' Lucy thought about this for a while.

'If we're right about him knowing Price in some way and being scared of him, he probably worked for the crime ring that used Price as a hired killer. They must have access to people who use hacking to find out about their victims. If Price is a violent schizophrenic and nothing we have found out about him in Barry contradicts this, then everybody should fear him. He'll be unpredictable and paranoid.' She sat up and looked at Huw, 'does the Michael Green murder mean that the gang routinely use hacking for extortion or getting to people and Green was simply a threat to their business because he'd found out? That would be motive enough and they already have a means to execute it in Price?' She continued to cradle her cup. 'That could explain how Colossus hacked your email address; he was or perhaps still is, part of the gang.'

'Colossus knows full well that if there's any hint of disloyalty in these organisations, he could expect a not so friendly visit from Mr Price or one of their hit man,' he said. Lucy seemed to warm to this idea.

'The gang seem to have been involved in the murder of at least five people, probably more if the search had been continued for similar cases. Nobody has been arrested or even identified. If Green knew why they were so good at it, how they did it, he'd be a very big threat to their whole operation indeed. They had a strong motive to kill him.' Lucy seemed to think that they'd understood roughly what Colossus was and his part in this and they also realised that they may have found the motive for the murder, the one that had thus far eluded Kevin Bryn.

'Why is the meeting here, where we live and work?' Huw still had niggles.

'He has your email address,' she paused, 'he must also have your home address.' A little shiver worked its way through Huw's body. 'He sent the email when?' Lucy looked at Huw, 'just after midnight? He could have sent it from anywhere en route or from wherever he is based. You can drive a long way in six hours. It's a piece of cake from London where the biggest crime gangs are based. He could come from Europe too, only a short flight away. I think he chose here because it would make it more likely that you came. He only needs Google to find any remote place to meet anywhere on the planet; somewhere he will feel safe. He found Whiteford Burrows; not a bad choice.'

Lucy stood up to signal that the thinking time was over and the action should begin.

'If what we have been thinking is mostly true, and I think it is, Colossus is not a threat to us, rather he thinks that we are his means to salvation. So we should definitely go to the meeting,' she looked at her watch, 'in about five hours time.' She chewed her lip before saying 'I should call DI Bryn right now; he will set up a team to pick Colossus up. Helicopters, dogs, the lot.' she sighed, 'It would probably be the armed response team and a horde of uniforms swarming over the beach. Colossus has a very good chance of being shot. You know how twitchy everything is these days. He certainly wouldn't escape. If he is caught, would he talk? From what he's said, he could never be safe from Price or someone like him, not in prison or out of it if he snitched. His only chance as I see it is for him to sink Price without anyone in the gang knowing how. That's what we're offering him. He tells us; well he tells you, and you, as far as he is concerned, will either attempt the job yourself, if you are what he thinks you are, or set some your accomplices to find him. I'm sure Price will have bent a few noses on his travels and there will be plenty of people out there who would like to see him gone. Colossus can wash his hands of it and just wait.' Lucy seemed satisfied with her analysis. 'In fact, of course, we will set Europol after Price wherever he is in Europe. He will certainly be caught or be killed in the process.' She looked resolved to act now. A real life tough cop thought Huw slightly in awe, standing right in front of me. I only come across this sort of stuff in thrillers. He shook his head slowly.

'What about Colossus?' he said. Lucy didn't hesitate; she'd worked it all out.

'If what we think is true, then if we catch him he won't talk. He won't talk unless we follow his plan the way he wants it, to maintain his anonymity. He is risking a lot here; which means to me that we get the information and let him go. He may go back to do whatever he does now, but the world will be rid of Price. If it's a choice between Colossus, who knows how dangerous Price is, who wants him out of the way, and Price himself, it's a no brainer.'

Lucy walked over to her bookcase and pulled out a 1:25000 Ordinance Survey map of the Gower Peninsula which she opened and laid flat on her table, sweeping off some magazines and newspapers.

'There we are.' She had opened the map to show the north west corner of Gower around Whiteford Burrows, a spit of sand, dunes and woodland which intruded into the Burry inlet and protected the salt marsh in the estuary from the wild seas of Carmarthen Bay. The storms and tides also occasionally exposed the remnants of the oak forest which used to fill the Bristol Channel some ten thousand years ago as the ice receded and sea levels rose after the last Ice Age. The rising sea flooded the forests with salt water and destroyed them, leaving just some stumps and a layer of peat to mark their passing all around the Gower coast. The wild and lonely beach on the western seaward side of Whiteford Burrows, runs from near Cwm Ivy in the southwest for about two and a half miles towards the northeast, where it reaches the tidal sands of the Burry Inlet. Pine plantations stretch along the peninsula in a series of woodlands growing amongst the dunes and wild flowers. At the northeast corner the dunes face eastwards towards the salt marsh over the tidal gash cut by the Burry Pill. The stream has cut a deep channel through the mud and sand which fills rapidly with water on an incoming tide and empties just as rapidly on the ebb. The salt marsh then runs east for another eight miles towards Crofty. On spring tides, it is flooded by the sea, which covers over the rough salt marsh grass and samphire. To the north, it grades into a sandy shelf where it meets the sea.

'So Huw, do you know it?' Huw leaned over the map and found Broughton Bay just to the west.

'No, I've taken my van to park about here,' he indicated a place near the beach where a small stream emerged, 'then carried my board across the beach to

221

about here,' he had his finger on Twic Point. 'There's a lovely break that curls around the corner on a north westerly, you can get a long ride on a good day.' He smiled at Lucy.

'I know it, great spot.' The break in tension was palpable. They were talking about normal things. Reluctantly, they returned to examining the map and focussing on the job in hand.

'Right, he wants us to park here,' she traced her finger along the road through the village of Llanmadoc and down a small lane to a cluster of houses marked Cwm Ivy. 'I've walked here before, but some time ago. There's a car park field there,' she said pointing, 'which would be empty I'd guess at that time of day.' She ran her finger along a track marked as a right of way and out to the beach. We can walk down here to the beach; we should be able to see the old lighthouse from there. I guess we..' She looked at Huw and then quickly back down at the map, '..sorry, I mean you, just walk out towards the sea and then along towards the lighthouse. I do know that behind the beach is an area of sand dunes and behind them some conifer forests.' She pointed her finger at them. 'It's all pretty quiet there, no direct access by car.' She suddenly stood up to think. 'That's it, that's why he chose it.' Lucy pointed to the PH on the map, she was animated now. 'That's the Britannia pub, there's a car park there, but there's also a footpath just around the corner which crosses the salt marsh out to that area of dunes.' She followed her finger along another right of way crossing the salt marsh. 'Ah! I get it. The reason he's been so specific about the parking and the arrangements. He

222

doesn't want you to see his car and he doesn't want you to meet him except out in the open on the beach. He will be able to see you coming from a long way off, but you won't be able to see him until he chooses.' Her face shone with certainty, 'He will park at the Inn and walk across the marsh, I'm certain of it. It's the only other parking spot for that beach. He can't get there any other way without us meeting and his arrangements pretty much guarantee that we won't, except on the beach. Clever, careful; he's chosen a good spot.' Lucy reappraised her plans in her head. 'So we go to park in Cwm Ivy at 6am, which means leaving here at about 5.15am to make sure we arrive in good time. You will then walk out onto the beach, meet Colossus,' she stopped to think. 'It would be good to wire you for sound,' but she immediately dismissed this. 'Take your phone and switch it on to record. We need a record of what he says.' She stood back and looked at Huw and said 'then you walk back to the car park and we take our booty back to the DI.' A frown crossed her face, 'Of course he'll be bloody furious; gobsmackingly, outrageously livid, but he'll get over it if he has Price' she said to reassure herself. She didn't look quite so confident now.

Huw had been twitching about for the last few minutes but didn't feel able to interrupt Lucy in full flow.

'Lucy, this is all a bit out of my league you know. I do want to nail some bastard for what they did to me, but meeting some international criminal on a beach on my own, Jesus!' He raised his hands and looked at her, 'I'm not sure I can do it.' He lowered his head. Lucy took his hands and held them, looking intently into his face.

'I know you must be scared Huw, but I'm sure that Colossus is not a threat to you, it's the other way round. He will be worried that you might be a threat to him, or he wouldn't have gone to the trouble of meeting at such a remote spot.' She looked at him hard, into his eyes; 'do you think the same way too? It's important that you do, you won't be able to do it otherwise.' She continued to hold his hands as his eyes told her he was running the idea again and again in his head. He eventually spoke.

'Yes, yes I do think that's how it is Lucy; it's just... Let's do it.' Huw looked very far from confident but he seemed resolved. Lucy tried to break the spell of fear gripping Huw.

'Pretend you're surfing the rocks at Overton, now that *is* dangerous.' He gave a wan smile. 'You and I will be there together at the car park and as you walk out to the beach, I will work my way through the woods and into the dunes so that I can watch you walk along the beach all the way. I'll have you in my sight all the time.' She squeezed his hands to reinforce the words. 'I'll be walking with you but out of sight in the dunes. You'll be gone from the car half an hour at most.' He laughed an uneasy laugh; 'and we'll get that bastard Price' she said with a final squeeze. Huw nodded, trying to smile; but he was churning inside. Lucy suppressed all thoughts of what she knew full well she should have done, which was to tell her boss and hand over the job to him. She also knew full well what a disaster for her and her career it would be if anything went wrong. She couldn't justify what she was doing except on the flimsiest of logic, but she had set out her path and she would follow it. She'd always done that in

224

her life, impulsive and determined, and usually it had worked.

Lucy had decided, that after Colossus had parked his car near the Britannia pub, he would walk quickly out across the salt marsh on the seawall footpath and settle into the dunes, so that he could watch Huw's approach and assure himself that he was alone. If Huw were to start walking from the car park at Cwm Ivy at 6am, he would be on the beach close to where they expected Colossus to be emerging by about twenty past. Lucy therefore argued that Colossus would be in place in the dunes just after they arrived at the car park. He would obviously arrange it so that they wouldn't see his car as they arrived. It was nearly half-past four now and too late for useful sleep. They were both pretty wired anyway and couldn't sit still for long or settle to anything. They busied themselves with packing a flask of coffee and some breakfast sandwiches in a rucksack and deciding on what to wear. It would start to get light in less than an hour. They went through the route that each of them would take again and again, refining their actions so that they both knew exactly where to go and would both know where each other was when Huw made his way along the beach. The plan was for Lucy to settle into the dunes from where she could watch the meeting though binoculars, but not so near that she could bump into Colossus accidentally. As soon as Huw and Colossus had finished she would make her way back shadowing Huw along the way back from her path in the dunes. Lucy would then call Bryn to give him the good news and take what she imagined would be a severe, but good-natured bollocking, for going off on her own.

She also expected acknowledgement of her quick thinking to exploit an opportunity which arose unexpectedly and her independent judgement in securing the means of capture for Price. It would, Lucy recognised, be Bryn who would actually get the accolades and her Super Maureen Fellows; but that's just how it worked. He would be pretty pleased with his DS. This scenario played continually as a background commentary through her mind. She needed this to justify to herself what she was doing.

He packed his gear in the small white van he had hired the previous day and set off at 5.15am towards Whiteford. He parked at a pull-in overlooking the marsh and where he could look down onto the lane from Llanrhidian that he expected Thomas to drive along. When he had confirmed his arrival, he would walk quickly out across the dyke in time to intercept Thomas walking along the beach from Cwm Ivy. If Thomas didn't turn up, he would set something more certain up; but he was sure that he would. He understood people, their needs, their concerns. There was a poetic symmetry to dealing with Thomas this way that appealed to the artist in him. It would also confirm the overwhelming sense of control he felt of other people's destiny. The murder would confuse the local police like the first one had and they wouldn't find anything to implicate him this time either. Another unsolved murder orchestrated by Colossus. He decided that he would then delete the alias Colossus as a member of the forums and in a few other places he had used the name. It had run its course; it was going to be the start of a new era. He would do that after he'd sorted out Mr Thomas.

Huw and Lucy left her flat at about 5.15am, deciding on the VW in the end because it gave them space to change in. They aimed to get the car park, a little, but not too, early. They would hold back if they found they were making good time. They drove across to Cilibion from the south Gower road and through Llanrhidian turning off after less than a mile to Cheriton. Lucy got down onto the floor in the back as they went through the hamlet.

'We don't want him to see two of us 'she said, 'if he's already here and looking for us to pass.' Huw grunted; it being about the only sound he could make at the moment. They passed the Britannia, Huw was unable to resist scanning the car park as he went past. Empty. Immediately after they had passed, a man emerged carrying a rucksack and walked off down the hill. Any locals seeing him that early would have thought him just another bird watcher going out to the bird hide on Whiteford Point. They might, on reflection remember the rucksack, but probably not anything else.

Kevin Bryn and the rest of the team gathered in the ops room along with their Super, Maureen Fellows. For the first time since last week there was an animated buzz of conversation. She thanked them for coming in early and introduced their DI for a detailed rundown of the operation which they aimed to start at 7am to raid simultaneously, the premises of SteepleTek and Hughes's house in Penmaen. Fellows then went down to reception to meet the magistrate who had agreed to come in early to check and sign the warrant. She would monitor events from Central and keep the Chief Super in Cockett informed. She seriously doubted that he would be there yet. Bryn was in bouncing form, literally. He rubbed his hands, and practiced his full range of facial expressions as he wound his way between the chairs and around the room talking animatedly all the while.

'Gray, take Constables Ferrari and Williams with you to the SteepleTek unit at The Technium Centre. The SOCOs will be with you when we've finished looking at the house. Collect any documents, memory sticks computing equipment, phones; you know the score. Bill's team will get along later to gather trace and bag up. Hold him if he's there. Wear over suits and gloves. Tape the doorway, nobody else is to enter the premises; treat it as a crime scene.' He looked at Ferrari, 'Clear?' She nodded. 'OK off you go. Enter the building on the dot of 7am when we,' he indicated the other team with his arm, then stopped talking abruptly and looked around him, looking faintly confused. 'Where the hell is Lucy?' The others looked reflexively about them, some shaking heads; 'anyone?' They all shook their heads and looked at Bryn. 'Dai, call her house phone and mobile now. Has anybody received any messages?' They all looked at their mobiles, all knowing that they hadn't. Bryn had stopped dancing for the minute. Dai shook his head; 'unavailable message on the mobile, answer phone on home number sir.' Bloody, bloody hell, Bryn cursed to himself. 'Dai, tell the sarge to keep trying, every ten minutes until he gets her, both phones. I want to talk to her as soon as.' The absence of Lucy had taken the shine off the briefing and left the team members unsettled. Bryn started to wind up again. 'OK, nothing we can do now. Dai, you come with me to the house.' He nodded at Bill Wood and the SOCO team. 'Off we go then.' The two teams left the ops room in a disorderly straggle and made their various ways to two white *Heddlu* vans parked in the compound. Gray's team lagged behind to let Bryn, Dai and the SOCOs get away first. They had further to go.

He watched the VW van go past carrying the now familiar registration number given to him by Price last week. A week in crime was almost as long as a week in politics, he thought to himself. He saw Thomas in the driving seat and nodded to himself. It was the first vehicle that he had seen since he had arrived going the opposite direction to the thin commuter traffic at that time of the morning. It was a direction which led to a dead end. That knowledge had determined his decision that Thomas park in Cwm Ivy and himself at Llanmadoc where he had alternative escape routes if anything unexpected happened. He got out of the van and went round to the other side to pick up his rucksack from the passenger seat. He slung it over his shoulders and walked briskly down the hill and into the side lane which led down to the seawall. He jogged gently to make sure that he reached the start of the dunes in time. He then chose a spot tucked into the dunes, close to, but out of sight from the path. He had an uninterrupted view along the beach in both directions. He prepared himself for the meeting.

Lucy got back into the front seat only when they pulled into the field to park. It was 5.50am. They both got out from the van and walked down through the gate onto the gravelled track leading out to the beach. They didn't want to linger and lose their nerve. A wide avenue of conifers, guarded by a bungalow nestling in the trees, appeared on their right, but they continued on to a further gate which led from the track directly onto the beach and alongside the dunes. A few yards along Lucy stopped.

'This is where we part lovely boy' she said, holding his hands again, 'it will be fine. You carry on along this path and follow the tide line along. It's not too far off a spring tide, so the sea will be well in now. I'm going along here,' she pointed to a footpath which went back through the low dunes towards the woods they had just passed on the track. 'I'll go into the woods there and walk along parallel with you in the dunes. Don't walk too fast' she smiled, 'I'll be going up and down the dunes.' She switched her mobile off. 'I'll leave it off until after the meeting, call me then, I don't want him hearing it in the dunes. He'll probably be quite close when I stop to watch the meeting.' She gave him a solid kiss on the lips. They were both quivering a little beneath their bravado and they could both feel it. 'Let's go, see you in half an hour.' Huw gave a tiny wave and said a feeble 'bye' before he put his head down and started walking slowly. Lucy was already half way to the edge of the woods.

Gray, Williams and Ferrari arrived at the door to the Technium Centre in SA1 at precisely 7.00am. The SteepleTek offices occupied a unit on the second floor. Gray showed the warrant to the security guard at the front desk and asked him to give them access to the SteepleTek unit. They put on protective coveralls and followed the security guard up in the lift. He opened the door to the unit using one of the master keys on his chain. Gray scowled at him as he attempted to walk in, shaking his head, and the guard stood back embarrassed. Ferrari thanked the security guard and told him that he was to let the staff who normally worked at SteepleTek into the building as usual, but to send away any other visitors with an excuse. The guard told them that there were usually two staff who arrived at about 8.00am. Ferrari warned him firmly not to alert them in any way when he let them, but to call her, Ferrari as soon as they left the foyer area. She gave him her card. 'Keys please' she said holding out her hand and passed them to Gray. Gray put them in his pocket and he and Ferrari walked in. Gray indicated with his head that Williams was to guard the entrance and put up some crime tape.

Bryn and Dai timed their arrival at the house to a few seconds before 7am, and were followed almost immediately by the SOCOs' van. They and the SOCOs were already wearing their protective suits which they had changed into at the small car park above Tor Bay. They all jumped out from the vans and Bryn started banging loudly on the front door. No answer. They looked at each other and Bryn nodded to one of the SOCOs who ran back to get the ram. Bryn carried on knocking until the SOCO saved him the bother by crashing the ram into the door and splintering the frame at the second blow. Bryn went into the hall first, shouting 'POLICE, STAY WHERE YOU ARE!' He ran towards the back of the house shouting again and then sent Dai upstairs; who shouted a few times more and then appeared at the top of the stairs.

'Clear here sir', Dai looked at Bryn. 'He's probably on his way to SteepleTek' said Dai. 'He'll be in for a bit of a surprise I expect' he said, smiling. They stood back to let the photographer take pictures of the house as it was when they'd first come in. He took about twenty minutes and OK'd each room as he finished so that the SOCOs could get started on dusting for prints and collecting any trace which might carry DNA evidence; hairs, toothbrushes and razors. Bryn sent Dai to check all drawers in the house for documents and computer equipment, especially memory sticks and phones.

Gray and Ferrari had a preliminary walk around the unit to get a feel for the space. Ferrari took pictures with her mobile phone of everything around them as they went. There was an open plan laboratory space with work surfaces littered with what looked to Gray like the makings of electronic circuits. Beside them were two computer workstations with notebooks open just as the last users had left them. There were other machines connected to the computers, probably printers Gray thought. There was also an office with a single computer and filing cabinets and many framed pictures of tall buildings from around the world. They started by examining the work desk carrying the computer and printer. Gray looked in drawers on one side and Ferrari on the other. They took out each drawer in turn, checking the contents carefully by putting the drawers onto the desk and emptying the contents. One of the drawers on Ferrari's side was locked so she went back to laboratory for a large screwdriver and made short work of the drawer front. Gray thought what a splendid thief she would make as she worked her way through the contents with her gloved hands. She picked up a pile of standard brown envelopes which were sealed at the top with self-adhesive flaps and held loosely together with an elastic band. She shouted out as soon as she saw what was written on the first and second envelopes.

'Sir, take a look at this!' Ferrari laid them out onto the desk writing side up. Gray looked at the envelopes and then back at Ferrari smiling.

'Got the bastard' he said grinning dementedly at Ferrari and using a definite article for the first time in days. He picked up one of the envelopes with his gloved hand; 'Christ Almighty.' The first envelope was labelled 'Naples March 2010', the second 'Berlin June 2010'; Gray picked up the one marked 'Llangennith May 2013' and carefully opened it with his penknife. He placed the envelope into an evidence bag and held a small black plastic object which he had found inside by its sides in his gloved fingers, looking at it intently with a distinctly disappointed expression on his face. He might not know what it was but he knew that it might have fingerprints on it. 'What the hell is this?' Ferrari laughed, did he really not know what a microSD card was. Gray could see her amusement and hoped that in good time, her grandchildren might well do the same to her.

'Ha, ha sir, don't you have a digital camera?' she asked; nothing in Gray's experience linked the word camera with this object in his hand. He'd certainly never seen one before. Ferrari looked enquiringly at Gray with her gloved hand held out palm upwards. 'Sir?' Gray put it in her hand and Ferrari pulled her mobile phone from her pocket, opened a slot in the side and inserted the object into the phone. She did a bit of sliding with her gloved fingers on the screen and a close-up, perfect image of marram grass growing in sand, appeared there almost miraculously. They both watched entranced. Just as suddenly, the grass receded rapidly into the distance to show a vista of dunes and beach with waves breaking on the shore. The image lurched dizzily sideways across the screen making Gray feel decidedly queasy. Suddenly, the sand on the beach moved quickly closer and slid alarmingly from the top to the bottom of the screen, until it swung madly across the sun, to reveal a solitary figure, walking towards them in the distance. The figure got steadily nearer until Gray gasped as he recognised Michael Green. Neither of them could take their eyes from the screen for a second. Michael Green's face became the main object in the image as he slid inexorably closer. When the top half of his face nearly filled the screen, his eyes suddenly focussed on the camera and widened. But before the mind behind the eyes could evaluate what it was seeing, a small dark hole suddenly appeared in the centre of his forehead and the image lurched and then twisted away with a sickening yaw. Ferrari dropped her phone as Gray ran to the cloakroom on the landing outside followed quickly by Ferrari who both managed to get there before they leaned forward over the washbasins to retch. They both heaved until they had nothing left to lose. Gray stood up straight and wiped his mouth with his handkerchief. He could hardly speak; he had been totally unprepared for the queasy, lurching unreality of the image followed by the shocking finale. It was one of the most cold-blooded things he had ever seen. Ferrari finished retching and spitting and wiping her face; she looked across at Gray. Police officers rarely get to see the murders they are investigating actually happen.

'Beats Straw Dogs sir; I had no idea what was going to happen. Poor bugger.'

'Better see how your phone is doing Ceri.' They put on fresh gloves and she picked up her phone and removed the SD card into another evidence bag, her phone seemingly not the worse for wear after its adventure. They then put the other four envelopes; 'Geneva June 2011', 'Naples March 2010' and 'Brussels August 2011' and the Berlin one into four other evidence bags and sealed and signed them. Neither of them had the stamina to look at another video. They were still both too disturbed to make normal conversation for a few minutes, until Gray broke the silence by saying that he needed to go outside and talk to Bryn.

Huw was getting nervous that Colossus hadn't appeared, he'd slowed his walk to an amble as he passed the place where Lucy had thought he would emerge. He was feeling distinctly uncomfortable now and his heart rate was still well over a hundred. He'd used the counting of them, against the second hand of his wristwatch, as a therapy as he walked along. It helped to take his mind off this crazy venture. The booming of the surf added to his sense of unease. He looked at his watch, twenty past. Lucy had thought he'd have had the meeting and that he'd be on his way back by now. Perhaps Colossus hadn't come after all. Their manic night time planning now seemed exactly that, caused by a lack of sleep, adrenaline and too much coffee. How could they have thought this Colossus person would come to meet them? They'd just over-reacted. The email must have been some kind of joke. These forum hackers were completely mad anyway; the email would just be someone's idea of a laugh. It was like leaving some silly image on somebody's computer when you hacked it, to say you'd been there. A sense of relief started to permeate him. They would meet back in the van, hug, have a good laugh and plan what to do next. He would certainly relish a cup of that coffee now and he was starving. He would walk for exactly five more minutes then turn, phone Lucy and then walk back to the van.

Lucy could see Huw walking tentatively across the beach, looking round him all the time, obviously nervous. Poor dab she thought, we will certainly make up for the worry tonight. She mirrored his passage along the beach until she judged she was getting close to where the path from the Dyke would emerge through the dunes. This was where she expected Colossus to be lurking, waiting to walk out across the sand to meet Huw. She walked much more slowly now, crawling to keep low at times and stopping to listen, but knowing that any sounds would be drowned by the surf and hiss of tide raking the sand. She did not want to bump into him. She judged that she should now stop and find a nook to follow Huw through her binoculars and she settled down into a depression in the dunes. Huw was nearly level with her now and level with where she expected Colossus to emerge from, not too far away. She waited, heart beating fast. She was starting to get nervous that he wasn't going to show. Huw was faltering now, having also expected to have seen Colossus coming towards him by now. She looked around her nervously and caught out of the corner of her eye a flash of something just above the dunes and close to her. It was moving. A skylark, she immediately thought, until she saw it disintegrate into a flash of orange and dark with a loud report. It was followed immediately by an intense thump into her left shoulder which threw her backwards onto the sand. They were the last sensations, which she would only recall later, in broken fragments, before she lost consciousness.

He had sat waiting patiently for Thomas to appear and was rewarded by the appearance of a solitary figure, definitely male, walking as directed. He experienced a twinge of excitement. He waited until he was nearly opposite him then moved his fingers over the screen of his mobile phone and concentrated on the screen. The image panned across the dunes. He suddenly sat up straight. Somebody, hiding in the dunes just behind him, maybe only ten yards away, appeared on the screen. Fucking hell, this wasn't in the plan. The other figure turned towards him at that very moment and he tapped the screen in panic, hearing the crack almost immediately afterwards. The figure, which he now saw was a woman, was thrown back onto the dunes. Fuck, fuck. He looked in disgust at the screen, which now showed just a close-up of sand. He was furious that Thomas had dared to ignore his instructions, had messed up his plans. He would regret that decision when he found the woman. He would learn that it wasn't a good idea to try to outwit Colossus.

It was time to leave, but where to? He took a few deep breaths to settle himself. He wasn't going back to the village, Thomas might have that covered too. The VW van was probably full of his team. He'd make his way along the old forestry track to the far northern end of Whiteford Point and work his way down the beach to Crofty. It was a long walk, a wet and muddy walk, but in three or four hours he'd come out at the small industrial estate there and could easily pass himself off as one of the cocklers or bait diggers. Call a taxi? No, get on a bus into town and disappear. A million thoughts poured through his brain, he'd sort that out on the way. He'd have plenty of time. There was a café there; he could clean himself off a bit, say he'd got lost. This was certainly a place where you could get lost. He was about to run off back into the dunes when he thought about his equipment. He couldn't leave it there, he knew that they'd be able to put the pieces together which led to him. He wasn't about to make it that easy. He piled his gear back into the rucksack and jogged off. The sooner he got into the pine forest, the safer he would feel. He'd work his way north staying in the trees. His only regret and it wasn't for the woman he had killed, was that his plan had been disrupted. They'd have another unsolved murder. He was almost laughing as he jogged away, the adrenaline making him as high as a kite.

Gray passed on the essence of what he now knew to Bryn, who he could hear whoop. He imagined him spinning around the house. He shook his head. Bryn was excited now and asked Gray to go over what he had seen again.

'Brilliant you two; is there anything more at your end Gray?'

'Computer, documents, memory things. SOCOs have plenty.'

'Right, make sure Ferrari is OK.' Gray nodded with a grunt and added that Hughes hadn't turned up at the unit for work yet.

'Then where the hell is he?' shouted Bryn to himself nearly deafening Gray in the process.

One of the employees had arrived at around 8.15am, somewhat dismayed to find the entrance door to their laboratory and office wide open and guarded by a policeman in uniform and a strip of crime tape. Constable Williams had diffidently held her back from entering the offices. Inside, she could see an older man and a tall

238

woman both wearing white coveralls and plastic shoe covers. The man barked for her to stay outside, the premises were being searched under warrant. He came to the door and asked her for her name and address and a brief description of her relationship to the company. She said that her name was Jo Morris and she was lab dogsbody, secretary and general run around. She was quite straightforward about it. Her boss was John Christopher; John was MD and did customer care. There was a technical consultant Dr Hughes, who designed the software and electronics and carried out the building surveys with her. Gray knew about him. Gray asked if Mr Christopher or Dr Hughes were due in today and was told that John was out on a job and that she didn't know whether the consultant would be in at all today. He asked for her and John's address and wrote it all down in his notebook. He warned her that any personal items of hers inside might be retained for evidence. He told her that she would have to remain there, he pointed to a seat by the doorway in the small landing area outside the unit, until the SIO, DI Kevin Bryn, decided what he wanted to do with her. He wasn't sure when that would be. Gray called Bryn to tell him that one of the employees had arrived and that he had details of her and the MD, John Christopher. He added that she had shown no signs of evasion or guilt in her conversation. Bryn told him to send her home and warn her that she would get a visit from the police tomorrow. The office would be closed until further notice. They found a store room at the end of the laboratory that was stacked with equipment that Gray couldn't immediately identify on benches to either side.

Gray left it for the SOCOs, they had all they needed and more than they'd ever expected to find.

Bryn called Maureen Fellows. He told her what they had discovered, finding it hard to disguise his elation at the evidence. He told her about the shocking video clip.

'Good work laddie,' she'd returned to Superintendent mode. 'It's looking good for a conviction if we can find the wee jobbie. We'll get as many hands as you need to look at the evidence. I want this bastard.' Bryn noted the offer with a smile and said he would carry on there with Dai Swab and send the SOCOs to the laboratory when they had finished at the house.

'We need to get Hughes's photograph out with traffic and beat officers and out to other forces and to Immigration. We don't know whether he's already run off, perhaps he got wind... no, I can't believe he could have known that we were planning raids this morning, we only arranged it late last night.' Fellows was silent for a few seconds.

'OK, leave it with me Kevin. Get back here when you can.' Bryn and Dai finished going over paperwork in the desk and on the bookshelves. They collected all of the computer storage that they found and took every sheet of paper that wasn't a book or a magazine. The SOCOs took the computing equipment and taped it into plastic. There were plenty of prints on every surface. This would keep them and the CPS busy for a while and he would certainly make sure that Fellows kept her promise about bodies. He wasn't thinking hard as yet, about where Hughes might actually be if he wasn't at the office or his house.

The five minutes were up and Huw looked warily about him. Nobody; it was just after half past six. He pulled his phone out and called Lucy, there was good signal. Damn, he got the unavailable message. He thought for a second or two then turned about and walked and ran back towards Cwm Ivy. She'll have forgotten to turn her phone back he thought. He hoped. He arrived breathless at the van after running up the slope to the field where they had parked. No sign of Lucy. The calm he had experienced on the beach had completely deserted him. He was close to panic. He felt exactly like he had on the beach last week. All his actions were paralysed by overlapping and conflicting thoughts. He ran back down the hill. He would backtrack along the route that Lucy would have taken in the dunes. Perhaps she was lost. He kept this thought in his mind, to keep at bay any others. He found a stile into the woods at the end of the path that Lucy had taken and climbed over into the dunes. This was an area of moss, grass and wild flowers that carpeted the dunes and was interspersed with small copses and more mature pines. Its beauty on a May morning passed him by. There were a series of tracks running parallel to the beach in the general direction he thought she would have followed. They would have allowed her a view of the beach and of him as she went along, except in rare places where the dunes in front were too high. There were some footsteps in the sand, but he couldn't be sure if they were hers. He made his way along for about ten minutes. He could see, when he climbed a taller dune, that he was approaching the flat area he had noted on the map, at the end of the dyke path. He started calling her name out loudly, then stopped to listen for a few seconds before moving on. The usually calming sounds of the surf now frustrated him and stopped him from hearing any replies to his shouts. He wandered with increasing panic, shouting and stopping for what he thought must have been another twenty minutes. It was a large and difficult area to search when you were in amongst the dunes. He thought he heard a wailing noise and each time he climbed high he stopped to listen, more carefully now, trying to filter out the surf. It was definitely there. He moved more quickly now, stopping to scan the immediate surroundings in detail on each high point, calling her name.

She was folded up in a hollow in the dunes close to the beach. A large bloodstain covered her whole upper body and had soaked into the sand. She was groaning weakly. She was alive, his heart jumped with relief. He realised only then, that he thought that she had been killed. He saw the wound was a gaping mess on her shoulder, but probably too high for her lung and her heart. She had lost a lot of blood. Hadn't he heard the shot? He cradled her good shoulder and tried to make her more comfortable, putting his jacket over her to keep her warm and talking gentle endearments to her continuously.

'I'm here now, it's me Huw, I love you and you'll be fine when we get you into hospital.' He kissed her forehead, the only part of her face not spattered with blood. He dialled the emergency number and twitched while he waited for it to answer. He blurted out that it was an emergency; his girlfriend had been shot and they were on Whiteford Burrows, in the dunes. He tried to explain exactly where they were. 'Hurry for God's sake. She's lost a lot of blood.' The dispatcher went silent for an endless minute, then said she'd contacted the air ambulance and it would be scrambling now from Fairwood and be there in a few minutes. She continued to try to calm him down and to get name and address details for both him and Lucy. 'She is a police officer, DS Evans, based at Central I think. DI Kevin Bryn is her boss, talk to him. Tell him it's the gunman.' The dispatcher told him to keep his phone line open and report any changes in Lucy's condition, talked to him, reassured him. She said, incredulously, that it was the second time in a week that she'd received an emergency call about a shooting on a Gower beach. If Lucy hadn't been moaning, he might almost have laughed the way that people do when faced with a crisis. 'It was me the last time too' he said. The dispatcher swore quietly, apologised and was rather less talkative after that, except to check every two minutes or so that the police officer was still breathing. 'She's still moaning,' he said, stroking her hair.

Bryn was in the car on his way to SA1 when he received a call on his mobile at the same time the radio crackled into life on the police frequency. His face turned ashen and his body stiffened as he listened.

'STOP! Turn around, we're going to Llanmadoc, Cwm Ivy, now quick as you can, another shooting, Jesus! Put on the siren; do your best lad.' He continued to talk into the phone, making rapid commands to raise the police helicopter and the armed response unit. He was told that Fellows had done it as soon as the message from the dispatcher had come through to the station. The air ambulance had already been alerted. Both were on their way. He thought that the helicopter run by Dyfed Powys

243

police was based at Pembrey and would get there first. He assumed that Fellows would know this too. He asked that they request the helicopter to pick him up at the Cwm Ivy end of the beach after they had confirmed the site of the shooting. He relayed to Dai the shocking news about Lucy.

'Jesus Christ Dai, what the hell is Lucy doing on the beach at Whiteford, no wonder we couldn't raise her this morning, when did she get shot? It could have been any time last night.' He was rambling a bit now wringing his hands. 'How badly hurt is she? She's alive, I just didn't ask.' Dai let the rhetorical questions float past him and gave Bryn's arm a reassuring squeeze.

'She'll be fine *bwt*, the ambulance will be there before us. That's what matters' he said. Bryn continued to drum his hands on his legs, in time with the rise and fall of the siren howl.

Huw clung on to Lucy rocking her gently in his arms singing the lullaby his mother used to sing to him 'Tura lura lura, tura lura lie..' keeping her calm and keeping him occupied. She had stopped moaning over five minutes ago and Huw found it hard to keep singing; the lullaby now punctuated by shudders of breath. He had put his phone down to focus his love on Lucy. The ambulance had arrived within ten minutes of Huw's phone call and the pilot had worked it slowly sideways along the line of dunes until they saw Huw waving wildly in amongst them. He had heard the air ambulance approach from behind. A wave of relief washed over him. He had let Lucy down gently onto the grass and clambered up on top of the high dune next to him. The Air Ambulance touched down as close as it could to them, on the flat sand of the beach. Huw watched as the paramedics ran across and scrambled up the dunes in front of him. The woman who had comforted him on Llangennith beach looked up at him and her eyes briefly registered recognition, followed by a shake of her head. She comforted him again with meaningless words, while feeling for vital signs and injecting a syringe into Lucy's right arm. She inserted a cannula into the back of her hand to which she attached a bottle of plasma. She asked Huw to hold it up high, partly because it needed to be and partly to give Huw a sense of doing something useful. Only after putting an oxygen mask over Lucy's face did she cut away some of the cloth on her shoulder to better expose the wound and the source of blood loss which leaked blood now only in a weak dribble. She gave her colleague a tight-lipped look as he held the tissue apart as she used the same scissors to start cutting into the flesh so that she could apply a pressure pad to block off the punctured artery. Her colleague told Huw to continue to hold the plasma bottle while he ran back down to the ambulance to collect the stretcher and another bottle of plasma. He would alert Morriston Hospital to prepare the surgical team that might, and he stressed again might, holding Huw's arms and looking into his face, save her life.

He stopped as he came to the edge of the woods. He would be without cover from now on. He could see the edge of a wide water-filled channel which ran fast back into the sea. This was Burry Pill, the stream which had gouged out a jagged scar across the marsh and met the sea at the northern end of Whiteford Point. The tide was only just on the ebb. There was much more water than he had expected and he wasn't a strong swimmer, especially with a rucksack to drag him down. Just do it, he said to himself and waded into the stream before his brain could think of reasons not to. He waded until his feet no longer touched the bottom and then started swimming. He panicked as he was swept steadily seawards until his feet reclaimed the bottom some thirty yards further on. He dragged himself onto the mud banks on the far side; stopping on his hands and knees for a few minutes to catch his breath. This would be an easy place to drown he thought. For a second he contemplated it. He also thought about abandoning his rucksack, but knew it would be found sooner or later by fishermen or cocklers. He couldn't risk it. The beach marking the edge of the salt marsh was over a mile away from the steep limestone hills which formed the land boundary proper. He could look ahead to see that he would continue to struggle along the shore, having to wait sometimes for the tide to ebb before he moved on. The beach was difficult, but he knew that the salt marsh was treacherous. It was riven by a complex of deep mud-filled channels which formed a filigree of inlets which filled and emptied with the tide, generating currents that it would be impossible to swim against. The depth could change from a few inches to fifteen feet over a yard of ground. He'd stay where he was and make his way slowly. It could only get easier as the tide ebbed.

The Dyfed Powys helicopter arrived some three minutes later from across the Burry Inlet and seeing the ambulance already on the sand, side-slipped across to the Cwm Ivy end of the beach to look for DI Kevin Bryn and his team, as they had been asked to do. Bryn's police driver had pulled up against the locked gates to the track down to the beach and Bryn and Dai had to trot down the track and out to the beach with the constable trailing behind. The pilot saw a gawky man in an ill-fitting suit, emerge at a run from behind the pine trees and spill out onto the beach. He was alongside a shorter younger man with unruly dark hair, who he thought was probably too young to be the DI. They were followed by a police officer in uniform. He brought the helicopter down and left the rotor turning slowly until his colleague had opened the door and beckoned them inside shouting at the uniform to run along the beach to the ambulance. There was room only for four. It then rose with a surge of power and banked towards the ambulance, settling down some thirty yards away from it. Bryn leaped out of the helicopter before it had settled, escaping the grip of the co-pilot who had tried to stop him and stumbled onto the sand. The beach had been much further away than he'd anticipated. Lucy was being carried gingerly down the side of a dune on a stretcher carried by two green clad paramedics with a third person in a bloody anorak who he now recognised, with absolute amazement, as Huw Thomas. He was scrambling along at their side, carrying a fluid bottle which was attached to Lucy's arm. Bryn shook his head, to dispel the notion that this wasn't some ghastly dream. What the bloody hell was going on? He never got a chance to talk to Thomas, who didn't seem to see him at all. Thomas was inside the helicopter and the outer door had slammed before he had time to say anything, or even to look at Lucy. He had to back off as he heard the engine power up and saw the rotor start to move. He turned round and covered his face as the helicopter rose and twisted away from him firing sand around it.

He got the pilot of the police helicopter to patch in to the air ambulance radio. A female voice identified herself

247

as the pilot and he asked her what had happened. She told him that they had arrived to find a woman with a severe gunshot wound to her left shoulder, which had damaged an artery which delivered blood to her arm. She had lost a lot of blood and was in severe shock with low blood pressure. She and her colleague had partially blocked the artery and given plasma. The woman was still unconscious and she thought had a fifty-fifty chance of pulling through. A team were on standby at Morriston Hospital, which she expected to reach in three minutes. She had never seen a gunshot wound like this, causing so much local damage she said. Bryn asked her if she had talked to the man with her about the shooting. She said he was also in shock and hadn't made a lot of sense, something colossal she thought he'd said, but she'd had other things on her mind at the time. They'd flown over the site before they landed and didn't see anyone else. Her tone suddenly changed to abrupt. She had got to go; she was preparing for landing. The handset went dead.

Bryn yelled in frustration.

'Can you get this officer to Morriston Hospital, now?' He asked the police pilot, who after checking with his base, told Dai to get up and get strapped in. He was also wheeling off to the east a few minutes later.

'OK constable, Cowley was it?' He nodded. 'Backup should be here soon, go back to the car now and find out who has the keys to the gate at the top of the lane urgently. There will be vehicles coming down here soon. Open the gate and stay there on the radio. If you can't open them, run them down. Tell control that I have mobile signal. Run!' Bryn took out his phone and talked to Fellows.

'I'm on the beach here ma'am, DC Williams should be arriving at Morriston by helicopter any time soon. He will talk to the witness,' he paused, his voice and expression becoming sombre. 'Lucy is seriously injured I'm afraid ma'am, the paramedic couldn't be sure that she'd survive.' His voice faltered. Fellows hadn't realised that a shoulder wound could be life-threatening and Bryn listened to a series of Glaswegian expletives at the other end. It also Bryn took a moment to regain his composure. 'I take it armed response are on their way?' he nodded as she responded, 'Good, Constable Cowley should have the gate entrance to Whiteford open. The witness is none other than Huw Thomas,' he said incredulously, 'do you know anything about this ma'am?' then grimacing and shaking his head, said 'nor me. We will need the helicopter back here ma'am to join the search for the gunman. If he didn't get off immediately in his car, he probably made for the marsh or went off across the dunes. Dai might find out some more from Thomas. There aren't many places to get away on foot. It's a hard route, dangerous on this tide; not something I'd try unless I was desperate. If he came by car he must have parked at Cwm Ivy or Llanmadoc and walked out. There's no other way unless he flew in. Can we get cars positioned along the marsh in case he is trying to make it on foot? They will be able to see anyone coming in off the marsh.' Fellows said that she would get on to the Chief Super as soon as he hung up. If he wasn't at a bloody Masonic lodge meeting, she added. 'Hughes wasn't at his office or at home, I've got him down for this shooting. DS Evans must have found

249

something out and gone solo. Bloody idiot. If he used his car he will be miles away by now, if he walked he'll still be out there.' Bryn looked at his watch; nearly half past eight. 'We need to get his car details and photos out there now, ma'am. I'll contact DS Crossman. If he's out there we'll find him. He listened for a while longer and nodded, 'Yes ma'am, I'll wait here. I'll direct operations from the Landrover.' Bryn put the phone back in his pocket and looked around him grimly.

He pressed the speed dial for Bill Wood and told him as much as he knew. He told Bill and his SOCO team to come out to look at the site of the shooting. Bill said that the team were still working at SteepleTek and would be there for a while yet. He would come out on his own and hoped to be there within the hour. He cut the call. Bryn told Gray to set up a UK-wide alert.

Lucy was rushed through the hospital to an operating theatre, where she was quickly anaesthetised and a surgeon started clearing the wound. The plasma bottle had been taken from Huw as soon as the helicopter had landed and he had trotted to keep up with the trolley holding Lucy. He was stopped at the entrance to the theatre and taken to a side room where a nurse helped him to clean off and gave him some sweet tea to help with the shock. He watched him carefully as Huw drank to see if he needed more treatment. He reassured him that Lucy was in the best place and that Ms Edwards was their top vascular surgeon. It was a calming strategy he used routinely for all frightened relatives. It calmed Huw down enough for him to stop shaking. A knock on the door announced the entry of DC Williams. They looked at each other for a moment, each unsure how to react. Dai hadn't recognised Huw at the beach and now looked distinctly perplexed. Huw Thomas recognised Dai as he came in, as the man who had swabbed him for gunshot residue over a week ago. They both started to speak together, but Dai, who had more practice getting the first sentence in, won.

'Mr Thomas,' he said warily, 'you were at the scene of the shooting with DS Evans?' He could still hardly believe it. Huw nodded.

'What on earth happened b'there *bwt*?' Huw looked up at him and made a weary sigh.

'Long story, officer.' Huw paused and realised that what he said now might well affect how DI Bryn treated Lucy. The worst of what either of them had ever imagined could go wrong, had gone wrong. 'All I know officer, is that I received an anonymous email saying that a character, who called himself Colossus on the internet forums that I use, said that he knew who and where Price was. He said he'd meet me early this morning on the beach to tell me. I only got the email after midnight this morning, so there was no time to plan properly. I called Sergeant Evans straight away. He said that there would only be one chance.' Dai was still listening; 'Sergeant Evans, said she'd come along; she didn't like the idea of me going alone. I tried to stop her, I told her she'd get into trouble, but she is hard to stop officer.' It was near enough to the truth to be sustainable and gave the best spin to Lucy's choice of action that he could summon on the spot. 'We both panicked and now Lucy has been shot and might die. Oh God!' Huw dropped his head into his hands and blew his nose with his handkerchief to wipe

251

away tears that had come easily again. Dai sat down next to Huw and spoke in a gentle voice.

'Come on *Bwt*, let's hope she'll be fine', he put his arm around his shoulders. 'Tell me what happened on the beach.' Huw described the walk out and that Lucy was shadowing him along the beach, walking parallel on the dunes. The growing uncertainty he felt, as nobody appeared.

'It must be Colossus who shot her. I don't know who he really is' Dai shook his head again trying to make some sense of what was happening. 'She must have stumbled across him as he waited in the dunes to meet me and he shot her. He must have made a run for it. I didn't see him at all, before or after.'

'So, you have no idea which way he went?' Huw shook his head. Dai was still struggling with the information, of quite why Lucy was there in the dunes, what this Colossus character might have to do with Price. Had Price come back for a second killing? Was Thomas involved? Being a witness once might be accident, but twice was surely careless. 'We thought Colossus would park at the Britannia pub then walk across to meet me. We were parked in the field at Cwm Ivy. His car will be gone now if he went back to it. If he ran off he could have gone any way, I just never even saw him. I only found Lucy later by searching the dunes. Oh God, what have we done?' Huw's apparent calm had fallen away and he started shuddering with shock and genuine misery. Dai went out to call Bryn with the little information he had, nodding into his phone as he looked about him in frustration. Bryn told him to hold Thomas as both witness and suspect. He was the only witness at a shooting again.

Dai could hear his voice rise in pitch and imagine Bryn shaking his head as he spoke. He told Dai to summon a car from Central to bring Thomas in and they would keep him in custody again. Dai was then to come out to Whiteford to the Landrover on the beach which he was using as temporary HQ. This case was becoming a nightmare. The only thing Dai was sure of at the moment was his name. He called the nurse to check that Thomas was well enough to leave the hospital and told her that they would be taking him to Central. He asked if there was any news about Lucy. The nurse touched his arm and shook her head, not yet she'd said, early days. He tried to drink some tea, while he waited for the squad car to collect them both, but he couldn't settle. He needed to be out at the scene of the shooting. He could think of nothing sensible to say to Thomas. In fact, he could think of nothing sensible at all.

The Dyfed Powys helicopter had returned from delivering Dai to Morriston and was sitting back on the beach. A police Landrover, which had brought in a uniformed search team, was now there too with a map laid out over the bonnet and a group of uniformed officers clustered around it. Bryn had been with two uniforms up onto the dunes to find the site of the shooting. They followed initially the skidded footprints of the paramedics as they had half slid and half walked down the side of the dunes with the stretcher. This was difficult terrain in which to make a systematic search, with dune after dune all looking the same and visibility in any direction limited to a few tens of yards. They had crossed each others paths frequently. It took the three of them ten minutes to find the blood stain in the sand and to mark off the area with tape. Bryn knelt down to have a preliminary look. There was a lot of blood. Bryn could see the many scuffs from the paramedics around the blood stain and quite by accident saw in the very next hollow, flattened grass and footprints. To his untrained eye it looked very much as though someone had settled themselves in there. There were footprints leading to the hollow from the south and a second set that led away northeast. He called for the constables to tape this area too and the space between it and the bloodstain. At least the tide would not cover this crime scene, at least, not for a few thousand years.

Gray, Ferrari and Williams had returned to Central. Gray was to act as home base, he would make sure Thomas was safely held in the cells and inform his family. Bryn asked him to conduct a preliminary interview on tape after his solicitor had arrived, if he requested one and after reading Thomas his rights again. Constables Williams and Ferrari would also base themselves there, to assist in the interview and be ready to drive off at short notice if they were required anywhere else. Gray would coordinate events at base dictated by Bryn from the Landrover and keep the Super informed. Bryn smiled as he tried to imagine the conversations between Gray and Fellows. A car was on its way to collect Dai from the hospital and Constable Cowley had told him that the armed response crew had just gone through the gate. The team were assembled. Armed Response were in a large van and would park on the forestry track by the new National Trust bunkhouse. Their CO said he would walk out to

Bryn to survey the area and to discuss tactics. The men would stay in the van in radio contact. Gray called back to tell him in as few words as possible that there were now cars placed at each road access to the marsh. Bryn was familiar with the terrain. He looked out from his cottage over it every day. He knew that they would be able to use binoculars to scan the marsh, to follow anybody moving out there. He was short of manpower and had only two spare cars to monitor traffic coming out of Gower. He reasoned that if he'd gone back to his car as soon as he'd shot Lucy he would be well away by now. But, if he'd taken a long way round on foot to avoid the inevitable police response, he might still escape by car. He had one squad car to cover each of the north and south roads out of Gower. It wasn't perfect, but it was all that they had.

Bryn talked through the options with the pilot and the CO of the armed response team, poring over the map on the bonnet of the Landrover. They decided that he would most likely move quickly northeast to Whiteford Point, cross Burry Pill and then make his way steadily east along the shore of the marsh as the ebbing tide permitted. They didn't think it likely that he'd go west, because he knew that was where Thomas and Lucy had come from. Bryn told them that footprints leaving the site of the shooting were heading northeast and that seemed to clinch the matter. Bryn told them that a witness had thought that the killer would park in Llanmadoc. He had his money on Hughes, but he wasn't sure enough to name him to the search teams. He wasn't sure of much at this moment. He may have got back to his car and made it away, but Bryn still had his money on him escaping on foot across the marsh. So, they decided that the helicopter would quarter the marsh from Burry Pill along to Crofty. The pilot thought he could cover the whole area in about an hour, but his fuel would be low by then and he would have to return to Pembrey to refuel. Visibility was good. He was confident that he and his co-pilot would see the gunman if he was there. If he was on foot, there were only a few safe routes across the marsh with a tide running. There were not many people who knew those routes and they counted on the fact that he would not be one of them. Bryn had cars placed close to these possible access points and he was reasonably confident that they would spot him as he came off the marsh long before he got there. The uniformed search team that Fellows had sent were deployed as a line of officers spaced about thirty metres apart. They would sweep their way slowly along the sand peninsula from the site of the shooting to its north eastern end. They had two dog handlers. Bryn had reluctantly allowed them to give their dogs the scent by letting them wander over the murder site where the gunman had hidden in the dunes. Bill would certainly say something rude about that later. Bryn thought it likely that he would be picked up on the marsh in the next couple of hours. The armed response team would only be called in if they had a sighting and would scramble to where they were needed.

He called Gray to keep Fellows up to date on the plans and for him to follow their progress on a map as Bryn updated him. The helicopter took off once more and the uniforms moved off with their sergeant. He was to be first contact if they saw anything. Bryn sat back in the

Landrover and was given a very welcome cup of sweet coffee by the young driver. He called Gray again to ask him to check with the hospital on Lucy's condition every hour and to let him know the result. He shut his eyes for ten minutes and was woken by the arrival of Dai who had been dropped off beside the armed response van by one of the cars. He talked to Dai again about his discussion with Thomas at the hospital and was as confused afterwards as he had been before. None of it seemed to make any sense. Bryn ran him through the search strategy and Dai wondered whether Price had returned for a second killing. Bryn thought that the absence of Hughes at both his home and his company offices suggested that it could be Hughes that they were chasing on the marsh. He sent Dai to settle himself at the end of the dyke path just in case he tried to make it back that way. He should warn walkers off the path and suggest that they walk elsewhere. Constable Cowley was doing the same at Cwm Ivy. There weren't enough bodies to cover the whole coast in the other direction from Broughton round through Llangennith and on to Port Einon. All of these places were accessible on foot along the coast path; all had multiple entry points to the road. They had made their play; they just had to hope it was the right one. Bryn asked for another cup of coffee.

He had only just crossed Burry Pill when he heard the unmistakeable sound of a helicopter and ducked down against a steep muddy bank, his heart thumping. He watched the air ambulance fly overhead and heard the modulated sound of it hovering and finally settling down near the dunes. He hadn't thought this through; there was nowhere to hide on the marsh from helicopters, nowhere at all. He looked back across the Pill to the trees he had just walked through on the other side and was tempted for a moment to swim back across and creep in there. A quick analysis of the likely outcome persuaded him that he would simply be trapped in there, difficult to find, but trapped. They would use dogs and the place would be swarming with police soon. A few minutes later, he first heard, and then saw, a police helicopter emerge from almost directly across the Burry Inlet and head straight towards him. At the last minute, it too curled off towards the dunes where he had just run from. He nearly panicked as it came closer and finally realised that he simply didn't have a choice. He would take at least three hours and maybe four to get anywhere approaching safety along the edge of the marsh with not a single hiding place on the way. He could slip down into a gully to evade police on foot, but with helicopters in the search, it would be suicide. The only place they couldn't see him was in woodland. As he reluctantly reached these conclusions he ducked again as the air ambulance curled overhead followed shortly by the police helicopter, both heading east this time. He was scared now. His only chance as he saw it then was to get back into the pine trees and sit it out until darkness fell, about ten hours from now. He used the last of his reserves of energy and willpower to get back into the very cold water which was now ebbing fast and to wade and swim back across into the woods. He looked at the bird hide with longing as he clambered wet and tired up the muddy banks on the other side, but that would have been very foolish. He would plan his escape route out when he was hidden in the trees. He hoped that he would have plenty of time.

Bryn could hear the helicopter now in the distance starting to quarter the marsh. He sat there trying to think what he would do if he was making his escape, running through scenarios, thinking where he would go. He realised that you could never have enough resources to search an area this big in such awkward terrain. They'd done their best, he could only sit back and wait. His phone rang about twenty minutes later. The sergeant had received a call from one of his dog handlers. The dog seemed to be following a trail through the pine woods along the old forestry track. Bryn moved his finger on the map until he was sure he knew where the sergeant was describing. He cut off the call and told the Landrover driver to go back out though the gate off the beach and follow the avenue of conifers off to the left. They came up to the armed response team in their van and Bryn told them about the call and that he would follow the track to its end near to the disused lighthouse. The CO started to activate his team, but Bryn said he'd call them if they found anything. Bryn was sensible enough to that know it was sometimes necessary to have an armed response capability but wise enough to know that humans and guns could never be trusted. He preferred to keep them in reserve until he was sure that they were needed. He definitely didn't want his prime suspect shot or anybody else for that matter. They bumped and bounced along the rutted track which ran alongside the salt marsh, then cut inland into the conifer plantation, where the track meandered around old dunes now stabilised with mature pine trees. This was even more difficult territory than the grass-covered dunes at the beach. They didn't see the dog and handler until they were almost on them and only by looking carefully, could he see the nearest officers either side in the line sweeping through the forest. They talked to the handler briefly, who was clearly holding back his dog and said they would follow at a good distance, reminding him that the suspect might well be armed and to stop and report if he saw anything, anything at all. Every five minutes or so, they moved a few tens of yards forward keeping roughly in line with the sweep. After twenty minutes they emerged into the open at the causeway which led over towards the bird hide. The dog strained the leash and pulled his handler over towards the hide until they stood at the edge of the wide channel cut by the Burry Pill. It had flooded at high water and was now draining fast. The handler looked at Bryn as the dog started to bark and whine and to walk around at the edge of the gulley in random directions, wagging its tail and then tried to retrace its steps almost back the way it had come pulling hard again on the leash. The handler yanked it back firmly and made a curt command and the dog reluctantly stopped straining and sat at his side.

'Lost it,' the handler said, 'it looks as though he's crossed the water onto the marsh. He must have swum part of it' the handler said looking dubiously at the fast-flowing murky water. 'After you sir' he said risking his career and smiling. Bryn ignored him on this occasion, too tense to acknowledge the humour.

'Will we be able to pick it up on the other side?' Bryn asked, rubbing his hands again in frustration. The handler compressed his lips and shook his head slowly.

'Very unlikely sir; if he swam across, he will have masked most of his natural smells and wet sand is not good for following trails anyway. By the look of the tide sir, he was probably in water on the other side too, so no footprints.' Bryn looked upstream at the fast flowing channels in the salt marsh and the deep muddy gullies and then out to the fast ebbing tide in the estuary now exposing a narrow beach on the edge of the marsh. He'd take the beach any day. He called the sergeant and told him to collect his team and to rendezvous with him at the bird hide. He then spoke to the CO of the armed response team to tell him that the suspect had crossed the Pill onto the salt marsh side to the east, but that they'd seen nothing yet.

'OK, wait here until the rest of your group arrive Constable and when it's safe you can wade across.' The sergeant and the rest of his team arrived shortly and Bryn told him to reform a line on the other side and sweep their way along the beach for the next hour or so or until further notice. His men should only cross the channel when it was safe. He walked back to the Landrover and sat looking over the marsh. 'He's out there somewhere. We'll have him' he said to Constable Cowley but he didn't feel as confident as he sounded.

He had chosen a deep depression in amongst the dunes as far away as he could from any of the many sheep paths he could see and sat himself down. The tree canopy provided perfect cover from aerial observation and he couldn't see more than about ten yards in any direction because of the steep-sided dunes. He briefly considered climbing into a tree, but the foliage was sparse. He'd be seen from a long way off, not a good idea. He started quickly to gather fallen branches and twigs carrying sprigs of old brown pine needles and to bring them into the dell. When he was satisfied, he lay down and pulled them as best he could over him and his bag. It was far from perfect, but he didn't think he'd be spotted unless somebody walked directly at him. He lay still trying to calm himself, trying to calculate the odds. The sound of dogs and then later of cracking branches and crunching twigs told him what he had expected, that an organised search across Whiteford Burrows was in progress. They'd either find him or they wouldn't. It was as simple as that.

There were eight officers including the dog handlers on the sweep and six armed response officers plus the drivers and Bryn and Dai. If nothing came up, they'd have a food break at 1pm. Bryn radioed Constable Cowley and told him to get to the village shop and ask them if they could arrange food. He should warn them that a bunch of about twenty muddy, tired and hungry police officers would arrive at about 1pm. He looked at his watch. That would be in an hour or so. He was itchy to do something. He called the sergeant and asked if they'd found any tracks or if the dogs had picked up anything. He was told that they'd found nothing yet and that they were about two hundred yards past the channel. Bryn told the sergeant to be back at the Landrover in forty minutes for food. He watched the helicopter get larger, turn and get smaller again as it scanned the marsh. It looked as though it had covered most of it now and it would need to return to be refuelled soon anyway. He sighed and got out for some air and to move his legs about a bit. He walked over to the hide and pulled open the door quickly, shouting 'Police, you're surrounded, throw down your weapons and come out with your hands up'. The driver, who wasn't at all familiar with this DI's idiosyncratic behaviour, was startled from a doze. Bryn then went into the wooden hide, smiling at his own foolishness. He peered out through the horizontal slots through which many a twitcher had poked a telescope to watch migrating birds feeding on the salt marsh.

Gray had allocated Thomas his old cell, as he thought of it and had allowed him to call his father, who would get his solicitor, Mr Parker, to come in as soon as he could. Thomas was very distraught when he was brought in and had said little, except to answer simple questions required of him when booking him in and to beg for information about Lucy. Gray asked Ferrari to look in on him every fifteen minutes. He was worried about him. Mr Parker and his father arrived some while afterwards and he allowed his father to visit him in the cells with Ferrari as chaperone. It was an emotional encounter for Huw and only a little less so for his father. They had hugged as soon as they met and his father had tried to console him. Huw was distraught about Lucy, not about his own predicament. Ferrari ushered his father out after ten minutes saying he could see him again after the formal interview. What happened then would be up to DI Bryn and the Super. His father asked Gray if he had any news from the hospital to give to Huw. Gray knew he shouldn't pass this personal information on, but felt for the lad and said that he would talk to him before the interview and that he knew he was concerned. Gray could definitely remember what love was about.

Gray called the hospital again to be put on hold by a nurse while she found the surgeon.

'Sergeant Crossman? Hello, this is Ms Edwards. I operated on Lucy Evans.' Gray tensed in his chair to listen.

Lucy now in intensive care, and I am optimistic about her survival. We caught her just in time. I have repaired the artery and some of the tissue damage around the site as best I could. You may be interested to note that I found four fragments of bullet, one which had punctured her subclavian artery and two of which had shattered her collarbone. The fourth fragment was lodged in her scapula. She had needed a metal plate to hold the fragments of her collarbone together. She also needed four pints of blood during the operation and her blood pressure and oxygen levels are now stable.' Gray slumped back with relief.

'Lucy has been extremely lucky that the cervical nerves which control her arm are, as far as I can see, undamaged. The shoulder joint has sustained serious damage and will certainly restrict her arm movement for a while if not permanently. She should otherwise be able to use her arm normally when the physical damage repaired itself.' The surgeon paused.

'I have never seen a gunshot wound like that before, is it some kind of dum dum bullet?' Gray leaned forwards to speak, but was cut off.

'I realised that you would need them as evidence and you can collect them from the nurse.' Gray, being a man of rather fewer words than the nurse, thanked her and said that a uniformed officer, Constable Ceri Ferrari, would be there to collect the evidence. Gray thought that Ceri would want to sit with DS Evans to comfort her until her parents arrived. She would also want to talk to Lucy if she was awake and well enough to talk.

He first phoned Bryn to give him the good news about Lucy, he could hear Bryn shout out when he heard, announcing the news to all around him. Bryn had obviously put the phone down and was probably doing one of his crazy walks. It took some while before Gray could re-establish contact. It was a huge relief to both of them, Bryn couldn't stop talking. He told Gray to send Ferrari along to the hospital to comfort Lucy if she was awake and to see if she needed anything. Gray told him that he had already done exactly that, great minds and such like and that she would also collect the fragments of bullet which the surgeon had kept and which sounded identical to those which had killed Michael Green. Lucy's parents had separated and were both now living in different parts of the country, her father near Chester and her mother now in Leeds. They had been told by Gray soon after the shooting and were expected at the hospital sometime in the next hour or so. Bryn was sitting in the village shop café now eating a ham and salad bap and drinking coffee, his sixth cup today. He looked at his hands to see if they were shaking. They were, but since he'd never really looked before, he didn't know whether they shook normally. There were about twelve police officers from the sweep along the beach, some extremely muddy and the armed response team, fresh from their morning reading the paper or just dozing in their van. The café in the village shop was a little gem. Bryn hadn't been there before. It was a cooperative run by volunteers, who had done them proud by making sandwiches and cutting cake, after Constable Cowley had warned them of the impending invasion. They were already laid out with the makings of tea and coffee on the outside tables when the first of them had arrived.

He heard the movement of people coming closer, forcing their way through the under-brush in amongst the dunes. There wasn't much talking, but he could hear the breathing of the one who came closest, only a few yards away and he could see the navy cloth between the twigs. He held his breath for as long as he could and then the moment was past. He exhaled and laid still for a long while as the noises receded into the distance. He had heard a diesel vehicle make its way slowly through the woods, but it didn't get close. He could still hear the chatter of the helicopter as it came closer and then retreated, performing some search pattern over the marsh, he guessed. The barking had receded into the distance. The dogs had been his greatest fear; he had a visceral dislike of them and had needed all his will power not to whimper when he heard them. He was deeply relieved now that he had made the decision to cross back over Burry Pill. He wouldn't have stood a chance out there. He shivered at the thought of the cold and merciless tide and the cloying grey mud. He had feared that the dogs would be set free in the forest, but he guessed that they had remained with their handlers. What neither he nor Bryn knew was that his decision to double back after crossing the tide had confused the dog handler but not the dog. The dog had easily picked up his return trail and was off to follow it back into the woods, when it was brought to heel by the handler. He settled down to a long wait, the fear of discovery remaining real, but diminishing, as the day wore on. He judged rightly, that the search teams would assume that he had made his escape somehow. The snatches of conversation carried on the wind and the sound of vehicles eventually stopped so that he found himself alone in the woods by late afternoon with only birdsong and the rumble of surf to trouble his senses.

His fortuitous escape he put down to superior planning and was therefore confident that his escape from Gower would also proceed smoothly after dark. He had fooled them again.

Kevin Bryn was going over in his mind what they had done and what they should do next. He reasoned that there wasn't much point in sending further search teams out onto the marsh which was now essentially drained of tide and therefore safer to walk on. If there was anybody there who had escaped detection by the helicopter, they would have been seen from their vantage points along its length, by using their binoculars.

'What about a boat sir?' Dai ventured. Bryn hadn't considered this at all and he scratched his chin.

'We could get the Loughor inshore out Dai, they could scoot along the length of the marsh quite quickly;' he was warming to the idea, 'they would be able to scan the seaward side and we're covering the landward side with cars. Good idea Dai.' Common sense intervened to interrupt his flow and his shoulders sagged. 'But I think a bit too late now.' He looked at his watch which told him the gunman had been on the run for at least five, maybe six hours. 'He could have walked to anywhere on the marsh by now, so I think he must have got away quickly after the shooting. We would have seen him by now if he was still there'. He started to get up to move. 'The helicopter saw nothing, we've found nobody, no tracks on the marsh, bugger all.' He had his hands in his pockets, as he nodded with his head to indicate the muddy search team. 'There's been no sightings from the cars along the marsh, nothing from the cars on the main roads in or out; what a bloody mess.' He shrugged his shoulders.

'Come on Dai, we'll talk to the uniforms in the cars along the marsh, get a feel for how much they can see, convince ourselves one way or another that he's gone. If there's nothing there we'll call it off.' He looked and sounded tired and low. 'OK boys, sit tight, thank you for your sterling efforts. Daz is on me.' Bryn looked at the sergeant and told him to stay put and that he would call him to continue the search or to abandon it within half an hour. He went across to the CO of the armed response team. 'Thanks boys, good to have you on call. I can't see that it's likely we'll need you again today. But that will be for the Super.' Dai indicated to Constable Cowley that they were about to leave and that he should finish the last two sandwiches or take them with him. They climbed into the car and drove off down the hill, the white flash of a van parked above the road on the right catching the corner of Bryn's eye, but not registering on his consciousness.

They drove to Landimore on the landward edge of the saltmarsh. They arrived at the squad car which had been parked all day at the foot of the lane, with an open vista onto the marsh. This was the bottom of his own lane and he knew it well. Whiteford Burrows were clearly visible from here through the early afternoon haze. It wouldn't be easy for him to have escaped their attention on the flat marsh or easily passed them coming off the marsh. But he also knew that he could, if he'd been careful, have made his way along one of the deep runnels and into the woods out of sight to the west. They simply couldn't cover everything. 'Has anybody been out to the old lookout tower?' Bryn was pointing at a small building right at the edge of the marsh which stood on stilts. It was the lookout tower used to observe shells fired across to Whiteford in WW2. The two constables shook their heads. 'OK boys get out there to have a look. It's a long shot, but the only place to hide out there. Constable, radio the sarge in the Landrover, tell them to call by here on the way back to base, they can help. You can follow them back to Central when you're done.' The car at Llanrhidian, the next observation point along the marsh, had a similar wide and uninterrupted view as did the car at Crofty. Again, he thought it unlikely that anybody could have come in off the marsh without being seen. The last squad at Crofty had talked to a party of cocklers moving out in a 4x4 about an hour ago, otherwise nothing. He radioed two of the cars to go to Swansea. One was to remain on lookout at the SteepleTek premises and the other to wait at Hughes' house until further notice. 'OK Dai lets get up to Morriston, I want to see how Lucy is doing.' Bryn told Gray that they'd got nothing and that he was calling off the ground search but leaving cars at the house and offices and the ones already on the roads into and out of Gower. Gray would have picked up his pessimistic tone.

Bryn called Maureen Fellows on the drive to the hospital to report the complete absence of any sightings, except for the dog scent on the burrows, which he said must have been a false trail. He told her that it would be difficult for any person walking on the marsh to avoid being seen, but that they simply hadn't had enough resources to be certain. There were a large number of access points on foot, between where the squad cars had been parked, into the woodland on the steep hills along the estuary. He could have gone the other way towards Llangennith; he could have escaped in the first half hour after the shooting before they arrived. He thought then to himself, but didn't voice it to Fellows, that it would have needed hundreds of searchers on foot and many more vehicles to make the search even 90% secure. There never would be those resources and so there just didn't seem any point in saying it.

'I'm calling in the search teams and suggest that you call the armed response boys off ma'am. We have a description of his SUV, we know where he lives, we know where he works; we'll get him ma'am. Gray set up the nationwide alert a couple of hours ago. I'm also sending two cars to watch his house and the unit in the Technium Centre now. I could do with some bodies to stake them both out for at least the next 24 hours. Unless he has another bolt hole, he's on the run.' Bryn thought he'd covered all the bases, but knew that this was something which only happened in fiction.

'I'll leave the cars monitoring the roads out of Gower overnight too ma'am, he might just be sitting quietly somewhere waiting for the excitement to die down.'

Fellows offered him some bodies for as long as he needed them and tried to offer him some solace, but Bryn didn't want to be cheered up yet.

Ferrari was outside the Intensive Care Unit at Morriston hospital on a chair when Bryn arrived. She told Bryn that Lucy was still barely conscious, that her parents were now both sitting with her. She had said little and kept drifting back into sleep. The surgeon had been to see her and had said that she was making satisfactory progress. She thought that Lucy might be out of the ICU tomorrow, if things continued the way they were. So good news, but it certainly wasn't the time to talk to her about what had happened on the beach yet. He would save that for tomorrow. Ferrari asked if she should stay the night. Bryn was touched by the offer and thanked her, but couldn't think of a good reason for her to do so, he didn't imagine Lucy to be at risk and her parents were here with her now. Her parents presumably would do shifts or the nurse would push them off to a hotel or back to Lucy's flat in Caswell if she was sleeping. Bryn needed to see her for himself though, to make sure that she was alright. He knocked quietly on the door and pushed it open. He introduced himself to her parents, but was looking at Lucy as he spoke. A tear nearly squeezed itself from under his eyelids as he saw her face, asleep, with a calm expression, a faint smile. He felt that he was intruding on a very private thing. Beautiful he said to himself. He would not have coped at all well if she had been killed or was still in danger. He left the room quietly with a nod to her parents. Had he been asked immediately afterwards to describe the parents, he would have been at a complete loss.

Bryn went with Dai and Ferrari to the hospital canteen. He had a powerful urge for something hot and comforting, an urge to eat food to cheer himself up, an urge which seemed to be shared by the others. For a second, he understood the dilemma for people who eat addictively for comfort. They all chose lamb stew with mashed potatoes and sat in a corner to take stock. The day had been dramatic, but not quite in the way that Bryn had thought it might be at the beginning. Bryn told Ferrari about the shocking telephone call he had received earlier. Ferrari said that she still squirmed when she recalled the video of Michael Green's murder. She said that none of them had any inkling of what Lucy was about to do nor of any arrangements with Huw Thomas. She was as baffled as Bryn about the appearance of Thomas. Bryn, with his antennae tuned more closely to Lucy than maybe the others, sensed that Lucy and Thomas had a personal relationship outside the case. He added together in his mind the moments of coyness recently, the blushes he had seen and he added the decline of his offer to supper to justify his faint but definite feelings of jealousy. There were long periods of silence between the bursts of conversation, where food was chewed and thoughts mulled over. There was no obvious direction for the conversation to take. There was either too much to talk about, or too little, nobody seemed sure. Bryn had difficulty explaining to himself what they had done today, let alone to Ferrari. At the time it had all seemed to be a series of logical decisions based on the incomplete facts they had to hand and the resources they had available. Now, he wasn't sure. He had fully expected to find Hughes on the marsh. He had imagined it in detail, the cold and bedraggled fugitive, relieved to have been found. He was visualising it now. But that wasn't how it turned out. They'd actually found nothing except the footprints leading out of the hollow where the shooting took place. They led towards the salt marsh and were maybe picked up by the dog. He wasn't a dog expert. He was again wrestling with notions of his own competence. Had he let this case trickle through his fingers again as he tried to grasp it? Experience had taught him that these moments of uncertainty and reappraisal were often the very catalyst for new insights into the case. But it is also in the very nature of insecurity, that the solace of this understanding can only be perceived in hindsight. He tried to let his mind go blank and, as before, something nagged from the depths, some kernel of understanding, as yet not fully ripe. He carried on eating with none of this torment visible on the surface, except as a faint ripple of concentration on his brow which played gently with the ridges of skin.

'I suppose you've noticed sir, that the circumstances of Lucy's shooting are essentially identical to those of Michael Green.' Bryn looked up sharply at Dai. Of course he must have thought that somewhere in his head but it hadn't crystallised out quite so starkly. He stopped chewing.

'Lucy gets lured to a lonely site where they are unlikely to be seen by witnesses and then gets shot, with the same type of bullet. Thomas said he and Lucy had parked at Cwm Ivy, and that they'd been sure that he would park at Llanmadoc. Hillend and Broughton sir, identical MO as Green's killing. It's just a different beach, with only two access points by car.' Bryn was about to ask, why then had Lucy not realised that they were walking into the same trap as Green, when he realised that he had only seen it that way himself, after Dai's observation. He stopped the utterance just before it emerged.

'Why was Lucy shot Dai, it should have been Thomas, the one on the beach?' Dai, held his cutlery in his fists, resting on the table either side of his plate, chewing rapidly what he already had in his mouth and swallowing.

'Must have gone wrong sir, maybe Lucy stumbled across him b'there, surprised him.' Why she had been there on the dunes they weren't quite sure yet. Ferrari chanced her arm.

'Could it be Price sir?' Bryn had been mulling this since news of the shooting. Could Lucy and Thomas have been following some enquiry that threatened Price, had he got wind of it? His once satisfying image of Hughes as the fugitive, exhausted, with his hands up on the sand was being edited to see if Price's face fitted. After swapping the faces back and forth a few times in his mind, he didn't think it did, but he really had no rational reason to think so.

'I don't think so Ceri' he said, not expanding in case it led him into further and more difficult mental terrain. They continued to eat. Ceri and Dai ordered apple pie and custard for pudding. Bryn was content to watch them in an unfocussed way whilst he toyed with the scenarios forming in his mind. He was happy for the silence. He continued thinking while they collected and drank their coffee and talked together about Lucy and what she might like them to take along to her when they visited tomorrow.

It was evening now and the sun had almost set behind him over the hills of Pembrokeshire just visible in the distance. He hadn't heard anybody for over an hour now. The last sounds he had heard seemed to be conversations between walkers or birdwatchers. He was pretty sure that they were not police. They'd given up the search. He'd won again. His terror earlier in the day and the miserable few hours shivering under a pile of branches and twigs with the sound of police, helicopters and dogs around and above him had been replaced by a supreme confidence. He heard himself laugh. He carefully moved away the branches a few at a time, stopping to listen and then continuing until he had cleared them all to the side. He sat up and stretched his arms and turned his head from side-to-side to free his stiff neck. He waited a few minutes, concentrating intently on the sounds around him, then stood up and massaged his legs and walked in small circles to get the circulation going again. He'd wait until it was nearly dusk, not too dark; walkers didn't come back from beaches in the dark. He wanted it to be just dark enough to soften images and for him to find his way back safely.

The three of them had a last conversation with the nurse saying that they'd be back tomorrow, hoping to talk to Lucy then. They left for the car with Bryn sat quietly in the front and Dai sitting in the back.

'Central sir?' Said Ferrari, looking sideways at Bryn who nodded with his lips compressed in thought. She took off fast from the car park towards Llangyfelach Road and the city centre. Bryn's head bounced up and down as she speeded over bumps and around bends before it turned sharply towards her and said.

'Ceri, back to Gower. We're having supper in the Britannia pub, my treat.' He had a smile on his face. It was usually a good sign. Ceri rolled her eyes in the mirror at Dai who responded in kind. He sat back to enjoy the ride. Ceri turned off quickly right then across the back of town to Gowerton and the Gower peninsula. They arrived in heavy rain at about half past seven and Bryn ordered drinks in the bar. He excused himself and left from the front door to return about five minutes later with a quietly confident expression on his face. Dai and Ceri swapped raised eyebrows again. They climbed the few steps to sit at a window table in the restaurant, Bryn had asked for that. The conversation was about anything but the case, Bryn would steer the topic away if it showed any signs of drifting in this direction. He was lively now and full of humour. He asked Ceri about her terraced house in Mount Pleasant which she had bought recently. Her police constable's salary plus a loan from her father for the deposit was sufficient to buy in this dramatic but run down corner of town almost directly above Central. It was a high crime area but had magnificent views across the whole of Swansea Bay to Mumbles and across to Devon on the south side of the Bristol Channel. If you didn't need to park your car there at night and were five feet eight, fit and feisty like Ceri, it was perfect. It was ten minutes walk to the town centre, twenty minutes to the beach. She was enjoying her new house and considering a lodger, but at the moment she said she was enjoying the solitude. Bryn and Ceri had the mussels starter and bream main course. Dai ignored again the inner calling for lighter and healthier food, planted there years ago by his mother and ate the paté and had burger and chips. They had another drink; two sauvignon blancs and pint of Pedigree for Dai. They had finished eating now. Even Dai declined the pudding, though perhaps more from guilt, than from a lack of desire. Bryn stood up sharply.

'OK now, off we go, quick now,' and moved off abruptly, nodding to the waitress that he'd be back and led them quickly out of the pub and into the front garden. Ceri and Dai shrugged their best Gallic shrug at each other. They could see a figure just disappearing up the steep hill into the dusk. They caught up as he was opening the rear door of a white van.

'Dr Hughes I presume' said Bryn with a smile, which was wiped off very quickly as the man swung round and Bryn could see that it was not Hughes at all. The man looked decidedly uncomfortable as the group of three which included a tough-looking woman in police uniform stood there staring at him in the rain. Bryn had the presence of mind to hold out his ID. 'I'm very sorry to startle you sir, DI Bryn from Swansea police.' He cleared his throat, 'as you must realise, I was clearly expecting somebody else.' The man seemed to relax then smiled.

'No problem officer, you gave me a scare is all. I was just returning from a walk over to Rhossili. Is there anything I can help you with?' Bryn looked sheepishly at the others.

'If I could have your name and address sir? Is this your van?' The man said that he had hired it for a couple of days to explore Gower, that he had come over to Swansea by train from Bristol yesterday. He gave his name and a Bristol address. 'Can you check out the van number Constable,' said Bryn trying to regain some gravitas. Ferrari radioed base and requested a check on the number.

'The van is registered to Town Car Hire in Swansea sir.' Bryn nodded at Ferrari.

'Thank you for your cooperation Mr Bristow, enjoy the rest of your stay.' Bristow nodded and smiled at them, walked to the driver's door and drove off up the hill.

'That was bloody embarrassing. I'm very sorry girls and boys, I had a hunch and I got it wrong.' He shook his head and sighed. 'it stops me getting overconfident I suppose.' He stood there shaking his head, then walked quickly back down to the Britannia to pay, trailing a slightly disappointed and wet straggle behind him. They thought that they were in for the arrest. The reality had been a let-down. They looked at each other and shrugged again as if to say, but we've been bought a free dinner by the boss. Nobody mentioned Hughes.

They drove back to Central, Bryn remaining silent in the front seat and occasionally muttering to himself and shaking his head. Gray was still in the ops room when they returned holding the telephone to his ear. He beckoned them over.

'Hughes arrested, home now.' Bryn's face opened up like the sun bursting out from behind a cloud as he grabbed the phone from Gray and meandered off nodding saying 'Yes, yes; bringing him in now? Splendid.' He handed the phone back to Gray to put back down in its cradle. 'Luck seems to be smiling on us poor mortals. I must have done something good in my youth. Hughes has just been picked up at his house. He arrived there on foot about ten minutes ago. He must have walked over from Whiteford. That's about a three hour walk over to Reynoldston then along the ridge to Penmaen. He's arrived at just about the right time I'd say. He wouldn't have known about the searches in his house and SteepleTek. He must have thought he was home and dry,' he looked up and giggled, 'well home at least. I bet the uniforms gave him a scare. Splendid, magnificent.' Bryn squeezed his shoulders up and shuffled his arms back and forth like a steam train. 'OK Dai, we'll welcome our new guest after the sarge has booked him in. Bag his clothes and boots and take a hand swab for gunshot. The traffic boys have read him his rights.' Bryn called the Super at home to let her know what was going on; she said she'd be in within fifteen minutes.

He had made his move after 7pm and moved forwards a hundred or so yards at a time towards the seawall path across the marsh, stooping to carefully scan the surroundings each time. He couldn't see anyone ahead and didn't see anyone crossing the marsh on the path. It was a doddle. He looked like a walker, he would be taken for a walker so long as he nodded a friendly hello to anyone he met; not that he met anybody. The rain had started to fall and he was looking forwards to getting inside again; it had been a long wet day. He was walking past the last cottage down by the marsh at about 8.30pm and emerged close to the pub and turned uphill towards the van. He didn't even look about him much; he was convinced the police search had been withdrawn, convinced that he had escaped.

Hughes was led in wearing handcuffs and the sergeant booked him and had him sign for his belongings. 'We'll need your clothing sir and your boots. Constable Williams will take you to the cell and find you some clothes. Our DC will take a hand and mouth swab when you're in the cell.' Hughes looked angry, but realised enough to know that shouting wouldn't achieve very much.

'I'll have my phone call please sergeant.' He talked for a few minutes and then told the sergeant that his solicitor couldn't arrive until the morning.

'I'll have to check with the DI about that sir; take him along Williams.' Fellows arrived soon afterwards; she was beaming. Her first murder result; she had established herself and could now look the Chief Super in the eye. She felt very well disposed towards her DI at the moment. Bryn and Ferrari were beaming too. Fellows took Bryn to one side.

'The sergeant says that Hughes has had his phone call to his brief; she'll be here in the morning. He can sweat it oot in the cells for the night, is that fine with you Kevin? You all could do with a wee sleep.' She paused to lean nearer, 'what are we going to do about Thomas?' Bryn smiled and said that he thought Thomas would prefer to sleep at home tonight and that maybe the sergeant should release him on police bail again and deliver him home; require his presence tomorrow morning.' Fellows nodded, 'I'll tell him on my way oot.'

His heart rate did not return to normal until he was on the common driving towards Swansea. A close shave, but what a performance! He whooped and banged his hands on the steering wheel. He had thrown the rucksack down the slope into the woods at the very last second as he saw the group moving towards him out of the corner of his eye. The copper was either smart or lucky, but he had seen his face, even if he had no idea who he was. The police would know about the shooting now if she was taken to a hospital, unless Thomas had taken away the body to dump it. They wouldn't know who to look for, but this was not good. It was Thomas and Price he was most worried about. They would move quickly now he'd shot and probably killed one of their team. Thomas had probably found her soon after the shooting which was about twelve hours ago. He'd had hours to plan. Price might even be here now. Whichever way he looked at it, he had to get out. Home was out of the question as was SteepleTek. They'd definitely keep an eye on those. They'd sent the woman to come to get him. It was either her or him. He wouldn't waste any sympathy on her. Price and Thomas wanted him out of it and it was only luck that saved him. He didn't like that at all, relying on luck. He definitely didn't like being screwed at his own game. He would draw out cash as Mr Bristow. He'd clean up as best he could in a public toilet and buy new clothes, toiletries and a small suitcase at the 24h Tesco in the retail park. He'd leave the van there and call a taxi to take him to Carmarthen and book into a hotel. From there, tomorrow, he'd probably take the train to Fishguard, for the crossing to Rosslare. He would decide how best to enjoy the cold plate of revenge over a nightcap.

Thursday

Bryn ate toast and fruit with a cup of coffee then drove off in his Bentley to Central. A good car to drive after an arrest, he thought. He wound down the window and enjoyed the warm spring air, the lambs in the fields on either side and the birdsong, which he could hear clearly above the tyre and engine noise. The team were in their customary places in the ops room when he arrived for his regular briefing and he was greeted by a ripple of whistles, clapping and cheering; not all of it ironic. He wandered over to a chair; Gray had been chosen to deliver the eulogy.

'Good one,' and then sat down. Bryn nodded his thanks.

'One word Gray and I would have died a happy man, but two; I don't know what to say, except well done team. We know who killed Michael Green, we know how he did it, we have enough evidence to convince a court.' He stopped and looked a little less cheerful, 'but we don't have Price nor do we know why. Dr Hughes, as you know is downstairs and he is the prime suspect for shooting Lucy.' Bryn looked at his watch. 'As soon as his brief appears I hope that we'll find out more about that and his involvement in all the killings. Gray tells me that Lucy is awake and recovering well. She will be moved from the ICU into the recovery ward today and if all goes well, could be home soon.' The team burst into applause and whistles. 'I look forward to hearing what our DS has to say for herself.' The team quietened down. 'Dai, you and Ferrari will be in the interview room, I'll give you a call when I've talked to the Super. Dai we need you to look at the financial records of the company, see who they pay and who pays them. Check Company house records; who owns the company, who are its officers, when was it set up. Does it look straight? We'll get our forensic accountant people to look in detail later. For now I just want a picture painted of how they operate. Check Hughes's finances too. Bryn walked out to a hum of speculation.

'Enter.' Fellows was sat behind her desk and stood up when Bryn walked in. 'Take a seat Kevin,' she said indicating a comfortable carver placed in front of her desk for the purpose. The prodigal son.

'So tell me what happened Kevin, I'm intrigued, how did you figure it was Hughes, how did you know where to find him?' She sat back with a wry smile on her face. 'Or not,' she added. Bryn scratched the side of his neck and scrunched his face up.

'Well yes, ma'am, just following a hunch.' He didn't much like talking about the hunches and ideas that sometimes broke a case. He had no more idea of where they came from than Fellows did.

'It's worked 'til noo,' she said more kindly.

'It was an itch which crystallised as I was walking, that I never got any satisfactory answer from Hughes about this company he was supposed to have set up and which many people had mentioned. His casual answer that it was a consultancy he ran from home just didn't feel right. So yesterday I just had get out of the office and go for a walk on the beach to clear my head. It had to be something to do with his history and I had Hughes and Watkins top of

283

the list. I just goggled the names on my computer..'
Fellows' eyebrows elevated a few millimetres, Bryn
paused, '..and sat quietly by myself going down the long
list of links looking for an answer. Sometimes it's the
simplest things that work. I found the company Hughes
had set up in Swansea, SteepleTek, which he quite
specifically didn't mention to us, and had a look at the
website. It's a company that uses drone helicopters to
survey the outside of tall and inaccessible structures like
skyscrapers and towers. The company video is a view
from a drone camera as it surveyed a building and I
thought 'that's it!' That's how they got to the victims
without anybody seeing the gunman. The gun was on the
drone. That's what was in the rucksack Price was carrying;
it's what Hughes must have carried today.' He paused for
Fellows to imagine the scene. 'So those videos we found
were taken from a camera on the drones as they closed in
to kill. The handler can activate the gun when it is close to
the victim.'

'Wow, that's too spooky.' The succession of
expressions on Fellow's face, from horror to
understanding, told Bryn that she realised that this
information not only allowed them to understand how
Michael Green was killed, but also, probably how the
European murders were committed. Fellows nodded
slowly. She got it.

'The SOCOs found drones at SteepleTek,' he paused,
'but they don't seemed to be armed. I'm waiting on Bill to
give me a preliminary report.'

'This is a problem then Kevin?' Bryn twitched.

'We have the video clips of the shootings found in his
office. Those are pretty damning. We should have enough

to convict Hughes. He must have a separate store for the armed ones, or maybe I missed something. I expect to get it out of him at the first interview. He must know now that he is doomed.' He looked up at Fellows and a shadow passed across his features. 'I wasn't aware that DS Evans was following a separate line of enquiry ma'am. It all seemed to happen late last night. I am assuming that for some reason she didn't have an opportunity to tell me anything, that she had a very good reason not to tell me. She's in recovery ward, so I'll find out some time later today when I talk to her.' Fellows frowned then nodded.

'Aye,' she said.

'A DS is supposed to show initiative' she paused, 'but not this much. It had better be good Kevin. This will be a disciplinary.' Bryn nodded, he knew that full well.

'How about finding Hughes, Kevin, you'd called the search off?' Bryn gestured that this had not gone so well.

'I had put my money on him heading east into the marsh to escape. That's the way his footprints went and a dog picked up a scent from where he was sitting when he shot Lucy. It all looked good for a bit. Then when we didn't find him..' He stopped to reflect, 'There's about eight square miles of woodland, marsh and dunes. Even with helicopters we couldn't be sure. So in the end I wasn't so surprised when we didn't catch him. Disappointed, but not surprised. I thought a nationwide search would pick him up somewhere, sometime. We had the evidence to convict, we had his identity, his DNA from the house, his photograph, we knew his car, we had his financial information. He couldn't keep hidden for very long.' Bryn made a wistful smile. 'We followed a dog on the marsh. It had seemed pretty confident about the

285

scent, as had the handler. Then we got to the edge of the Burry Pill channel, full of fast running water and the simplest explanation was that he'd gone across. Perhaps he did. The handler was clearly convinced and I let him persuade me. All the while his dog was running around excited and trying to go back into the woods. It was pulling hard at the leash until the handler jerked it hard, told it to heel and the dog reluctantly sat down beside him. That was it. The dog had wanted to follow the trail back into the woods. It came to me that Hughes had swum across the Pill and come back to try to lose the scent and that the dog had picked up the trail of him going back into the woods. That's why he was straining to go back. The dog was right and the handler was wrong. Clever really, Hughes must have sat there smiling to himself after we took the bait and ran around like lost sheep. He just had to sit it out until it got a bit darker. It was risky, but safer than the marsh.' Bryn looked up to see if Fellows was still awake. 'I also had an image of a white van parked up the hill opposite the Britannia pub which wouldn't go away, even though I couldn't actually recall seeing it. If there was a revelation, it was that. I thought Hughes would sit there hidden in the woods and wait until we called off the search. He was right on all of that. He'd then go back to the van and drive away. So I went back to the pub where I thought he would emerge from the marsh. When we got back to the pub to eat, I went out to check whether a white van was really where my subconscious said it was and there it was. I had obviously seen it but just not registered it. Dai and Ceri thought I was only there to buy them dinner. So I just waited at a window table for him to appear and you know the rest.

Ha, ha. It wasn't him, just a walker.' He looked as sheepish as he could, given that, despite his false hunch, they now had Hughes in custody.

'How the mighty are fallen Kevin, it's nae a big problem; it was a good hunch, just the wrong one that's all.' She leaned towards him. 'You were only wrong about the van though eh? A white van was just too good to ignore' Fellows grinned at him. 'Anyway, he must have done exactly as you supposed and walked off the marsh at dusk, except that he walked home? It's a funny business crime detection, no matter how the forensics improves, it's the insights and intuitions which still make the difference. Yours were working well Kevin, well done laddie.' Fellows stood up. 'Let me know what the interview brings up. I'll put out a press statement to the effect that we have arrested a man for the attempted murder of a police officer and for conspiring in the murder of Michael Green. Is that OK Kevin?' Bryn nodded. 'Have we charged Hughes yet?'

'Next thing ma'am'

'Oh, what about Thomas, is he still in the frame?' Bryn looked perplexed and shook his head.

'Thomas?' He sighed loudly. 'No ma'am, he's just an unlucky witness I think. Well, lucky witness, the bullet that hit Lucy was probably meant for him. Until I talk to Lucy I don't know whether he has actually broken any law, except possibly obstructing a police enquiry? I will interview Thomas later. I've only heard a garbled version from Dai, from when he was in shock.' Bryn decided not to mention his suspicions about Lucy and Thomas. He wanted Lucy to get off lightly he had decided. She had learned a pretty fierce lesson about going freelance. He was definitely more hurt than angry.

Bryn and Ferrari had gone down to the cells to charge Hughes formally with the attempted murder of a police officer and conspiracy to murder Michael Green. He said nothing in return and was locked back in his cell. A woman in an expensive-looking tailored suit jacket and skirt and who carried a fine leather briefcase, appeared at the front desk and introduced herself as Gloria Richards, here to represent Dr Hughes. The sergeant asked Williams to take her down to Hughes's cell and to remain outside. He called Bryn to let him know. They would commence the interview in half an hour to give Ms Richards time to discuss the case. Bryn was pretty clear on how he would approach the interview and was hoping that Hughes would be in a confessing mood when he realised that a conviction itself was not in doubt. He called Bill Wood to see what preliminary information there was on the equipment the SOCOs had found in the laboratory before he talked to Hughes.

'Not sure what to make of this bit of kit Bryn' said Bill. 'The store room at the back of the laboratory was full of them. It's pretty much a standard helicopter drone with four propellers driven by electric motors. You can get similar ones at Maplin and other high street stores. Those drones are radio-controlled, have a camera, a bit of electronics which stabilises flight and controls the motors. It's manoeuvred with a joystick. They will probably fly for ten or fifteen minutes. The video image is usually played back through goggles that the operator wears, so they feel as though they are actually flying it. This one is definitely rather more sophisticated. The heart of it is a smart phone which acts as the video camera but also seems to be used as the computer which controls the motors on the drone to make it go where the operator wants. These phones have motion sensors so they know the orientation of the drone. The motor control electronics is plugged into the data socket on the phone.' Bryn was now peering around the room for something interesting to look at. 'I'm guessing that the operator in this case would use another smart phone to control the one in the drone using the cell phone 3G signal to transmit rather than radio control. So in principle at least, it can be controlled and monitored from anywhere on the planet which has a 3G signal. I suppose you would call the software an app these days. Some bright bugger at SteepleTek must have written the code. He would probably see the live image from the drone camera and control it using his screen.' Bryn was wakened from his boredom when a shiver went down his spine as he recalled the video. 'We haven't had time to look at this part of the system yet, but we will. That's about it for now.' Bryn tapped his teeth with a pen and it took a few seconds for the implication of Bill's comments to sink in fully. 'So, basically, it's just a model helicopter then? A legal helicopter?' Bryn was standing completely still.

'I'm afraid so,' said Bill trying at the same time to sound encouraging.

'Thanks Bill, I'd hoped for a weapon' said Bryn.

Bryn had been looking forward to confronting Hughes during the interview with forensic evidence from a lethal drone. He now knew that they had at present, only weak circumstantial evidence that Hughes shot Lucy. He had been away all day and had arrived back muddy at a time consistent with having been at Whiteford. His company designed and made drones and they had found video presumably taken from the drone of the killing of Michael Green in his office. Pretty strong circumstantial evidence, but it would be ripped apart by a defence team in court. They still had no forensic evidence as yet from the dunes and all they had was a toy helicopter of the type which was used legitimately by SteepleTek in building surveys. The call from Bill had come as a big disappointment. Bryn had also assumed that Hughes had collaborated in the killing of Green by Price; that they worked together. The drone provided the means for both shootings. The thought that Hughes might wriggle out of it was intolerable to Bryn. He clenched his fists and growled to release the tension. He went to pass the news to Maureen Fellows who also realised that they had a little way to go to pin this one down and would need to wait on Bill and his SOCO forensic team. They had celebrated a little prematurely. It would be a very painful wait. She nodded at Bryn and he left to take charge of the interview.

Hughes was escorted into the interview room and sat to the left of his brief at one end of the basic wooden table which was bolted to the floor in case interviewees felt the urge for exercise. Bryn sat at the opposite end with Dai to his right, the side to which he could wink most effectively. Constable Ferrari set the video recorder going and stood by the door. Bryn announced to the tape those present in the room, when and why.

'Dr Hughes, we obtained a warrant this morning to search your house in Penmaen and your offices at SteepleTek; which, for the benefit of your solicitor, makes helicopter drones which are used to survey high buildings. Would you like to tell us where you were this morning at 7am Dr Hughes?' Hughes looked at his solicitor who nodded.

'I was walking. I left the house at about a quarter too. I've been walking all day.'

'I'm sure you have Dr Hughes. That's a bit early for most people I'd say; where were you walking?' She nodded again not looking round.

'I walked along the coast path towards Caswell, had something to eat at the cafe. I came back the same way.' Bryn did a mental image of the walk in his mind.

'That wouldn't have taken.' He did some mental arithmetic, 'fourteen hours.'

'It didn't, I carried on walking up the Bishopston Valley and had a beer and dinner in the pub. I came back late to find your lot parked by my house. Who pays for my front door?'

'I wouldn't worry about that yet Dr Hughes. Did anybody walk with you, did you meet anybody? Can anybody confirm that you were on this walk?' Hughes shrugged.

'Probably not; unless somebody remembers me from the pub; it's not my local. It was busy.' Dai took some notes.

'You were pretty muddy when you arrived at the house?' Hughes sighed.

'The track up from Pwll Ddu is very muddy..'

'Our forensics will confirm where you were Dr Hughes, from your boots; we'll check with the pub. I think you were nowhere near Pwll Ddu. I asked you a few days ago whether you'd set up a company in Swansea. You answered no and you signed the statement Dr Hughes. You do run a company in Swansea because we've just searched it. Why did you lie to us?' Ms Richards awoke from her reverie.

'I didn't lie Chief Inspector, I am not the MD but I own a share. I do run a consultancy from home. I may have been economical with the truth.'

'Dr Hughes has answered your question Chief Inspector.' Bryn raised one eye and carried on.

'In your office at SteepleTek we found a locked drawer containing amongst other things five envelopes each marked with a month, year and a place. Each date and place coincided with an unsolved murder. One of them was the murder of Michael Green, the others we know of from our liaison with Europol. Each murder was unsolved because there seemed to be no plausible way that a gunman could have come close to their victim. Could you tell us about the envelopes Dr Hughes?' Hughes looked distinctly less comfortable. Bryn continued, 'we know that one of the murders, that of your once colleague Michael Green, was carried out by an old school friend of yours, Mark Price. We're pretty sure that we can get a conviction on that. Quite a coincidence, wouldn't you agree?' Ms Richards was looking at him concerned. They obviously hadn't discussed this at all.

'I would like to discuss a matter with my client Chief Inspector, say ten minutes?'

Bryn smiled sweetly at her. 'Of course Ms Richards, Constable Ferrari, would you escort them to the cells. Back here at,' he looked at his watch, '10.15am?' Ms Richards nodded as she left. 'Interview paused at 10.05am for client to discuss the case with his solicitor.' Bryn sat back with his head in his hands. 'Dai, can you ask Gray to follow up his notes taken at SteepleTek? Ask him to check out Jo Morris and John... what was it?'

'Christopher.' Bryn mouthed the surname and continued, 'DVLC, council tax register that sort of thing?' Dai nodded and went out. Hughes and Ms Richards came back in with Ferrari. Their body language suggested a rather cooler relationship than when they had first appeared in interview room 2. Dai followed soon after. Bryn re-introduced them to the tape.

'Shall I repeat the question Dr Hughes?'

'That won't be necessary Chief Inspector.' She turned to Hughes who looked pained.

'No comment' he said. Ms Richards nodded smugly. Bryn held his hand out to Dai indicating that he had the floor. Dai confirmed this with a glance and then took a small black object from an evidence bag.

'Do you know what this is Dr Hughes? Ms Richards? They both nodded. Hughes squirmed in his seat, his eyes pointing anywhere but at Ms Richards. Ferrari shifted on her feet by the door. She knew that whatever Hughes had said to his solicitor would not prepare her for what she was about to witness. 'It is a memory card from the envelope marked 'Llangennith May 2013' found in a locked desk in Dr Hughes office.' Dai slipped it into the slot on his mobile phone. 'It has been dusted for prints,' he added enigmatically. He moved around beside Ms

Richards so that she and Hughes could see the screen and started the video file. The marram grass came sharply into view causing the solicitor to jump back in surprise. The view panned back and then sideways before it raced along the beach to bring Michael Green into view. 'This is Michael Green, the murder victim about 5 seconds before his death.' Hughes and Richards were glued to the image looking horrified. Hughes flinched, anticipating the finale. Ms Richards gasped and pulled her head backwards, covering her face with her hands and remained like that for what seemed like minutes. She then calmly removed her hands, wiped her face with a handkerchief and sat quite still. Ceri looked concerned and offered to fetch a glass of water, to which Ms Richards nodded her head gently. Bryn was describing the showing of the video for the benefit of the tape, which would certainly have picked up the gasp and long period of silence. 'Interview suspended 10.34am. Rest break' he said to the tape. Ceri escorted Gloria Richards to the washroom.

'You've seen the video already I take it,' said Bryn sitting back pinching his lips between his fingers and looking at Hughes who remained head bowed.

Ms Richards came back in looking slightly less glamorous, but in control again now. Bryn restarted the interview and asked if Hughes could explain the presence of the microSD memory cards in his locked office drawer. Ms Richards shook her head at him. She leaned forwards to speak.

'No comment.' She had recovered herself well.

'Very good inspector; let me get this straight. You have found out that my client is a part of a company which uses helicopter drones for surveying buildings. It is a legitimate company, registered with Companies House. My client is their chief consultant. He resented your intrusion into his house and in an unwise fit of annoyance refused to answer your question accurately. I'm sure he regrets any inconvenience this may have caused.' She stopped to survey the effect of his words on the police officers who showed no recognisable emotion. 'He has told me that he knows nothing of a shooting on the beach. He was walking all day yesterday for pleasure.' She continued confidently.

'You claim to have discovered that a Mr Price shot Michael Green and I will assume that you have evidence to prove it. My client had already told you that he was in school with him. He does not know anything about how the memory cards got into his office drawer.' Ms Richards stood up and indicated to Hughes that they were leaving. Bryn sighed, nodded and stood up too.

'Interview terminated 10.43am. Take them back to the cells Constable.' Bryn asked Dai as they were leaving the room to call Bill to try the keys that Hughes had on him when he was arrested and the ones they had found in his house, to see if they open the office drawer in which the flash cards were found.

Bryn took ten minutes to calm down enough to talk to Fellows. Neither of them had expected such a spirited defence and Bryn said that he'd been taken aback by the confidence. They realised that they had no direct forensic evidence to implicate Hughes, only circumstantial evidence that seemed to add up in only one way, but Bryn thought Hughes would crack under the pressure of evidence they already had. They had thought that they could tie his absence for the day with the killing on the beach. He had the means, but they didn't have the proof. A jury might see his story as entirely plausible. Bryn knew that they couldn't guarantee a conviction unless they had firm forensic evidence. Bryn dearly wanted to curl up in a corner and sleep so that he could awake to find the case tidied up and Hughes and Price shut away. How pride comes before a fall he thought. He would reflect later that hearing Hughes's run through what could easily have been his defence highlighted the gaps in a case that they had, amongst themselves, assumed to be essentially watertight. They realised yet again that they were completely dependent on anything that they or the SOCOs dug up or found on the computers or in the paperwork.

He dragged himself back to the foyer where he asked the sergeant what the arrangements were for Mr Thomas. He was due in for 11.30am the sergeant told him. 'Ferrari and I will interview him in room 2 sergeant at 11.45, thank you.' Bryn walked outside and took off towards Swansea railway station to the café opposite. He would buy a newspaper, order a latte and sit and read on an outside table for half an hour. After this morning, he hoped that there weren't going to be similar surprises at the interview with Huw Thomas. He looked around him at people going about their lives, with no concerns about murderers and victims and wondered, not for the first time, what it would be like to be free. He started to read the obituaries to cheer him up. He resolved that he would go to see Lucy after the interview with Thomas when he knew more about what had happened. Lucy was in a dilemma, which would need some careful finessing with Fellows if she was to save her career. In his present gloomy mood he needed to project himself beyond that to something that he could look forward to. So he pictured himself later in the day making a nice supper which he would eat by the woodstove with a glass of something red, a Malbec perhaps; in his own house, on his own. Sheer bloody luxury. The half hour went much too quickly and he was soon walking back along to Central.

Thomas was sat at the table in interview room 2 and both Ferrari and Bryn were disposed to the side of him at Bryn's request. Bryn wanted to diminish the adversarial layout of a conventional interview. It was just a friendly chat. Bryn thought he should be direct about the possible consequences and told Hughes that in principle, he might be guilty of police obstruction, and that he Bryn, would decide whether any charges were to be brought. He also pointed out, unnecessarily, that DS Evans might be subject to disciplinary proceedings, depending in part on the outcome of this interview. He looked up steadily at Thomas at this point, to make sure that he understood the implications of what he was saying. He said that the discussion would not be taped, but would be recorded as a statement on paper and would require his signature. Bryn wanted as much leeway as he could get to prevent a disciplinary, as he hoped he'd hinted to Thomas, without actually saying it. Thomas looked at Bryn and nodded indicating that he had understood. He went through what had happened from the beginning, making clear that he had been the one to drive the process along because he was angry at his original arrest and wanted to do his bit to catch and convict the killer who nearly had him charged with murder. He mentioned the hacking of his computer in particular. He described how he thought that he might lure anybody involved with Green by putting out messages, using his alias, on the various hacker forums he used himself and knew now that Green had used. The first posting was to see if anybody out there knew of and cared about Green. The second posting enquired about Mark Price, a name that was now probably known only to his close associates and was intended to provoke a more energetic response. He admitted that Lucy had inadvertently dropped Price's name into a conversation, but was sure that she hadn't meant to. He thought he had received no responses to the Price posting until he received a rather chilling email from an alias called Colossus. He had brought the email along to show Bryn. While Bryn was reading the email and rubbing his chin, Thomas told him that he'd received it in the early hours of Wednesday morning and was scared stiff. He'd phoned DS Evans immediately. She had told him previously, when she had handed his computer back, that if he had any worries at any time, to contact her. He looked up at Bryn after saying this, to see if he'd provoked an unfavourable response. He hadn't, or at least not one that he could see. She had told him to bring the computer over to her home straight away so that she could look at it.' Bryn raised his eyebrows at the mention of home, but remained silent. It just confirmed his intuitions. 'This was in the early hours of the morning. He then told Bryn that he'd told DS Evans that he was going to the meeting with Colossus to help nail Price. He said that he'd talked long and hard to DS Evans to convince her that Colossus wasn't a threat to him. In the end, in exasperation, she had said she would accompany him in case anything happened. She would shadow him in the dunes, watch the meeting. She would bring back any information from the meeting to her DI. He then said Bryn knew what happened next. DS Evans must have accidentally disturbed him in the dunes and the bullet that was meant for him had hit Lucy. Bryn had noticed only too clearly the quivering lip as he said this and the switch from using DS Evans to Lucy. Case proven. Bryn sat back to look at Thomas, shaking his head slowly.

'It didn't occur to you that this was an identical scenario to the one you witnessed at Llangennith, except that this time, you were the intended victim?' He said this without a hint of hypocrisy. Thomas shook his head.

'Of course I have thought about that since, but at the time I was just caught up in the moment.' He hung his head and then looked up at Bryn. 'Have you caught him yet?' It was Bryn's turn to nod.

'He's downstairs.' Thomas looked relieved.

'I never saw him you know.' Bryn nodded. 'How is DS Evans?' Gray had told him last night that she seemed out of danger; 'what will happen to her?' Bryn looked upwards for inspiration.

'She's being moved out of the ICU today. I understand that she's recovering well.' Huw bent his head forward in relief. 'She will get a bollocking from me and if the Super agrees, that will be the end of it. Damage limitation. It has probably permanently dampened her enthusiasm for solo performances and yours too I don't doubt. I can't see what good a disciplinary would do. She's a good detective, we want to keep her.' Bryn sighed, 'You are both very lucky to be alive; you know that now.' He looked across at Ferrari. 'Take his statement Ceri,' he glanced across at Thomas, 'I want you to put down what you have just told me, no more and no less,' he looked at Thomas again to see that the message had got home, 'and then every single detail of what you did and saw from when you arrived at the car park in Cwm Ivy. Understand?' Thomas nodded gratefully. 'I suggest that you talk to somebody knowledgeable about protecting your computer against hackers,' he said, as if he habitually gave technical advice about computers. He left the room with a smile on his face, the little humiliation had made them quits for the moment. He was a little happier now. He concluded that he could base everything he said professionally about Lucy to Fellows, on what Thomas had said he was going to do independently, with or without DS Evans. He could make a case to the Super, that in the heat of the moment, she had made a reasonable decision to accompany him as protection. He would express the view when the shooting was investigated, that whilst he hadn't known straight away about the immediate intentions of his DS, because of the circumstances, he might well have backed her decision in principle. He would of course, have insisted on using a little more muscle in practice.

Bryn walked out to his car and drove off to Morriston Hospital. He went to the shop in the foyer and bought chocolates, a computer magazine and a Guardian. He then added a newspaper to give her plenty of puzzles to do. She didn't like to be idle. Lucy was talking to her father, who was sitting next to her, when he went in. Lucy looked up and smiled in a guarded way at Bryn. She looked so much better, although she winced when she tried to adjust her position. Her father stood up and shook hands with Bryn as they introduced themselves and then left Bryn to it. He said he'd be back early in the evening just to see that she had everything she needed. Bryn sat awkwardly next to her and put the papers and magazines on the chair next to him; 'just some things to stop you twitching when you get bored.' He smiled at her experimentally. 'Is there anything else you want?' Lucy dropped her eyes and muttered.

'Sorry sir, I was very stupid, I lost my head.' She looked up again with a vulnerable expression that touched Bryn somewhere deep inside. 'We..' Bryn cut her off and switched to a business-like tone.

'I've spent the last hour with Mr Thomas, who said that he'd told you he was going to meet some person he had contacted on the internet. He said that he wanted your advice, something to do with finding Price. I understand that you thought he was walking into danger and insisted that you went along with him, to keep an eye on him. It was very silly, but very brave. You should have told me, but I understand that you had very short notice.' He held his eyes on hers without blinking. 'Is that right?' he asked still holding her gaze. She eventually nodded. 'Thank you sir, I don't know what to say.' She put her hands up to her eyes to wipe away some tears. Bryn gave her a tissue from the box on the side and waited for her to collect herself. He put on a hearty voice now to dispel his own emotion.

'So we won't be seeing you for a while in Central I suppose?' He was clasping his hands together tightly on his lap. 'What do the medics say? Lots of rest? Lots of pina colladas? A bit of competitive tiddleywinks with the nurses?' They both squeezed out a smile.

'You won't get rid of me that easily sir.'

Bryn knew that he could do little without further information from Bill Woods. It had been a physically and emotionally tiring day and he needed some respite. He stopped off at the supermarket in Penclawdd for cream and a few tomatoes and at the shellfish stall in Crofty for fresh mussels. He picked up a crusty white loaf at the garage at the top of the hill. He hadn't been home this early for a while. He was living out the fantasy he had imagined at the café opposite the railway station. He felt that he had probably found a way to protect Lucy from serious disciplinary consequences and he felt more relief than he had anticipated. He deserved his supper and was now in the mood to enjoy it. He pulled out a bottle of Malbec from the larder to warm on the table and a bottle of rosé to cook with. He lit the woodstove; first things first. He was deeply pleased to be at home on his own, with only the prospect of his own company and a decent supper to be made. The gloomy afternoon was swept away as the flames from the stove flickered in the room. He went upstairs for a shower to wash the day away which had gone from dreadful to better as it had progressed. He returned downstairs in his fleecy dressing gown and a pair of slippers. He noticed that his legs were sparsely covered with curly dark hairs. He smiled to himself as he visualised the rather louche image he must present to any observer. There was a time not so long ago, that he'd have put a finger in his mouth at the very thought of dressing gown and slippers. Today though, it was just right. He unscrewed the cap on the Malbec and inverted the bottle twice to put some air in it then left it in a warm part of the room. He pulled the cork from the bottle of rosé and then tipped the net of mussels into the sink, where he discarded a couple of open ones and scraped off the bits of barnacle and beard. He then rubbed them together to scour the surface clean, washed them in running water and put them to one side. He put on the radio for the 'pm' programme then took an onion and three cloves of garlic from the larder and chopped them both. He'd forgotten to pick the parsley and so had to expose the new gentleman of leisure to the gaze of any neighbours that might have been looking, as he grabbed a handful from a pot growing by the back door and sprig of thyme from another. He chopped the herbs and poured himself a glass of Malbec. He moved the pepper mill closer to the little pile of ingredients, opened the foil cap of the cream then sat back on the sofa to enjoy the wine listening to Eddie Mair amusing himself in the interests of free speech in the background. Two glasses later, he stood up to saunter over and put the herbs, onion and garlic into a large saucepan. He pulled what he normally would use as a serving bowl onto the woodstove for a few minutes to warm. He then ground in half a dozen generous twists of black pepper followed by a half pint of rosé into the saucepan. He cupped his hands and put in all the mussels and set the gas as high as it would go. He put the lid on and waited expectantly. He could soon hear the mussels moving in the pan and smell the evaporating wine with its tang of herbs. When all the mussels were opened, he ladled them into the warmed bowl and continued for a few minutes to reduce the wine a little. He then poured in

303

half a cupful of cream and brought it back to boil and poured it over the mussels. He carried the bowl and the loaf to the table where he went steadily through the pile of mussels scraping off the meat with half a shell used as a spoon. He dipped the bread into the juice at the bottom until the bowl was entirely empty. He passed his eye over the battlefield of a table. He lowered himself onto the sofa and laid his hands around his full stomach and let himself drift off into a doze. It was interrupted only when the Archers theme music roused him and forced him to turn the radio off.

Friday

Dai had been following up the company paperwork on SteepleTek. Companies House records showed three shareholders with one share each in the name of Jean Christophe, Robert Hughes and Marc Renaud. The company had been registered in 2009. The company secretary was Ms Gloria Richards, Hughes's solicitor. The financial records showed that it had made a very decent profit in each of the three trading years. Dai was going through the bank statements which he and Bryn had taken from the office and had piled into boxes for analysis before handing them over to the forensic accountants. He was looking for anything which stood out to him which they might follow up immediately. Dividends had been paid to all shareholders in April and regular payments by direct debit were listed for the usual telephone, broadband, rent for the unit in the Technium Centre, loan repayments to NatWest Bank and to City Lets in Swansea. Did they rent another building? Dai telephoned the agency and after listening to paper shuffle for a few minutes was told that the payments were rent for a lockup in St Thomas. This was just across Fabian Way from the SteepleTek unit. Dai asked the agent to meet him there with a key in half an hour pointing out that he was investigating a murder. This was enough for the agent, who had the simple choice of either sitting in his office bending paper clips or being actively involved in a murder enquiry. He didn't need any further incentive. The lock-up was in a terraced street looking down over the Kings Dock. It was hidden behind scruffy metal gates daubed with graffiti and secured with a substantial padlock. The agent unlocked the padlock and the deadlock on the inner door and pushed it open. Dai put his arm out to stop him entering. If he was expecting to see a body, then he was disappointed, because all he could see in the gloom was a pile of mechanical paraphernalia. Dai asked him to wait outside as he fumbled for a light switch to see what was there. On a bench on one side, were a series of what Dai would have called model helicopters, each of which had four propellers pointing upwards. They lay mixed in together with what might be various tools required to assemble or adjust them. Dai wasn't a handy man. On the bench on the other side, in a cardboard box, Dai found 0.22 calibre ammunition. The box was next to a vice which was surrounded by a sprinkling of coarse copper powder and above which, a fine-bladed hacksaw was hanging on a hook. Despite his inexperience with metalwork, he could unravel the story behind what he saw. He had less success trying to understand the selection of various white plastic tubes and blocks, which were laid out on the surface around the vice, alongside trays of electronic components and wire. He called the sergeant at Central for uniforms to come to tape off the lock-up and protect the crime scene and for the SOCOs to come to take everything away and look for other trace evidence. Dai thanked the agent and sent him away, keeping the keys for the lock-up for which he signed a receipt. He instructed the patrol officers when they arrived and then went back to Central to talk to Bryn. He was feeling pretty pleased with himself, he knew he had found what his DI was waiting for.

Gray had been back to the Technium Centre to talk to the security guard and then back to Central following up the details Jo Morris had given him. He found her details easily enough in DVLC and local authority records and they matched the data she had given him as he had expected. But, he could find no records for John Christopher. He would need to take a statement from him too at some time. He called the mobile number Jo Morris had given him. A voice with a faint continental accent answered. Gray explained who he was and held the handset away from his ear as he received a barrage of anger in response. The voice said that yes, he was the MD of SteepleTek and that he had not been able to get into his office this morning because he had found a group of people carting away his computers and paperwork. How was he meant to work? He had jobs booked. Gray could only say that he was sorry for any disruption, that they had a warrant to search the premises as part of an ongoing enquiry and they would hand back the offices as soon as they had finished. He was not at liberty to give him any further information at present. Gray managed to convey this information in a minimum number of words, as if it were some kind of test. This seemed to calm Christopher down. Gray said that the SOCOs would probably need another day in the premises, but that they would be holding the computing equipment until they had checked their contents, which might be several more days. Gray said that he would need to talk to him. Where and when would be convenient? They arranged to meet at the offices later in the morning. Gray sighed loudly as he dropped the phone back on its charger and rubbed his face with his hand. He was surrounded by notes and photographs and files of statements which he and others would spend the next few days collating for the CPS. It was they who would ultimately decide whether the case went to court. He let himself calm down, then set to working through the files. A photograph caught his eye. Where have I seen you recently he thought, it wasn't quite right but it troubled him enough to take it across to Ferrari, who was collating the statements she and Williams had taken from witnesses at the Marina and at Hillend. She didn't recognise the face but said she'd think about it.

'Give me some time Gray, I usually get there in the end if I've seen him before' she said handing it back and Gray took it away sifting through his memories. He put it to one side, shrugged and tried to carry on where he had left off. Soon afterwards he had forgotten about the photograph. He was about to put a pile of information to one side, as not relevant to the CPS case, when it clicked. He had seen him outside the Technium Centre this morning. Of course, Ferarri wouldn't have seen him this morning. He wandered back to his desk and matched the image number with the list of names. He shook his head. He couldn't have been there he thought. He must be mistaken, just a passing likeness. The photograph was neither very large nor very good anyway. By reflex, he put the photograph in his pocket.

Dai was failing to restrain a ridiculously broad grin as he told his DI that he had found the gun factory, as he called it, in a lockup in St Thomas. The company accounts showed that the premises were rented by SteepleTek.

'So sir, maybe the legitimate company is in the Technium Centre and the illegal bit in St Thomas.' Bryn also broke out into almost a rictus as he as he quivered and rocked on his toes.

'Do you know Dai? I think you're absolutely right. You can't have guns and bullets lying around your office for your building company customers to see. It isn't the sixties Dai.' He positively twinkled with glee and kept rubbing his hands together as if to conjure up more magic. 'So this is where the murder drones are made or serviced or whatever. I can see the Evening Post headlines now "Angels of Death Found in Lockup".' He smiled as looked skywards to see the headline written in his mind. Perhaps he also imagined the story, praising the Swansea murder squad, written underneath it. 'I think I might make my way over to see Bill to see what he makes of it all. And you Dai had better get back to the accounts, you might solve some more mysteries before I get back.' Bryn waltzed slowly across the ops room to ask Ferrari if she'd be happy to go to the hospital again, to check that Lucy was alright and to see if she needs anything. She could also pass on the news and the good wishes of the team. He gave her a £20 note; 'get her something you think she'll enjoy.'

Gray nodded at the security guard and told him he had an appointment with John Christopher, the MD of SteepleTek. The guard looked puzzled for a moment.

'Jean Christophe sir, he's French.' Gray blushed as he realised that he'd done what generations of the English had done and anglicised anything they couldn't pronounce. Gray checked his watch, Christophe was due any minute. He sat down on one of the comfortable sofas and picked up a copy of a newspaper that somebody had left behind. He had started to read an article on some banking scandal and realised with a start that he'd been reading for over fifteen minutes. No sign of M. Christophe. He called the mobile number he had used earlier which came back with a 'number unobtainable' message. A little irritated, he waited another ten minutes and tried again with the same result. He walked over to ask the security guard whether he had received any messages from Christophe. The guard shook his head.

'Sorry sir.' To relieve his frustration, knowing it to be fruitless, he pulled out the photograph in his pocket and pushed it in front of the guard. He would wait another ten minutes, then leave.

'Looks a bit like M. Christophe,' said the guard after a few seconds, with convincing French pronunciation, 'but he's too young' He shrugged and passed it back uninterested. Gray grabbed it and turned back towards the sofa. He stopped for a couple of seconds in the middle of the floor, shouted 'shit!' loudly, causing the guard to jump back. Gray turned around to face him.

'Address' he said aggressively, 'you must have an emergency contact address and number for Mr Christophe?' The guard bent over his computer and tapped some keys on his keyboard. He wrote the information down painfully slowly for Gray with pencil on a piece of paper. Gray called the mobile again and then the fixed line number on the piece of paper in front of him. No answer. 'Shit!' Gray, a man of few expletives, a man of few words of any kind, ran outside and called Bryn.

Bryn was having a sandwich in his office and starting reluctantly on the pile of paperwork that he would need to sort for the CPS, when he was interrupted by a call from Gray, who sounded rather more animated than he usually did. He listened to Gray's rapid and terse description and his analysis of what had happened this morning.

'Get back here pronto and put out a nationwide call; airport, ports, railways. I'll get a squad car out to his place now, but, as you said, he'll have probably done a runner.' Bryn went along the corridor to tell Fellows that they were now looking for a suspect known as Jean Christophe, manager of SteepleTek, who was probably on the run after finding out that they were on to him. He would have been alerted by the search yesterday which he had evidently seen and certainly by Gray's call to arrange a meeting. He could be the missing link between Price and the murders. They would have a meeting in the ops room in half an hour. He greeted Gray on his arrival and heard the story for a second time, but at his insistence, more slowly. Gray held out a crumpled photograph towards Bryn, as he told him it was a photograph of Rhys Edwards, Green's school friend from Barry school days, who had disappeared with Price. He explained that the security guard at SteepleTek had recognised him and watched as a look of amazement spread across his DI's face. It wasn't because of the name.

'Bloody hell Gray, he was there right in front of me yesterday! He was the man we stopped going to his van, the man I thought would be Hughes. He called himself Bristow. Bryn did a small jump and landed like a skier. Bloody fool! I let him walk away.' He continued to curse himself until Gray suggested he added Bristow's name to the nationwide alert. Bryn nodded and worked himself back into positive mode. 'All the bits are coming together Gray, all the bits that have taken the piss out of us for the last two bloody weeks. I can see the Promised Land glinting in the distance through the mist.' Bryn had his hand held over his eyes as if he were peering into the distance. He brought it down quickly when he realised what he was doing. 'This whole bloody case has been a grudge between schoolboys that ended up as murder.' He shook his head as if to say that it wasn't like that in his day. 'Better get that description out there now. I'll get Dai to talk to his continental friends and get the two names Edwards might be using out to Europol. They've got something to work with now. I wish we had Lucy to age that photograph, and blow it up, he added, 'but it's all we've got at the moment.' Bryn stopped twitching long enough to remind Gray that Edwards had been described by Price's mother and by others as a violent psychopathic person. He was probably the person who had shot Lucy. He was dangerous. He should definitely put that out with the details.

Bryn called Bill Wood. He was still at the lockup.

'How's it going Bill?' Bryn was sitting at his desk, one elbow on the table.

'OK Bryn, good. The lockup was a bit like Hamleys without the music and cuddly toys. We've got four working drones plus spare bits and pieces, we've got one box of ammo and perhaps most importantly, we've got plastic parts for what I am sure are guns. I'll call you later about that when I've had a proper look. I think you'll have the evidence you want. There's prints everywhere and plenty of trace DNA from hairs and coffee mugs.' Bryn stood up and turned slowly in a circle.

'That's good Bill, very good. In fact DNA is what I called you about. Do you remember the sample from Mrs Edwards, from last week? Well, at the time I didn't think we'd need it, but things have changed rather quickly now. Can you look it up, first thing when you get back and check it against the DNA we collected from Birmingham? We'll definitely need to check it against the stuff you found at the lockup' Bryn nodded and turned some more as Bill confirmed what he would do. 'OK Bill; thanks; talk to you later.' He put the phone down and mouthed 'yes.' He felt calm for the first time in two weeks. He then called dispatch, to check on the squad car sent out to the address in Newton the security guard had given to Gray for Jean Christophe. There was nobody in. Bryn told them to remain there and treat it as a crime scene. He would get a warrant to search it as soon as he could. He went off to the briefing meeting in the ops room.

Bryn was back to his ebullient self; twitching and bouncing around the room as Gray and Dai and Constable Williams came in followed up by Maureen Fellows who was as yet unsure of what to make of the new turn of events and stood to one side.

'Gray, bringer of new insights, that stalwart defender of the people, has stumbled across a truly surprising finding. Pass the photograph around Gray, don't hog it to yourself.' He passed the now dog-eared photograph around which went to Williams and then to Dai, who looked long and hard at it, his face eventually opening up into a huge grin.

'He looks like the guy at the white van opposite the pub, but much younger' he looked up puzzled, 'how did you get that?' Gray looked as smug as was possible for him and squeaked.

'Jean Christophe, aged seventeen.' Dai looked even more puzzled and looked around to see if he was the only one who was lost here; he wasn't. Constable Williams looked lost too; but then he often did. Even Fellows was straining to understand and shook her head as Bryn looked across at her, his eyebrows raised in query. Eventually, Bryn laughed and took the photograph from Dai.

'This is Jean Christophe, alias John Christopher,' he winked at Gray who scowled back. 'Shall I continue Gray? A rhetorical question of course. Jean Christophe works at SteepleTek; in fact he is their MD. He is the third person with Hughes and Jo Morris, the lab technician or whatever who work there. He was away apparently, working, on the day of the search by Gray, Ferrari and Williams,' he looked at them in turn. 'Dai and I recognise him as the man who we stopped at the white van in Llanmadoc who had just walked off the marsh. The man I expected to be Hughes, the man I expected to arrest for the shooting of Lucy;' he paused, 'the man I let go because I was so sure it would be Hughes.' He shrugged off his mistake and held up the photograph. 'This is the photograph we got from Mrs Edwards of her son who disappeared at the same time as Mark Price. He was seventeen when this photograph was taken at Barry school. He would be about thirty two now, near the age of the man we saw at the white van.' He paused to let Dai fully absorb the information. He wasn't disappointed, Dai stood up; he couldn't help it.

'This is amazing, so Rhys Edwards is now Jean Christophe who works at SteepleTek with Hughes. So the three Barry boys, Price, Edwards and Hughes are probably responsible for at least five murders and one attempted murder?' Dai shook his head. Fellows was getting up to speed now and her smile showed that she was in on the act too now.

'So we have two on the run and one in the cells doonstairs. Well done Detective Sergeant Crossman; well spotted. You may just have got your SIO out of the shite.' Bryn could grin now, he certainly wasn't yesterday. Gray looked utterly contented.

'Dai, you have some news too which touches on this?' Dai looked around.

'Yes sir; the Company House records show that SteepleTek is owned three ways, shared equally between a Marc Renaud, Jean Christophe and Robert Hughes. They all receive substantial profits from the company each year according to the summary of accounts published there. Renaud and Christophe are French citizens.' Dai looked across at Bryn to see if he wanted to continue the story; he nodded at Dai to continue. 'So we might reasonably ask whether Marc Renaud is Mark Price?' Bryn clapped at further proof of the wisdom of his choice of acolyte.

'Yes Dai, a worthwhile thought; Europol will be very excited by that suggestion. It might well save them many months of legwork. You might become famous in the annals of international crime. Dai Poirot, remember him? They'll say to their grandchildren. Dai Poirot the man who single-handedly,' Bryn looked around at the rest of the team, 'well nearly, identified Europe's most notorious gang; the Barry Boys.' He sighed and looked upwards and outwards. Dai looked ridiculously happy like a puppy whose tummy is being tickled by a child. Bryn nodded at the assembled team, as if to say there's more and then at Dai for him to continue.

'I'd only just started to look at the financial records of the company and noticed amongst the direct debits, monthly payments to City Lets. It turns out that these are rent for a lockup in St Thomas.' He paused for effect, maturing in front of their eyes. 'The agent opened the lockup and inside there were several helicopter machines and a box of bullets. The SOCOs are b'there now.' Dai sat down feeling uncomfortable in the spotlight. Bryn picked up.

'So, we really were stumbling a bit when the drones found at SteepleTek were just that, surveillance drones. It looks as though Dai has found the base for the illegal bit of SteepleTek, the bit that conducted the assassinations, the bit that killed Green. Not a bad haul in a morning's work. Good work both of you.' Bryn looked across to Fellows who was walking into the centre of the room.

'Fine work yous. I'm still catching up for the minute, but if I've got it right, we know the names being used by Mark Price and Rhys Edwards, the murderer of Green and the attempted murderer of Lucy. We've got the forensics to secure convictions, is that right DI Bryn.' Fellows looked across at Bryn who nodded. 'Yes ma'am, we know the aliases of both Price and Edwards. If they use these names for their records in Europe then they shouldn't be too hard to find. We have a detain on sight notice out for Edwards; lets hope he doesn't get away.' Fellows clapped her hands and looked all round. 'Aye, well, let me know what happens. I'll enjoy telling the Chief Super.' Bryn settled down a bit and became more serious.

'We don't have any positive identification of Edwards yet.' Dai put his hand up and Bryn, smiling and in a benevolent mood, raised his eyebrows for him to continue.

'We have his mother's DNA sir and we will have DNA from the lockup. We can match them.' He sat down.

'We do Dai, we do; I don't like to steal your thunder, but I've just asked Bill to check out matches with Mrs Edwards urgently. He'll do it when he's finished at the lock-up after the meeting. Well done though. 'We won't know until tomorrow at the earliest. The trace in the lockup and the unit should be crucial too. I think the SOCOs will have another long night and our Super will be in for a big overtime bill.' Bryn put his finger to his lips and the buzz of conversation slowly died down. 'Bill, bringer of joy said that they'd found drones in the lockup and what he thinks are gun parts as well as the ammunition. I think we are on our way at last. Well done everyone.'

Ferrari came back from the hospital to report that Lucy was in good form. Apart from a very sore and stiff shoulder she was fine and would probably come out tomorrow. Ferrari said that the doctor had said that there were no infections at the wound site, but they couldn't yet say how restricted her arm movements will be or how long she will take to recover fully. She would be getting some long term physiotherapy on her arm. Ferrari said that Lucy thanked everyone for their good wishes and cards and Bryn for the Belgian chocolates Ferrari had bought on the way out there. Huw Thomas was with her and they seemed very happy together, was there something she had missed? Bryn felt a definite twinge of jealousy as the others had an animated conversation about the possibility of a relationship between the two. Ceri said that she'd go back to Lucy's flat and tidy up and put some food in the fridge, a bottle or two of wine and some ready-to-cook meals. She collected a ten pound note from everybody there and joined in the general hubbub of conversation to find out what had happened while she was away. Lucy would certainly enjoy hearing all the new evidence on the investigation and would be as surprised as they had all been at the name of the person who had shot her.

Bill called Bryn mid-afternoon to give him some important bits of information. The plastic parts were definitely gun parts and it looked as though they would fit onto the drones in the lockup. These were similar to the one he had looked at from the laboratory at SteepleTek, but modified to carry the gun. There were also half a dozen bullets in the box which had already been sawn at the front in the form of a cross, as they had anticipated from the recovered fragments. There were part fingerprints on some of them too. The chilling thought passed across Bryn's mind that this would have been six new victims. Most interestingly, Bill said that the DNA sample from the swab taken from Mrs Edwards matched the sample recovered from the hire document from

Birmingham. So Edwards had been the hirer of the van. They already knew that it wasn't Price, so that was another question resolved. Bryn would ponder on the Birmingham link, but at the moment, he thought it probably meant only that they were being careful, trying to confuse any evidence trail. Well, he could certainly confirm that it had. But it did mean that Edwards could now be formally linked to the murder of Michael Green. Bill signed off saying that the team would be working through the night rather than work over the weekend and he expected to match the samples found in the lock-up by early tomorrow. He'd talk to Bryn on Saturday morning. Bryn thanked Bill again and wished him a fruitful vigil. Bryn sauntered across the ops room to confirm with Gray that he had got the information about Edwards out to UK-wide police forces and Immigration who would be on alert to stop M Christophe or Mr Bristow. He confirmed with Dai that the same information had been passed on to Europol. He went along to his Super's office and told Fellows that Rhys Edwards had hired the van in Birmingham and that he hoped that Bill would confirm that the DNA found in the lock-up would match that from the hire document. Fellows shrugged, she said that she'd rather had Hughes down for the van hire because it would link him to the Green murder, but this was definitely better. She said that they should put out a press statement with Edwards's photograph, warning members of the public not to approach him. There was not much more they could do but wait. Perhaps Bryn should have another talk with Hughes now that they knew about the lockup.

Hughes and Ms Richards had been talking for much of the afternoon and came into the interview room looking resigned. Bryn and Fellows had decided that they would pile on the evidence as it emerged until Hughes had no option but to admit his guilt and then try for mitigation. It might be now, it might be tomorrow, but come it would they thought. Bryn formally opened the interview with Dai beside him and Ceri at the door.

'Dr Hughes, can you tell me about the monthly payments made by your company to City Lets?' Hughes looked to his right to seek approval, which he received.

'No I can't, I know nothing about them, our secretary Jo Morris deals with payments and accounts. It could be storage I suppose; we don't have a lot of space in the unit.'

'If I told you it was payment for a lockup in St Thomas rented under the name of SteepleTek?' Hughes looked around sharply at his solicitor with a questioning expression on his face; she nodded to him.

'As I said, I don't know anything about the payments, but it does sound like extra storage for our equipment. We try to use the unit space for research and development.' Bryn sat back in his chair.

'Would it interest you to know that we found a set of modified drones in there?' Hughes shrugged as if to say, like I said, storage. 'We also found some ammunition which matches the type that killed Michael Green and injured DS Evans?' Hughes face definitely paled, he was looking straight ahead. 'Our chief SOCO thinks he's found the makings of guns? Does that ring any bells?' Hughes leaned towards Ms Richards who shook her head.

'No comment, I would like some time with Ms Richards.' He stood up.

'Sit down Dr Hughes, you may have as much time as you wish, but we have a lot of forensic evidence building up all of which implicates you. I suggest that you use your time with Ms Richards to tell us what you know. You will be convicted of conspiracy to murder Dr Hughes, but you might be able to mitigate the sentence by saving us time and resources.' Bryn settled back in his chair again with his arms folded. 'One of your co-owners, your MD I think, a Jean Christophe, hired the van that Mark Price used to kill Michael Green in Llangennith.' Bryn stopped to allow Hughes to speak. He remained silent and looked down at the table. 'This same Jean Christophe, the MD of SteepleTek, co-owner of SteepleTek, looks remarkably like one of your old school buddies. Does this mean anything to you?' Hughes mumbled into his hands so that only Gloria Richards could hear.

'No comment.' Richards started to get up urging Hughes to do the same,

'I would like to clarify some issues with my client, Chief Inspector,' she said. Bryn laid his hands out to signify that she could if she wished, but said, 'you might like to tell us tomorrow what you know about your co-owners of SteepleTek, Marc Renaud and Jean Christophe. Sweet dreams Dr Hughes. Interview terminated 17.15pm. Escort Dr Hughes and Ms Richards back to the cells please Constable Ferrari.'

He went into the ferry terminal at Fishgaurd and bought his ticket to Rosslare. He sat in the waiting room reading a paper for a while with the other passengers. At the boarding announcement, he

pulled on his shoulder bag and went across and handed his passport, made out in the name of Bristow, to the customs officer in the booth and smiled at her. She checked the passport and waved him on with a return smile. He walked along the corridor towards the ferry, lit white by the afternoon sun against the dock, feeling the elation of freedom course through his body.

Bryn went back to the ops room to confirm that the team all knew that they'd be on overtime this weekend to collate paperwork for the CPS. He left the room smiling to the predictable, but half-hearted groans erupting behind him. He would have a pint and some supper in The Dog. He would talk happily about nothing in particular for a couple of hours. With this cheerful thought Bryn left the building.

Saturday

Bill called at just before 7am. 'We've been at it all night and I'm just off for a few hours' sleep, but time for fizzy at last Bryn. I think we've got the last pieces of the jigsaw here.' Bill was getting into his stride early, 'the sting in the tail of this drone is literally a plastic gun; a single shot device triggered by the operator via the phone computer. There has been some talk in the news media lately about a plastic gun design which can be made using a 3D printer. The design is actually on the web; have you seen it?' Bryn shook his head, but didn't say anything. The ensuing pause was long enough to prompt Bill, who was aware of Bryn's technophobia, to continue. 'Anyway, the advantage of a plastic gun is that it is light enough for a small drone to carry easily and it's probably accurate enough at close range to be lethal. You have to remember that the average pistol weighs more than a kilo, so the plastic gun is a game changer. The plastic gun also answers one of the little queries raised by ballistics early on which has been on my mind ever since. I told you that ballistics couldn't find rifling marks around the bullet fragments.' Bryn was losing interest again. 'The answer seems to be that the plastic rifling is hard enough to spin the bullet enough to send it straight, but not to mark it.' Bryn was a little lost but he would never have said so and didn't want to interrupt the flow. 'Anyway' Bill said 'We have found the CAD file for a variant of this internet gun design complete with firing mechanism on the SteepleTek office computer. All he needs to do is download it to the 3D printer they have in their laboratory and hey presto, it makes the gun parts. It looks as though they all screw together to make a complete gun and it looks as if the gun would fit the mounting pieces we found on the drone. We will actually use these drawings later today on the SteepleTek computer and 3D printer to make a new gun and check that it fits the drone. We will check that the drone flies and that we can fire the gun. That should convince any jury I think. I'll send you a video.' The mention of the video again evoked a shiver along Bryn's spine, but it was a huge sigh of relief that Bryn felt like making, rather than a hoot of joy. This had been a long time coming. There were many times when Bryn thought that a solution had finally drifted out of reach, in a morass of un-provable possibilities.

'Bill you're a champion. Just when all around were losing their heads you come up with the goods. Have a good sleep Bill; call me when you wake up. I think a celebration might be in order later if you are awake in time.' Bill groaned, but added some icing before he put the phone down.

'Oh, I nearly forgot.' What Bill? Bryn thought smiling. 'The DNA from the lockup matches the sample from Birmingham and from Mrs Edwards. I'll confirm the results later. You're looking for the right man.' Bryn nodded his thanks, saluted, clicked his heels and put the phone down. A little later, Bryn hummed as the rain beat down on his windscreen falling from the low cloud which obscured the upland ridge to the south as he drove along the north Gower road. He hummed through the news on the economy; he hummed through the sports roundup, he was still humming as he walked into Central.

The sergeant looked up puzzled, from his paper, holding his finger on the sentence he was reading, as Bryn, still humming, drifted past with a nod of greeting. Bryn went straight along the corridor to pass the new information to Maureen Fellows.

Maureen Fellows was bent over a stack of papers on her desk when Bryn entered and pushed them aside with apparent relief as she ushered him into a chair. 'Bill has just confirmed what we hoped he would; the drones in the lockup are not just surveillance drones, they have been modified to carry a gun and the ammunition we found matches the fragments used to shoot Green and Lucy. Lots of technical stuff ma'am, I'm sure he'll explain it to you. The DNA in the lockup matches the hire document and Rhys Edwards, so his old school buddy hired the van Price used in the Green murder and worked the lockup in St Thomas where the gun parts were found. So it looks as though the Technium laboratory was used for the legitimate part of the business and the lockup for the illegal stuff. I think we'll have Dr Hughes back in, did his brief come in this morning?' Fellows nodded. 'This is looking good Kevin. So, can we nail Hughes? We still don't have any direct forensics for the shootings; but plenty of circumstantial, eh?' Bryn was quiet for a few moments. 'It seems impossible to me that he could be unaware of the existence of the lockup and the activities which stemmed from it. The shootings were carried out by his fellow shareholders; there are only three of them for Christ's sake.' Bryn was clearly rattled. 'He must be involved and we'll get there, whether or not we catch Edwards or Price.' He shrugged.

'I'll get Dai and Ferrari in on this and have Gray in the box again; do you want to watch ma'am?' Fellows shook her head, 'your baby Kevin, talk to me afterwards.'

Bryn requested the pleasure of the company of Dr Hughes and Ms Richards in interview room 2. Dai and Ferrari took their by now familiar positions. Bryn introduced the company to the tape.

'Dr Hughes, a number of things have become clear today which now make your commitment to trial inevitable. Our forensic team have discovered a CAD file on your office computer,' Ms Richards looked across at Hughes with a puzzled expression on her face. 'Would you explain to Ms Richards what a CAD file is Dai?' Dai looked distinctly pleased at having been asked.

'Certainly sir, a CAD file is a Computer Assisted Drawing file miss. The CAD program is used by engineers to make precise technical drawings for the manufacture of complicated things.' Dai sat back and smiled.

'Thank you Dai, this file was found on Dr Hughes's office computer,' said Bryn raising his eyes. 'The file is a set of drawings specifying the manufacture of parts of a plastic gun which screw together to make a complete gun. It has been in the news if you follow that kind of thing. Would you like to carry on with the story or shall I Dr Hughes?' Bryn looked across again and said for the benefit of the tape. 'Dr Hughes is shaking his head.' He continued, looking at Hughes. 'The drawings would have been used on the 3D printer you had in your laboratory; is that right? No answer?' he informed tape machine again. 'Our Detective Constable tells me it could make the parts as many times as you like. The bit our tech boys like is that the plastic gun is light enough to be carried by the drone. Your drawings are being used as we speak by our forensic team to print out the gun parts on your 3D printer Dr Hughes. They will test whether it fits properly onto the drones we found in the lockup rented by your company and if the drone can lift it. They may even check whether your phone can control the drone and fire it. I expect they will have a lot of fun, being just grown up children the most of them. What do you think of that Dr Hughes?' Bryn produced the most neutral facial expression he could in the circumstances, but the makings of a smile were clearly there to see for any connoisseur of semiotics.

'I can also tell you that I have just learned that DNA found in the lockup and on the hire contract for the van that was used by Mark Price to kill Michael Green, matches DNA from samples we took from a Mrs Edwards, who now lives in Ely, late of Barry. You surely haven't forgotten your old school friend Rhys Edwards.' There was still no response from Hughes. 'I expect that we will also be able to provide evidence that the bullet fragments found in the bodies of Michael Green and DS Evans were fired from such a gun and were modified in your lock-up.' Bryn stopped now and raised his eyebrows first at Dr Hughes and then at Ms Richards. They looked hard at each other and Hughes nodded weakly at Ms Richards.

'My client would like to make a voluntary statement Inspector, to assist in any way he can the enquiries of the police.' A huge weight suddenly lifted from Bryn's shoulders, he felt as light and airy as a bird. Paradoxically, he wanted to weep with relief. It was at moments like this that he suddenly realised what a huge pressure he had been under. These emotions, deep as they were, flitted only momentarily across his features. He would savour them later.

'Go ahead Ms Richards.' She looked over the notes she had on the table in front of her and then directly at Bryn and Dai to emphasise the significance of what she was about to reveal.

'My client has written this statement which he has asked me to give to you. It is signed.' She slid it across to Bryn and settled back into her seat. Hughes leaned forwards and started on a long and complicated story. Both Bryn and Dai, anticipating a lengthy soliloquy, settled back in their seats to enjoy it.

'I was in school with Michael Green, Mark Price and Rhys Edwards as you know. They were all in the computer club at Barry school and we would share lots of ideas together and write programs together, make gadgets. Michael and I worked together mostly on software to control various gadgets using radio control and the new lightweight mobile phones. We used to argue about who had done the most work, whose ideas were most important. Even though he was a year younger than me, the good ideas were his. Basically, I used a lot of Green's software ideas to start up SteepleTek without telling him. He was a bright sod. I knew Price and Edwards, but nothing about their disappearance in the sixth form. I did know that they were involved in criminal stuff in Cardiff and that they were both pretty nasty people. They came back from the French trip really excited. The teachers couldn't find them in Paris much of the time and even wanted to send them home. When they were back in school, they talked constantly about the gangs of youths around the outskirts of Paris who did everything from drugs running to contract killings. They were obviously inspired by it and had talked to these kids, I don't know how. They weren't even terribly fluent in English at that stage. Then they just disappeared. Nobody knew where to, but some of us suspected France because of that trip. Maybe that's how France came into the myth. After my PhD in Birmingham and during my postdoc in Cardiff I started doing security consultancy work to pay for my real interest, which was to set up a company using the new smartphone technology and the new lightweight battery and electric motor systems that made cheap and silent drones a practical reality for the first time. Wales was just setting up the Technium Centre idea and one of the best ones was in Swansea. I submitted my ideas and got some pump-prime funding and a unit in the Centre in SA1. This was the start of SteepleTek, using drones to survey structures which were difficult to access, by using this new technology. That was 2009. I was one of the first companies offering this surveying service and tall buildings were going up every week all over the world. It saved the engineers and builders from physically getting up the building to check on details or problems. We could just send up a drone with a camera on it. The company was doing very well. Price or Edwards somehow got wind of this. Soon after I'd registered the company I got a series of threatening emails from them essentially blackmailing me. They said that they knew I'd used Michael Green's ideas to set up the company and I should start paying them a monthly fee to keep quiet about it. Green was still in Cardiff then. This was my new baby, I was terrified that they could blow my new company out of the water and I had no idea what they might do if I refused, and so I paid up. The company was making money very quickly. I could easily afford it.' He looked around to see three very attentive police officers and one of them wriggling his finger at him to continue. 'It didn't stay at money for long. Soon afterwards they said that they had uses for the drones we made. They said I should send one over with all the phone control system and software. They obviously liked it and had me send another over soon afterwards. I didn't know at the time what they doing with them. It was some time after Michael Green had moved to Swansea, probably last year, that I received an email from him saying that he knew about SteepleTek and of my involvement and said he also knew that I was using some of the software he had written and wanted a share in the company. He wasn't interested in a royalty, he wanted in. Now Michael Green seems to be a very decent person, but he is a controller. It's why we argued over the software development, it was always his ideas which had to be the best. It was why I couldn't imagine sharing a company with him. I didn't know what to do.' He paused to sip some water; Bryn nodded him to continue. 'I told Price what was happening and they simply said that they would deal with it, no bother, as I suppose I knew in my heart that they would.' Hughes swallowed hard and took another sip of water. 'They never liked Green, he used to patronise them in school as small town oiks. He was smooth on the surface but hard underneath. They told me in a telephone conversation that they would get Green out of the way, that they'd enjoy it. Nobody would know anything; nobody would tie it to me or to them. They said it was what they did as a business in France and they'd never been caught. I said for them to go ahead, but I didn't want to know anything about it. I was under a lot of pressure from Green at the time. I then received an SD card by post, like the ones you've seen. It had a recording of our phone conversation on it which was, on listening to all of it, clearly about me agreeing to a contract killing of Michael Green. Price said that they'd do it in the UK and they would come over and set it up. They were now Marc Renaud and Jean Christophe, French citizens. They probably had been for years. Not only did they have the recording but they said they had evidence that SteepleTek drones had been used for several contract killings in Europe, paid for by various gangs presumably. Again, I didn't want to know. They insisted that I watch one of the videos of the killing in Naples. It was horrible as you now know; it's why I flinched when you showed the killing of Michael Green. I knew exactly what was coming. When they arrived about three years ago now, they wanted access to the laboratory and joint shares in the company; split three ways. I felt I had no choice. I couldn't claim now that I didn't know what it was all about. I just couldn't get out and walk away. I genuinely thought Price and Edwards would kill me if I didn't agree. I said to them that I would only run the legitimate survey business, which was all I cared about. They could have access to the technology and joint ownership, but they couldn't run their illegal activities from the Technium unit. That's what the lockup must be about; it was where Edwards made and developed the lethal drones. Edwards was and is a psychopath, but he's pretty good technically. He redesigned the guns he found on the internet and firing mechanism and modified our standard drones. He told me about it all the time so I couldn't say that I didn't know. He made sure that I was implicated all the time. Ms Richards here as company secretary arranged the legal stuff, but she had no idea of the story behind it. As far as she was concerned, it was just a way to bring in partners to fund the company. They weren't short of money. The incorporation of them as two new shareholders was completely legitimate, it was registered with Companies House. Jo Morris the secretary and technician knows nothing either. I am currently developing gps drones that can go as far as the battery allows; which is quite far now. They can be controlled directly through a mobile phone at long range. I dread to think what Price and Edwards would do with those, I dread to think what drones will be doing in ten years time come to that. I know that Edwards was interested in face recognition software. The nightmare scenario is that psychopaths like Edwards or any reasonably technical person can make a home-made drone which can be controlled from anywhere and pick out a face in a crowd and simply shoot at it.' Hughes's voice broke down now; his confession released the pressure he had hidden behind the layers of deception, for far too long. The room was silent for a while contemplating the scenario painted by Hughes. Bryn imagined being stalked by a drone which knew his face or his walk or his laugh. The expressions of the others in the room suggested that they were thinking the same thoughts. He shivered involuntarily.

'What about Michael Green, Dr Hughes?' Bryn asked roughly.

'Price went back to France where I assume he is now and then returned when Edwards had set up the killing. Edwards communicated with Green as a fellow aficionado via various online forums. He got him to go out to Llangennith and you know the rest. Well done Chief Inspector. I find it is actually some relief for it all to be out in the open. But I dread incarceration.' The room was again silent until Bryn announced the interview over at 10.52am. The surreal science fiction atmosphere was broken by the comforting everyday scraping of chairs and squeak of shoes on vinyl as Ferrari shuffled out behind Hughes and Richards to take them back to the cell.

Bryn, who was rubbing his hand over the lower part of his face to test for feeling looked across at Dai who still looked stunned.

'Didn't expect that *bwt*,' he said, completely seriously. They both burst into peals of laughter which had been dammed up behind the tension of the last two weeks. They snorted and shuddered uncontrollably for several minutes with tears streaming down their faces. Bursts of snorting erupted from one or other of them intermittently for the next few minutes. It erupted every time that they looked at each other. Only when they had cleared their throats and rubbed their heads to remove the last shudder of laughter did they stand up. Bryn said that he needed to see Fellows and share the good news, which initiated a long, but final bout of uncontrollable laughter.

Fellows had finished reading the statement. 'This is more than you could have dreamed of Bryn. We have evidence to convict all three and I don't imagine the other

333

two will be on the loose for long with arrest warrants here and in Europe. What do you make of Hughes now?' Bryn stood looking around him for inspiration.

'I think what he says sounds pretty plausible to me, but he is of course still definitely an accessory to murder, maybe even a co-conspirator. That will be for the CPS to wrangle with, I'm pleased to say. I believed him. His obsession with his technology and his arrogance allowed him to ignore his exploitation of Green and made him vulnerable to the advances of Price and Edwards. Another person might have reported the blackmail.' He shrugged, 'who knows what we'd do in the same circumstances? They threatened his new baby.' He sat back with his hands behind his head. 'We can talk to Jo Morris to get her take and we will convict Edwards and Price if we catch them. They will definitely be charged with murder and attempted murder here and in Europe. I can't see why it would benefit them to implicate Hughes in things he hasn't done, so Hughes may get away with accessory.' He stretched his arms up happily and smiled at Fellows who beamed back.

'Well done laddie. Tell the crew to meet in the ops room at 2pm for a wee talk.' She gave him a gentle hug. He had never been hugged by a Superintendent before and it wasn't as bad as he might have imagined.

Bryn brushed aside the knowledge that they would have been able to convict Edwards and Hughes even if Lucy hadn't gone on the fools' errand with Thomas. He submerged the thought that one of them could easily be dead now. He was a pragmatist; you had to be in the police force. What was done was done. It would be Lucy and Huw Thomas who had to live with it. Bryn slipped out to call Lucy on her mobile. He didn't want to be overheard by anyone in the station. She said that she was now home and feeling absolutely fine as long as she didn't catch her shoulder on a door or move it without thinking.

'Lucy, we have nearly wrapped up the case now, there is lots for you to catch up on. It was Edwards who tried to kill you. Green and the three suspects are all Barry boys.' Bryn still couldn't quite believe it himself. He gave her a brief description of the evidence uncovered by Gray and Dai and the new forensic evidence. He listened as Lucy tried to assimilate all the new information, to deal emotionally with the knowledge of the name of her assailant, the man who nearly killed her.' She asked lots of questions, slowly coming to terms with the shooting and with the history. 'Look Lucy, we'll have a long chat sometime soon and we can go through all the evidence in detail then. I called because we are having a little celebration here. I'd really like you to be here. Are you fit enough to come along? It will start at about 2pm.' Bryn remembered the last time he had invited Lucy and still a flush of embarrassment swept across his soul; even more so when she didn't reply immediately.

'Actually sir, Huw Thomas is here. He brought me back from the hospital a couple of hours ago.' He paused and looked up to try to find in his soul the good Kevin Bryn and said enthusiastically.

'Bring him along Lucy. He needs to know the story too.' He almost meant it. Lucy laughed.

'Thanks sir, I'm bored already, we'd love to.'

Bryn walked next door to the metro store, calling Bill on the way to invite him and his team. He bought all the sandwiches and most of the cakes left on their shelves, which he carried back to the ops room. He then went around the station gathering up the team for an impromptu picnic. Bryn, Dai and Ferrari took turns to tell the story according to Hughes and the room filled with the excited chatter at the unravelling of the case. Everybody had something of their own to add. The SOCOs arrived just as the team had started attacking the food on the table and joined the throng.

Fellows arrived just before Lucy and Huw Thomas and put two bottles of whisky on the table with a bottle of water which would remain untouched. Glasses and mugs miraculously appeared beside them. Fellows poured the first drinks herself; one each for Bryn, Ferrari and Dai and one for Bill Wood, Lucy and for Gray. The last stiff one she poured for herself. She indicated to Williams to pour the rest for him and the SOCO team and for Huw at whose sight she raised an eyebrow and looked at Bryn, who was conveniently looking in another direction. Fellows raised her glass; *'iechyd dda, slainte mhath,* good health all of you; brilliant.'

She stood back and shouted to the assembled company. 'Constable Williams, before you get bladdered, call for taxis for the team. Then you can all bugger off when the whisky's finished, I want you fresh tomorrow to get sorted for the CPS.'

'Yes ma'am' said Williams grinning.

She finished her tot in one and disappeared from the room to cheers and hooting from the throng. Two bottles of whisky between twelve police officers do not last long. It was just as Maureen Fellows had intended.

He went down the walkway out of the terminal from the immigration area. He liked Ireland; he might stay a while, before deciding on whether to go across to France. Price knew where he lived and who he was. He would have to construct a new identity for himself and a new life. He didn't want the bastard Price finding him. He had money held in various accounts around the world, money wouldn't be the problem. He was getting fed up with the drone business anyway. He turned the corner to leave the terminal along with the other passengers. From amongst the crowd, two of them were somehow close alongside him and took his arms, gently but firmly. One smiled.

'Monsieur Christophe, welcome to Ireland.'

Made in the USA
Charleston, SC
27 November 2015